Lee never gave up on the cryptids and the Forteana.

Though neither did she go mad for it, like some Birdman-hunting Van Helsing. She kept on as she had been, wrote articles for local papers, then some national papers; contributed top-ten lists of weird shit to websites; was paid enough to make the rent and buy a sandwich. And every so often she imagined Mal reading those pieces and laughing at her. It made her feel close still, even when the fourth anniversary of her disappearance had come and gone.

Until Mal called.

Or someone called who sounded like Mal used to sound, a voice indelibly engraved in Lee's memory. She wanted to meet, with no time for catch-ups and pleasantries and Lee's *What the fuck do you mean by this? Who is this? Why are you... What are you—Wait!* Just a place, a time—pedestrian, ridiculously mundane. And a choice: to go, or not to go.

Lee went.

Praise for
THE DOORS OF EDEN

"Full of sparking, speculative invention. *The Doors of Eden* is a terrific timeslip / lost-world romp in the grand tradition of Turtledove, Hoyle, even Conan Doyle. If you liked *Primeval*, read this book."
—Stephen Baxter, author of *World Engines: Destroyer*

"Inventive, funny, and engrossing, this book lingers long after you close it."
—Tade Thompson, Arthur C. Clarke Award–winning author of *Rosewater*

"What a ride. Talks like big-brained science fiction and runs like a fleet-footed political thriller."
—John Scalzi, author of *The Collapsing Empire*

THE
DOORS
OF
EDEN

BY ADRIAN TCHAIKOVSKY

SHADOWS OF THE APT

Empire in Black and Gold
Dragonfly Falling
Blood of the Mantis
Salute the Dark
The Scarab Path
The Sea Watch
Heirs of the Blade
The Air War
War Master's Gate
Seal of the Worm

ECHOES OF THE FALL

The Tiger and the Wolf
The Bear and the Serpent
The Hyena and the Hawk

Guns of the Dawn

Children of Time
Children of Ruin

The Doors of Eden

THE DOORS OF EDEN

ADRIAN TCHAIKOVSKY

www.orbitbooks.net

Copyright © 2020 by Adrian Czajkowski
Excerpt from *Children of Time* copyright © 2015 by Adrian Czajkowski
Excerpt from *Nophek Gloss* copyright © 2020 by Essa Hansen

Cover design by www.blacksheep-uk.com
Cover images by Alamy / Getty / Shutterstock
Timeline illustration by Adrian Czajkowski
Author photograph by Ante Vukorepa

Orbit
Hachette Book Group
1290 Avenue of the Americas
New York, NY 10104
www.orbitbooks.net

First U.S. Print Edition: September 2020
Originally published in Great Britain by Pan Macmillan and in ebook in the U.S. by Orbit in August 2020

Orbit is an imprint of Hachette Book Group.
The Orbit name and logo are trademarks of Little, Brown Book Group Limited.

The publisher is not responsible for websites (or their content) that are not owned by the publisher.

The Hachette Speakers Bureau provides a wide range of authors for speaking events. To find out more, go to www.hachettespeakersbureau.com or call (866) 376-6591.

Library of Congress Control Number: 2020936628

ISBNs: 978-0-316-70580-6 (trade paperback), 978-0-316-70578-3 (ebook)

Printed in the United States of America

LSC-H

Printing 2, 2021

To lost chances.

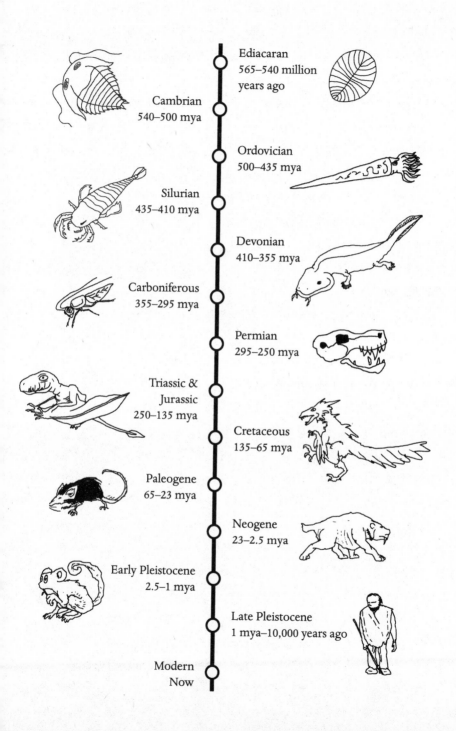

Ediacaran
565–540 million
years ago

Cambrian
540–500 mya

Ordovician
500–435 mya

Silurian
435–410 mya

Devonian
410–355 mya

Carboniferous
355–295 mya

Permian
295–250 mya

Triassic &
Jurassic
250–135 mya

Cretaceous
135–65 mya

Paleogene
65–23 mya

Neogene
23–2.5 mya

Early Pleistocene
2.5–1 mya

Late Pleistocene
1 mya–10,000 years ago

Modern
Now

Prelude: The Ediacaran Period

Excerpt from *Other Edens:
Speculative Evolution and Intelligence* by
Professor Ruth Emerson of the
University of California

For three billion years the only life here has been microscopic. Bacteria have been leaching sustenance from strange chemicals in the bowels of the Earth or the depths of the sea. Ice comes, ice goes; the atmosphere for most of this time is a heady mix of chemicals either toxic to life or simply useless to it. There is life, though. For almost half the aeons since its formation, this world has known self-replicating organic entities. They've been bustling and thriving and dying and trying to outdo one another in a ferocious, invisible war for survival.

Life sometimes seems destined, to we fortunate ones who live at the far end of time's telescope. But what were the chances of success? Hard to say, and the no man's land between inorganic process and organic existence is a region, not a hard dividing line. We fondly believe there is no reversing that step, however, after a few very basic criteria are satisfied. Imagine life as a manual that includes instructions for replicating itself. The replication process is fallible, of course; everything is in this world. That leads to mutation and the possibility of change, and so to evolution. Here, a mutation can give one minuscule knot of organic chemistry the opportunity to replicate more efficiently than its neighbours. Its offspring faithfully copy the fortuitous error and thereby inherit it. Even without the evidence nestling in the heart of every living cell, the logic itself should be infinitely persuasive. Evolution is inevitable once you have an imperfectly self-replicating system in an environment of limited resources.

For the longest time, all the dramas of this particular world could have played out in a drop of water, life was of so small a scale. We have some evidence of a few flowerings of more complex life developing. But either the ice came back, acidity rose or oxygen levels fell—and these early signs collapsed like enlightened empires before the tides of barbarism.

Three billion years passed like motes in a god's eye. Life expanded to fit the meagre niches the world provided. And a constantly changing cast of life forms fled from one another, devoured their fellows like miniature tigers and traded genetic material like shady black marketeers hiding contraband in their trench coats. These life forms exploited the inorganic substrate of the world. Later, they exploited the organic matrix that was the graveyard of a million billion fast-lived generations of their forebears.

Then in this Archaean microbial age, some unicellular visionary made an explosive discovery—akin to mankind's discovery of fire, in terms of its impact. A volatile, poisonous chemical was tamed. Since the dawn of the Earth, this chemical had voraciously attacked any element it came into contact with; now it became the servant of developing life. This first metabolizing of oxygen might have been a defence mechanism. A process that incorporated the dangerous substance rather than falling prey to it. Perhaps your ancient ancestors took wolf cubs from their mothers with a similar goal. And what a world of opportunity opened up! Oxygen is a shortcut to a higher energy lifestyle, a ticket to getting out of the bacterial ghetto to live the high life. Our cast of characters becomes more complex as a result. Life gets a new paint job, alloys and go-faster stripes, now there is something more powerful under the hood.

Next, single cells find advantage in numbers. Simple bacterial mats carpet the floors of every sea, shore to shore, washing up on lifeless beaches in a scummy slick of organic matter that cannot even decay properly yet. Then cells cling to each other, sharing the work so enough of them might even resemble some larger coherent being. But the next storm or riptide breaks them down again, to reform slowly, later. Some developing cells cling to those bacterial mats and rocks and sieve the water for organic detritus; some drift in the current. Cells evolve that can only survive in the company of their fellows, doing some small specialist role like an office worker who only deals with form G. But because the rest of the alphabet is also monitored, the paycheque still comes through every month. Multicellular life evolves exponentially, now it has that hard, oxygenated liquor to fuel it. Everywhere, a garden of life arises—the very first Eden. But it doesn't support life like ours, or even our ancestors'. This is life of another caste entirely. A world of quilt-bodied things that lie supine upon the sea floor, or inch slowly across the bacterial mats without limbs or muscles, feeding upon them without mouths. They are a global community of organisms alien to us, and they live without tooth or claw, without eyes, without organs.

Our world was like this once. Go back six hundred million years and you wouldn't know the difference. But this is not our world.

In this world, something awoke.

PART 1
DOWN THE RABBIT HOLE

1.

Her name was Lee, short for Lisa Pryor. Which, technically, was short for Lisa Chandrapraiar. But when her grandparents came to England from Pakistan, the immigration authorities had been having a rough day and so Pryor was what went on the paperwork. Her parents still called her Lisa, but Mal called her Lee and that was the important thing. After a while her other friends did too, because what Mal said tended to stick.

Mal was short for Elsinore Mallory, because her parents came from a particular social stratum where that was perfectly acceptable. However, she never forgave them for it.

They were nineteen. Lee was studying zoology at Reading, Mal was reading English Lit at Oxford—an establishment so exclusive that they had a whole other verb for what you did there. They'd only been friends in school because Lee's parents had pushed hard to get her somewhere good and Mal's parents had lost their starched white shirts on some dodgy stock market deal, so couldn't afford to send her to an expensive private establishment. The moment she'd first met Mal was engraved in Lee's mind: a thin white girl sitting on her own because she was, frankly, pretty much insufferable at age thirteen. She'd come over from a very posh school that had told her she was better than everyone else. Being thirteen, she'd told her new peers that too, and had been surprised to discover they hadn't agreed.

So Mal had been alone in the cloakroom, shoulders hunched inwards, head down, reading Lyall Watson's *The Nature of Things*. And Lee had a tatty second-hand copy of that very book back home. She had never run into anyone else who'd read it; it was bonkers too, pure Forteana about the secret life of the inanimate world. Here, for the first time ever, was someone else who was interested in *that* stuff.

Mal had looked up defensively, anticipating more mockery from the chubby Pakistani girl who was staring wide-eyed at her. Yet somehow she'd understood exactly what Lee was after. From that moment, they'd been inseparable. Lee's parents didn't know what to make of her, and Mal's certainly didn't know what to make of Lee, but neither of them cared.

There followed years of sharing everything, from Dungeons and Dragons campaigns to their first intimate experience. This deepening of their relationship had seemed inevitable to both of them, but none of their parents ever guessed at it, locked into a mindset where such things didn't happen.

Their other shared pastime was hunting monsters.

It started off passively, reading the *Fortean Times*, watching old reruns of Arthur C. Clarke's *Mysterious World*, trawling the internet. There they found rumours of yetis, Mokele-Mbembe, the Jersey Devil and stray big cats. Two years before, though—before *The Thing That Happened*—they had started holidaying together. They had been seventeen, and Mal could always cadge some travelling money from her parents. They thought Lee was a good chaperone who would prevent their daughter from getting into compromising situations. In this they were absolutely and exactly mistaken. But it meant that when the pair of them wanted to go backpacking in Scotland, or visit Gévaudan to practise French, it all sounded perfectly respectable. Nobody knew they were casting themselves into the wilderness, desperate for a look at beasts that almost certainly didn't live there.

Looking back, Lee couldn't have honestly said whether they believed any of it. She could never quite recapture the mindset they'd had, not after what happened. They weren't seriously looking to actually find proof, not exactly. They wanted to be the ones to take that vaunted blurry photo that might, in a certain light, look a bit like something was there: the ripple on the loch, the faintly anthropoid shadow in the woods.

And then, after we'd done it a couple of times, Mal picked a target for our next jaunt, and we actually found our monster.

Later, making a tenuous living writing cryptozoology articles for magazines and websites, Lee would explore the literary tradition where "monster" was a metaphor: the monstrosity inside us all along, the true villain being human nature, all of that. And she would feel like a fraud, because that wasn't the kind of monster she and Mal had encountered. They met the other kind, with terrible claws and savage teeth. And how many other cryptid-hunters had experienced that moment, confronting the fugitive panther, standing before the ape-man, realizing that the true joy was in the quest. The actual finding holds only terror and loss.

*

Lee had been away from Mal for most of the summer term, sending her mournful emails and indulging in lonely midnight Skype calls. Mal had settled in better, up to her eyeballs in

LARP and the university debating society. They'd been an item for years, but now they were apart and in that stage in a relationship where you constantly wonder, *Is this more important to me than to her? Am I too needy? Am I trying to tie her down?* These worries always disappeared the moment Lee actually got to speak with Mal. Nevertheless, every day she was away, Lee was newly terrified that Mal would suddenly remember she was white and posh—and go back to her own people, like some brief alien visitor to Earth.

Then exams were done, term was done, and Lee was willing the train faster all the way to Hemel and home. Her parents and siblings were given a five-minute window of her time before she was off, westward to Bracknell and the big old house Mal's folks were still holding on to by their fingernails.

Mal, at that time: she was like porcelain. You'd think that she'd break into pieces with a little shove. For the longest time Lee had thoroughly envied her metabolism, because that girl could *eat*. Twice as much as Lee, whose mother would tut and nag about dress sizes and what nice boys might or might not want (a matter of supreme indifference to her), and yet Mal remained waif-like. She was so pale you could almost see through her; she dyed her short hair platinum because it annoyed her mother, and because she had a love-hate relationship with standing out. She hated strangers staring, hated the thought of people making judgements about her. Yet at the same time she couldn't dress down and drab, like Lee usually did. A part of her had to be seen and heard, to know she was real.

Before university, of course, Lee worked out that Mal was so slim because most of what she ate she purged right out again. She became quite ill one summer, and her parents were frantic that someone would guess there was something *wrong* with her. She had private doctors and therapists, and they even packed her off to a kind of rehab centre for very rich people with eating disorders. Lee remembered living through that time as if under a shadow, taut with a strain she had nobody to talk to about. After the business with the too many pills they took her out of the centre, though, and stopped locking her in the house. Lee was able to see her again, and Mal was better after that.

When *The Thing That Happened* happened, Mal was still skinny, but you couldn't see her bones quite as much. Lee's worries about Mal meeting some Oxbridge wunderkind and running off with her had abated. More than that, Mal had been making plans.

"Lee," she said, with that grin that went through Lee like sticking fingers in the mains socket. "We're going on holiday."

And of course they were; that was their tradition, to pack cameras and night-vision kit and go play cryptid detectives on some well-worn trail. This time, though, Mal had found something different. No Loch Ness Monsters or Lambton Worms, nowhere with a gift shop where the cryptid in question was immortalized as a gurning plushie. They felt their old yearning for new territory stirring.

That undiscovered country, as the bard said, from whose bourn no traveller returns...

*

YouTube was not, of course, undiscovered country. Discovery was entirely the point of YouTube. And if you looked hard enough, you could discover just about anything on it, although sometimes you had to wade through a lot of porn to find what you were looking for. One thing YouTube had, if you entered the right search terms, was a plethora of the Unexplained.

Mal and Lee were no longer wide-eyed naifs when it came to that sort of thing. They'd spent a dozen hysterical evenings over the last couple of years trawling the net to find cryptid videos, mysterious sightings of unknown species. Lee's firm impression was that nine-tenths of the "unknown animal" videos on YouTube boiled down to (a) gross jellyfish, (b) bad special effects and (c) actual readily identifiable animals with the bad luck to be encountered by someone who'd apparently never seen a nature documentary. One of them, under the heading of *MISTERY ANIMALS!!*, had been just a regular heron. And the look in that heron's eye had said, "Don't you be pulling that internet shit on me," or that's what Mal had claimed.

So when they were huddled together on Mal's bed, blinds drawn and her laptop balancing precariously across their knees, Lee hadn't exactly been holding her breath.

The video Mal had found was titled *Birdman of Bodmin?*, and at least all three words were spelled correctly. The alliteration was a nice extra.

"This is going to be dumb," Lee decided, leaning into Mal.

"Just watch." And there had been a jag of excitement in the other girl's voice that said that however dumb this dumb video was, they would be heading to Bodmin Moor that summer.

It purported to be footage from a security camera. Black-and-white nocturnal video of a suitably grainy quality, so that the viewer didn't have to try very hard to start seeing things in the static-laden gloom. The viewpoint was immobile, angled to look down the stone wall of a two-storey building: there were suggestions of rectangular windows, and across from them, a corrugated wall, perhaps a barn. There was a gap of about ten feet between the buildings, cluttered with what might be farm implements and tarpaulined crates, a kennel on its side, a bicycle missing its front wheel. At the far extent of the view, after a security light was triggered, Lee could just make out the looming hulk of a Range Rover, crusty with mud. Or that was how she remembered it in retrospect. She could never quite square the precision of her recollection with the grainy quality of the video. Memory screwed you over like that.

She'd scoffed at the time. Not so hard as to get on Mal's nerves, but that was how the Forteana side of their relationship worked. One of them would propose something and the other would gently knock it down. And this video had been a classic, in terms of the cryptid cock-tease. Fixed camera angle, so things could be happening just off-screen, plus bad-quality images full of ghosting and phantom movement. The viewer could read in a whole conga line of Sasquatches.

The camera was supposedly attached to the house of a sheep farmer on Bodmin Moor, down in Cornwall. The video's description went into impressive amounts of detail about the lonely farmer whose livestock was being attacked by a mysterious (note the correct use of the letter y!) animal. And that was also a red flag in the credibility stakes. When someone went to these lengths to embroider a narrative, it tended to be because the facts resolutely refused to speak for themselves. Much of the original footage was steeped in gloom: moonlight filtering in to show the outlines of things, but nothing definite. There was no sound. Then the motion sensor triggered and everything lit up, but nothing was there—someone had misaligned the camera and sensor, no doubt. It was another absolute standard in the "fake videos of spooky things" oeuvre. The more you could make the viewers' imaginations work for you, the better.

This happened a couple of times. And maybe the farmer was going nuts, or maybe he was asleep or off in the big city displaying his prize trick-performing pig. Lee remembered getting a bit fidgety after the second jump-scare-ha-no-false-alarm, and started rolling her eyes at Mal, who poked her in the squidge at her waist and told her, look, here it is.

Everything had been gloom for a minute and a half, and in that gloom Lee could see movement, if she was so inclined. Truthfully, she could have seen anything. Squint and that suggestive shadow was creeping forwards, slow enough to fox the motion sensor. Blink again and it hadn't moved a pixel. Or was that something occluding the Range Rover's licence plate, a hunched shape that might be a dog or a humanoid figure on hands and knees? *Birdman of Bodmin?* queried the title, and that alone peopled the darkness with all manner of outlandish shapes. Bird cryptids were rare, after all, and what was a *"Birdman"*? Lee remembered the flywheels of her imagination spinning, denied anything solid to sink their teeth into.

Then the light went on again, and something was suddenly there, frozen in the brightness. Lee couldn't see it properly, half behind a tarpaulin. The light was so bright that it leached away detail. Most likely it was some art student's CGI project and everyone'd been had. But something was there, bigger than a bird, a little smaller than a man, insofar as there was any frame of reference. They both saw it: a hunched, prickly shape, with a suggestion of limbs, of wings that were more like arms despite the ragged sleeves of plumage. A head lifted high on a serpentine neck—or maybe it was just an arm inside a puppet.

It bolted, shooting between the Range Rover and the house's wall, knocking over a crate as it went. That was the thing that had hooked Mal and sent a thrill down Lee's spine. It didn't move like anything they'd ever seen. It wasn't flying or hopping like a garden bird. Not the long lope of an ostrich, or a bloke in a chicken costume. The whatever-it-was legged it straight across that narrow alley and into the concealing shadows. There was nothing of man to it, and precious little of bird. Lee was left with an afterimage of a feathered body covered in ragged plumage and a whirl of legs—its long tail almost a blur, emphasizing just how damn fast the beastie was. And that head, heavy on the muscular neck, looking back at the camera. It was as though it knew it was being watched, the eye flashing a rapid tapetum reflection before it vanished.

There are certain codings for how a creature moves that are designed to awaken a deep and ancestral unease. Lee had seen them all in those fake videos. Make something that's too close to human for comfort; make something that jolts into sudden, scurrying motion like a spider. Design something that bends and flexes wrong, but not too wrong. There was a language of horripilation in creature design; ask any SFX studio that's done a horror film or two.

This thing, the Birdman, displayed none of those tricks. Its body was built from a different alphabet, another language entirely. That was what caught them both. It was a fake—obviously it was a fake. But so long as neither of them said as much, they could pretend it might be real.

By that evening they'd booked a hire car and a bed and breakfast in a small village called, delightfully, St. Teath. They were going to Bodmin to hunt—not for its infamous Beast, but the Birdman.

*

At the B&B they were told, to their faces, that breakfast wasn't included. Neither of them dared ask what the other "B" was for, though they had fun inventing options. Lee remembered nobody cared that they were two girls booking into a room with a double bed. She didn't know if their hosts were pleasantly broad-minded or if they, like Queen Vic, honestly didn't think of women as being *that way inclined*.

Next up was to work out where they were going. The thing about dodgy YouTube videos of fake cryptids is how many important details they don't include in the description, and Lee and Mal weren't about to go wandering Bodmin Moor looking for "the farm." They spent a day travelling from village to village, showing stills from the video and asking if people recognized it, until in a pub, one sunny lunchtime, someone gave them a queer look (so to speak) and asked if they were there for the beastie. Straight out with it in broad daylight, like they'd never seen a horror film in their lives. This was a prime opportunity to put the wind up some tourists, and yet here was this cackling old boy just *telling* them about the local bogeyman without any ominous build up or *They do say...*

Thinking back, four years on, she could laugh. However, when things went to crap this encounter had felt like the awful warning they'd ignored.

The old boy had been so helpful because the farmer in question was known locally, and not in a good way. A weird loner who didn't get into town much, and enjoyed bitter boundary disputes with anyone luckless enough to be his neighbour. So when he'd turned up months before at the local police station, claiming there was a monster on his farm, everyone leapt on this opportunity for fun. The old boy spent a half hour talking about it and bought some decent local perry to go with the story. He also marked the farm on their maps and provided the name of its owner—one Cador Roberts. He sounded like a Welsh hill chieftain, except apparently he was mostly a grumpy middle-aged man, stuck out on a sheep farm on the edge of the moors.

They returned to the B&B to spend the evening inventing lurid tales of what might be found on Roberts' land. They wondered whether he had faked the video himself or if someone had been gaslighting him—there seemed no shortage of suspects, from the way the old boy had gone on. Roberts had given his CCTV tapes to the police station, apparently. But they'd ended up leaked to a YouTube channel— so maybe the whole online exercise was to piss off Roberts should the man ever get near a modem.

In the morning they put their hiking gear in order, buying maps, water bottles and sandwiches from a local garage. There was a track that led to Roberts' place, but they'd been told authoritatively that their little hire-car hatchback would not survive the trip. They planned to take the road as far as they could, walking the rest of the way and aiming to be at the farmhouse by noon.

They could, of course, have gone trespassing, looking for Birdmen. But farmers tended to own shotguns, especially those with possible cryptid interlopers. And they had a secret weapon, should Roberts think they were part of the village gaslighting brigade, out to poke fun at him. They had a copy of the *Fortean Times* from January that year, in which Lee had an article about The Beast of Gévaudan. It was her first published piece, and she was inordinately proud of it. Roberts would see they were serious cryptid-hunters.

*

The walk took longer than they'd thought. They were having such fun getting away from all the nonsense that was most of their lives that they didn't notice it was well past noon until they spotted the farmhouse. There was a chill in the air, too, that had been absent the previous day. The country was beautiful, but you had to like bleak to really appreciate it. It was all ups and downs, with plenty of places where the rocks had clawed their way right out of the earth. The land was scrubby too, green and yellow. The occasional houses were all grey stone boxes with too few too small windows, as if purpose designed for storing mad wives in the attic. And they were ruinous; most of the buildings Lee and Mal saw had been abandoned generations before. The Roberts family obviously had more staying power than most.

Later, Lee had to acknowledge that the whole venture was a spectacularly stupid thing to do, for entirely quotidian reasons. They never considered the possibility that Roberts would be an axe-murderer, or even that a random non-Roberts axe-murderer might happen upon them. They were after monsters, and weren't frightened, because neither of them expected to find any.

Knocking on the door didn't yield any results, and they decided Roberts was probably off on sheep-related business, which they really should have thought of earlier. At that point, though, their options were to wait an undefined length of time for permission or to seek forgiveness later, so they went around the house to find the vista the video had shown. They weren't being stealthy—chatting away nineteen to the dozen, in fact, because it was an adventure and they were doing it together.

They found the spot almost immediately. Some of the junk had shifted, but there was the alley between house and barn, and, there, the actual CCTV camera. They took their own photos and examined the muddy ground, as though expecting to find incriminating footprints.

They did find footprints. And they weren't human.

Lee still had the photos on a datastick somewhere. They weren't exactly a smoking gun though. None of the footprints were complete, and they overlapped one another—but if someone had made them with a fake wading-bird foot, they'd really gone to town. The prints had two long toes and one short one, as though the inner toe had broken off halfway. Mal and Lee exchanged looks, and there was something between elation and terror in the air. Even messy and infinitely interpretable, this was *new*. This would get them in the *Fortean Times*. This would get them a speaker's spot at Weird Weekend or even air fare to a big symposium in the States. This would make their names in the field—they knew it.

Mal picked up a bad smell beyond the general farmyard odour and followed it round the side of the barn. Lee's subconscious was busy comparing reality with her memories of the video, feeling something was missing.

When Mal let out a horrified noise, Lee dashed over, already feeling sick in her stomach. The scent of dead meat was overpowering even through her hay-fever, sweet with rot. Most definitely she could hear the legion of busy flies. She was horribly certain it was Roberts.

It was sheep, though. A little flock had been penned in here, in what looked like decidedly makeshift accommodation, and something had got in amongst them. They were very dead, and for a moment that was all Lee could think about, because there was blood everywhere, painting the walls even, and some of the bodies seemed to have just about exploded. Mal lost what was left of her lunch right then, staggering out of the barn and retching, but Lee just stared. She'd seen roadkill before, and her neighbour's hamster, when it did that hamster trick of dying for no reason. Now she was looking at the brutally torn-up carcasses of at least seven sheep. She felt almost clinical about it, like she was Sherlock Holmes ready to make gnostic pronouncements about the murderer. And the more she stared, the more she really did think like that, because she was noticing things, even as Mal called for her to come away. Horrible as the sight was, this wasn't just death for death's sake. There were far too many visible bones, and they were hacked about, not torn by the teeth of animals...

"Flensed," she said, and Mal gave her a baffled look. Then Lee lost her nerve and didn't explain the thought sitting in her head like a toad: this is what you get when you butcher bones, not when you gnaw on them.

She looked at the horrible, crimsoned walls, seeing places where the blood hadn't just spattered. She took one photo before she had to get out into the air: a few smears and lines, really. Nobody would have thought anything of them, save that there was purpose there. Something had made those streaks, way past the high-water mark of the killing. And they'd see marks like that again.

Lee's theory was right then: some sadistic bastard really was gaslighting poor Roberts. Someone had come in and cut up his sheep and put fake footprints about, or maybe it was the man himself, after the insurance.

At that point something bolted from the barn. It shot past them at such speed that it was almost gone around the building's edge by the time they spun round to watch. Lee was left with an impression of it, a sense of something grey and ragged with a long tail. But of course that was what the video had primed her to see, and the next moment she didn't know whether it had been real or just in her head.

Mal looked horribly pale, but also determined. She wanted to find something more, now. Lee was right with her, her brain belatedly stepping in to hand her a note about what they hadn't seen yet.

"Range Rover isn't here." Roberts must be doing farm things, and there was a set of tyre tracks heading away from the house, over the rugged moors. They exchanged looks, wide-eyed. They knew they were crossing a line, but that was what the cryptid-hunting game was *about*, after all. Being on that brink, feeling the chasm of the unknown yawn at their very toes—before taking that prudent step back.

With daylight left, they went to find Roberts, armed with nothing but a hiker's guide and a personal alarm that, out on the moors, nobody could possibly hear.

After an hour of walking they saw Roberts' big grey-blue car, muddy and battered and in the middle of a field. No sign of the man himself, nor any potential Birdmen. However, they had also apparently stumbled upon a Site of Special Historic Interest. Three standing stones stood in what Mal's guidebook charitably called a circle, yet was only ever going to be a triangle.

"The Six Brothers," Mal read out, looking at the trio of monoliths. "That's what the locals call 'em. Hello? Mr. Roberts?" Her call fell away weirdly into the air, seemingly swallowed up before the sound could travel. She turned to Lee. "Is it colder?"

It *was* colder. They stood there in shorts and T-shirts and shivered, dickering over whether to get more clothes out of their rucksacks. Lee looked up at the early afternoon sun, seeing it bright and fierce in a clear blue sky. The cold seemed something *other*, as though it was leaching in from elsewhere. Or so Lee remembered later, with the benefit of hindsight.

Mal approached the nearest stone, which wasn't much taller than she was, flat and irregular, nothing like the decent workmanship of Stonehenge. "Six brothers," she said derisively. On the inner faces of all three were lichen-clogged scratches that might have been local graffiti or Stone Age ritual magic.

The Range Rover's door was open. Lee slowed her approach, sniffing frantically through her allergy-clogged nose in case it was another murder scene. There was no body slumped half out of the driver's seat. There was no sign of Cador Roberts at all. She even got down on her knees to look underneath, finding only that the ground was somehow freezing cold and soaking wet.

"Lee," Mal said. She was standing by the stone, not quite touching it, and she was very still. "You can see forever."

"Hmm?" Later, Lee would try to reinterpret that pronouncement into something profound and prophetic, but probably Mal just meant the view. The stones marked out a rise in the moorland, and they could see for miles. What they could not see, however, was any sign of Roberts. The thought was almost as frightening as the sheep slaughter. Why would someone dump their car here and walk off into the tawny forever of the moors?

"I think we're out of our depth here," Lee decided, and then a rolling line of shadow raced over, as if clouds were obscuring the sun. That sky had been entirely clear a moment before, but weather could turn suddenly on the moors, Lee told herself.

Then it began to snow.

There was a moment where the summer sky above Lee was mostly blue, and yet snowflakes were spiralling down—and she was such a city girl that alarm bells were still failing to ring. Then Mal shouted. Lee turned towards her and got a face full of blizzard.

Abruptly the wind was tearing around her, out of nowhere. It brought great skirls of snow, like the waves of the sea, raking her skin and flurrying at her clothes with a thousand sharp fingers. She staggered forwards, leaning into the wind to make progress. Mal was in the midst of the storm, hunched between two of the stones. She had her phone out, trying to take a picture of the weather. Why not? It was a prime Fortean phenomenon: unseasonal snow from an almost clear sky. Perhaps it would start raining frogs and fish next.

Lee collapsed at Mal's feet and tried to wrangle coats out of their packs—flimsy cagoules because they'd packed for rain, not for Scott of the Antarctic. The temperature had gone through the floor and her fingers were already numb. She managed to hook the hood of one coat over Mal's head and fell over into the nearest stone trying to get her own on.

The stones... That was what no amount of keep-calm-and-carry-on could handle. Before, there had been three wide-spaced stones in a field. Now there were suddenly six. Six Brothers, like the locals said. The stones were having a family reunion.

The one Lee was leaning against, a new one, had something painted on the inner face. The snow was doing a good job of washing off the redness it had been daubed with, but the artist had been following lines ground deep. She saw a curved sign—then she reinterpreted it as a figure, leaping high with tail and beak pointed downwards and one leg extended, all depicted in a few elegant lines.

"Lee," said Mal.

"Mal, have you seen *this*?"

"*Lee.*" Mal's voice was simultaneously tight and quiet, and very insistent.

Lee looked up and there were the Birdmen.

They were in the centre of the stones. No. They were where Lee's internal compass told her the centre of the stones ought to be, but things were... wrong—it felt somehow like a paper cut to the eye when she looked in their direction. There were at least three of them, although the whirling snow, *their* snow, made it hard to be sure. They were a little smaller than people, and quite a bit lower because of how they were built. She saw long legs, but a body canted forwards, counterbalanced by that sweep of tail. And that wasn't a bird's spray of plumage, now she saw it close-up, but an actual tail, stiff bones and all. Their heads were round, surprisingly large behind their beaks. Lee stared into almost perfectly black eyes, huge and set forwards, a predator's.

They were impossible, like a monk's marginalia or bestiarist's fantasy come to life. They were closest to giant ravens or, no, jackdaws, because their plumage was a scatter of black and white spots and bands. But her mind refused to take in more detail. Because they weren't animals at all.

They had capes: animal hides secured at the throat and under the belly, shapeless as ponchos. One had a pack, something bundled in skins and lashed down. Another had something, a rod, maybe a spear, balanced in the crook of its bird-arm. It wasn't a wing but had a sodden sleeve of feathers to it anyway. The hand was a crook of claws, like a taxidermist's joke.

The central one, the largest, stepped towards Mal. Lee remembered the video, and the same alien language of muscle and movement was on display here. She had forgotten the snow, the cold—had mind-space only for the play of those lean muscles, the scales where the feathers tapered above the knee, the three-toed foot with its inner digit held daintily off the ground. It evoked the pinky finger of a matron aunt taking tea. Save that aunts didn't have hooked claws like that, not in this era. Not in this *world*.

She'd initially thought the central Birdman had a big hooked beak like a—well, "like a raptor's" wouldn't edify anyone, really. Like an eagle's, say. But it wasn't a beak. It was a blade, crooked like an elbow, metal. *Bronze*, crudely hammered. And Lee saw immediately, with a zoologist's eye, how those clutches of claws would be good at holding on but terrible for manipulation. But plenty of birds can be clever with their beaks if they need to be.

It was five feet from Mal, who was trying to back away very, very slowly. No blood was visible on the bronze blade, but both of them reckoned they knew what had happened—first to Roberts' sheep and then to Roberts. And that was when reality shouldered aside all the wonder and the dreams of Fortean fame, because they realized it was going to happen to them too.

"Look out!" Lee shouted. "Mal, *run!*"

They ran. Mal had had the foresight to dump her pack, and that meant she was taking the lead, then slowing for Lee's shorter legs to catch up. The snow seemed to rush towards them no matter which way they fled, and they lost the Range Rover and the track almost immediately. Mal was heading uphill and Lee laboured after, seeing fleet shadows left and right, their pursuers pacing them effortlessly. She heard them, too, calling each to each. Not the keening of hawks nor the brittle croaks of ravens, but a panoply of whistles and clicks, clucks and chuckles, as versatile as parrots. It sounded like laughing.

Mal stopped suddenly and Lee almost ran into her, which would have sent both of them plummeting ten feet down a rock-studded slope. It wasn't the drop that stopped her, though. It was the view.

It was recognizably the moors, even though snow lay in the hollows. Down below, where a vigorous stream cut its course, a herd of animals had gathered to drink. They were big as shire horses, with something of the same ponderousness, but shaggy to their ankles with drab coats of feathers. Their necks were long and their crested heads small. Two or three stretched up to keep watch over the surrounding countryside while the rest drank. They did not see the two girls, or rather, the humans meant nothing to them. But when the Birdmen materialized on either side of Lee and Mal, the beasts gave out anxious knocking sounds and the herd began to move off.

Mal hadn't seen the Birdmen yet. She was pointing at something in the middle distance. The snow had ebbed, so they could make out drifting lines of smoke. Lee saw structures: something like yurts, perhaps; a cluster of animals corralled nearby and industrious movement.

Then, from almost at Lee's elbow, one of the Birdmen spoke. *Hak*, it went. It took a few steps along the ridge of the rise. It had a scalloped flint in its mouth, and now it wiped it on the ground as though sharpening it, its gaze never leaving Lee.

Hak.

Run.

Lee backed away, plucking at Mal's cagoule. Two Birdmen now crouched amidst the rocks, watching them keenly, the third behind them somewhere, and abruptly Lee could not stand before that thoughtful stare a moment longer. That evaluating, calculating regard, eyes deep as wells—glittering with cruelty and murder, perhaps. But also with undeniable intelligence.

One of them settled, rocking on its haunches, and Lee suddenly remembered a friend's cat. It would wriggle almost exactly like that before a pounce.

She ran, and Mal was a step behind her, just a step. She would swear to it.

*

They treated Lee for hypothermia and exposure, later. She didn't remember much of it, didn't remember getting *out*, if *out* was the right word. *Out* and *in* implied a relationship to

29

regular directions that couldn't possibly apply. As soon as she was able to string two words together she asked about Mal, and they asked her the same. The locals were sharp enough to spot when two girls went onto the moors and only one came back.

She remembered the local police, the hospital staff, all those earnest faces. *Of course we'll find your friend, miss, just tell us everything you remember.* The words boiled up inside and choked her, because she couldn't tell them. They'd think she was mad, that she was guilty of something. She talked about the Roberts farm and the moors. She talked about snow, because that on its own seemed just the right side of Crazy Town, even though it was July. She talked about getting lost. Somehow her mouth stitched together a consistent tarpaulin of fabrication that could be draped over what she *actually* remembered, so the result had the same general shape but concealed all of the details. She discovered a gift for mendacity that she'd never known she possessed.

She wondered, lying alone in her hospital bed, if she'd doomed Mal somehow by lying. But if Mal had been anywhere they could have found her, then Lee's story might as well have been the real one.

They interviewed Lee three times, three different earnest, comforting police staff going through variants of the same questions, with her trotting out her true-enough answers—and she was bone-tired, shaking and upset. She could tell they were all *Poor girl, losing her friend,* and not one of them guessed she'd lost *her lover, her heart, her whole life.* She made herself stay awake, desperate to see Mal come through the hospital room door, unscathed, even if she blamed Lee for leaving, even if she hated her, even if she never wanted to see her again.

At about seven the next morning, Lee was exhausted enough that she'd started seeing Birdmen, ragged and warlike, in the corners of her eyes. And in came a policeman who looked no older than she was, asking questions with an embarrassed little smile. *Sorry, miss, be done in just a moment.* And Lee realized he wasn't here about Mal; he was asking about Cador Roberts, also missing. He didn't seem to quite know who she was, just asked about Roberts—how Lee knew him and when she'd last seen him. She didn't and hadn't, so couldn't help him.

Something broke then. Some vital rubber band of discretion snapped and flew off. She told him everything: the video, the sheep, the Birdmen, the impossible fucking vista of the snow-swept moor and the thundering, feathery reptilian beasts. She saw him write her off as stark raving mad quite early on, but he'd been well brought up—and she was the goddamn Ancient Mariner and wouldn't let him make his excuses and leave. She talked at him for twenty minutes straight, and out of force of habit he scribbled it all down in his notebook, although she'd bet it went in the station bin the moment he got back. After that, when Lee had finally vomited up all those words her lies had corralled within her, he actually gave her a smile, a top-of-the-range placate-the-madwoman model, and told her he'd be in touch. Thankfully he never was.

The search went on for two weeks. They found Mal's pack by the three stones of the Six Brothers. They didn't find her, of course. She'd gone in a direction not picked out on the compass rose, off all maps. Lee remembered Mal's dad, pitching up hot and angry after driving for hours. She remembered the look of absolute loathing he'd turned on her because Lee had been found and his daughter had not. She remembered looking at her own reflection the same way for many, many mornings. Mal had been the centre of her life, the object of her desire, the light that made all the petty, grim darknesses of the world bearable. As the days went on and the search became an exercise in public relations, Lee remembered looking into the future and seeing…nothing. A life without Mal, something she'd never planned for. Stupid teenage lovelorn girl, but she had loved, and then she'd lost, and right then she didn't think the former made the latter in any way better.

They never found Mal. That made it worse for her family, because to them she was lying out on the moors somewhere like a stray sheep, vanished impossibly into that little knee joint of wilderness at the southern tip of the British Isles. But Lee knew she was *elsewhere*—could even console herself with the thought *It's what she would have wanted*. A bespoke fate for Elsinore Mallory, to which no other human being had ever been consigned.

*

As the years went by and Lee—by her own estimation—miraculously didn't open her wrists in the bath or chug the contents of her parents' medicine cabinet, she mythologized the disappearance. It made things easier. She was The Girl Who Stayed, Mal was The Girl Who Left, like they were immortalized in *Doctor Who* episodes. She used to dream of Mal as though she was still out there somehow, as though she'd come back.

And Lee never gave up on the cryptids and the Forteana.

Though neither did she go mad for it, like some Birdman-hunting Van Helsing. She kept on as she had been, wrote articles for local papers, then some national papers; contributed top-ten lists of weird shit to websites; was paid enough to make the rent and buy a sandwich. And every so often she imagined Mal reading those pieces and laughing at her. It made her feel close still, even when the fourth anniversary of her disappearance had come and gone.

Until Mal called.

Or someone called who sounded like Mal used to sound, a voice indelibly engraved in Lee's memory. She wanted to meet, with no time for catch-ups and pleasantries and Lee's *What the fuck do you mean by this? Who is this? Why are you ... What are you—Wait!* Just a place, a time—pedestrian, ridiculously mundane. And a choice: to go, or not to go.

Lee went.

Interlude: The Wanderers

Excerpt from *Other Edens:*
Speculative Evolution and Intelligence by
Professor Ruth Emerson of the
University of California

Over time, the tranquillity of the Ediacaran period's sessile, quilted forms met its end. The low-energy biology of those supine species was replaced by an acceleration into the world of tooth and claw, competition and predation. This was the death knell of the Ediacaran epoch, when one species discovered that harvesting material from its defenceless neighbours was vastly more efficient than filtering detritus for a living.

There was an explosion of biological disparity. No more were quilts the fashionable things to be seen in. Whilst some creatures still sat and sieved, the world was moulded by new pressures. Life had an urgent need to move—towards, for predators; away, for prey—to hide, ambush, devour and protect.

Welcome to the Cambrian period.

Some species became swift, flexible, muscular: slender ribbons of life eeling through the water. Some burrowed into the sediment. Still more used a strategy borne of desperation: let the predators break their teeth and blunt their claws on their hard shells. Unwanted trace elements and compounds that had been building up within organic bodies like all-over kidney stones were secreted on the outside as armour. These creatures would be first on land, first in the air, in any timeline. For this is just one timeline.

In our world, those ribbons of flesh inherited something

greater. The internal rod they attached their muscles to became, eventually, part of the spine. They became *us*, over the course of half a billion years. But not in this world.

Why? There is never a definitive moment when a finger is on the scales, tilting them away from the course our own history took. Perhaps it is only chance that dictates which seed of time will grow and which will not.

The great predators of this Cambrian seascape are the anomalocarids. They too have a carapace. Their bodies are pen-shaped, like squid, flanked by rippling waves of flattened fin-legs that propel them swiftly through the water. They have huge stalked eyes for spotting their prey, which in this world is most things that move. In this timeline, perhaps they are a little faster, their eyes more acute, their arms swifter to grasp than in others. Our putative ancestors, little boneless eel-things, never do well here. They cling on as sessile sea squirts and similar atavisms, but no fish develop in these seas; there are no jaws, no dorsal fins to scare the swimmers, no slow coelacanth cousin hauling itself onto land, modified swim bladder pressed into service as a makeshift lung. No tyrannosaurs, no mammoths. No *us*. This is not our world; this is not our story.

Nor is it the story of the anomalocarids, if it's revenge you want. They too will pass, or at least recede into irrelevance.

To win the arms race of *this* Cambrian is to have the strongest shell. It is to be hauled up from the sediment by the anomalocarids' fearsome arms, ground between their spines, gnawed at by their toothed ring of a mouth, then abandoned for flimsier prey. From such a forge, here is what will fight its way to dominance.

They are segmented beings, with a head like a crescent

moon, a body of three lobes, a shell of calcite and compound eyes where each facet is a tiny tubule of stone. At the start, nothing in particular distinguishes them. They remain trundlers on the seabed for a long, long time. But they *have* a long, long time. They have, though they cannot know it, half a billion years on their long road to now.

When at last they take to the land, their shells fend off the killer radiation of the sun and their respiratory surfaces hold enough water for brief seaside strolls. Their articulated legs are initially only strong enough to drag their jointed bellies in the sand, but that will change. Their predators (other trilobite descendants as well as the gamely persevering anomalocarids) are slow to follow. By now there is a burgeoning plant ecology out there for grazing; a few million years later there is a burgeoning herbivore ecology. Life makes its way up the beach with increasing confidence. The land is conquered by a succession of variations on woodlice and horseshoe crabs and silverfish, derived trilobites experimenting with terrestrial locomotion.

What might not be evident is that many of the trilobite descendants have solved one problem that none who come after—in any timeline—will ever crack. They are immortal.

Why, after all, do we die? Yes, there are technological remedies. There is the virtual life everlasting that is "uploading," and we'll see more of that; there is the bloody-minded persistence of medical science without limits, procuring a bespoke longevity for those who can afford or mandate it. But these Cambrians simply evolved out of death by natural causes.

So again, why do we die? Because each time our cells divide, we eat into the chemical caps at the ends of our chromosomes. And as we wear away these telomeres, we accelerate towards an end point where the grabby hands of our cells' biochemical mechanisms can't get purchase on them. They fumble and drop them until, giving up in disgust, they refuse to replicate any more. Even where such degradation fails to happen, we reach another sticky end: cancers, cells out-dividing their neighbours, hostile and uncompromising.

The trilobite descendants, or at least one lineage, practically sweat telomerase—rebuilding their battered chromosomes every time their cells divide. They still die like flies from predation—sooner or later *something* will get you—but built into their design is this truth: they don't *have* to die. The philosophers that they *will* one day produce will never face the existential question that haunts *us*. The question of why, no matter how good the show, the curtain must always come down.

Their biggest challenge—the one that limits their size and kills them despite their genetic chicanery—is moulting their exoskeleton, when all that hard support turns soft. Grow large enough and the effort of shrugging out of their entire *skin* is eventually fatal. And that, surely, is the end of the road for the Cambrians.

Except for one lineage of trilobite descendants, still passably trilobite-like despite the intervening millions of years. These Cambrians moult their shells away in flakes, shedding pieces heavy with corralled bacteria and parasites, growing constantly without ever needing to discard their entire hard wardrobe in one go. They grow big; they grow old. Give them a few million years and they're as big as whales in the sea, as big as elephants on land.

Big doesn't mean smart, of course; ask any sauropod. But

they achieve a kind of sentience around the time our own distant ancestors are exiting the sea. Their sentience is a strange thing, a personal thing. As they master their world, so they learn to avoid the countless deaths by misfortune that would otherwise cut short their lives. Communication between individuals arises from intellectual desire, not social need. Their technology, as it develops, focuses on self-modification and improvement, further taking the reins from mere brute evolution. They become masters of their own growth and shapes, changing themselves for new environments and purposes, growing their exoskeletons into the tools they need to unpack the universe.

By the end of the Permian period they are the inheritors of a culture with a million years of unbroken sophistication— ossified and brittle, with an assurance of its own endlessness. The end of the Permian is when Earth devours its children, though, a time of colossal environmental upheaval and extinction on a global scale. The Cambrians are not ready. Individuals ten thousand years old expire in the long heat-death of a mass extinction. Vast carcasses float and decay in the waves. On land, assemblages of fallen, hollowed segments mark the deaths of these lords of creation.

The surviving Cambrians regard the world with bitter betrayal. Something new has come to them: an understanding of what it means to be complacent in an uncaring universe. From their sheltered refugia they expand out again, forced into an unwonted but necessary proximity with each other. They are finally becoming a civilization, where before they were only ever distantly polite individuals. They fear, now, and because they do not die they do not mythologize that fear or forget its causes. Instead, they improve their senses until they can see forever into the night sky. With their naked eyes they view and measure the minute disruptions that alien planets make to distant stars.

Around the time dinosaurs rule our Earths, the Cambrians are walking with their many legs upon the moon. They taste the harsh atmosphere of Mars and amend their biology to suit. They grow themselves photon drives and solar sails. And in space, they grow *really* big. Gravity has always been an inconvenience to them.

Long before we are even a dream in the eye of an ape, they have spread out through the galaxy, truly the greatest of all the Earths' children. But then, they had a head start, after all. Half a billion years is a long time.

And if you saw a *really* big one…just imagine. Through the dust clouds and debris of some far star system, there is an articulated body a hundred kilometres from blunt prow to trailing segmented tail. Its stony carapace is pocked with impact craters and dust abrasion, in places grown into outlandish horns and curving spines longer than skyscrapers according to alien necessity or sartorial preference. It cruises past planets under its own power, devouring asteroids and converting their mass into pure energy to power its eternal flight. And within the vaulted chambers and organs of its body, within the hundred-metre-thick shell, there is a mind vaster than you can imagine. It regards the universe with a patient curiosity, a being that knows it has all the time there ever will be to discover everything there is to know. Because they are realistic about their accomplishments, they consider themselves the lords of all creation. They are now proof against any mere global catastrophe, immortal as long as the universe itself persists.

Until one day, in some far orbit, a discovery is made by one such arthropod descendant...philosopher? Scientist? God? A discovery of such dire import that it breaks a million years of silence and burns a planet's worth of energy in its haste to communicate the news to its vastly distributed kin.

It is coming to an end. It is all coming to an end. And both their mastery and immortality are finally revealed as a cruel sham.

2.

I

Julian Sabreur was, he had to admit, no young Sean Connery or even Roger Moore. Perhaps a little Daniel Craig about the eyes and chin, if Craig had dark hair and narrower cheekbones. At just shy of forty, he felt that he should have left such comparisons behind with the rest of his adolescent baggage. When he first started shaving, though, he'd taken to staring at his newly adult features, saying "Moneypenny," or "Shaken, not stirred." Even doing the sudden point-the-gun-at-the-camera bit from the credits. His dad had walked in on this once, to his eternal chagrin. Still got brought up at Christmas dinner, that one.

So now the eminently adult Sabreur, Julian Sabreur, could not banish the thought of 007 entirely whenever he took up the razor. It was just one of the many things he would never, ever share with any of his colleagues. Except Alison, who he'd told two years ago. They'd both been drunk and off-shift at New Year's, she still reeling from her divorce, he from the death of an old friend and mentor. And there hadn't been anything like *that* between them, even if Josie had cast suspicious looks Julian's way come January 3rd when he finally came home. But he couldn't talk to Josie about his work, and recently he couldn't talk to her about much at all—apart from John's long crash-dive towards GCSEs or whether they should sell or rent her late mother's flat in Scarborough. Instead, Julian spent his time defending the country. It sounded very grand, put like that, but was mostly forms and reports and meetings.

The most dangerous-looking part of Julian's face was the faint scar above one eyebrow. It was jagged enough that one subordinate had, for about two weeks, taken to referring to him as "Harry Potter" behind his back. Until Julian had called him in for a Meeting Without Coffee to explain that (1) that sort of thing was generally not conducive to a chap's career prospects and (2) if he didn't understand that people *talked*, then maybe the Security Service wasn't the right place for him. Julian had inherited the tradition of Meetings Without Coffee from his late mentor, Germaine Willoughs, who'd had it from his own and so on back, probably, to the days of Kipling and the Great Game.

It was his turn to do the school run this morning, and once John had been abandoned to the last miserable few yards with the bell already sounding and Josie had vanished to the coffee shop she called her "office," he had time to catch up with work. Working from home two days a week seemed an odd luxury for someone in the Service, but he had a secure phone, and so long as he didn't leave his encrypted laptop somewhere, it wasn't a problem. Julian considered that 007 would not be on Her Majesty's Secret Service wearing yesterday's joggers and a faded Marillion T-shirt. However, 007 was foreign service rather than home. Probably they had different standards.

There was a stack of reports waiting for him on one Billy

White, including one from Alison. She hadn't flagged it as urgent and he knew how thorough an analyst she was, so he decided he'd skim everything else first, then give it the time it deserved.

Billy White, born William Tams Wellish, should have been small fry, but somehow he'd found a pond to be a big fish in. There was the usual police record, plenty of wrist-rappings for criminal damage, a little ABH, threatening behaviour. His wife had also suffered suspicious injuries including a broken arm, but she'd insisted she was just "clumsy." These days he had lawyers, which meant that his appearances at the nick and in the dock had ebbed, even if his actual activities had only grown. Right now, White was the darling of greatgeorg-england.com—the missing *e* a constant visual stumble every time Julian saw it written down. The website greeted visitors with a wealth of St. George regalia surrounding a sensation-alist news feed which collected every conceivable scare story about how England was under threat from...just about anyone whose ancestors had come over post 1066.

Alison's initial intel gathering had already followed White through two dozen websites and message boards, highlighting links with the already radicalized, both here and abroad. White had never been stupid enough to make one of the dangerous lists; his involvement was always just second-hand enough to keep him from the spotlight. Julian had monitored several far-right potential troublemakers in his career, and he knew White wasn't quite in the elite of those circles. He'd never made it to a local council seat either, though he'd stood in the last election, and he wasn't smooth enough to wrangle a mainstream media platform outside of the usual websites. Julian reckoned he knew the signs of someone making that transition, though, going from foot soldier to commissioned officer in the nationalistic war. All of which would have been entirely a problem for the regular police and outside Julian's remit, had not Billy clashed with an individual on a very different government watch list.

Julian caught up with the most recent addenda from the Extremist Analysis Unit, which still reckoned White would huff and puff but not actually blow anyone's house down, or indeed up. Next he needed to check what White's antagonist had done overnight that might have added more fuel to this fire.

Dr. Kay Amal Khan was never going to be one of Billy White's favourite people, even back when she was a he. Julian remembered her from way back, when she was still deep within the DST crowd—Defence Science & Technology. A slender man with a pencil-thin moustache and sideburns; he'd been awkward, gangling, frustrated—a brilliant mind unable to express itself. Academically and in the workplace he'd ended up losing the spotlight to more forthright colleagues. But Julian and his superiors were well aware who was really giving them the clever sums, and who therefore needed to have an eye kept on them. Following Khan's transition, she had... come out of her shell, Julian supposed. She was like a different person, and that included not backing down or taking shit from anyone. Her social media profile (which the analysts endlessly dissected) now read like a war journal. She regularly clashed with bigots and white supremacists, hence the current reason she was giving Julian Sabreur a headache. More than one of his team was muttering about "PC gone mad," too. Traditional values being hardwired into the Secret Service, it wasn't hard to find people there who scowled at the whole idea of Khan and obstinately clung on to their masculine pronouns.

Julian had met Khan twice himself, once before and once after. Prepping for the second interview, he'd braced himself, expecting to experience his own establishmental knee-jerk of prejudice, which he knew must reside within him. And then Khan had turned up, a tall woman, elegantly dressed in a turquoise-and-gold kameez. Loud, quick to laugh, foul-mouthed, a world away from the retiring young man Julian remembered. Halfway through the interview, when she went out for a cigarette (because she smoked now), he had to admit that being a woman suited Khan a whole lot better. She was obviously far more comfortable in her own skin and making more progress with her rarefied work.

As for Khan's faded-red-carpet treatment by the security services, she was a world-class authority within a tiny niche of experimental mathematics, one of only three people who had ever made any headway with whatever the hell it was, and the only one HM Government could call on. She was therefore gently discouraged from meeting too many foreign nationals or going on holidays abroad.

Catching up with the Extremist Analysis Unit's report took Julian to midday. It told him that while White's followers were still rattling sabres against Khan, this was likely as far as it would go.

After that, he began on Alison's report over a sandwich and tea. As usual she'd gone down the rabbit hole, far deeper than the EA Unit, but Alison Matchell had a good track record of catching rabbits. She'd picked up activity on three more online boards, highlighting a claim that White would sort out Khan, and soon. All hearsay, but Alison had linked the commentator to foreknowledge of a handful of violent attacks in the past.

Alison had proceeded to analyse these previous incidents. Then she extrapolated her conclusions. Billy White wasn't just an ambitious right-winger. She believed he had a handler, though who this was or why they'd want to use Billy this way, she couldn't say. Recent incidents had been written off as steam by the unit—faecal matter had been posted to Khan's new workplace at UCL, and someone had lobbed a brick through a window at her previous address. Alison read it differently.

Alison was simultaneously an excellent and a terrible analyst. Terrible because analysts were rigorously trained out of relying on gut feeling, which opened the door to unexamined prejudice and guesswork. Excellent because her guesswork was extremely good—as was her analysis. She had something of a sixth sense that Julian had come to rely on, and he appreciated that she was never anything but honest about the fact that she ended up pulling on some very tenuous threads.

On the other hand, Operation Glassknife, as he called it, had a budget. Unless he was certain White was going to be a problem, he'd been instructed to leave it to the police. Julian stared at Alison's report, rereading paragraphs at random, juggling priorities and outcomes. The thing about James Bond, when you got down to it, was that *he* had carte blanche to go and do stuff. And M didn't ride him about budgetary overspend.

Julian tapped a number into his phone.

"DI Royce speaking."

"Kier, it's me." Julian waited to see what kind of a mood the man was in.

"Oh shit, what now?" Still with Royce's faint aftertaste of

Caernarfon, despite the fact the man had been based at the Met for twelve years.

"Nothing, nothing, just calling to catch up," Julian said, devoid of sincerity. "How's the wife? Kids?"

"Still not speaking to me," Royce said flatly. "Dog's still dead, too, before you ask. What do you *want*, Jules?"

"Got any lads sitting on their hands near Primrose Hill?"

In the staticky quiet he could almost hear the man thinking that through. "Not so's you'd notice, not right now. All quiet on the northern front, isn't it though? And I know you've not called to tell me otherwise because we have *channels* for that, Jules."

"We absolutely have," Julian agreed. "And I will absolutely bring all the relevant paperwork to the next Joint Service meeting and put in the request for your assistance. I'll table it as soon as I get off the phone, in fact. And I am absolutely not suggesting that if you had a few spare lads from the On Call Investigations Unit, they might find the street food second to none over that way. That would obviously be completely outside my brief..."

Royce had been counter-terrorism duty officer on two past operations on Julian's watch. The two of them had been like cats and dogs at the start, but had each ended up in a position to make the other look good. Favours were owed both ways, the kind that never quite went away.

"How much of this are you pulling out of your arse, mate?" Royce asked at last.

"Possibly all of it. In which case I will owe you twice over, and I will come to apologize in person."

Another thoughtful pause, as of a man who had to balance his own budgets and account to his own chiefs.

"Plenty of cultural flashpoints over thataways," Royce mused. "Be good for a few of the new lads to get a feel for the area."

Julian felt a knot of tension he hadn't quite acknowledged uncurl. "It's probably nothing."

"Well, knowing you, we'd all prefer if it *was* nothing," Royce agreed. "Long may it remain so, say I."

After Julian got off the phone, he discovered that no less a personage than Dr. Kay Amal Khan herself had emailed him direct, demanding to meet with him. This wasn't the first time either, as Khan had long since lost any tolerance for the slow mill of regular channels. Sabreur sighed. Today was clearly going to be all about Khan. She simply preferred to deal with people she'd met before, but Julian composed a message for someone else to find out what she wanted. The old guard in the office, the ones who didn't like what Khan represented any more than Billy White, would snicker about her having her eye on him. They'd doubtless use it to undermine Julian's position and dignity, all those old boys who felt he shouldn't have been jumped up to his current post. For a moment he considered ignoring Khan's email entirely, toeing the office line to avoid the looks and whispers. Then he hated himself for it. And it was only a short stop from there to joining in and making his own life easier. It was depressing how he could scratch the surface and find just a little bit of Billy White staring at him in the mirror.

He forwarded Khan's email. At this stage, and without a confirmed threat, it wasn't protocol for him to meet with Khan. After that, it was time to ferry John from school to his badminton club.

That evening, and despite the glower from Josie, he took

the Tube across London to Shepherd's Bush. He wanted to relax and talk, and home wasn't a place where either tended to happen these days.

Alison lived in a decent-sized flat which she'd retreated to after her divorce, paid for by a combination of salary, settlement and inheritance. Because her concerns about personal security went above and beyond the call of professionalism, he called ahead, letting the phone ring four times before ringing off then redialling.

"Matchbox," he said.

"Spiker." Her voice came to him distantly amused, as always. After they'd first met, she'd gone a year before realizing she'd misheard his surname.

The rattle of bolt and chain after she'd checked him out on the cameras was a familiar ritual. Despite the fact that there was nothing sexual between them, Julian felt a stab of guilt as the door opened, right on the heels of the rush of well-being he always got from being here.

Alison Matchell, then: middling height and a few years his senior. The taut boniness of the woman he'd first known was now filling out, as though she'd been under the pressure of some dense and punishing atmosphere throughout her failing marriage. Her blonde hair was bobbed, framing a thin face dominated by antique spectacles with mother-of-pearl-inlaid frames.

"You look brutal," she told him, by which she probably meant just frowny. "Am I making up a bed on the sofa?"

"What? No!" And another stab of guilt, because this was exactly where he'd go if things ever got to that with Josie. Alison would have the sofa ready in an instant, a safe house long prepared for emergencies.

She gave him a measuring glance and hoicked a bottle of Chardonnay out of the fridge. "Does that mean no signed copy of *Beguine*, then?"

"I...didn't ask. Next time, sorry." Because, of all things, Alison was an avid reader of Josie's books, which had not had the expected result of endearing her to Josie.

"Tell her it's her best one. Very racy. I approve." It was not common knowledge at work that Julian's wife made a decent living writing erotica, another Sword of Damocles over his poor, abused dignity.

Julian took a glass and sipped. Alison's three monitors were all on, displaying a mishmash of websites, reports and scrolling chat. "Still online?"

"Always. Burning the midnight oil twice as brightly at both ends, you know me," she agreed. "Screw it for this evening, though. The world'll just have to not set itself on fire until civilized o'clock tomorrow morning." And yet he could tell, by the way she sat, that a sliver of her attention was still on the screens, no matter what. It was the meat and drink of the conversations she had with her Service-vetted therapist and the final knife in the back of her marriage. Alison was a professional worrier. It meant that as an analyst she turned over a lot more stones than most of her peers, but she couldn't turn it off. "I don't watch the news, you know?" she'd told him years ago, when he was the one providing safe haven. "An analyst who can't read the headlines without breaking out in a cold sweat. Because I've got no control over it, at that remove. At least when I'm working I feel I've got leverage."

The conversation hovered about work like a fly over food for as long as either of them could keep it up. Yes, John was doing well enough at school. Derek, the departed Mr. Alison, was being a pain in the arse about contact with the girls again, unless by now it was just the girls themselves. Alison's latest Netflix obsession turned out to be something he'd seen two years before. And eventually Alison just jabbed him painfully in the arm and said, "Say it."

"Dr. K got in touch." Because this was something he needed to air, and there was nobody else he was willing to talk it over with.

"Told you she would." Alison topped up their glasses. "Say why?"

"Probably wants to let me know we're not doing enough. Which might be true, but it's all we can do within budget."

"Budget," she echoed. "James Budget, licenced to spend as little as possible. She'll get your personal email next."

"How?"

"Science-fu," Alison supplied unhelpfully. Julian reflected that this might be close to the truth. One of the major applications of Khan's work had supposedly been codebreaking— by some kind of arcane data transformation that just sidestepped conventional security. Plenty of high-ups in the Service had been alternately rubbing their hands and crapping themselves over the possibility. Khan was no hacker, but if anyone could magic up email addresses out of pure maths, it was her.

"Just go get permission to meet somewhere secure. Better sooner," was Alison's advice. *Before she causes some godawful data breach* went unsaid, as did a great deal of what actually passed between them. They were old hands, and they'd known each other too many years. Even here, in Alison's fortress, sensitive information remained implicit wherever possible.

"It's probably nothing," she added after a while.

"I know." Meaning—and understood—that he'd take it seriously nonetheless.

Alison's grey cat, Simms, sauntered out of the bedroom and gave them an unimpressed stare, eerily similar to Josie's expression on his exit earlier that evening. Alison tried to make a fuss of him, but Simms was in one of his standoffish moods and instead desultorily mauled the desk leg.

Julian was going for the dregs of the wine, but he knew instantly when Alison's body language changed. A moment later she was off the sofa and staring at her screens, as Simms scooted off to hide under a chair.

"Fuck," she said. "Spiker, just been messaged by my source. Says White's on the move, means business."

"Your message-board source. Who you're not supposed to be liaising with directly because that's not your job."

She grimaced back at him. "Sometimes you have to get your hands dirty."

You don't, Julian thought, but said nothing as Alison stood back from the screen, biting her lip.

"Word came down from on high, my source says. Then White just grabbed him and they're on the move. Going to sort out K."

Julian stood stock still for two seconds, digesting this. It was all unverified sources. He couldn't ask Royce to go in mob-handed on nothing more than this. Not with an analyst liaising direct with someone else's suspect source. The whole thing stank of White trying to smoke out some half-sensed enemies, and Royce wouldn't thank him for throwing that at him. Julian needed something concrete.

"Where from and when?"

Alison was already ahead of him, calling up online maps,

London streets on one screen, the messenger window on another. *Where are you?*

Left club all2gether 6ofus 2herplace now

"Club" meant the snooker hall where Billy White held court, Julian guessed. Alison was already drawing best-fit road routes between there and Khan's Camden flat. Julian was calling Naia Osmaili.

After a chance involvement in an operation three years back, Julian had cultivated Osmaili carefully, making sure any help she gave was generously rewarded with flowers and those chocolates she liked. She wasn't in the security services and she only had the haziest idea of what Julian actually did. But from her position as a technical adminis-trator for Transport For London, she could call up footage from every traffic camera in the city's network, and so much more quickly than going via the police. Not exactly what she *should* be doing, but Osmaili was a serial voyeur of other people's lives. Her night shifts were spent illegally recording accidents, crazy pedestrians bolting through moving traffic and, in one case, someone who turned out to have planted a car bomb. Julian's team had looked into her after the bomb squad had been and gone, and she'd been on his contacts list ever since.

Alison had identified a dozen cameras on likely routes and her source had confirmed White's transport as *whitevan reg LDO9smthing*.

Osmaili was the keenest pair of eyes in the business, so Julian passed her the information. It felt like an unforgivable breach of good tradecraft, but so was getting Kay Amal Khan killed. Alison was on her phone now, getting brief, punctuated texts from her source as he jolted about in the back of White's van. She'd tried Khan's number, but the physicist wasn't picking up.

Osmaili had her own phone camera turned towards her screens, giving Julian the best view of what she was looking at.

"Remarkably obliging, this chap of yours," Julian observed to Alison as they watched Osmaili monitor the routes to Khan's flat. He pictured the administrator lounging in her office chair, squinting at the screens and glancing over her shoulder in case her supervisor was near.

Alison's silence told him she'd been hiding things and felt guilty about it. "I've been cultivating him," she said. "He's a thug called Cleary. Been in with people like White most of his life, his family included. Claimed a change of heart." She was leaning over Julian's shoulder intently, her hair pricking his cheek.

"Found God?"

"Half of these guys already *have* God. But he beat someone half to death last year. Like an initiation..." Her lips moved as she read the newest text. "Didn't sit well with him. Tried to turn himself in, and someone got him hooked up with us."

Then Naia Osmaili was in Julian's ear in a hoarse whisper that suggested her boss was doing the rounds. "There! White van there! Is that it?"

He squinted: white van, yes; the registration was hidden by the tailgating hatchback behind. However, it was driving carefully, letting other vehicles pull out ahead of it, the way people in London so seldom did. Almost as if the driver *really* didn't want to be pulled over.

He conferred with Osmaili again. The camera view obligingly skipped two junctions down the road and they watched the van amble up and indicate. As it turned, Osmaili read off the plate. It matched the partial Alison's source had given them. The cloud of possibilities collapsed into a single certainty. *It might be a set-up. The source might be lying to see what we'll do. This could even be a hoax, leading to us kicking down the door to scare the crap out of Khan.* He had a single exchange of looks with Alison, knowing she was heading down all the same blind alleys. Her hand gripped his shoulder.

"You trust your source?" And then, even as she replied in the affirmative, he was thanking Osmaili and ringing off.

White's people were now far too close to where Khan lived. *Perhaps they're just going to break a few windows. Perhaps they'll paint a couple of "go home queer" messages on the wall. Perhaps, perhaps...* And then he was dialling Royce and hoping the man would pick up. Now he had established the threat beyond reasonable doubt, he could call it in to Royce and the SO15 officially so it was all above board. That done, Julian snagged his coat from the back of Alison's door.

"Leave it to the professionals," she told him, and she was right. Matters were in the domain of the police now. Royce's lads who just happened to be kicking their heels at Primrose Hill would be told he'd received an "anonymous tip-off" and could take a look. And most likely it was nothing and they'd have to apologize for getting Dr. Khan out of bed.

James Bond would have gone. In fact, Bond would already *be* there, without relying on other people, because Bond was omnicompetent. Julian Sabreur was not.

"I'm going to the area," he said. It was a wretched halfway house and he knew it. "Just...nearby. In case."

"In case what?" Alison was at her computers, pointedly logging out. "You're not a crime scene investigator. You've done what you can, Spiker. Besides, you need to call in and update whoever's on late shift, tell them Op Glassknife might have gone south."

He could feel his adolescent dreams of action herodom floating away like autumn leaves. He adopted a crisp smile. "Caught up in the moment, there. You know how it is."

"I know." And she shrugged into her own coat. "Come on then. I'll drive."

He lost most of the journey to that familiar adult tension that was a mix of "I should be doing something" and "I have possibly screwed up" with a side order of "I have just generated so much damn paperwork for someone, and that someone is probably me." And, very deeply and distantly, because he kept it chained like a malodorous dog at the end of the garden of his mind, there was the memory of a single moment. He'd been working on the traffic footage and Alison had been breathing in his ear, hair brushing his cheek—the two of them yoked to a single purpose. He put it with all the other things he couldn't afford to keep but wasn't able to throw away.

Alison's driving was a Zen balance between aggression and caution. She was hyperaware of everything on the road, exploiting every opportunity while leaving not even a ripple of horns or anger behind her. Her jaw was clenched, because when she was out of the house everything became a potential threat. She found a parking space and the two of them had an unconvincingly casual coffee, within ten minutes' walk of Khan's address. The late-shift barista plainly thought they were breaking up with one another, from her sidelong glances. Alison was covertly checking her phone every couple of minutes. Her source had gone silent.

Come on, Royce. And even as he thought it, his phone

buzzed. *Probably it's nothing. Probably he's calling to bitch at me for wasting everyone's time.*

"Royce?"

"Goddamn, Jules." The Caernarfon ran stronger when Royce was under pressure. "Just…what the piss is this hole you've dug for me?"

Julian stood abruptly, almost upsetting the table. "What's the situation?"

"I have two bastard *corpses* on my hands, Jules, and another two waiting for the ambulance. You and I are going to have a talk about unofficial favours."

Julian went cold. "Khan—?"

"What?" Royce's voice, briefly mechanical with bad signal. "Oh, your woman's fine. No, not her."

"Your people—?"

His tone of utter chagrin was obviously mollifying in some way, because Royce sounded less punchy when he said, "No, my lads are fine, but—"

"Royce, we're coming over."

There was an ambulance strobing blue fire across the street when the two of them hurried up. Royce's SO15 boys were handling access and keeping a crowd of late-nighters and rubbernecking neighbours at a respectful distance, and Royce himself stood with a handful of uniformed officers outside Khan's building. He caught sight of Julian and excused himself from the huddle. Julian knew Kieran Royce as solid and unflappable, a broad, balding man whose face relaxed into an avuncular smile whether he was feeling jolly or not. Right now the smile was nowhere to be seen.

"It's a goddamn war zone in there, mate," he complained. Paramedics were stretchering someone out of the front door, the features all too familiar from Julian's daily briefings. Billy White.

"What the hell happened?"

"Sixty-four-thousand-dollar bastard question," Royce agreed.

The extent of their knowledge was this: Royce had rallied his people but they'd arrived too late. White's lot had forced the lock on Khan's apartment building and gone in. They'd taken not just weapons but gaffer tape and plastic ties, which suggested they'd been intending to snatch Khan and take her elsewhere for the real fun.

Looking at the timings later, Julian reckoned that Royce's people might have been in time to catch White's lot leaving with Khan if things had played out differently. Instead they'd arrived to find the front door open, and then progressed with all due caution up the stairs to Khan's flat. Khan's door had been kicked open—her neighbours were starting to peek out, and one had called the police—and inside was the aforementioned warzone.

White had gone in with three heavies, and they'd been taken apart so brutally that one of the paramedics was talking about a bear attack he'd once seen. White and one other were found dead, the other two insensible. All outward signs suggested they'd been beaten savagely with whatever was to hand, with sufficient force to break bones and crack skulls. It was as though they'd encountered a frenzied berserker. Khan's flat was trashed, barely two sticks of furniture still connected. "So now the hunt's on for some meth-crazed lunatic," Royce summarized, "but at least it's my problem and not yours. I'm guessing this wasn't what you were expecting, Jules?" *Or you'd have warned me*, was the unspoken rider.

Julian was agreeing when Alison nudged him. On the far

side of the ambulance, sitting on a doorstep in her dressing gown, was Kay Amal Khan. She was cadging a light from one of the onlookers, but shooed the girl away when she saw Julian. The glow of the cigarette seemed to form wavering figures of eight in her shaking hands.

*

"I told you I needed to speak with you," she said.

The fallout came in waves, spread out over the next few weeks. Op Glassknife was over save for the filing, with Billy White out of the equation. Julian had a tense meeting with his director, Leslie Hind, a woman who tended to stare angrily at people as though trying to set them on fire with the power of her mind. Julian had given her plenty of staring material, and she dragged him over the coals slowly in respect of his various breaches of protocol. The operation had been successful in real life, but it looked like a fuck-up on paper and that was bad for departmental metrics.

While Alison liaised with SO15 about the chances of retaliatory measures by White's people, Khan had enjoyed a few days at a safe house, shuttling back and forth to interviews with the Met, helping them with their enquiries. The transcripts were already on Julian's desk.

The doctor was wearing a subdued skirt suit when she came in, and he could tell she was still rattled by the whole business. Her hands were constantly fiddling with cigarettes and lighter and she alternated between refusing to meet Julian's gaze and glaring at him.

"So what really happened?" he asked, pushing the transcripts over when she didn't volunteer anything.

"Every word nothing but the truth, Jules." She brought an unlit cigarette to her lips and scowled. "Do you not have one meeting room I can fucking smoke in?"

"Kay, what *happened*?" She'd told the police that when White came beating at her door she'd locked herself in the bathroom with a kitchen knife, and without her phone. She'd heard what sounded like all hell breaking loose in the next room. Then eventually she'd responded to the cautious calls of Royce's people and come out to find the scene of devastation.

"*That* happened." She gestured to the transcript Julian had in front of him. "Just like that."

"Kay, when White arrived, there was someone already with you," Julian pointed out. "Now either you let them in or they forced their way in, but—"

"I swear, I was alone when my door was kicked in," Khan insisted fiercely. "Unless someone was hiding in the broom cupboard. You think that's likely, Jules? Cos I do not."

"Two people died—"

"You think I did it? Or you think I keep a, what, a body-guard? A super-jealous boyfriend? A... gorilla?" Khan's voice broke. "Jules, there were dead bodies in my *house*. And I'm going to have to go back there and..."

"Kay, why did you want to speak to me?"

"Why didn't you want to speak to me?" Khan raised a sardonic eyebrow. "You thought the great queer was attention seeking, is that it?"

"I thought there were proper channels." But he knew she was right, at least a little. "Here I am, Kay. Talk to me."

"I was approached."

Julian went still. "But not by White?"

"No, but just as this White business was kicking off online.

I was approached by a woman in a bar. Only instead of wanting to try out a new kink, she said her employers wanted to speak to me. Wanted my professional opinion on something. Very important, very hush-hush. She was dressed like a moody goth, but she looked like she'd been forced into it at gunpoint. She looked...feral." Oddly, she smiled. "And yes, obviously, I can do a full description. I can even do you a sketch if you want, for what it's worth. No contact details were given. Said she'd find me. Spy stuff, Julie. Pure spy shit. She knew who I was, though. She was talking about CITS. Which is such a terrible acronym that it only appears in classified reports. The reports that only get read by you people and nobody else should be able to even get hold of them. Not unless they've cracked CITS already and need people like me because they're winding up to do something with it."

Cryptic Informational Transformation Space, supplied Julian's memory helpfully. It was what Khan had been working on at the government laboratory. He was still none the wiser about what it meant.

He felt a new operation coming on, in which he would be neck deep. "There was just this one contact?"

"And now this." A jab of the lighter indicating dead bodies and a wrecked flat.

Julian sighed. "Go back to the beginning, tell me everything you can, every detail."

II

The transcript of that meeting found its way to Alison, along with a grab bag of other evidence: police interviews, scene-of-crime reports, autopsy results, camera footage. She was currently in limbo between Op Glassknife and whatever new operation might sprout up from Khan's revelations. It seemed likely that when it had gone through enough meetings to become something tangible she'd be brought in on it. In the meantime she pulled what strings she could to keep informed. She didn't like living in a world she couldn't get a handle on— it didn't feel safe—so she would pry obsessively until those handles were discovered or installed. Back when the girls were tiny, before she'd joined the Service, she'd run her own trace agency from home, tracking down absconding debtors, long-lost beneficiaries and truant husbands who owed too many maintenance payments. Every success made her world more ordered and therefore more controllable. Controllable was secure. It slowed her heart rate and backed up all the anxiety medication.

The autopsies contained nothing surprising, save the coroner's estimates of the force applied. White and his mates had been beaten with Khan's furniture, and then with bare hands. These were large and heavy-knuckled, judging by the signature marks they had left. Of the two survivors, one had lasted two days before succumbing to haemorrhaging from a cracked skull; the other was stable but had yet to wake up.

The other man dead at the scene, besides White, had been Patrick Cleary, Alison's source. He had, she thought, deserved better. He had been trying to turn himself around, and had been brave enough to work against a man like White to atone. And he'd died not to serve that cause but at the hands of some unidentified third party.

She considered what Khan had said to Julian. Had that third party turned up to recruit or even kidnap Khan themselves, only to get into a scrap with White? They'd then run off before the police arrived? The timing seemed suspiciously coincidental, but coincidences happened even in the most ordered of universes.

Then there was the camera evidence. There was no good street view of Khan's building, but the woman had been sharp enough to keep a camera system overlooking her front door. The quality was decent. It showed White and his lads turning up, pausing to gather themselves and then shouldering the door open on the third try.

Then, nothing for about five minutes, because the camera didn't have sound.

Then *they* came out.

Two new figures: a woman and a man. She had long hair, tied back, neither very pale nor very dark. The grey of the footage made colour impossible to determine, and she was bundled in a puffy jacket. She looked almost straight at the camera, without any awareness of it. Alison isolated the image thoughtfully. Khan was a competent amateur sketch artist. It certainly looked like the same person who'd tapped her in the club.

The man with her was about the same height but twice as broad. His long leather coat was split at the shoulder blades, most likely from some particularly energetic part of beating Billy White to death. The camera resolution didn't show the stains, but that coat must have been gory with blood, and the police were already searching nearby bins and skips for it. The camera only caught a partial profile, but that was enough to pick the man out as strikingly ugly, broad-faced, weak-chinned, heavy-browed. Alison shivered at the sight: a latter-day Karloff in full monster make-up. Surely not hard to track down.

They hadn't entered via the door though. The police had already gone back through everything still on the camera's memory. It looked as though the pair had been there for longer than the device could record, or they'd maybe crept in through a window. Except Khan's place was on the second floor and there was no sign of forced entry except for the door. So had Khan lied, and let them in...? More unknowns awaiting a tidy resolution. Alison had been in the game long enough to know that some mysteries were never resolved. She would, at some point, have to either come to terms with that or go mad. But right now her drive to turn the world into a puzzle, where every piece fit, was what matched her so well to her job.

There wasn't enough of the man's face in the footage to run through recognition software, but the girl was another matter. The police would be looking into it, of course, but Alison had a bad habit for an analyst of scaring up her own intel when it suited her. Yet another blot on her record, balanced only by her good results. And if someone was trying to poach Khan, it really was a national security matter.

Knowing she should close up shop and get some sleep, Alison closed her browser. There was another window behind it, showing a scrolling page of... text? Code? Instinctively she went to close it. However, another window had opened up within it, and another within that, like a digital Russian doll. She went cold and hit the trip switch on her internet connection, for what little good it would do. There was a third nested window now, with even smaller text running rapidly in weird, random conglomerations of ASCII pixels. It was as though her computer was possessed and trying to enunciate demonic language.

Convulsively, she yanked the power cable. Her heart began to hammer as the screen stayed lit, impossibly, even as the lights on the computer hard drive died. The distorted characters inhabiting the inner window were speeding up exponentially. In the slower code in the outer windows she began to catch snippets: names, dates, coordinates.

A large slice of her psyche was denying that any of this was happening, preferring to believe this was a tiredness-induced hallucination—or even the introduction of some neural agent into her system. The rest of her, concerned with gathering intel no matter how impossible, fumbled her phone out. She started taking photos of the screen with shaking hands.

Forty seconds later, the screen died at last. When she booted the machine up in safe mode, it worked perfectly. Then came a thorough scan, a search through the memory, attempts to look over recent histories...but there was no evidence that anything untoward had happened. Only the photos on her phone stood as mute testimony.

She put her head in her hands, breathing heavily. It wasn't that it had happened; it was that it had happened *again*.

Interlude: The Philosophers

Excerpt from *Other Edens:
Speculative Evolution and Intelligence* by
Professor Ruth Emerson of the
University of California

What if—bear with me—a civilization of gigantic immortal spacefaring trilobites *didn't* evolve? I know, it seems hardly credible, but imagine, if you will.

Our own timeline shared the events of the trilobites' time until it didn't. Until that point in a shared Cambrian where the arthropods sealed their eternal dominance in their version of history. Whereas in our timeline the plucky vertebrate descendants survived and prospered, and went on to...

But it's not time to tell that story yet. For here's another divergence point, budding away and writing its own timeline. This is another Earth we never knew, which gave rise to something that could know itself. And there will be others, each sharing a history with ours right up to the point it doesn't—diverging from our history one after another, each one the "real" Earth to the things that evolve in it.

In this Earth's timeline, sentient trilobites didn't evolve. Their kin exist, certainly, and they will persist here for longer than in our world, but they are not masters of the world.

You wouldn't have recognized the trilobites' Cambrian seas as belonging to your planet, even though your planet once held those same waters. In this Ordovician period, forty million years later, life is beginning to look like a modeller's rough maquettes of something you'd see out of a submarine's portholes. In this timeline there *are* fish, though weak-chinned and jawless things, armoured like tanks. There are coral reefs. There are things that look like lobsters, although they are more like scorpions.

And there are giants in these seas. If you were there, in your submarine, you would see them looming like blue shadows against the gloom of the deep water, or snuffing out the sparkling daggers the sun casts through the waves. Like whales, you might think, having no other basis for comparison. Indeed they are, though: slow, vast, twenty, thirty, fifty feet long, perfectly poised within the water.

Most of that length is shell, straight or spiralling like the horn of a gigantic unicorn. They ghost ponderously through the water point first, as though steeling themselves to ram an enemy below the waterline. In your world they are a fleeting memory, supplanted by jawed fish, sea scorpions and other swifter creatures—but their relatives are still with you: the squid, the octopi. In these seas, the long, pointed shell glides past and, at the open end, you see an eye the size of the very porthole you gaze out of, huge and detached in its regard. It presides over a parliament of writhing arms, with which it picks over the sea floor or snatches prey from the water. An orthocone.

In this world, the early orthocones did not simply rest on their laurels before giving way to your piscine ancestors. They grew immense and cunning, brains outpacing their huge bodies, their organs rearranging to fit an ever-increasing cere-bral volume. The evolutionary pressures on them are readily apparent. They must keep a leash on their unruly pack of limbs, and they must master a skinful of chromatophores—at first used for crude camouflage, then for brute signalling between courting couples, and at last for primitive speech. The early orthocones slide silently past one another like billboards, flashing threats, warnings, queries. Later species will begin to sound off at one another, generating gas within their shell chambers and mantles and agitating it against their septa. They'll produce basso profundo groans that can be detected across a hundred leagues of ocean by another of their long-lived, lonely kind. Over ten thousand years, the ocean fills with their conversational flatulence. They speak constantly but meet only to mate, a process steeped in slow, graceful ritual: the intertwining of arms, the rippling of patterns on the skin. A dance of days for one clutch of eggs, which will hatch into three score of miniatures carried off on the tide, never to know their parents. Yet the sea resounds with the speech of their kind, and they learn it over their long childhoods. The few that reach adulthood join in a select global community of hermit seafarers.

And what of our own ancestors? By the time the orthocone descendants have reached a level of self-awareness we might recognize, the fish, scorpions and the rest have had their chance to become fierce and dangerous. Vertebrates come to the land very late in this world, and still without jaws.

Even as they do, the continents of Earth are clasping together in a single mass like the jaws of a trap. The world is heating up, volcanos belching out poisons to darken the sky from pole to pole. The great dying time that falls on all Earths descends, with the inevitability of a clock striking midnight, to strip land and sea of their biodiversity.

The orthocones perceive that their world is changing, and they debate and discuss, their deliberations rolling back and forth from shore to shore of their world-ocean. They are towering intellects by now. Knowing one another only by their conversations, they have been choosing mates by the quality of their slow, reverberant repartee for thousands of years. A depth of intellect is like a peacock's tail or the blue backside of a mandrill, for them: infinitely attractive. Countless generations have selected for intelligence and gone on to deliver a newer generation, slightly brighter still. By the time the extinction clock strikes, they are perhaps the most complex intellects any timeline will ever see.

And they win, in the end. They think their way to a solution, even as the seas around them go sour with poisons and the land burns to sand. They build a global network of vast abyssal walls and ditches and ridges. They create whole artificial mountain ranges, mounded up by no other means than clutches of tentacles controlled by genius minds. They alter the currents of the seas to create safe zones, cool zones, oxygenated nurseries. They suffer, but they survive, and because of their efforts countless other marine species also live, even the poor, forsaken trilobites.

On the land, things are worse than they might otherwise be, because the orthocones don't care about it and use it as their heat sink. Whatever life has clawed its way out from their tentacled shadow simply dies off. In the end the world lurches out of the dying times and into a better future, where terrestrial life will never amount to much—and where the seas are ruled by the orthocones in their wisdom.

Where are they now, though, those towering minds of the oceans? Where are their spaceships, their industries, and will they ever put a squid on the moon? Nowhere and nothing are the works of the orthocones. Nowhere save in the constant murmur of their erudite consideration. They never leave the sea, which is the medium of their thought. Even though they have reshaped the world to their liking and for their survival, they did it by hand. They have no technology; despite their many dextrous arms they barely craft tools. Our ape ancestors of three million years gone were greater makers than these cephalopods will ever be. These intellects will never look up and see the stars, yet they effortlessly understand and communicate profound truths about the nature of existence that we cannot grasp, and we are the poorer for it. They have gone beyond us to a realm of contemplation that we, the ape-children with our bloodied stone axes, are not fit for.

3.

I

Lee Pryor sat on her bed in her studio apartment in Hemel—the one that her parents still contributed towards despite all their grumbling. She stared at the knees of her jeans, trying to work out just *what* this might turn out to be.

Not for one moment had she considered not going. The phone line hadn't been great, but she knew Mal's voice. And really, what was the plausible alternative? That, four years later, parties unknown were trolling her?

Except that was entirely possible. She had made a meagre living out of looking into the unexplained, and she'd seen plenty of examples of how far people would take a hoax. How they'd devote vast amounts of time and money to something that would only result in the most fleeting attention from strangers on the internet. Plenty of those people knew her, Mal's disappearance was public record, and there were hoaxers and Fortean buffs who had absolutely no grasp of what was or wasn't fair game. Some of them had fallen through their hollow earths and Atlantean theories into all sorts of real-world political philosophies. Some of these philosophies didn't have much room for someone like Lee Pryor. And so, yes, it could be something set up to piss her off.

It could also be something else.

The meeting place was a cafe in Camden—not too far from her own haunts, on those rare occasions she decided to check up on the LGBT community in that corner of London. She reckoned that internet murderers probably didn't ply their trade in front of large crowds of people. However, she'd have to take serious stock if she got a text asking her to go into a dark alley and close her eyes.

She couldn't believe how calmly she was taking all this.

She slung a bag across her shoulders. She had her phone, her purse, her e-reader and an illegal locking knife given to her by a six-foot Swedish woman who'd joined her hunt for giant serpents in the Storsjön lake the previous summer.

"Right," she told the room, as though she wouldn't see it again. *Because let's suppose . . . let's just suppose it is Mal . . .* Mal had gone "somewhere." And if she had come back, then perhaps there was now a two-way door from *there* to *here*—although why Camden would suddenly be twinned with Narnia was anybody's guess. Maybe Lee *herself* wouldn't be coming back, and she should be thinking very seriously about the various people her absence would upset or at least inconvenience. Instead, she felt a swirling spiral of excitement in her stomach.

What if it is Mal, and she's been Somewhere Else?

Which translated as, *What if I really do remember everything, and I didn't go crazy on Bodmin Moor.*

Ten minutes later and she was on the train to Euston, trying to read but finding her eyes skipping over the words. Around her, the carriage was three-quarters full of people. They were going into town for late shifts or were dolled up for parties or clubs, out on the razzle. They were doing all the gloriously mundane things people did when they didn't know the world had magical stone circles or monstrous Birdmen in it. Lee kept glancing at them and felt like leaping up and yelling, "I'll be able to prove everything soon! And you'll be sorry you laughed at me." But she didn't, of course, because that wouldn't have been very British of her.

The sky was cloudless, baking, when she got out at Camden and waded through the homeward-bound commuters. She was there in plenty of time to prepare the ground, check for ambushes, all that spy stuff.

Scouting for ambushes turned out to be difficult when the place was packed, though. Mal had specified a cafe where every coffee came with three Italianate descriptors and the barista had an improbable moustache, each side curling up almost high enough to frame his eyes like spectacles.

Lee slid into a seat as the current tenant was vacating it. She was still ahead of the time Mal had given, but she scanned the crowd, just in case. Nobody looked familiar. She had been buoyed this far on a tide of optimism that abruptly left her and headed out to sea again. Instead, she had a bleak epiphany. Some rational auditor stepped into her mind and evaluated the precise odds that her four-years-lost friend had called her from—let's face it—beyond the grave and asked her to meet up in a coffee shop in Camden at ten o'clock at night. Put like that, it didn't seem exactly reasonable, did it? It didn't even seem like a good hoax. She looked inside herself and recognized what she had been feeling a moment before. The old excitement that came without any real sense of reality or peril. Because part of her always knew it wasn't real, that there would be no proof, not even an out-of-focus photograph. It was just another cryptid hunt. She could pretend to believe, as usual, all the way up until she returned home and got on with her life, without the world being any different.

She stared into the dregs of her mochaccino and felt her whole tower of thought slide sideways into the abyss.

But I remember, she insisted to herself. All around her the hubbub of people's everyday conversations rose like the surf. *I saw the Birdmen.* But she'd gone back to the original video, and she had to admit it hadn't looked that convincing. And wasn't it more likely she'd invented the snow and the monsters and the doubled perspectives? To believe that she'd lost hold on reality, in her grief, was a hypothesis that fit perfectly with the general parameters of reality. Whereas to believe the other thing meant that everything else about the world was called into question, and did she *want* that, honestly?

It's not about what I want. It's about what's real. But was it, really? She should accept that she'd had a breakdown, that Mal was gone, that nobody had called her. She could then, perhaps, move on.

Because there was that one other thing, which she had stoically ignored until now. She remembered the call—she told herself she did—but her phone didn't. There was no entry in her phone's history for any incoming contact. She might as well have spoken with a ghost.

Right. Well, then... She should just go. No point wasting more of the evening. She abandoned her table, almost colliding with the moustachioed barista as he came to take her cup. He smiled at her, recognizing someone who'd been stood up, albeit not someone stood up by a freak of their own defective subconscious. It was that shame, perhaps, that moved Lee to order another and sit back down. Shame, and a stubbornness her parents had been remarking on since she was five.

The lean, broad-shouldered man across the cafe sat down too and stared furiously into his newspaper.

Lee froze, then got her e-reader out and tried to do the same thing. He had been sitting down, she was sure, just one of the anonymous punters desperate for an overpriced and over-explained shot of caffeine. But he'd been about to leave when she did, and changed his mind just as suddenly.

She stole a glance at the man. His face was invisible behind one of the more lurid tabloids. He hadn't cut out little eyeholes through which to spy on her. She felt foolish. And yet she couldn't rid herself of the certainty that he'd been about to follow her.

She stared furiously at her book again, taking in none of it. Ten o'clock had been and gone. She tried to get some research done but, eventually, she was forced to acknowledge that the cafe had mostly emptied out. She looked around suddenly, hoping to catch Tabloid Man unawares. In the intervening time he had left without her noticing, and she ended up glowering at a pair of young men who seemed genuinely intimidated by her.

She could feel herself teetering over a great well of despair. She had worked herself up for this; she had borrowed hope at a ruinous interest rate—one that she had no chance of paying back. She had, she forced herself to admit, been spectacularly stupid from start to finish.

She got up. No sinister figure stood to follow her. She put down a couple of quid on the saucer and shambled out of the cafe. Time to go home.

She saw the lights—enough flashing blue for an emergency

services convention—and linked it instantly with Mal. She couldn't help it. Maybe something had happened to her on the way.

Following the flash and the occasional siren whoop as a new vehicle pulled up, she ended up on a street behind all the glitz and bustle, houses converted into tiny flats each worth as much as a small island nation. There was a scatter of police cars and ambulances, and a throng of uniformed people going in and out of one building in particular. Two dozen others were out on the street, some passers-by and some evidently neighbours, including a sleepy-looking old woman swaddled in a duvet. Lee pushed forwards, and then moved faster because they were bringing someone out of the house on a stretcher.

For a moment she saw Mal there—not just Mal, but the Mal of four years ago in her hiking jacket, argent-dyed hair cut spiky short, face pale as death. The vision was so clear that she took it for real before her eyes caught up with her mind and tackled it to the ground. She was looking at a man, first off. A big, overweight man covered in weals and blood, as dead as anyone Lee had ever seen. His skull looked the wrong shape, and one of the paramedics was desperately trying to get a sheet over him as they hauled him out. The stretcher crew looked not only grim but hurried, and as soon as they were clear of the door another pair were in with another stretcher.

Lee snuck close to the other gawkers. It was plain from the way the neighbours were dressed that the casualties being evacuated weren't this street's normal stock in trade. One of the ambulances pulled away, and then the police were throwing up a cordon, all grim faces and intractable politeness.

When that invisible line had been drawn, Lee saw a woman on the outside of it, sitting on a doorstep and fumbling in her purse. She was tall and bony, Indian heritage or somewhere close. Her hair was half up, half wildly straggling, and she had a coat over her shoulders, a silk dressing gown beneath. She was the only person paying no attention to what was going on.

She looked up as Lee approached: she had a strong, aristocratic-looking face, and the lines on it suggested that under other circumstances she was the life and soul of the party.

"You haven't got a fucking light, have you?" she asked hoarsely.

Lee didn't smoke but enough of her friends did, so she was able to ferret out a cheap plastic lighter and hand it over. The expression of gratitude she received was like a shot of distilled good karma, but then she had to steady the woman's hands as she lit her cigarette. Lee held a respectful silence as the woman took a long, shuddering drag.

"Fuck," she said, almost reverently.

"Was that your house?" Lee asked.

There was a flash of suspicion from the woman, but then she inhaled another lungful from the cigarette and mellowed. "My flat," she admitted. Her hands started to shake again, and she clamped one around the wrist of the other.

"Did *you*...?" Lee's eyes were wide. This woman seemed slight and the victims she'd seen had been huge.

The woman stared at her blankly, and then let out a single hack of horrified laughter. "*Me*? Take on them? Did you *see* them?"

Lee nodded. But the woman could be a ninja or a HEMA quarterstaff champion as far as she knew.

"I don't know what happened," the woman said hollowly—and, to Lee's ears, not entirely convincingly. "I don't know how I'm going to explain this. Fuck." She scowled at her smoke, and Lee passed the lighter back to her. The remaining ambulance crew were bringing another body out.

"I'm Kay, by the way," the woman told her.

"Lee."

"You ever get the feeling there are cracks in the world?" Kay asked, straight out, as blunt as that.

Lee choked and stared at her, as though the woman had scooped out all her ready responses with a spoon, leaving only the crazy she'd been sitting on for four years.

Her response, or lack of response, tightened something in Kay's face. Lee recognized defences going up.

"You'd better go," Kay told her. "Or they'll want to talk to you. *I* don't think you're anything to do with this. But they'll want to check. Thanks for the light."

"What about you?"

"Well I want to talk to them, so that's okay." Kay smiled. "But go."

Lee backed off, and sure enough there was someone angling towards Kay: a dark-haired man in a long coat who looked...determined.

You ever get the feeling there are cracks in the world? And the answer to that was "Yes." The answer to that was "My girlfriend fell into one somehow." She suddenly wanted to run back, to find Kay—if the woman hadn't already been bundled off by her gloomy-looking minder. She wanted to demand answers: What had she meant? What cracks? *Where did Mal go?*

She was in the dark still, knowing only that she didn't know.

Then she reached Camden Town, and at least one area of uncertainty crystallized, because the metal lattice gate was drawn shut and she'd missed the last Tube. It seemed impossible for that much time to have fallen out of the bottom of things, but her phone told the same story. She tried to think how long it would take her to walk to Euston.

When she turned away from the station, Mal was there.

Lee made a sound she'd otherwise only expect to hear from someone dying: a guttural cough. There was Mal, fifteen feet down the pavement, the immovable object that the handful of other late birds were weaving around. She wore a grimy padded jacket, dull orange under the streetlamps and too big for her. Her jeans were torn, not artfully for fashion but ripped down one leg from the knee, and with a jolt Lee saw something underneath, a dark bandage. Her hair was long, like it hadn't been since she was fifteen, tied back and mouse-coloured, no more platinum or peroxide.

Her face hadn't changed. Oh, it was older, and there was a scar down one cheek—like a fish hook had caught there and been yanked free years ago. Those years were in her eyes, too, and in the hard lines about them, as though she'd lived through a decade while less than half that time had passed for The Girl Who Stayed. And there was a new expression on her face, or else it was a new lack of expression, a closedness that she'd never had before. Hardly the same woman at all. Except it absolutely was. Lee wouldn't mistake her, not now, not ever.

Her heart seemed to have seized up.

Then Mal opened her mouth, and Lee expected... anything: the secrets of the universe, the keening of a hawk, the blind data sound of an ancient modem, anything, so long as it matched the strangeness of a four-year absence with no word at all.

And she said: "Has anyone talked to you, about me?"

"What?" Lee gaped.

"Lee, listen," Mal snapped. And her voice was hard, now, far more so than memory supplied. She darted closer, moving oddly, as though flitting around objects Lee couldn't see. "I don't have much time. Has anyone else been in touch? Police? Or people saying they're police?" It wasn't that the coat was too big, Lee saw; Mal was too big. Wherever she'd been, they had a gym. She was broader across the shoulders. The hand she reached out with had scarred knuckles and unfamiliar callouses.

"Mal, I *waited*!" Lee told her, shrinking back. "What... How can you just come back and ask...?" And she had waited: hours in the cafe and years in Hemel, in the real world. "Mal..."

She found herself staring into the face of a cold stranger, and for a moment was simply out of options—neither sane nor mad, neither real nor unreal. Her imagination and her rationality both disowned the scenario.

"Lee, listen to me—"

"No! Nobody's been asking, nobody at all!" Shouting on the street outside a shut station. People were crossing the road rather than getting mixed up in what might be a drunken rant or a lovers' spat or a full-on mental breakdown. "Least of all *you*, Mal! Because you went. You went, and I've... I..." To her horror, she burst into tears. "Screw you, Mal! How—How—How—" But the words were being washed away.

She felt strong hands holding her as though she might

break, one on each arm, an awkward distance still between their bodies. Mal's face swam in her vision, weirdly twisted like she was trying to remember how expressions worked.

"I'm sorry." That voice in her ear. "Lee, I'm sorry."

"Sorry...?"

"Because they'll come, they'll ask," Mal said. "I wanted to find you earlier, but...things happened, things we had to take care of. Lee, it's all coming down. I..."

"What? You had a mission? You had to deliver the fucking Death Star plans or the world ends?"

For a moment there was absolutely no admission in Mal's pale, stone-impassive face of any shared cryptids hunted, dungeons crawled, nights spent tangled together outside of parental scrutiny. Not even a flicker for Star Wars. She simply didn't know what Lee was talking about. Then the cracks came, a twitch about the eyes, a tug at the corner of her mouth. She snorted in that way she had that made her eyes bulge, because she had spent most of her life before she met Lee keeping the funny inside. Because nobody else around her shared it.

Without transition she was hugging Lee, bony chin digging into her shoulder. The new strength in her arms was almost frightening, as though some beast inside her was only waiting for the full moon to make its escape.

"Something like that," she said in Lee's ear, voice choked. "Something very much like that. And I'm sorry. Even after this contact, they'll find you. Maybe they'd have found you anyway. Lee, deny everything; tell them you don't know."

"I *don't* know," Lee insisted. Mal smelled of curdled sweat and woodsmoke and a spice she knew with absolute certainty she'd never scented before. "Are you...living on the streets? Do you need somewhere to go?" Abruptly that was her lodestone, the only possible port out of this storm. Mal'd had a breakdown, years before. She'd lost her memory. She'd been living rough. She'd only now remembered Lee and managed to get in touch. "Come back with me. I can put you up, I can...Anything, Mal. Anything you need. Let's get something to eat. You need medicine?"

Mal put her at arm's length, but only to look at her. "You haven't changed," she said, and Lee didn't know if she meant physically or this helpless outpouring of babble. She opened her mouth to say something, to restate all the offers she'd just made, but a tall, skinny youth lurched into the pair of them, reeking of beer. He slurred a lewd proposition to one or both of them. Without hesitation Mal straight-armed him in the chest, sending him skidding six feet on his back.

Lee stared at her, owl-eyed.

"I don't need help, Lee. And I *am* on a mission. The world *is* going to end." She said it with that mocking quirk to her mouth, like she always did when she was taking the piss out of herself for being too serious. "I have to go. I've stayed too long already, and I—Yes, yes, I'm coming."

This last was cast over Lee's shoulder. She twisted around and let out a shocked cry because there was a man there and he was terrifying.

He was broad as a weightlifter at the shoulder and waist, shrouded in a long leather coat. A baseball cap did its best to shadow a face simultaneously brutal and compelling: heavy-browed, broad-nosed, weak-chinned. His skin looked bronze in the streetlight, darker than Mal's, lighter than Lee's own. His eyes were very deep-set, glittering like beetles. There was a smile on his wide mouth and it didn't help.

"Uk," Lee got out. There was a spatter of something across

his cheek and up into his hairline, like a birthmark. Like blood. And blood *was* on the air, that metal smell of it. She had never before had such a sense of another human being's dangerous physicality. He looked like he could crush bricks in his bare hands.

She belatedly recalled what Mal had said. *Things* we *had to take care of.*

"Mal...?"

"He's with me. He's a friend." And Mal let her go, leaving Lee feeling as though she was falling even as she stood there. "We need to go. We have to catch the last train out of here. Lee, I'll...There'll be another time, I promise. There will."

And then the huge man was past them, shifting from stillness into swift motion without warning. Mal hurried after him, one pale glance back at Lee, who was stood frozen on the pavement. She didn't want to go after the man, now she'd seen his face, seen him move as though the buildings around him were a ghostly mist he was kindly consenting not to disrupt by just barging through. But Mal was going too, and she couldn't just...

She ran, calling Mal's name—"Wait! Take me, too! Take me with you!"—without caring where that path might lead. "Mal, I can help you! I'll do anything!" she shouted, to the great amusement of other less sober night owls, some of whom had obscene suggestions about just what she might do. Mal and the broad man were getting further away, even though they were barely hustling along and Lee was running flat out. They were receding in a direction that had no name, but she'd seen this before, she *had*, it wasn't just some fantastical misremembering! It was Bodmin Moor all over again, except in the heart of Camden.

And

Gone.

There was no sudden magicianly gesture or occlusion, but they had been *here* and now they had gone *there*. Lee was left standing, panting and shuddering, knowing that there was indeed a crack, a door, a portal. She was on the very brink of it, but it would not open for her.

II

Lucas May had been in the army, though not, as he tended to tell people, in the SAS. Instead, he'd done his time in the logistics corps, organizing the movement of people and things from place to place, which probably gave him a more useful skillset.

After twelve years' service he'd already had his escape trajectory plotted. He'd run into a few opportunities abroad, rubbing shoulders with private security types—who always seemed to be better paid and less heavily supervised. Specifically, he'd found himself in a position to do some favours for useful people, and he'd been headhunted practically before his boots hit civvy street.

On paper, Rove Denton was a private security firm. It did have some overseas operations, mostly providing bodyguards and discreet site security. A particularly keen eye would note that RD personnel never did get deployed to the real hotspots of the world, but more often to cities of relative wealth and comfort. There, they specialized in introducing their rich clients to the seamier side of life, protecting them more against over-inquisitive paparazzi than actual harm. May had heard plenty from returning colleagues. Some loved it, because when there was vice and pleasure splashing around, everyone tended to dip a hand into the fountain. Others came back faintly disgusted, because sometimes the tastes of their clients ran far past personal lines of morality. And it was the job of RD's foreign service to cover up anything comprom- ising, up to and including the odd body.

May himself had stayed home after signing up with the firm, and reckoned he'd made the right choice. Less chance to indulge, but better prospects. He'd proved adept at finding or obscuring, whatever the job called for. He'd warned or misdirected journalists, bought off mistresses, kept secrets and run anonymous threat campaigns to get activists to back down. Some of his peers had been keen on the heavy touch, going in fists first whenever they could. They tended not to stay. In contrast, May's preference for violence as a last resort saw him promoted. And in due course, he was transferred sideways into the boss's personal cadre.

For a couple of years he'd just enjoyed his good fortune, without really understanding why Mr. Rove was suddenly relying on *him*. Only a chance remark tipped him off, during one of his many face-to-face meetings with the boss. The man had made a passing reference to *that business in Cyprus, eh?*, and May had gone cold all over.

Not exactly a high-risk posting for a British serviceman. Except there had been one night when he'd been on duty, towards the end of his time in the forces. It was after he'd picked up his habit of doing little favours for people like RD's clients. There had been a very rich man whose employees were taking delivery of something off the British Cypriot coast. May had command of the watch and he'd ensured the team got out and came back in without interference, using one of the base's boats. Even put them up in the base while they waited for their helicopter out, all the paperwork faked up neat as you like. He'd taken a look at the cargo, though. He'd assumed it was drugs, or maybe antiquities, but there'd been a nagging worry that the crate might contain people, and he had his limits.

It hadn't been people. The crate stank powerfully of some kind of preservative, and inside was...a thing, a lobster the size of a man. Except it had clothes of a sort: a half-shredded poncho or coat made of something like canvas. There was metal amongst its hideous mouthparts, possibly a device or ornament. He had closed the crate and nailed it down, but they'd known he'd seen it. Rove himself had known. More importantly, he'd appreciated that May hadn't breathed a word of his discovery, even though he believed he'd seen a dead extraterrestrial.

Rove's mention of the incident had brought him out in a sweat. It meant there was more of *that* out there, and if his apparent ability to cope with the weird had secured his promotion, he was on a career path he would never have willingly chosen. Since then, part of him had always been treading carefully, lest the ground give way beneath his feet in the worst way. Right now, the weird was ghosting through his current job like wolves in the trees either side of a fleeing sled. He hadn't been bitten yet, but on the downside, he now had to report a failure to his boss.

In the beginning, Mr. Rove had liked face-to-face meetings with his lead subordinates, not trusting phones or video chats. He met Lucas in rooms without windows, with a white noise generator, after a thorough sweep for bugs and with all proper deference. And that had been all right. Rove was one of those long-time rich guys who knew where he stood and expected his inferiors to know that where they stood was definitively below him. However, he paid well enough and his instructions were clear and blunt.

In recent years, personal meetings had become rare and finally petered out. Now his mysterious plan was advancing, teleconferencing with his subordinates was an acceptable security risk.

May hated this part.

After the debacle at Camden ending in the death of Billy White, he had given his team their instructions and then gone home. A text had arrived from Rove Denton's usual auto-mated number. *Await contact.* Duly primed, May had spent the small hours staring at the wall until it happened.

It had been a condition of his most recent contract with RD that he left one wall in his flat unobstructed by pictures or furniture. At the time it had seemed eccentric, in the way all rich people were eccentric. Maybe, he'd reasoned, it was feng shui.

It wasn't feng shui. It was this. As he stared, he seemed to be looking into the wall, as though the paintwork's whorls and imperfections were a vast landscape and he was a satel-lite high overhead, squinting down at a great snowy waste. He felt a lurch of vertigo, imagining himself falling into the endless plain far below. By way of some nameless sense, he felt the *distance* expand far beyond the bounds of his flat, the building, the whole street. And there, in that other direc-tion, was Mr. Rove.

Daniel Rove was close on sixty, by May's reckoning, but looked a well-preserved forty at most. He was trim and toned, narrow-framed. He'd worn glasses when May first met him, a neat little affectation he'd outgrown since. He was still wearing his understatedly expensive suits, but the dim background behind him had changed: no longer the boardrooms or the huge chambers of Rove's various residences. There was a constant sense of motion around him, as though a vast, out-of-focus factory floor spread behind him in the darkness. The ceiling seemed perilously close to Rove's hairline, irregular and lumpy with vents and industrial processes. May honestly wondered if the man had his own private space station now, or perhaps a volcano lair.

Rove's air of energetic bluntness was the thing that never really changed.

"So, piss-up, brewery, May?"

"I'm sorry, sir." May had seen Rove spitting mad a couple of times, and that had been bad news. People in Rove's personal guard didn't get to tender their resignation, not with what they knew. His own elevation had come after a "reassignment," and May had never found out how much of a euphemism that was. He did know you couldn't run or hide. Once you were *in*, then Rove would always find you eventually.

Rove made an impatient gesture, and May took a deep breath.

"White did what we wanted. He moved in, almost professional. I have full confidence that he'd have snatched Khan and brought him out. My team was in place. We'd have taken Khan off White's hands and Khan would have been shaking our hands, sir, as rescuers. We'd have had him delivered to you without a hitch. Except…"

"Yes, *except*." Rove would have heard at least something by now, via his other channels.

"White's dead; someone took him and his people out. There's one left that might tell us something. I've a man at the hospital, watching. My team said two people came out of Khan's flat, right after the fighting. They left the scene just before the police arrived. And they were fast, sir. From White going in to these two coming out was under two minutes. They took out four big guys that quickly."

"Who were they?"

"One big man, one mid-sized woman. My man said he reckoned she could handle herself but it was probably the bloke who did the heavy work. Our team tried to follow them, but...they vanished. We got some photos, though."

"I've seen." And Rove wasn't angry, or not at May. "What of your surveillance of the variable?"

"Sir?" Because that hardly seemed relevant now. "She... spent the evening in some hipster coffee place. Just played with her tablet for most of it. Whoever she was waiting for stood her up, obviously. Looked like she was going to leave early on, and I thought she'd made me. But then she sat back down and stayed there, pretty much until the White mess kicked off. I...let that monopolize my attention then, sir. I thought it was more important."

Rove reached out and made a couple of precise, insectile motions in the air, which May knew by now was some advanced VR rig he used. "Her."

An image of the young woman he'd been watching earlier popped up, to the left of Rove's face, and May nodded.

"Her file's being couriered over to you now. Along with..."

Another picture popped up: a pale girl with white spiky hair. May stared at it for a moment, thinking, *Is it? Isn't it?* But he'd had plenty of experience in disregarding changes of hair and make-up, imagining thinner, fatter. All the things that could happen to a human face without touching the precise alignment of features which triggered recognition in the brain.

"It's her." The girl leaving Khan's place with her bruiser friend had looked a hell of a lot tougher, and years older, but there was no mistaking her.

"The variable is that one's contact," Rove said. "But it looks like they didn't get to meet. I think it's most likely that the variable's clueless so far. Which means you can trump up some reason to approach her."

May nodded, already piecing something together. Turning up at people's doors claiming to be someone legitimate, all part of his stock in trade. And mostly it was to have a look around or gather a bit of intelligence. Occasionally, it was to plant a bug or incriminating evidence. Or, more rarely, he might stage a break-in turned homicide. Because there were always people prying into the affairs of Daniel Rove, and he was a private man with very little patience for impertinent questions.

"What do you need doing with her, sir?" he asked.

"Bring her in."

Interlude: The Warmongers

Excerpt from *Other Edens:
Speculative Evolution and Intelligence* by
Professor Ruth Emerson of the
University of California

This is not your world, though some twists of its fate may seem familiar.

The great orthocones rose and fell, here as in your own past. They never attained sentience, instead gliding gracefully into biological obsolescence, overtaken by fleeter, more vigorous life.

Here, in these Silurian seas, the fish still look armoured and alien. And they have good reason to go kitted out in mail. This is a story about top predators.

The humble scorpion relatives which lived on the sea floor in the shadow of the orthocones have stepped up their game in this timeline. Some are tiny, some bigger than you are. They are fierce, active hunters, keen of eye and equipped with a Swiss Army knife of tools for shelling fish and molluscs. In your world they had their time and were gone before they might trouble your nightmares. But this is not your world; this is theirs.

There are metrics of success that would place ants, beetles or bacteria at the top. However, we are all naturally biased to value large, fierce animals, those that can adapt to change and exploit opportunities. The eurypterids, sea scorpions, are all of that, and their realm is littoral, all the world a beach. They live both sides of the tidal divide, emerging from their burrows to fish the waters when they are in and sieve the sand when the waves soak away.

Soon land becomes an interesting place too, as a more congenial atmosphere rides in on the back of the first crude forests. A grab bag of sea life evolves to move inland—not least to escape these damn scorpion monsters that patrol the beaches, like murderous border guards. The eurypterids follow on their ever-stronger legs, progressing from a dragging crawl to a spider-quick scuttle, their appalling cutlery drawer of arms held high for death and dismemberment. We would recognize them as the dominant animal group of their world, but for a long time they are beasts of very little brain. Sometimes ferocity is enough.

In the Permian days of mass extinction, this timeline changes gear. Countless species of eurypterids vanish. Of the survivors, one is of particular note. This descendant of the sea scorpions has colonized much of the world, but only in the narrowest of strips. And, now the world has contracted to a single contin-ent, there is far less in the way of beachfront real estate for the ambitious predator.

As their world shrinks, their populations become denser. They live in submerged burrows side by side, jostling elbows and clashing claws. There are fights, and this becomes a real threat to the species because they are spectacularly well equipped to tear apart large shelled animals, most definitely including each other.

One subspecies learns to live with its neighbours. Its members negotiate with one another, assert dominance or back down. They recognize individuals, assess their fitness, remember the results of previous clashes. Their brains become more convoluted, shaped by memory creation and decision-making. Soon enough the strong amongst them are not merely driving off the weak, but co-opting them for more efficient hunts, sharing morsels from their kills to feed their new minions. As the world recovers, they are the one species to have thrived through the great dying. Appropriately, for they are the greatest killers.

Their coastal communities spread, and for another fifty million years they are always on the point of becoming simply predators, losing the fragile meniscus of society that necessity imposed on them.

A dominant culture emerges. By now they are far more terrestrial than aquatic, breeding on land and laying hard eggs, letting their hatchlings battle for survival in the nursery pens. They are not scorpion-shaped any more. Instead they are hunched over vulnerable lung-like membranes, tails curled beneath them, backs still a column of armoured segments. Stalked eyes bob and flick over a melange of appendages that are limbs, mouthparts and weapons: blades, pincers, fangs, spears and clubs in constant chittering motion.

By the time the dinosaurs of your world are glancing anxiously up at the sky in case that dot has grown larger since yesterday, there is only one eurypterid way of life across all the globe: a fierce one. The territoriality that once marked individuals is now espoused by communities. Each clawed polity knows only two states: war today or preparation for war tomorrow. A fight for resources is subsumed into a fight for *us* against *them*.

They fall readily into a kind of feudalism. A warrior class rules and a declawed underclass serves, dependent on a nobility who possess a literal right to bear arms. The eurypterid states harness sinew and plant material to launch sharp flints at one another. They smith copper, then bronze, then iron. Every technological development is achieved over a mound of corpses, every advantage is turned towards the subjugation of a neighbour. Dynasties come and go; empires rise and fall.

Later, they have an industrial age of sorts, discovering the uses of fossil fuels made from the crushed and compounded remnants of their own long-ago ancestors. Their societies are already pre-adapted for factory lines. A century later, and the world is at war.

The eurypterid soldiers march into battle like scuttling tanks, weapons mounted on their curving backs. Their heads are hooded with instruments, goggles over their stalked eyes like periscopes. Or else they control great machines that tear up the land with barbed legs or tracks, stopping every time they crest a rise to unleash a storm of fire or poison or sheer explosive force. They are in the air too, monstrous zeppelins raining murder upon the cowering peasants of the other side. They cruise the seas in segmented submarines that grapple with steel claws and tear each other apart. The warrior elite are no longer Those Who Fight, but Those Who Command. Everyone fights.

Should we visit this world now, however, that is not what we would see. Their Great War To End All Wars was fought and lost long ago, before our earliest ancestors came down from the trees.

But they are still there, those sentient descendants of sea scorpions. They live on the beaches, mostly. Most continental interiors are still too damaged for habitation—haunts of chemical weapons, radiation or plagues. The great hulks of their war machines lie rusting, and nobody is left in the world who recalls what they were.

The remaining eurypterids hunt what prey remains; they fish the oceans they didn't taint with their long-ago war; they beat tools out of the wreckage of the past. And when one community meets another, they fight. Despite all that went before, they have not learned.

And who knows what happens next, because we cannot see the future. Who knows if they *have* a future, or if the whole cycle will start again, the most dismal repetition of history. Perhaps next time there will be no survivors at all.

4.

I

Alison had asked Julian over for dinner, which in practice meant him turning up with two bags of groceries and cooking for the pair of them. Alison herself bounced between the poles of greasy takeouts and salads so plain they'd make a diet plan wince. It wasn't that she couldn't cook but, post-divorce, she couldn't be bothered with the fuss.

Josie was at one of her monthly writers' groups and Julian had a minder in for John, along with an optimistic thought that he might be back first and thereby be clear of hard looks and awkward questions. When Alison called him, though, rather than him just turning up on spec, it meant she had something she needed to get off her chest. They were each other's crutch, and he was aware that if work knew just how much they saw each other out of hours then eyebrows might be raised. It would be easier if Alison visited him occasionally, even though there seemed no real chance of Josie warming to her. Alison didn't like getting out of the house much, though. And they couldn't talk shop properly with Josie and John around. Or that's what he told himself.

All completely innocent, he insisted, like a mantra, as Alison let him in.

"Stir-fry," he said. "Hoi sin, bok choi, something something bean sprouts."

"Something something," she echoed wanly. "My favourite." She locked and bolted the door before hanging awkwardly at the boundary of the kitchenette as he set everything out.

"Is it Derek?" he asked over his shoulder. "He's been in touch again?" A pause as he carefully lined up a handful of oil and sauce bottles, in the same way he did with pens on his work desk. "Or is it Cleary?" The source who had died. "Stewey Leminkin and SO15 were cut up about that, I hear. But police will keep tabs on White's associates, and we'll keep watch over Khan—and never the twain will meet, hopefully."

"And what about whoever was behind White?"

He paused a moment before decanting some peanut oil and turning the heat up. "I know he kicked off very suddenly for a man working himself up, but as you said in your report, there's nothing to show he had a handler." Alison's protracted silence needled him. "Matchbox?"

Her expression was oddly flat; he knew it of old. Alison's flaw was digging too deep, going beyond the evidence into personal suppositions.

"Stewey got a rap on the knuckles, way I heard," he remarked. "For getting you involved with his source."

"I asked—"

"I know. And my feedback was that without *that*, we might be looking for Khan's body instead. But you know how Hind is. Everything by the book. And no grand conspiracies."

"I know," she said, that expression still there.

"Lay off the unverified sources for a while," he suggested, making a pun of it by waggling the hoi sin bottle at her.

"What if I had the motherlode of unverified sources, Spiker?"

When he looked over, she was actually glancing about, as if fearing unfriendly ears, even here.

"You cook," she told him. "I'll show you later."

Alison saw a therapist, he knew. It was one of the few things that she went out for these days. Her job was drawing meaningful patterns from a vast morass of complex interactions, and people's lives (and large sums of government money) often hung in the balance based on her recommendations. Get too far into the mindset and you started seeing patterns everywhere. Was it still paranoia when it wasn't you that *they* were out to get, but the whole country? And yet Alison was keeping it together, more than a year since her last crisis of confidence. Seeing her so brittle twisted something inside Julian, just as when John was buckling under school stress or Josie wasn't talking to him. He wanted to fix things, but he didn't have the tools. That twist was twice as hard when it was Alison. Josie was tougher, he reasoned evasively.

Over dinner, she showed him what she'd found: a series of photographs of her computer monitors, hastily taken with her phone.

"I had to do it this way," she said briskly. "I knew there'd be no trace of it afterwards."

Julian frowned at the images. "Were you hacked?"

"I don't think so. Not in the sense you mean. The opposite, maybe. I...think I was accessing a network."

He squinted. "I give up. I have no idea what I'm looking at. Looks like Windows had a seizure."

"That was kind of what it felt like," she agreed, still so utterly calm that he knew something must be pinned down and thrashing beneath the surface. "I was...accessing something connected to it. I think *something* was trying to talk to my operating system in a way it could understand—talking down to it, if you like. And only half successfully, because there's a lot of gibberish. But there's...I think it's doing my job for me. I think it's sketching out connections I couldn't see. Look, this is Cleary." She was pointing at a photograph of her screen.

"How's that Cleary?"

"It's his social security number. Here I'm pulling back, and there's White—and two dozen others. Those two who were at Khan's place, more were from the greatgeorge site. I think."

"You think?"

"Spiker, hold your horses, okay? It's like it can see what I'm trying to do, what I'm trying to fit together, and it's helping. Look, this is what happened after White's details popped up."

Julian blinked, still straining his eyes. "I just see numbers, and then lots of splats and spiders in ASCII."

"These numbers map onto the registration of a group of companies. So it's giving me identifiers that make sense to me, or that it thinks will."

Julian polished off the last of his sauce with a mop of bread. It gave him time to think of a response that wouldn't antagonize. "How did you work that one out?" he asked neutrally.

"Because I already knew to look, to follow the clues I was given." She hesitated before continuing. "Because this isn't the first time this happened to me. Before, I didn't know there wouldn't be any trace of the...incident, so I didn't take photos, and I never told anyone. I hadn't met you, then. There was nobody I trusted to tell. I thought I was going mad."

He digested that along with the last mouthful of stir-fry. That twist inside him tightened another notch. Nonsense, surely. The sort of talk that would get you taken out of service until a professional had a chance to look at you. Except she didn't look distressed or irrational; she wasn't even upset. This was Alison in full-on professional analysis mode, save that she might as well have been trying to trace the activity of spies out of Oz or Neverland.

"You keep saying 'it,'" he pointed out at last. "What's 'it'?"

"Who can say?" She tried a breezy smile that fractured almost immediately. Then, in a smaller voice, "I think it might be an artificial intelligence."

*

"You remember Schoen Fayre Invested?" This was after the meal, with Alison curled up at one end of her sofa, one knee drawn up and Simms pooled precariously on the arm.

Julian was still at the table, having flicked through his email to ensure nobody had started any wars since he'd last checked in. "Rings a bell."

"This was...eight years back. Stocks and shares guys. There was a stink about it. They shut down."

"Not really an area I keep tabs on, but I assume there was more than insider trading if they brought you in?" He frowned. "Or was this Derek's thing?" Alison's ex was Something In The City.

"This was...a bit of a hybrid job. I got involved first with my civilian hat on, and yes, through Derek, because he'd sunk some money into them—meaning his clients' money—and they were looking dodgy. Then your lot became involved. They didn't want me around, then they saw I'd worked out a whole lot they hadn't, so they stopped being coy with me. By the end of the job I was signing the Official Secrets Act and applying my talents full-time for Queen and Country." She settled further into the sofa. Simms glowered at Julian and put a proprietary paw on her arm.

Schoen Fayre Invested could boast neither a Mr. Fayre nor a Herr Schoen—the name being chosen at great expense through professional image consultants, to inspire the maximum amount of positive connotations in its client base. It was a new, small player in a city full of heavyweight traders, the brainchild of a telegenic technical wizard. The latter, Peter Swayne, had been in the running for *Time* magazine's "Man of the Year," and there were dozens of interviews showing his broad grin and tuft of beard. "It's all in the algorithms," he would say when asked why he was going into the stocks and shares business. "Chaotic systems like the FTSE are still predictable if you can devote enough computing power to them, yoked to an intelligent system capable of looking back over the last twenty years and extrapolating patterns." And he would talk like this for as long as anyone let him, fifty per cent buzzword and fifty per cent love of his own genius—all wrapped up in that charming smile.

Except the object of Swayne's desire did seem to be a reality and not just his fond imaginings, because SFI started making waves in the City. Financial analysts started looking very carefully at the figures coming out of Schoen Fayre. It seemed to be able to beat its competitors by vital microseconds in the rapid-fire virtual dogfight of the trading floor. But it also made occasional mad lunges into the writhing pool of publicly traded shares, snatching up a fistful of nothing-very-much that became pure gold within the day, within the hour. And SFI were outsiders too. Their people didn't go to the same clubs or patronize the same dealers as the regular stock market crowd. Other stockbrokers found Swayne insufferable, basically because he was telling the world media that the entire business could just be run by computers, without the need for well-paid executives. Needless to say, there were accusations of insider trading, but investigations failed to find anyone who might qualify as an *insider*. Swayne, meanwhile, parroted his line about it all being in the algorithms.

After about a year of this, however, SFI had a very bad day. Every trade went wrong. Swayne fell out with his partners and the shareholders who held the balancing twenty per cent wanted to know what the hell was going on.

Then they were back on form, and everyone tried very hard to pretend that it was all part of the plan, some financial and technical wizardry. And that Swayne hadn't lost a hundred million sterling of client money by betting on the FTSE equivalent of a three-legged horse.

Then it happened again.

By the time Alison came on the scene, there were already half a dozen other investigators poring over the data, some private and some acting on behalf of the authorities. The company had died by then and taken vast sums of other people's money to its grave, like a pharaoh of old. What everyone wanted to know was why. Was it a software error, or was it—the angle that brought Julian's employer in— deliberate outside interference? Perhaps a dry run for a wider crashing of the stock market?

However, there wasn't a perceivable pattern. None of it made sense, unless SFI was covertly retaining Nostradamus and Mother Shipton on the payroll.

Alison read through interviews conducted with the various

brokers employed by the firm who'd overseen these baffling but so often brilliant trades. At the start most had insisted on their own personal genius. After things went sour, they denied all responsibility, saying the decisions were mandated by Swayne's revolutionary expert system. A team of computer experts had already done their best to work out what the system was doing and had mostly drawn a blank. Nobody could work out *how* the machine was able to second-guess the market three times out of four, or why the fourth time was such a disaster.

Alison, inheriting this morass of bafflement from her peers, decided to create her own data, exceeding her given role in exactly the way she would do later in the Service. Specifically, she went to speak to SFI's system administrator.

SFI was a small enterprise doing its best to keep its costs down. Technical support was intended to be mostly outsourced, but as it happened, such expense had barely been needed because Charen Volkovska practically lived in the office. She'd made herself available twenty-four seven, in case anything went wrong. And during SFI's tenure, she had never taken a day's leave and had come in to work most weekends, when the offices were otherwise deserted. Her record went past "exemplary" into either "obsessive" or "suspicious." Alison had been expecting the latter but, after meeting the woman, settled on the former. Charen knew computers, and possibly not much else. She spoke in rushes of lumped-together words punctuated by long silences. She had been briefly interviewed before, but she didn't know about the trading arm of the business, nor did she seem to care. She was very, very interested in computers, and SFI's beating heart in particular, and that was all. She idolized Swayne, who, to his credit, paid her very well and had personally headhunted her. She came highly recommended so long as you didn't want someone who would play nicely with others.

Alison wooed her by tracking down her Iain M. Banks fanfic and complimenting her on it, which got her closer than any of the previous interviewers. In particular she discovered that Charen was still in and out of the SFI offices, despite having been theoretically laid off following the dramatic death spiral of the firm.

"It's not our fault," she said angrily. She was escorting Alison through the deserted trading floor, then into the hidden corridors and rooms beyond. Here, as she put it, the real work went on.

"Nobody's saying it's your fault," Alison lied.

"*Our*," Charen repeated. She had a hint of a Slavic accent still, which made her stop-start speech harder to understand when she got going. "And now they're going to come and try to turn it off again—because of something like money. We will have to do something."

Alison felt oddly certain that "we" didn't mean Charen and her boss, but the system itself. By now they were amongst the servers, in rooms cold enough that her breath plumed white. Charen rounded on her with a gleam in her eye. "Can you hear it thinking?" she asked.

Alison could only hear a multitude of fans and the air conditioning going full blast. "Does it have to be this cold?"

Charen laughed at her. "*This* isn't cold. This is just the system waiting. When it gets working, then it's *really* cold. That's when I put my jumper on; that's when I put my coat on. There's ice." Her smile should have seemed deranged, but Alison recalled it as weirdly innocent.

She found the logs for the server room temperature.

Nobody else had thought to look at them, because why would they? Either something was broken or the room fluctuated from fifteen degrees above to seventeen below. Alison did a little research on the cooling systems involved and worked out that this was impossible. The heat from the machines should have kept the place uncomfortably stuffy at the best of times. Except she'd stood there, in that chill. Not frostbite temperatures, but still colder than it had any right to be.

A small step, from there, to start correlating the temperature shifts with the trading. Things went wrong when the server room became warm, every time. One of her predecessors had even pinpointed to the minute when the computer's decision-making seemed to go off a cliff, and Alison could match it exactly to her temperature graph.

Charen looked mulish when confronted with this, during a formal interview. She pretended not to know anything about it, which Alison saw through. She wouldn't volunteer anything else either. Pressed further, she just stood up to go, the interview unilaterally over.

"They'll think you sabotaged it." Alison's last gambit, but it froze Charen in her tracks.

"How could they? How could anyone?" The system administrator looked around suspiciously, despite the audio and video recording she had been warned about. "We can't control the network. It comes and goes. We just ride it. But tell them that, they don't understand."

"Help me understand. Is this . . . Are you being hacked?"

Charen laughed bitterly. "What even is hacking? Is there some crazy kid out there playing *WarGames* with our system? No. Is there a black hat sending us denials of service? No. Nobody steals our passwords and tries to get at the money.

Any problems are down to the network. Mr. Swayne designed the system to read data and generate predictive patterns. It just needed better data. The network has all the data, all of it."

At this point, Alison knew she was rabbit-holing far too hard, and that her remit probably only extended to passing Volkovska on to her peers. The woman was plainly a little off balance, and that couldn't be connected to SFI's bouts of prescience. And yet...

This, as Alison explained to Julian, was where she decided to sidestep personal ethics. "The system's still running," she noted to Charen.

"*I* keep it running, only me." The woman clearly wanted to go back to it. "It needs to stay on."

"If *they* turned it off...?" Invoking that nebulous *they* that everyone fears in their own way.

"They can't. It would never...It can't be off. We'd never get the connection back. They'd be killing something, never to be seen again," Charen almost shouted at her. "They wouldn't. They *promised!*"

Alison had swallowed down her repugnance at what she was about to do. "You have to show me what's so special, Charen. And if I can understand it, I can sell it to the others. I can make them see why it *needs* to be kept on. But right now I don't understand." And she had no authority, not even an advisory role. SFI was dead, and its assets were going to be split up and sold to pay the fees of its liquidators.

But Charen seized on any small chance, as Alison knew she would. Two days later they were back in the deserted Schoen Fayre offices. Everything valuable from the trading part of the operation had been stripped out by then. But in the chill room below, the servers kept on turning; they would last as long as the investigation, because they were still the primary source of intelligence for just what the hell SFI had been doing.

"Here, you sit, put Wi-Fi on, I will show you everything." Charen seated Alison at a folding desk with her laptop, then shrugged into a heavy coat and vanished into the server room.

"Can't you just...?" Because surely whatever needed to be tweaked could be done as easily from a terminal? But apparently Charen needed to be close to the object of her obsession. *Priest and temple* was the comparison that flowered in Alison's mind. *A one-woman cult.*

Her laptop screen began to display some familiar data formats: the trading instructions from the computer below. Thanks to Charen, it was still running its inexhaustible analysis of the markets. If Alison had the ability to act on this information, could she become an overnight millionaire? Or would they lead off a financial cliff? She wondered what the temperature was down there, as a general indicator of the machine's powers of prognostication.

Her phone rang: "You see now?" Charen's staticky voice. "You're seeing this now?"

"I don't see anything new." And even as she said it, Alison realized she hadn't given her number to the woman.

"*Look!*" And then more distantly, Charen speaking to someone or something else, "Show her, please!"

Or maybe she is just crazy, Alison remembered thinking, just before it happened.

Her screen began throwing up windows like errors, except each contained more data. Every layer seemed to encapsulate the previous data in a perfect, instantly graspable and yet utterly inexplicable equation. Then she was seeing networks, complex webs of *if* and *then*. There were models, fractal patterns, geometry and telemetry that sought to describe impossible spaces extending in unknowable directions.

She saw everything. In that moment she came perilously close to becoming the second convert to Charen Volkovska's cult. For perhaps thirty seconds she saw what the woman had called the "network," a vast frozen ocean of computation in which SFI was encysted like a parasite. She saw the godlike perspective that turned the chaotic complexities of the stock market into a child's peg-and-hole game, where all you needed to do was match the shapes to dominate the markets.

At this point in her retelling, Alison obviously saw that she'd lost Julian, which was always the problem with the indescribable.

"You ever read Abbott's *Flatland*?" she asked. "A 3D, regular human encounters a 2D world, basically. 2D people can't conceive of 3D space, but he considers what he'd be able to do to their world. He sees their entire universe spread out in front of him, all at once. Walls and barriers are like lines on a page; nothing's secret from him. One more dimension is all you need to be a god. Well it was like that, only we're the 2D people and this network was seeing us from somewhere else, seeing all of us."

"You're saying...outside time? That's the fourth dimension?" Julian was doing his best to keep his objections buried for the duration.

"Not time, even, but...some other perspective," Alison tried. "It wasn't like it was seeing the future, it just had such a perfect and complete grasp of our present that it could make these predictions. But it was patchy. And when the network dropped, then whatever careful chain of trades it had set in motion couldn't be completed. That was because the grand plan couldn't be accessed, and so it all crapped out right then. The network cutting out *caused* the temperature fluctuations, by the way, not the other way around. The heat didn't cause the network to fail; the network brought the cold with it." Alison scratched Simms behind the ears, and he grumbled at her.

"So then what happened?"

Alison's laptop had snapped back to its regular view. Then all she could see was the trade data unspooling from SFI's system, unheeded and lost in the ether. When she scrabbled to see what she could salvage from those earlier revelations, there was no trace of it whatsoever. And she had absolutely no proof it had happened.

She had tried to call Charen but couldn't reach her. Eventually she had gone down to the server room, braving the blast of cold air when she opened the door.

Charen wasn't in there.

The only rational explanation was that she had gone out of the fire escape. Although Alison wasn't entirely sure where she stood on rational explanations, after what she'd seen. Certainly the investigation was never able to locate Charen Volkovska again.

Housekeeping: SFI was broken up. What wasn't widely known was that the computer assets were bought by a sequence of companies that also bailed out the disgraced Swayne. But Swayne's computers ended up as the exclusive property of one firm, and effectively one man.

"One firm?" Julian echoed.

"Pushed my resources to the limit to find out," Alison said, "but someone was really interested in what Swayne had... uncovered, maybe's the best term. Rove Denton."

"And now..."

Alison wordlessly showed him her photos again. "Whatever

this is, this 'network' of Volkovska's, it likes to identify things with numbers. But it uses numbers that make sense to us: social security, company registration. Unequivocal identifying tags that exist in our datasphere. And this is Rove Denton Ltd. You can look it up at Companies House. Rove Denton bought up SFI, and maybe they bought in Charen Volkovska as well, who knows? Rove Denton links to Billy White too, this transaction here...right before he takes it in his head to whack Dr. Khan. And yes, I know: the 'network' is the bloody emperor of unverified sources."

Julian was nodding slowly. "Well, quite," he agreed. "What am I even supposed to do with all of this?"

Her smile then was brief and fragile. "Well, you've done the first thing, which is to not just dismiss it all as some kind of 'episode.' Because I know how this sounds. And I could have faked these photos."

Julian weighed it all up, every word of it, and nodded slowly. "It does sound like that, but yes, I'm not dismissing it. Possibly awaiting further evidence, but...Rove Denton could be a lead?"

"I can't ask you to dig into them, not based on this nonsense," she said briskly, as though agreeing with a statement he hadn't heard himself make.

"Of course," he confirmed, and that was enough said.

II

In the office the next morning, Julian put in a request for whatever they had on Rove Denton, assuming they had anything. It was innocent enough, and he covered it as part of the initial preparation for Op Mouser, the operation that would be keeping tabs on Dr. Khan and taking hard looks at whoever wanted to poach her. It was Julian's show at the moment, and it was on-grid, meaning the director had allocated a decent slice of the resource pie. Khan had been out of the government's direct employ for years, but there remained an implicit understanding that the contents of her head were HM Government's property—as and when they might be required.

Of course, to work out who else was interested, it would be useful to understand what Khan was an expert *in*: that particular meeting point of advanced maths and theoretical physics which apparently had such implications for national security. He put in a request for more on that, too, without much hope. Most likely it was either above his pay grade or beyond his comprehension.

In the interim, though, a tentative ID had come in for one of the pair that had savaged Billy White's lads.

The one surviving casualty of that little affray had been conscious long enough to answer a few police questions, but he'd had little to add to that blurry security footage photo. As expected, the big, slab-faced man had done the fist work. But White's lad had no idea who he'd been or why he'd ambushed them—except that the man had obviously been a foreigner, and therefore the enemy of everything White represented. Even hiked to the gills on painkillers and with a dozen broken bones, it was depressing how quickly the witness descended into rhetoric. The police were reasonably satisfied that the man was being candid, though, and Julian played the recording through and agreed. The big man and his friend had been there for Khan, not White, and if not for White's blundering then maybe they'd have snatched Khan instead. A tangled web.

The man himself had not been identified from their partial profile shot. The woman was another matter. Julian's team, aided by facial recognition algorithms, suggested she was a good ringer for one Elsinore Mallory, the only drawback to the match being that said Mallory had been missing for four years, after disappearing on Bodmin Moor. Missing wasn't dead, though. Julian delegated the unenviable task of questioning her family regarding a genuine family tragedy: privileges of rank. Aside from them, Mallory hadn't had many contacts. A handful of university chums and one childhood friend, Lisa Pryor, who'd been with her on the trip.

Julian stared at Pryor's picture blankly. There was no reason why she should have looked familiar, but he was instantly sure he'd seen her somewhere.

He checked his diary, saw that this afternoon's meeting promised to be the particularly tedious and unproductive kind, and decided that he wasn't too lofty to delegate tasks to himself. He would visit Pryor, to see if that would shake loose the thorn of memory pricking at the inside of his skull.

*

Mid-afternoon and he was on his way to Hemel in the company of Detective Sergeant Grace Lawrence. She was one of Royce's people, also trying to track Elsinore Mallory for the White murders. Lawrence was a young black woman who plainly reckoned, with some justification, that Julian had been born with a silver spoon in his mouth, and wasn't afraid to jab him about it.

Half the drive was spent on the phone to Josie after John came home with a cut lip and a shiner. She reckoned it was Julian's turn to talk to the school about their anti-bullying policy. She also reckoned—not explicitly, but it hovered about her words like a ghost—that Julian could be doing more at home for John. In that, she was probably right. He made vague noises about the pressures of the job, national security, that sort of thing, feeling wretched as the words came out of his mouth, but unable to stop himself.

Lisa Pryor lived on the fourth floor of a reasonably intact block of flats, and that was more than Julian had expected. Her employment, such as it was, lay in writing lurid articles about the occult for websites and the occasional special-interest magazine. He'd watched a clip on his phone where a two-years-younger Pryor had been on the local news when someone reckoned there was a big cat on the loose on Blackbirds Moor, although Julian reckoned it would be hard to lose even quite a small cat there. Her activities meant she had an online footprint as big as some small-time pop stars. There were apparently about a million websites obsessed with weird creatures—and they all bled into the flat earth and other fringe sites, with a cavalier attitude to reprinting each other's articles.

He had toyed with the idea of calling ahead to save a wasted trip, but that thorn was still digging in him. Just in case Pryor was up to her neck in it, he didn't want to find that a clumsy overture had led to her fleeing the country.

At Lawrence's knock they heard someone moving inside. A door two flats down opened and an old man stuck his head out balefully, wispy hair flaring like a halo in the light from the window at the corridor's end. Julian smiled politely, and then Pryor opened the door. She was smaller than he'd expected, a stocky woman just younger than Lawrence herself, wearing jeans and a T-shirt showing a tentacled monster and a complex word full of consonants ending in *-con 2017*.

"Miss Pryor? Hi, I'm Detective Sergeant Lawrence." She launched into the usual spiel: friendly introductions, then showing a badge with a calm and reassuring manner. "Mind if we come in to ask you a few questions?"

Pryor nodded without actually clearing the doorway. Her eyes slid over to Julian, and he was sure, in that instant, that she knew him too. Then she gave a strained smile and backed into the flat to let them enter, and he wasn't sure after all.

He'd thought Lawrence would take the lead, but she brought out her phone and informed Pryor she'd be recording, then sent a challenging look his way. Pryor's flat was a bedsit: bedroom/living room, a tiny corner for a kitchen and then an en suite. The limited space was monopolized by bookshelves, double-stacked with books and then half obscured by piles of more literature and periodicals. It was unpleasantly claustrophobic. Nobody else seemed to mind.

"Miss Pryor—May I call you Lisa?"

"Lee. People call me Lee," she said. She was tense and twitchy, but then, remarkably few people welcomed the intrusion of the authorities. It didn't necessarily mean she was mixed up in this Mallory business, but still...

"My name's Julian." He wasn't as good at reassuring as Lawrence. "We're here to talk to you about some ancient history, I'm afraid. An old friend of yours, Elsinore Mallory."

Pryor nodded, a single staccato movement, and sat down on the bed. No surprise, he saw. Here to talk about someone four years vanished, and Pryor didn't think that at all odd.

"Would you care to tell us again about when you last saw

her?" DS Lawrence had taken the room's single chair, turning it round so that the desk and its monitor were at her back. Over her shoulder, Daleks trundled endlessly from the left of the screensaver to the right. "I know you went through this already, but if you could...?"

They listened as Pryor recited all that had happened on the moor. She stuttered a bit, but seemed weary and still hurt by it, rather than guilty.

"And when did you last see her?" Julian threw in. He was still standing, because it was that or sit on the floor, which he knew cast him as bad cop.

"I haven't. Not since then." Pryor made a good job of meeting his eyes.

"And she's not been in touch since she disappeared."

"No." Plenty of visual cues to show how tense she was, but he was sure she'd been expecting this since the pair of them appeared at her door.

Confident she was lying, Julian had an elaborate skein of leading questions in the back of his mind. But as he opened his mouth to show how clever he was, his memory finally kicked and he said, "I saw you in Camden three nights ago. Why were you there?"

Pryor's expression was gratifyingly rabbit-in-headlights, and Lawrence kept any surprise to a sidelong glance at him.

"Miss Pryor," she said. "We've reason to believe your friend has surfaced and is involved in something extremely dangerous, both to her and others. People have already been hurt. If there's anything you can tell us, we need to know it, for your friend's good as much as anyone's."

Lisa Pryor shuddered, still staring at Julian. "That was you. With the ambulance."

"People died there," he said bluntly. She'd been talking to Khan, and that meant he needed someone to quiz the good doctor again. "We can't overstate how serious this is, Miss Pryor." He was overplaying the act a little, as he tended to do if he wasn't careful.

"Please, Miss Pryor, has Elsinore been in touch, in any way?" Lawrence pressed more gently. "Help us to help her."

He saw the moment when her sheer stubbornness cracked open. There was only misery behind the shell. "I don't know," Pryor said. "I really don't know."

"Explain," Julian barked, and then, "Please," reining himself in.

"I got a call from Mal. That's what she preferred. Prefers. Mal. She said to meet. That's why I was there. I waited for her. Even though the call was...wasn't on my log, on my phone. No number, no record at all. And I went, and I waited. And she didn't turn up. And then there was...you, and all that, whatever it was, and that poor woman whose house had been broken into."

Julian nodded. Pryor sounded sincere enough, to his best guess. She was still tense, though, gripping her knees. Where was the release he'd expect to come with that revelation?

"Go on," he suggested quietly. Pryor's look was accusing, as though they'd made a deal to meet halfway, half the story as full and final settlement.

"You were there..." she tried weakly.

"If there's anything else, we need to know," Lawrence encouraged her. "If you were at the incident, you saw how that turned out. There are some extremely bad people out there, and we need to bring them in before this happens again."

"I thought I met her. On the street. Later." Now Pryor

wasn't meeting anyone's gaze. "I thought it was her, just…
out of nowhere, just…back. That's what I remembered,
next morning, after spending half the night getting home.
Then she'd simply gone away again. Gone where I couldn't
follow."

Julian's lips twitched in irritation. "What do you mean?"

"I remember things that couldn't have happened," Pryor
said dully. "I did before, when Mal went. And now I've done
it again. I remember Mal going away, into…into the Away.
And that can't have happened, right? And I remember her
calling, except she can't have called. You want a statement,
officers? I solemnly swear I do not know what the fuck is
happening or what is true. Or whether I'm just a brain in
the jar and you're all made up out of my head. Is that good
enough? Type it up and I'll sign it." Now she was looking up
again, full of an anger to which he and Lawrence were only
accidental accessories.

Julian was about to push her nonetheless, because anger
could be a useful skeleton key to all sorts of doors, but
Lawrence stood abruptly. "Thank you, Miss Pryor," she said.
"We'd like you to come down to your local station very shortly,
so we can talk this through in more detail. Would that be all
right?" Julian was trying to catch her gaze without showing
any disunity to Pryor, but Lawrence soldiered on. "We'll give
you a call in the next day or so, to agree a time. If you have
any contact from Mallor—Mal in the meantime, then you
must get in touch immediately, you understand." She fed a
card into Pryor's numb fingers. "I can't stress how important
that is. Whoever your friend is involved with, they are
extremely dangerous, and it's important she's separated from
them as quickly as possible."

Back at the car, Julian finally exploded. "What was that, precisely?"

"That was me being wary about interviewing someone who might have mental health problems without proper procedures and support personnel in place," Lawrence said. "Look, here. That stuff she was coming out with, did you see the interview she gave in Cornwall?"

"She practically repeated it for us verbatim."

"Not that one. Look." She passed her phone to him. "There was another disappearance on the moor around the same time. Turns out she got interviewed about it."

Julian squinted at the tiny font. His eyebrows slowly lifted as he took in the alternative details of what had happened to Elsinore Mallory, according to Lisa Pryor's imagination. If he hadn't seen Khan's flat's security footage, he'd now be wondering if *Pryor* hadn't caused her friend's disappearance.

"So we call her into the station with a professional on hand. I don't want to end up on the wrong end of a discrimination claim because we came down hard on a schizophrenic, or whatever she might be."

"She might just be lying," Julian said stubbornly.

Lawrence gave him a level look. "Real convincing story she spun in there."

He nodded reluctantly and checked his own phone, to see just how dull and time-wasting his missed meeting had been. The first message he opened almost had him through the roof of the car.

Despite the best efforts of the security services, Dr. Kay Amal Khan had slipped her minders and vanished.

Interlude: The Posticthyans

Excerpt from *Other Edens: Speculative Evolution and Intelligence* by Professor Ruth Emerson of the University of California

Each branching timeline brings us closer to our own. In this world, the sea scorpions are only a memory, the trilobites no more than shabby detritovores already reaching the end of their long run. We are not quite done with arthropods, but the open waters of these seas teem with fish that you can at least recognize as such, jaws and all.

Just as in the eurypterids' timeline, there is something magical about the boundary between land and water that nurtures complexity. The shifting biomes, dry to wet, wet to dry, mean twice as many predators, twice as many kinds of prey. There are opportunities for forays inland or out to the open ocean. To adapt to the surf and shore is to shoulder more burdens than to commit wholly to either land or water.

At first, these particular fish are mere opportunists, mudskipper-like things encroaching on the fringes of salt forests. Here, masses of unchecked ferns, horsetails and lycophytes tower in lieu of the trees that have yet to evolve. Insect life draws the fish here, a wealth of protein-rich food—if only it can be brought down to the water to be devoured. Bulbous, froggy eyes adapt over tens of generations to see above the waterline as well as below it. Brains bulge with the strain of calculating spit trajectories to bring down dragonflies and knock cockroaches off overhanging fronds. The air proves a potent medium for competing males to boast and bellow in. They co-opt aquatic organs to produce terrestrial sounds that would be deafeningly loud to us but are muted and dull to their makers' crude ears.

By the end of the Devonian the shores are lined with colonies of big, slick-skinned beasts like lumbering elephant seals. Monsters neither fish nor true amphibian, which seem at least half mouth. And those big heads hold big brains.

Their ancestors were catholic diners, appropriately enough for fish. As well as hawking for insects they grubbed in the mud for shellfish and worms and burrowing crustaceans. Their snouts sport coiling barbels which were first used to locate their prey and later on evolved to root it out and seize it, stronger and more dextrous over the generations. By the time they evolve the powerful brains that make them the object of our study, they have something like a hand of six muscular fingers attached to their faces.

They are quicker to develop than the trilobites or the eurypterids, and one convenient narrative is simply the way that they are bound to the transition between land and water. They now live primarily in fresh water, haunting the river edges, lakes and swamps that, in other timelines, will give later eras their coal seams and industrial ages. These are unstable biomes, always on the point of being too brackish, too anoxic, too dry, too hot. The Devonians evolve on a knife edge of need. Their breeding requires conditions the world is reluctant to guarantee. Even their respiration is conditional on their environment, for by adulthood they have lost their gills and breathe through their skins and the linings of their mouths.

As their intelligence develops it is driven by a need to control and stabilize their environment. They start with dams, dykes and other primitive terraforming, then progress to manipulating the chemical make-up of their surroundings, to which their barbels and skins are highly sensitive. While working with stone and wood, they are also experimenting with salt gradients and the curious bond properties of water molecules. Their alchemists unlock the secrets of electricity frighteningly early. In the cold climes they love, where their respiration is at its most efficient, they grow artisanal ice crystals in order to create machines which simply return to water when their makers tire of them. They electrolyse metals from sea water and lay down skeins of gold within the shifting interstices of icebergs. Ice becomes the key to their technology. Evolved from cold-blooded stock, they are nonetheless still adapted for cold-water living. Their blood is laced with antifreeze; their metabolisms burn fiercely to maintain the energetic demands of their busy minds.

Looking at these Devonians, you would not recognize something akin to you. At the height of their prowess you'd see a thing twice your size, showing something of the fish, something of the salamander. Something, even, of the slug, because they still drag their naked bellies in the mud. Breathing through their skin, inured to the cold, they have never developed or even conceived of clothing, and their adornment is found in patterns of colour and glow that they cultivate within their skin, tame fungi and bacteria become their body art. Their eyes are huge, mobile, set so they can view the world before, beside and even behind them, above and below the waterline. Their sagging chins and broad noses bristle with the barbels that are their brains' interface with the world.

They are one of the great technical civilizations, rising to prominence with shocking swiftness. For a time they hold the world's clock still and reshape the ecologies of the land as they see fit. They have no industry you might recognize, and yet the ice caps of the world are their supercomputers, filigreed with metallic and chemical logic gates that they cultivate like gardens, flurrying with electronic thought. Their machines are sliding block puzzles, regulated by melt and flow and freeze. You would never spot their great engines, and yet in a mere millennium they pass from the primitive to a level of engineering sophistication that neither you nor we can imagine. They even gain a foothold in orbit, sending up clouds of ice particles that self-organize into satellites with their own artificial minds. Most remarkably, for the longest time they do so little harm.

Early in their development, they nearly destroyed them-selves wherever their numbers grew too great, the overspill of their chemical industries poisoning the waters they relied on. They learned, regulating the numbers of their spawn, changing their breeding habits. They accept that their lives are fit for two narrow bands of polar and sub-polar coastal habitats, and the rest of the world is simply too inhospitable to trouble with.

As a digression, this insular attitude results in a rare moment when two separate species exist side by side on the Earth, both able to claim a measure of awareness and sentience. Around the equator are great fern and cycad forests, where dwells a species of colonial spider that has been evolving a mind of a very different kind. The forests are dense with their webs, which form an extended sense organ linking all the component parts of the colony. Later, these generations-old and constantly rewoven tapestries become a kind of exported cognitive engine. The spiders do not think, but between them the web they work on becomes a substitute mind—active when they move upon it and update it, falling to oblivion should they ever stop. And when the great tropical storms come to lash the equatorial forests, these weird minds are torn apart and die, and the spiders blindly weave fresh webs the next season until a new thinking being is born, knowing no continuity with what was lost. The Devonians observe this but can only tell that after the webs hit a critical mass of complexity, the conduct of the colony becomes abruptly more purposeful. It seems to be planning ahead beyond the dreams of any of the individual weavers.

Perhaps it is this observed outsourcing of intellect that prepares the Devonians for what must happen next.

It is their ill luck to rise to prominence in the very shadow of obliteration. Even as they perfect their icy difference engines, the world is turning. The continents are already clasped in their death knot; volcanic traps the size of continents vomit poison into the air and sea. The ice that nurtures their civilization retreats north and south; the cold water is warmer each summer. They begin to smother, then boil.

The great dying time, the Permian extinction, is upon them too now, and they are an especially susceptible species. Their thinkers, their scientists and engineers and fish-eyed dreamers, come together to croak and rumble out their theories and plans. They are, after all, masters of their world. Surely there is something they can do? With the aid of their great computers they determine that there is. There are many things, in fact, and they will do all of them. In desperation they set out to wrestle Death for the fate of the world.

United as a species working to the limits of its technology, they fight the warming of their planet at every turn. They alter the currents of the seas, seed clouds with ice and grow structures within the ice caps that alter Earth's weather patterns beyond recognition. They launch countless more composite satellites into orbit, forming mirrors to parry the rays of the sun. They plant inland mountains with glaciers and accelerate their growth artificially until the ice fields themselves become their armies, marching across the barren land in savage wars of attrition. The Devonian civilization will not go gracefully into anybody's fossil record.

They win, proving their mastery of the world beyond all doubt. They calm the volcanos; they cool the Earth; they expand the icecaps even past where they were before. Their species, after terrible losses, looks forward to a new golden age where anything is possible. A thousand thousand species have been lost to the fires, to anoxic seas, to drought or to the newly minted ice, but Earth's icthyan lords remain.

Their golden age lasts only a generation, in which they expand in all optimism to every corner of the Earth that is habitable to them. And those corners only grow more numerous as the years go on, so it seems to most of them that they are greater than they ever were, the iceberg coasts creeping closer to the tropics every year.

Their greatest scientists raise concerns, but for the longest time nobody wants to listen to the truth. Only when the ice is halfway to the equator do they leave off their long age of optimism and accept that they have only traded one problem for another. The processes they have set in motion have a global momentum too. They cannot just be turned off or even reined in. Every year is a little colder; every winter the ice reaches with longer arms, every summer it gives less ground in its retreat.

They do everything they can in a vain quest for equilibrium, but this new fate—which they built themselves—is too much for them to undo. And perhaps there was never a time when they could have escaped. Perhaps they only ever had the choice between two deaths.

There comes a time when the Earth can only beget more ice, the white sheen of it casting back the sunlight, so that the frozen land beneath is never warmed. The world enters the greatest ice age since the freezing times that came before the Ediacaran epoch. In your timeline, the Permian extinction killed perhaps eighty or ninety per cent of all species in the world. On these Devonians' Earth, at the end, there is nothing left beyond extremophile bacteria and algae—whatever can live in and off the ice. The forests, the fish, the insects: all the rich tapestry of life has either burned or frozen. And yet the ice-makers are not gone, not quite.

At the end, they were forced to look into that icy mirror and recognize that they themselves had brought the world to an end—and they had one final recourse. They could take refuge in their technology, because their computers would grow only more powerful with the gathering cold. Those who could be saved had their personalities and experiences uploaded into great polar engines, populating the supercomputers. In this way, they continued their existence within an eternal simulation of the world they'd destroyed. And this option was seen as desperate enough that the vast majority simply chose sleep and storage rather than any active virtual existence. As artificial intellects, far from seeking some infinite expansion throughout the galaxy, they had no purpose. There was no biological imperative to go on, to make more of themselves, or even to discover the secrets of the universe. They had no reason to *be*, and their memories were shackled to a world-destroying guilt. They made for themselves a frozen, everlasting hell of recrimination, with an infinite amount of time to ask, *Could we have done it differently?*

Then, after millions of years of agonized stasis, they received signals from outside. Random signals, incomprehensible signals: signals that indicated contact from...nowhere, everywhere, somewhere impossible.

And, eventually, a call for help.

5.

I

When the two officials had gone, Lee collapsed on her bed, thoughts chasing each other about the room like dogs.

It was hardly her first time being interviewed by the police, or even her first time since Bodmin. She knew the drill. Several of her friends were averse to speaking with the police and she'd covered for them from time to time. And if there was anyone she would cover for, it was Mal, surely. Except...

When they'd started, she was going to deny everything. After all, what could they prove, precisely? Then her nagging recognition of the white guy had suddenly clicked into sharp focus because he'd been there, at the break-in gone wrong or whatever it had been. He'd seen her.

But what did that prove, except that they thought Mal did it?

And now *she* thought Mal was involved in the break-in too...She tried to be loyal, but Mal had been *somewhere* for four years, and had never called or texted or even put a note through her door. She'd been dead. Lee had known she was dead. It's not as if there was a whole other world on Bodmin Moor where a girl could scrape out a living for four years without seeing anyone. As though Mal was just another cryptid whose presence she could fancifully believe in whilst her logical mind knew there was nothing there.

Yet Mal *was* back, in the company of a monstrous bruiser, and people were dead. She'd seen them stretchered out of that house.

She could see how her two visitors had played her: the calm, consoling woman, the hard-faced, looming man. They'd made her worry about herself and about Mal, and she'd cracked. It would be best if she told the truth, had said that traitorous little thought. So she'd opened her mouth and waited for the truth to hop out, like toads from the lips of a cursed girl in a fairy story.

She remembered very clearly meeting Mal outside the closed Tube station. In the same way, she remembered being at the Six Brothers with Mal years ago. And being on the far side of them, where the other three brothers lived, where the Birdmen were. She remembered those things, but her logical mind knew there was nothing there.

She had tried to tell the policewoman and her colleague about Mal's reappearance in Camden, and every word that she'd forced out had seemed thinner and thinner, waxy and see-through like greaseproof paper. She had scared them off, she reckoned. She'd just said madder and madder things until they were embarrassed to be in the same room. So they'd left.

But if she'd just imagined the Camden break-in, why would those officials be reinvestigating Mal after all these years? There had been stains on the broad man's long coat, and its hem had been heavy and wet with something other than rain or piss or spilled beer. Mal had been broad at the shoulder too, bulked out with muscle like she'd never had, scarred, tough.

Lee sat up. The police had more questions. People were

dead and she was a lead, if not an actual witness. And what might they let slip, as they grilled her? Might she discover enough to follow where Mal had gone?

Distantly, she marvelled that she had already swung all the way back: now she was telling herself it had all definitely happened, even the impossible bits. And she was champing at the bit to investigate.

There was a knock at the door and she stood up unsteadily. A large man in a shirt and tie could be spied through the peephole, a beige coat folded over his arm. He rapped again, knuckles close enough to her vantage that she flinched back.

"Hello, Miss Pryor?" he called. "Police."

Already? It wasn't the same ones, but she supposed she hadn't exactly signed up with them for a loyalty card or anything. Cautiously, she opened the door and looked up at him. He definitely worked out more than Julian whoever-he-was, broader and taller. There were sweat stains at the armpits of his shirt, and she imagined him vaulting up the stairs, thrilling at the free aerobic workout.

"Did your colleagues forget something?" she asked.

He had his phone out and his gaze flicked from her to it, as if checking her face against a photo. Her glimpse of it only showed something like a stopwatch. For half a second his face was expressionless, but then animation returned and he flashed her a wallet with his ID. "Sorry to come back so quickly, but our superiors want you to come along to the station and give a full statement. After that, we shouldn't have to bother you with anything. Best to get it all done with, eh?" His smile was easier than Julian's had been. *So, if they were good cop and bad cop, who's this? Gym bro cop?*

She didn't want to go, she realized. This wasn't just a

general reluctance to go with any police officer anywhere, from experiences of gay rights protests gone bad, reinforced by friends into civil disobedience and alternative lifestyles. Gym Bro made her nervous.

But she steeled herself. After all, this was the plan. She was going to find, by evasions, misunderstandings and sly jibes, just what the police knew about Mal.

"Fine," she told Gym Bro. "Let's go." She grabbed her bag and pushed into the hall, locking her door behind her.

In the juddering lift he stood like a monolith, taking up way too much space. She tried a few nervous conversational assays like, "I don't imagine I'll be much help...," but he parried them all easily with a smile and shallow encouragement. It was routine, be over soon, paperwork, you know.

The summer heat had made the whole building stuffy, and she braced herself for the hammer blow of the sun as she stepped out, shielding her eyes. But the air was chill, and she felt—imagined she felt—a flurry of cold grit against her cheek. She stopped very suddenly, and Gym Bro Cop sidestepped her neatly.

"Miss?" he asked.

And of course the sun was out and the air was warm as toast, and what had she been thinking, exactly? *Is this going to be how it is now?* Her own senses and memories were venturing out into terra incognita and bringing back stories she couldn't trust. She apologized weakly. *But they want to talk about Mal, so some of it must be real?*

There was a black four-by-four with dark-tinted windows, and Gym Bro Cop skipped ahead a couple of steps to haul open one of the back doors. Lee baulked for a moment, then reminded herself of her mission. *Find out what they know.* In case her friend was still real and alive. And it was the police, after all, so worst-case scenarios were limited here. A night in the cells, a little shouting by some seventies TV stereotype in an interview room, a wasted day, a few homophobic slurs. Only later would she realize just how comfortable her growing-up had been, that her worries extended so far and no further.

She got in, and there was another big man in the back, with rolled-up shirtsleeves and his tie pulled loose and awry. He gave her an unfriendly look as Gym Bro Cop slid into the front seat. Then the car started by some remote magic not involving keys.

They moved away from the kerb, and Lee glanced backwards to see two other identical cars fall in behind them. A motorcade of sinister black vehicles, for the sole purpose of taking one harmless young woman to make a perfectly routine statement at a police station.

"Um…" she said. The man beside her didn't even look round, but she met Gym Bro Cop's eyes in the rear-view mirror.

"Can I see that ID again?" she asked timidly.

II

Lucas May was cautiously pleased with how smoothly things were going. He was, he knew, a passably convincing policeman when he needed to be. He'd judged that this Pryor girl fell into a certain cosseted section of the populace for whom cooperating with the authorities was a knee-jerk reaction— no matter how much they considered themselves counter-culture. Sure enough, here she was in the back of the car, and only now questioning who he was. She'd find the doors locked, obviously, if she tried them. And any funny business would have Dominic back there keeping her in line.

It might have gone another way if not for the App. Entirely possible that Lucas could have turned up at her door, asked a few questions for form's sake and then gone away again. Except boss man Rove had downloaded it onto his phone. Lucas didn't much like the App. He especially didn't like the way it only appeared when Rove wanted him to have it, and vanished just as readily. It used no storage nor battery—and when it wasn't around, his phone would not admit to ever having it installed. And it was simple to use: you held your device near something or someone and it gave you a reading. Precisely what it was detecting, Lucas had no idea, and in his head the thing measured Weirdness. Things and people that had been in contact with Weird Shit gave off some kind of radiation, something the App could detect. And while he'd far rather have been on the side of the business that didn't need such tools, it was a useful thing to have.

Lisa Pryor was definitely flicking his Weirdness Geiger counter. Not the highest readings he'd seen, but she'd been in contact with *something*. That same "something" had killed three men and mauled a fourth. The girl implicated in Billy White's death was an old friend of Pryor's and, given the readings, they'd renewed their friendship recently. The spectral fingerprints were all over her, according to the App.

As he slung the car along the M1, heading for Rove Denton's usefully windowless office, he had his phone beside him. He was texting one-handed whenever the traffic let him. The texts vanished the moment they were sent, which was all very mysterious but a pain in the arse when you couldn't remember what you'd written previously. Rove's replies—sent with his own pointy fingers from wherever the fuck he was—appeared and waited to be seen before fading away like bad dreams.

There was a flurry of what he thought was steam or smoke across the windscreen, and he swerved slightly. Behind, Dominic swore. Pryor was tense now, hunched in. In retrospect he should have just shown her his ID again, because it was a good fake. Still, he felt that taking the hard line was playing fair. She deserved to know she was in the shit.

"Fuck's sake," Dominic spat. "Is that *snow?*"

"Don't be stupid," Lucas told him as another brief curtain passed over them, light as gossamer. "It's July. There's a fucking heatwave, mate."

He met Pryor's eyes in the mirror again and was profoundly disconcerted by how they'd lit up. *She knows something.*

Abruptly they were ploughing off the road, thundering down a bank to carve through a broad stream. They scraped half their paintwork off against a gnarled tree that simply hadn't been there before—and neither had any of its many, many friends. They were rattling and jolting over a topography of roots and mounded dead needles under a canopy of dense, interlacing boughs, the summer sun turned almost to twilight by their shade. Lucas wrenched at the wheel, weaving drunkenly between tree trunks, all those half-forgotten lessons about driving under adverse conditions surging back to him. Then they'd ploughed into another watercourse, coasted to the far side with water rising over the hubcaps and ended up axle-deep in mud.

A further flurry of snow passed over them and was gone.

Lucas stared out at the forest, gloomy and receding into darkness on every side. In the rear-view mirror he saw

Michael's car, drawn up on the other side of the stream. There was no sign of the third vehicle. Maybe it was still... back there, where there were things like roads and sanity.

Dominic was swearing steadily, and Lucas told him to shut up. He tried his phone: no signal, go figure. Behind, Michael and Becca had left their car and were staring about them. Lucas elbowed his door open, and cold air sawed into his throat. "Holy fuck," he rasped out. It was midwinter out there. He fumbled for his coat, the shock of the sudden temperature change like a weight on his chest. The air was full of flies, scratchy with unfamiliar birdsong.

He waved at the others.

"We'll come over to you?" Michael shouted. He was still in his shirtsleeves and his breath plumed dully. Becca was hugging herself and stamping.

"Stay there. Need a tow rope to get our car out of there," Lucas called. His voice fell away into the spaces between the trees and, just as he was thinking about all the noise they were making, something answered: a long, low bellow like the indigestion of a whole world. Like monsters. It hadn't sounded close; not exactly in the distance either.

Michael had the tow line, but a couple of failed attempts showed that he couldn't sling it over the broad stream. Nor was he keen on wading through it. Lucas looked around impatiently. In the gloom he could see things at the water's edge, heads low as they drank. They didn't seem to be further up on the Weird Shit scale than some kind of deer or boar. He eased his pistol out of the concealed holster slung under his armpit—although whether nine-millimetre rounds would stop even a perfectly normal wild boar was anybody's guess.

The unseen bellower let out another grand belch. It didn't sound closer, and the drinkers at the streamside weren't spooked by it, which he reckoned was a good sign.

In the meantime, some part of his mind had been examining the sodden ground. Not enough traction for towing their vehicle, was the unfortunate conclusion.

"Stay there, we'll come to you!" he ordered, catching Michael midway through rolling his trousers up. He rapped on the car window. "Dom, we're wading across to them. Cold as fuck, but it's our best chance to be under way quickly."

When he emerged from the car Dominic visibly shuddered with the cold, but the physical discomfort didn't reach his eyes: those were already wide and rigid as he stared at his boss.

"Under way *where*?" he spat out, voice shaking. "Where the fuck are we, Lucas? What the fuck, even?"

"Calm down," Lucas said. He'd thought Dominic had run into his own share of Weird, but then he didn't think *anyone* on his team had gone this deep, himself included. He was used to shit coming *in* from somewhere else, not him falling out of the world into ... fucking Narnia.

"Seriously." Dominic's voice was shaking. "Seriously ... go where? There isn't anywhere."

"Still better to all be in a car that can get the hell out of Dodge if we need it," Lucas said. "Come on—" And then Lisa Pryor slammed her door open, ramming it into his knee, and made a determined break for it. He grabbed her by the collar, more instinct than decision, and yanked her back so hard that she sat down and choked for a while. Without much sympathy he hauled her up and thrust her at Dominic.

"The boss will sort this out," he said, wishing he could be sure of it. "He needs us, and he wants *her*. So you look after her, and we're all getting out of this, okay? We simply keep safe until he tracks us down."

"You're sure?"

"Sure I'm sure." Lucas scowled at the stream, and then rolled up his trousers like a seaside tourist and waded into it. The water was groin-deep in the middle, and Dominic went over entirely and came up soaked head to toe. When the three of them emerged on the other side he half expected them all to freeze solid.

"In," he managed through chattering teeth. "In. Heater on, Michael."

They had spare clothes, thankfully, although these were more intended to deal with suspicious spatter marks than a ducking. He and Dominic got white T-shirts and jeans that made them look like ageing members of some bygone boy band, and Pryor eventually consented to change into a skirt of Becca's that wouldn't quite button up.

"Right." He checked his phone again. Still no telecoms network in Narnia, but Rove would surely be able to get through. A good idea to get the car out of the mud though, if they wanted to get going. He ordered Becca behind the wheel while he and Michael put their backs into moving the vehicle upslope. Dominic stood by, shivering, with a heavy hand on Pryor's shoulder.

Halfway through this, Lucas's instincts kicked in belatedly, because Pryor wasn't nearly as spooked as the rest of them. It was as though she'd been expecting it, recognized it. Even as the revelation hit him, Dominic barked out a shout of alarm.

They weren't alone.

On the far side of the stream, next to Lucas's abandoned

car, was a human figure. A human-*like* figure, he corrected himself. It was robed and hooded, maybe with a face mask— he saw the dim light catch on glass lenses. Short, very broad, freakishly so. He wouldn't want to go toe to toe with whoever owned that body, if they knew what to do with it. But that was why he had the gun.

"Hi there," he called out. All of them had drawn their guns now, and Dominic's pistol hand was shaking in a worrying way. "We've run into some trouble." He bit off the words *Could we use your phone?* because that probably wasn't what you said to a...technodruid, or whatever the fuck this joker was.

"Give us the girl." It was a woman's voice, or he thought it was. Very deep, though, and each word accented in a way he was absolutely sure he'd never heard before, not anywhere in the world.

"Not going to happen," he said, still friendly-like, still not pointing his gun at her.

"If you want to leave here, it will." The woman stepped forwards, and at least she moved like a human being. He didn't see any weapons, but he also wasn't born yesterday.

"It's not an option," he told her. "But I'm sure you want us out of your...lovely forest, so why don't you show us where the..." *Wardrobe* was the word his mind supplied, uselessly. "Where the exit is, miss, and we can be out of your hair."

She made a sound like guttural vomiting, which he interpreted as laughter. "It is not," she said, "*our* forest."

"Chief," Michael snapped.

But Lucas was already turning, because something big was coming, shouldering between the trees, something as big as the car.

147

It bellowed, that same gurgling roar he'd heard before. The source of that noise was absurdly small, swaying over his head on a long neck. However, the body was big as a bison's and almost as hairy, save that the hair was feathery. It had a tail long enough to be lost in the shadows.

Lucas stared up at the dinosaur. The dinosaur regarded the car with instant and motiveless rage and then surged forwards along the edge of the stream.

"Becca, out!" he yelled, and she piled out of the passenger door even as the monster reared up on its hind legs like an elephant at the circus. Its forefeet had one big blunt claw each and it brought them down on the vehicle—hard enough to drive the roof into the steering wheel. The airbag leapt out in a futile attempt to do some good and then exploded with an echoing retort. The dinosaur squealed in fright and took off across the stream, wallowing in the water.

Then he realized Dominic was yelling: Pryor had shucked off his grip in the confusion and was racing between the trees, zigzagging wildly. Dominic was aiming, but a dead Pryor wouldn't be of any use to them.

He swore, at Pryor, at incapable subordinates, at dinosaurs, and then he was giving chase. He was trusting to the others to be on his heels and hoping the technodruid didn't fancy the exercise.

Daniel Rove valued his elite workforce, this much Lucas knew. But what Rove really wanted was to probe Pryor's mind to find out what she knew, and that meant Lucas really, *really* needed to be where Pryor was when his boss caught up with them.

III

Even as she put the first tree between herself and her pursuers, Lee was aware this wasn't the smartest thing she'd ever done. Yes, the not-police had been in the middle of kidnapping her, and they were maybe associated with the thugs that had been stretchered out of that Camden flat. Sticking with them had few attractions, then. On the other hand...

She half expected gunfire, but instead there was shouting and the sound of pursuit. She was willing to bet Gym Bro Cop could outrun her in a straight race, so she started weaving between the trees. She headed for where they grew close and the shadows hung heaviest, with the mad idea of ducking behind a tree and somehow evading his notice entirely.

On the other hand, she might be running away from the only human beings in a hundred miles—perhaps in this *world*. She might have gone camping a few times, but that didn't translate to living off the land. And this wasn't even the land she might have learned to live off, because *that* land didn't have actual dinosaurs roaming about.

Gym Bro had miraculously failed to catch her yet, but she could hear him scuffing down the slope she'd descended, cursing her name. He was going to beat her to within an inch of her life when he caught her, she guessed, and the thought gave her an extra turn of speed.

Then she was out of the trees.

She hadn't expected it, and she was abruptly crashing down a bank, skidding on her backside. She dug the heels of her sodden trainers in to slow her before she went into the water beyond. Gym Bro exploded from the trees above her, pelting full tilt, and he almost put a foot through her face as he

149

stumbled over her. He ended up on the water's edge, turning with a gun in one hand and the other already reaching for her. Without thinking, she kicked and caught him on the hip. She'd been aiming for the groin, but it wasn't a move she had much experience with, and anyway the impact was enough. With a dismayed yell he went backwards into the mud-coloured river.

She slithered to her feet, a hair from joining him, and bolted off along the bank. Gym Bro's friends arrived, but they lost vital seconds when all three fell over each other to pull him from the water. At least one was being yelled at to follow her, but then they were all hooting and hollering and at least one gun went off. She risked a look back. But whatever had emerged to snap at Gym Bro's heels was already submerging, a curved grey back vanishing into the opaque water.

Then she was running, following the curve of the bank, knowing she'd have to go back into the forest to try and lose them, and that would mean a struggle up the crumbling, slimy bank. Her filthy hands were already numb with cold and the rest of her wasn't far behind. And she had nowhere to go. That was the kicker, really. She could run as far and fast as she possibly could and she'd still be nowhere at the end of it.

Gym Bro had been talking to someone out there, someone new. Perhaps, she considered, she might have had the wit to run *towards* them, rather than simply *away*.

A vista opened up as the forest thinned out behind her and the riverbanks fell away. The shape of the river was laid out before her as it cut its way through the clear, marshy ground ahead in the brittle sunlight. She saw hills and other watercourses, and a herd of something like tusked elk watched her incuriously from the far side of the river. Its curved course was speaking to parts of her mind not involved in the chase. She thought of standing on Waterloo Bridge, of the opening sequence of *EastEnders*, of…

I'm still in London, she realized. *Or where London will be? Or where it never was? Is this the Thames?*

"Mal, here!" someone called from the trees, and her heart jolted. Not just *someone*. *Mal* was calling her. She'd recognize that voice anywhere, even at her wits' end.

"Mal! Here! I'm here!" she gasped. She began clawing her way back to the forest edge. Gym Bro was yelling at her that he was going to shoot if she didn't stop. But they needed her alive—didn't they? He sounded pissed off, but also pleading, and that gave her hope.

She reached the trees. "Mal!" she called, and from further within the forest came that beloved voice, crying "Mal!" back at her. She was so happy to have *somewhere* to head for that nothing else seemed to matter, not even asking why Mal would be crying out her own name. She just blundered madly, bouncing from tree trunks, listening for that voice.

Then she began to slow, because she was hearing voices from more than one place now. Some of the voices were Mal's, while others were starting to sound like her own.

"Mal, help me!" she shouted, and something cackled from a branch above her head. She looked up, then fell over, raising an arm to defend herself. It was one of *them*. It really was. One of the things she'd seen, then tried to tell herself she hadn't, all those years ago.

The Birdman leant down to stare at her. It was grasping a branch in the talons of its hind feet, their sickle claws held daintily up. Its arms were tucked in like chicken wings, and she saw how two of its digits came together like pincers, not quite a thumb but enough to serve as a holster for two sticks with sharp stone tips. Its head up close was not so very birdlike, eyes tilted forwards, beak half open to show serrated teeth.

"Mal," it said distinctly, in Mal's voice, except it wasn't quite. A better mimic than a mynah bird or parrot, but it wasn't true speech. "Mal, here," and then, to her utter incredulity, "Clever girl."

"You're kidding me," she said. Was it actually quoting... *Jurassic Park*? She forgot the pursuit. She forgot the killing cold and that she had fallen sideways into a *somewhere* she manifestly was not supposed to be. She had spent years hunting fruitlessly for non-existent mystery beasts. Now she was face to face with a genuine, bona fide cryptid—and it was making *pop culture* references at her?

"Mal. Clever girl," it croaked, bobbing its head. It was watching her without meeting her gaze. Then, just as she registered the crashing that signalled the imminent arrival of Gym Bro, she heard a very clearly enunciated, *"Run!"*

She whirled around to see the big man and his friends stumbling through the trees. Gym Bro was soaked through and suffering for it, lagging behind the others. None of them looked amused, and the man in the lead—Dominic—was plainly considering shooting her after all.

As she stumbled away, something attacked him, dropping from the high branches to rake his face. He screamed, tried to dodge and ended up ramming shoulder-first into a tree. Lee thought it was one of the Birdmen, but the attacker was smaller, like a long-legged eagle. She took the opportunity to flee, screeching and cackling erupting all around her.

A shot rang out, and she turned to see a frozen tableau: two of her former captors were right on her heels, but past them Dominic stood over a broken feathery bundle. He was already putting a second bullet into it. In the next instant one of the Birdmen had swooped on him, using its beak to drive a spear between his shoulders with a shriek of rage that crossed all species boundaries.

Then Lee's closest pursuer grabbed for her shoulder, and she ducked under his grasp. As she dodged around a tree, she knew there was no way she was getting away this time. They were fitter than she was, and her feet were like great blocks of ice on the end of jellied legs. Still, some iron core within her was not giving up. And so she stumbled on, to win a few more seconds of freedom in an alien world.

She lurched forwards, and then lurched further forwards still. She felt disoriented and suddenly had the sense of not going anywhere whilst simultaneously falling into an infinite abyss.

Then the cold hit her.

It hadn't been cold before. She understood now that her assessment had been a foolish human foible, born of a comfortable life in a temperate climate. The trees had vanished too. She was now staggering drunkenly along the floor of a narrow canyon, and either side of her rose walls of ice. Light shone down from high above, a weak sun that felt as though it was twice as far away as it should be. And Lee thought helplessly, *Is this fucking Mars? Europa?* She took in a whooping breath of air that lived a long way on the wrong side of freezing, feeling as though someone had rammed an icy knife through both lungs.

She managed another few steps before she was on her knees, which stuck to the ice below her. Her body was shivering frantically, trying to generate warmth, but she reckoned "warmth" was something this place hadn't seen since maybe forever. She could hear her pursuers behind her, but reckoned they all had other things to worry about right now.

She forced her eyes open, feeling her tears freeze. The ice wall closest to her shimmered and moved—no, something was moving within it, fracture lines and cracks tracing the passage of unimaginable mechanisms.

She was on her side now, though she couldn't remember how. The cold seemed to be gone, although part of her was aware that her ability to feel it had withered away. This was a bad sign. Probably. Almost a relief, not being able to do anything about her impending demise. Her only regret was that she had finally been shown the true weird heart of things, and she would never know how it worked or what was going on...

She had wanted to see Mal.

Before the end.

Still, never mind.

Then huge hands lifted her up, and she stared into a shimmering faceplate. It didn't seem to be made of anything more substantial than rainbows and dreams. Behind it was a broad, robustly ugly face, a man—no, a woman? It had a wide mouth and heavy, overhanging brows.

Something happened, and she wasn't in the cold place anymore. The shift into the warm July she distantly remembered was shocking, and agony to her fingers and toes. She was on the ground—no, on a carpeted floor—and her rescuer was doing something...medical to her?

A pale light was coming from behind her, and she twisted her neck to see. She was looking off into the distance: into *a* distance that had no truck with the actual dimensions of the room she was in. She could still see the ice walls of the canyon she'd been rescued from, rising too far up to see their tops. From her current vantage point, she seemed to be able to see *into* the translucent ice too. It contained layers of structure, as though a whole translucent city had been frozen within, and she was some ice sculptor savant who could see all the possible shapes the ice might be carved into.

She could make out two of Gym Bro's friends, too. One of them was lying face down on the canyon floor, and the woman was kneeling. They were frozen; ice had formed a thin layer across their skin and frost rimed their clothes. Their dead faces were a ghastly blue-white. Then they receded, tucked out of sight as though physics had swept them away with a broom to tidy everything up.

Lee decided she could abandon her fingernail-hold on consciousness, and let go.

She woke to the smell of fast food, lying on a tatty sofa while the sun streamed in from an uncurtained window above. It was propped half open, but the familiar heat of the interminable summer was already baking the room.

How very British of me, she considered weakly. *I was freezing to death not that long ago, but already it's too hot.*

She sat up and realized she had no idea where she was: a small room crammed with furniture: sofa, desk, unmade single bed and a wardrobe. This was large, old and ornate enough to make her wonder if she really *had* come through it from another world. There were two doors, one ajar to what was presumably the loo, the other closed against the outside world. Nothing matched, and the lime-green wallpaper and turd-brown carpet weren't on speaking terms either. *I'm in...a bed and breakfast?* Because she had stayed in her share of rock-bottom cheap places, and this definitely had the feel of one.

She sat up with a groan, noting that the savoury smells were only the product of a litter of packaging left on the desk beside a laptop.

Force of habit sent her hand questing into her pocket, and she barked out a yap of alarm, straight into twenty-first-century problems. "Where's my phone?"

"You can't have it until they've monkeyed with it," someone said from the bathroom. A woman stepped out, still midway through applying make-up. She was dark, wearing a blouse and long skirt, and Lee blinked at her twice before recognizing her.

"You..." The woman from the Camden flat, last seen shakily igniting her cigarette with Lee's lighter. "Kay?"

"Correct, love," she said, regarding Lee doubtfully. "And you're...?"

"Lee. I'm...How did I get here?"

"Oh, now, that's the question, isn't it?" Kay said, sitting down at the desk and angling the laptop towards herself. "Can't tell you that. Don't fucking understand it yet. Which is a bother, really."

"Why?" Lee looked over her shoulder. There was nothing comprehensible on the screen. Oh, she knew the individual numbers, and she could spot familiar conventions like equals signs and nested brackets, but the actual arrangement of characters was a wall of random text.

"Well firstly, darling, I am the best theoretical mathematician and physicist you will ever meet. And I am fucking well *meant* to be able to understand impossible shit like this," Kay said sourly. "And secondly, I think the world is going to end, and I need to understand this if I'm going to make it stop."

PART 2
LOOKING GLASS
CREATURES

6.

I

Nobody could explain how it had happened. Julian had read through the reports of three agents who'd been monitoring Khan's safe house. She'd been entirely happy with the arrangements, as far as they'd been aware. She'd had someone on hand to get anything she wanted. Another field agent had been positioned unobtrusively in the building, catching up on paperwork. A third had been off duty and asleep, but reachable. Nobody had expected Dr. Khan to simply vanish.

There was no camera footage. The safe house had surveillance inside and out, but the recordings had...gone.

"So what happened?" Julian was debriefing Roland Rigo, an agent who he'd always felt was sound. "I mean, I know she slipped out without anybody seeing her, but...there must have been *something*."

Rigo rubbed at his lean hatchet of a face, a man who knew there was no way this would look good on his record. "Before? Nothing, Jules. I spoke with hi—her last, of the three of us. I got her a download of a book she wanted, and junk food. She wanted junk food all the time, said it was comfort eating, cos she was so stressed."

"How stressed?"

Rigo shrugged. "You can't always tell with someone, right? And he—and she was a bit high strung anyway, I reckon. But we'd been there a few days, and she was way calmer than she was at the start, at least." He grimaced at the corners of the room, as though looking for a way out. "Jules, she'd settled."

Julian nodded. "For the record, Roland, did she get any stick about being…"

"Trans?" The grimace deepened. "Not on my watch, and I don't think so—I know, I screw up the pronouns. She called me on it, believe me, but…I don't think that's it."

"And she didn't get any calls, any contacts? Any information about the case, a threat against family?"

"She didn't have her phone," Rigo confirmed. "No visitors except us, and we sure as hell didn't say anything. There was no way…" Under Julian's watchful gaze he shifted awkwardly. "She was on the laptop we gave her a lot. Offline, but she was on it. I wondered, afterwards, if someone got round us, somehow. If they were able to get a message to her."

"It's being looked at, of course."

"Of course," Rigo confirmed. "It was on, open, when I went into the room to look for her. The screen…But this is in my report, okay?"

Julian had zeroed in on that paragraph on first reading, vague echoes of Alison's experiences rattling about his head. "Tell me, in full." Because Rigo's reference to it had been cursory, embarrassed.

"I thought there was something on the screen. When I went in I looked at it, just quickly—I was after h-her, after all, wasn't I? But there was maths on it. I know I'm no expert, but it was like nothing I've ever seen. Later, when we went back, after we knew she'd done a flit, the symbols were gone, as if they had never existed."

"Wiped? Restored to defaults or whatever?" This was a secure laptop, the same kind that Julian used to work from home. It was supposedly bulletproof, as far as someone messing with it was concerned.

Rigo spread his hands. "They're looking still. According to them, it was as if the machine had just started up and then not been touched, just sat open for about ninety minutes. Whatever Khan was doing on it, any message someone snuck in...it's gone. And then there were the notes."

Julian nodded. "We'll have to leave that to the experts too. More than our pay grade..."

Rigo nodded grimly. Beside the laptop there had been a handful of sheets of paper covered in notations. He should probably be thankful that Khan had felt the need to work through something by hand or they'd have absolutely nothing to go on. Except nobody could understand it. Julian had already seen terse reports from two other Defence Science and Technology lab physicists who had confessed it was simply not their field. Nobody else in the DST would even venture an opinion; the whole point of keeping Khan safe was that she was one of the few scientists in the world whose field it *was*. The others were deep within the machinery of other nation states, so sending Khan's notes to them would probably be grounds for a treason trial.

He had no idea what Khan's field really was, and in a way that was the most terrifying thing. An area of science so rarefied that almost nobody understood it, but just comprehensible enough that it might be vital to national security. The thought brought him out in a sweat, thinking about mind control, death rays, volcano lairs...

Was that it? Had Khan been the villain all along, and this escape was part of her ingenious plan? Except he couldn't see how any of this could have been engineered by Khan, or by anyone, and Khan's exit felt opportunistic. She'd seized her chance without even collecting her notes or the computer.

Julian's instincts were telling him this was a multi-way clusterfuck, several factions after the same thing and treading on each other's toes. He ticked off the possible enemies: Billy White's greatgeorgengland mob were probably patsies rather than serious contenders, but someone was behind them. And someone *else* had beaten several of them to death. A big, ugly wrestler-type and an Oxbridge student who was supposed to be dead of exposure these four years.

He added it all to his notes, tabled the necessary meetings and jumped on board the accelerating train that was Op Herringbone—or Glassknife II: The Search for Khan. He had to report to his director, Hind, tomorrow. Her meeting request seemed formal and polite, but between the lines could be read the suggestion that this could be his only chance to explain his way out of a slapping.

After that, a text from Alison should have been a mercy. But *Come over tonight. We'll talk* didn't mean a pleasant evening with a bottle of wine and her latest Netflix fixation. It suggested a tense, late night of talking shop.

*

Alison's desk was strewn with photos and transcripts. All three screens were bright with scans of similar documents, and Julian could see at least a dozen windows open on each.

"What have they got you working on?" he asked, then for

form's sake added, "If you can tell me." If she couldn't, she wouldn't have left it out for his visit.

"This is your Op Mouser, while you've been off getting yourself into other trouble," Alison said. She was taking a break from the desk, sipping tea on the sofa and petting Simms. Julian rattled about in the kitchen until he had tea as well, putting the wine in the fridge.

"Josie?" Alison asked when he returned.

"Could see I was stressed as hell, bless her. Let me off this once."

He saw her customary sardonic look. Every month Alison decided that she needed to get together with him and Josie to smooth everything over, and Julian was equally opposed to the idea. Ninety-five per cent of that was him knowing Josie wouldn't take to it. And Alison actually turning up at their house might be the relationship equivalent of pushing the nuclear button. The remaining, wretched five per cent was the part of his mind he didn't let into the driving seat under any circumstances.

"How in trouble are you?" Alison asked.

"Not too much, not me. But...this damned business is the gift that keeps on giving, isn't it? Sprouting operations like mushrooms. It's looking like I'll get Herringbone and Stewey'll oversee Mouser, at least until they turn out to be the same thing."

"Which they will," Alison confirmed.

"Which they will," echoed Julian, "though I can't find any way of explaining why I'm certain of it."

"I don't suppose you can."

Both cases involved mysteriously disappearing communications which came and went without leaving any tracks at all. The message to White, the data archive that Alison had been given brief access to, the text message from Mallory to Pryor, and now perhaps some ghost message received by Khan. Someone was playing with extremely advanced tele-communications tech, something that could hide from scrutiny and walk through any security they could devise. That could, maybe, even establish a connection to an offline machine. The stuff of utter paranoia that, if it was true, would see them relying on huge libraries of paper files as though the last five decades hadn't happened.

Flatland, he thought, remembering Alison's anecdote about the stockbroker firm. He imagined the 2D security services of Flatland trying to defend their secrets against a 3D infil-trator. One who could look within their sealed safes, access their little flat difference engines...

"You look ill," Alison told him frankly.

"This case is making me ill." He gulped down too much too-hot tea and choked out, "What's Mouser turned up, then?"

"Mice," she said. "Far too many mice. Spiker. Someone's either done an exemplary job in record time or this is a stack of unsolved evidence that's been doing the rounds from op to op for a while. I've got material here from Ops Racetrack, Moraybleak, Cartwright, Bluepeel and Hertzelectric."

"Hertzelectric," Julian repeated. "Wait, was that...?"

"Willoughs," she said, naming Julian's old mentor. "This was the last operation he helmed. All of these are top secret, and several of them involve the Department of Sci and Tech. And while some of them had happy conclusions, all of them had at least one loose thread that nobody could ever tie up. Now it's Op Mouser's problem, and maybe yours as well."

"So what's the link?" Julian asked.

She passed him a photo wordlessly. It was black and white, showing a man he recognized instantly: broad-faced, weak-chinned, with deep-set eyes. The beard was heavier, but then it was an old photo. "Elsinore Mallory's accomplice." The man who'd likely killed Billy White and his cohorts.

"Except it's not," Alison said tiredly. "Because this is a photo of a corpse. This was taken during Hertzelectric, ten years back. It involved an attempt to physically abstract data from DST Portsdown by parties linked to the Russians, though that was never proven. It went wrong, needless to say. There was some shooting. One of the infiltration team got killed, two of ours hurt, and after the smoke blew over, our friend here turned up dead on the grounds." She passed over another photo, and Julian sucked air in through his teeth.

"Christ," he said. "Glad *he's* dead." This was the man stripped naked in the morgue. He looked appallingly muscled, not like a bodybuilder but a man born to strength: barrel-chested, pot-bellied, broad shoulders and massive arms and legs. And so hairy it looked like he was wearing a vest. The photo was also taken from a peculiar angle, which made no bones about the man being intimidatingly endowed.

"Coroner's report?" he asked.

"Those two photos are the sole surviving evidence of this man's existence," Alison said. "And we have *that* one only because the coroner's assistant was, frankly, a pervert who liked taking photos of dead guys with their tackle out. The body went missing afterwards. There was no ID anywhere within the man's possessions either, which also vanished, along with his fingerprints. Nobody could connect our dead guy there with Hertzelectric, or work out why he'd been there to catch a stray bullet." She thumbed through the file and brought out another photo, heavily dented and rust-stained where a paperclip had sat. This was in colour, grainy, showing someone's shoulder, someone else mostly turned away—Julian could only really see an unshaven jowl, an ear and tufts of red hair. And framed between them, a woman caught mid-laugh. She could have been the dead man's sister, although the hilarity made her look friendlier, like someone's eccentric but favourite aunt. Even with the poor quality picture, he could see the woman's huge square teeth. Her eyes were in shadow, sunk deep under her brow.

"This was an op that turned out to be money laundering, smuggling, that kind of thing. She was a Belgian, supposedly: importer, peripherally involved and never important enough to hunt down after she—wait for it—mysteriously vanished." Alison shrugged and plucked the photo back from Julian's fingers.

"They look so similar. Are we dealing with a criminal family here?"

"Makes you wonder, doesn't it." Alison shuffled the open windows on one screen and came up with a scanned transcript, at the end of which was a photofit picture that had obviously been clipped to the original. "Here's a statement from Emil Novotny, recorded last year. Czech hacker taken up on a drugs charge. He ended up plea-bargaining to reduce his sentence, admitting that he'd been hired to steal DST personnel files in 2012...just when Khan was working for the lab."

"He confessed *what*?" Julian demanded.

Alison grinned and topped his wine up. "Well, quite. And I'm not talking about the Czech guy doing 'into the Matrix'-style hacking, either. He just sent a plausible email to a cabinet minister who shall remain redacted, alas, who ended up giving him all manner of access privileges, because some of our elected representatives do not pay attention in their security briefings. Makes you wonder what you don't know, doesn't it? Anyway, this is the hacker's best shot at what his employer looked like, according to him. Needless to say, the investigation's gone nowhere since."

The photofit face looked like a child had Frankensteined it together out of ill-matched parts, showing a heavily bearded man with staring eyes like Rasputin's. But with the benefit of recent hindsight, Julian could see how it might be another member of the same group. He shook his head wonderingly. "Is this like... some espionage version of *The Hills Have Eyes*? Some inbred clan of... hereditary information brokers, or...?"

"I call 'em the Plug-uglies," Alison said firmly. "Although that is not going in my report. Look, I haven't screwed with your mind enough yet. See this."

She pulled up security camera footage—February 2015, from the date in the corner. It showed a spartan-looking corner of a mostly white room, the walls lined with cabinets.

"Department of Science and Technology, Sevenoaks," Alison said. The clip was only fourteen seconds long.

A figure walked into shot: broad and heavyset, wearing a dark shirt and trousers, with a satchel slung across their body. Julian would have said a man, but now he'd seen the photo of the Belgian importer he wasn't sure. Whoever it was knew what they were doing, though. They unlocked one cabinet and opened it, selected three files and stowed them in the satchel, then turned and left. Julian saw enough of the face to recognize if not an individual at least the same heredity as the others.

"What was taken?" he asked.

"Redacted," Alison answered brightly. "Context suggests one of the DST people—no, not Khan—had become paranoid about electronic records. Was keeping everything on paper. In one letter there's a complaint from tech staff that they can't find any sign of the electronic intrusions that whoever—also redacted—was complaining about."

"Been a lot of that recently," Julian noted glumly.

"This is the sole piece of evidence. There are cameras outside this room. I've got the floorplan: no windows, only one way out. No sign of this person entering or exiting. Just this. Which begs the question..."

Not "How did they get in?" but... "Why do we even have this record?"

"Because nobody's perfect?" Alison threw up her hands theatrically. "The really scary thing is, there was one super-diligent filing clerk working on Op Moraybleak. They'd been on Hertzelectric too and had a really good memory for, let's agree, some pretty memorable faces. They searched around and unearthed these cases here. However, there might be another dozen related cases that *haven't* been cross-referenced, just sitting there in our filing system. And other than including members of this 'group,' none of these cases link together—oh, there's a focus on the DST. Yet until that clerk put two and two together, they were all completely separate, just like Glassknife would have been. Except now we have... the Plug-uglies, who seem awfully interested in some of our scientists. Who may now have Khan."

Julian drained his glass. "And working for whom, exactly? Or do you think freelancers, highest bidder? How can we not *know* about these clowns?"

"Because they're not clowns." She had the Belgian importer's jolly laugh up on both screens. *The joke's been on us for at least ten years.*

"Even so," he managed. "Look at them. You'd not have much problem picking them out of an ID parade, would you?"

Alison had all the faces lined up across the paired screens: the corpse, the importer, the photofit, a still from the lab, another from the camera outside Khan's place—zoomed in to clip out Elsinore Mallory. For a long while the two of them stared at their rogue's gallery.

"You want to hear something really crazy?" Alison asked at last.

"I really, really want to say no," Julian said. "I've had my quota for one night. Is this evidenced crazy or the purely speculative kind?"

"Oh, speculative—the *most* speculative, born of bad data and guesswork," she said gaily, and he realized she must be at least a glass ahead of him. "And I'm not an ethnographer or anything, perish the thought. But look." She circled the cursor about two of her screens like a heat-drugged fly. "Look here, at, say, the cheekbones—his, then look at hers. And here's our chap from the lab. He has a broader face, even broader. Photofit guy...okay, a bad example, but you can see how Dead-ugly's leaner, hollower."

"They all look pretty similar to me," Julian said. "What's your point?"

"Maybe I don't have one," she said, her confidence collapsing abruptly. "Forget it. Stupid idea anyway."

"Go on, Matchbox, what was it?"

"It just seemed like—I mean, yes, they look alike, because we're picking up on the big differences between them and us, right? But if you start really looking, there's a lot of variation between them, on a bone-structure level. What if it's like we're, well, we're bigots like Billy White, only used to faces like ours? So we tell each other"—she put on a gruff, loutish voice—"they all look the same to me. Because we're only seeing the differences. And because, in Billy's case, he was a racist turd. But even so."

"You're saying we're seeing... what, they're not the same family, they're the same nationality? But... from where, Matchbox? Tell me, so I can cross it off the holiday list."

"I don't know. Nowhere. Stupid thought, like I said. An ethnic group from nowhere we know, turning up in ones and twos to conduct impossible thefts and kidnap top scientists. I mean, it's ludicrous, right?"

"Right," he agreed, and the two of them locked eyes as Alison patently tried to rid herself of her suspicions and, just as visibly, failed.

*

Julian had been the final protégé of Germaine Willoughs, who'd practically died in harness, only two weeks between his collapse in the office and his death in hospital. His had been a long life in the Service—escapades against the Soviet Bloc, murky doings in proxy states—the sort of career that could have crippled any number of governments had he ever decided to write his memoirs. At the end he'd been on the far side of irascible, impatient with a Service that was modernizing in leaps and bounds. His successors hadn't coped well with the chaos he'd left behind. It had taken Leslie Hind's appointment before anyone could swipe the reins and get the department under control. Julian was certainly not a favourite of Hind's, but she wasn't someone to throw away a useful tool because it had someone else's initials on it.

Being called in to see Hind always brought a stab of schoolboy guilt. She had that stare, a headmistress who knows precisely what you were doing behind the bike sheds. She was in her mid-fifties now, grey-haired and with a lean, raptorial face. Under her guidance the department's machinery ran smoothly. Nails that stood up received a hammering and squeaky wheels were replaced.

Her office was pristine. In one corner Hind's secretary was typing to the whisper of voices in her earphones. Along the far end was Hind's large desk: not Willoughs' mahogany behemoth from the days of the Raj, but something functional and severe. Hind herself was hunched behind it, reading the contents of a file, tilted so he could neither see its innards nor read its label. Her eyes flicked between it and her monitor while she sipped her tea.

"Mr. Sabreur."

He braced himself. *Meeting Without Coffee, here we go.*

She set the teacup down and flicked a finger at the other chair, which suggested things were at least on the right side of fatal. Gratefully, he sat down, feeling some of the naughty-schoolboy burden slough away.

"Operation Herringbone," Hind said. "Didn't see that coming, did we?"

"No, ma'am," he confirmed, heartfelt. "I've spoken with—"

"I've read the reports, of course. We've been careless." That "we" was a tenuous thing. Julian might yet be left alone at the oars of this particular leaking rowboat. "Your thoughts?"

"Too early for thoughts, ma'am."

She nodded with grudging approval, and was about to say something but changed her mind. Without visible signal, the secretary was at Julian's elbow, asking him if he wanted a drink. He eyed Hind warily, because one word nobody had yet applied to her was *indecisive*.

"I'm going to need you to be flexible on this one, Julian," she said.

He blinked at her, wordlessly accepting a coffee.

"Your previous assessments suggest you're not averse to cutting corners. Although as you tend to tidy up after yourself, it hasn't mattered. Your friendship with Matchell probably doesn't help in that regard."

Julian felt his loyalty kick inside him and pushed it back down. He saw Hind note the narrowing of his lips.

"However, this is an unconventional case," she said, in what was shaping up to be understatement of the year. "Cutting corners may be required. As may an open mind. At present we don't know the scale of what's going on. Worst-case scenario, this may turn out to be this generation's Burgess and Maclean."

"You think it's an inside job?" Julian asked.

"I think it's too early for thoughts." She sighed. "Tell me about Rove Denton, Julian."

For a moment his mind was a perfect blank. "Ma'am?"

"You've requested the file. The firm doesn't feature anywhere in Glassknife, or am I mistaken?"

Now what sort of trouble am I in? "They don't, officially," he said carefully. "It was...a cut corner, if you like. I had an off-the-record suggestion that they might be involved and I thought I'd check—to rule it out. No more than that. And then, obviously, things escalated with—"

"Quite." Without any apparent prompt, the secretary took off her headset and left the room, closing the door softly behind her, all the better to deny knowledge later. "Rove Denton is owned by Daniel Rove, an influential fellow. He gives talks at charitable dinners, set up some think tanks, major party donor, went to Eton with half the cabinet." Hind's expression soured as she spoke; she herself was not a product of the public school system. "Plays golf with the current Home Secretary," she added, and then, "our boss," for clarity.

"It has been suggested to me that idle prying into Rove Denton would not be a good use of departmental resources, and would represent something of an insult to one of the country's leading security specialists. Who, needless to say, have been tendering for Home Office work forever."

"I understand," Julian said.

Her expression suggested he didn't. "This conversation did not arise because of your own recent request, I should note. It came up last year, with a different Home Secretary who was nonetheless also close friends with Mr. Rove, after a separate request for the file. You might imagine, in fact, that several such requests have crossed my desk. Rove Denton seem to have a habit of being at the periphery of suspicious events, Julian. Almost as if there is a central core of information that we cannot see, which would link all those independent file requests."

He nodded warily.

"There is no Rove Denton file," she said. "However, there is a small collection of documents, existing entirely in hard copy, which does resemble such a thing. It has no official existence." Hind slid the file—unmarked, he saw—across the desk. "I am not officially instructing you not to look into Rove

173

Denton under any circumstances. You are, of course, deep into Op Herringbone and your mind is on other matters. However, if I discovered you and Matchell *were* investigating Rove Denton's activities, I would instruct you to desist immediately. Such unsanctioned digging would be entirely inappropriate...But should you, by utter chance, uncover something documentably suspicious or incriminating about the firm, bring it immediately to me." She regarded him bleakly. "The company has been across my desk so often that I can't scrub off the footprints. And nothing would give me greater pleasure than to put my suspicions on the record."

II

Pain in his arm dragged Lucas May into wakefulness, quickly followed by all the other aches and pains that had been politely waiting at his deathbed to see if he would make it. He felt as though he'd been beaten with sticks. His toes and the fingers of his right hand were screaming at him, and his left hand was...It hurt. It managed to hurt in a way no part of him had ever hurt before. He tried to lift it, and discovered that he was clamped to a bed. To something. It was a concavity like a cradle, narrow enough that his shoulders were turned inwards, short enough that his legs hung over the edge. The restraints felt like thick metal padded with rubber, something no-nonsense and industrial.

It was dark, but not pitch-black. There was a faint red radiance coming from somewhere, like emergency lighting. It gave him no clues about where he was, but his ears suggested it wasn't a big space. He could feel a constant shuddering through his skin, coming from everywhere: engines, ventilation, some kind of heavy machinery. The air tasted like oil and metal.

His nose was blocked with what he suspected was blood. After a few goes he managed to sniff it clear and was rewarded by a sharp reek that was definitely organic. He detected stale sweat, excrement, urine, and all of it bound into a grander stench that had something of the animal, something of desperation. He'd gone into a bunker, once, back in his army days. Thirty-nine people had hidden there with minimal food and water. Twenty-eight had come out, in the end, half dead themselves. They had crouched there during the shelling, as the entrance was buried, feeling the air grow staler. This place smelled like that. Like despair.

To call out or not to call out? But the question became moot as the hellish light waxed brighter. Abruptly there were shadows moving on either side of his cot, and he felt a stab of panic that he fought down. It took all his willpower to lie still, to pretend, maybe, that he was too groggy to break necks should they release his bonds.

Out of the corner of his eye he saw someone come close. Some*thing*: the movement didn't register as human. He rolled his eyes and strained through the gloom. The size of a child, but not the shape. The body was long, canted forwards, and there was too much head, too much neck. It undulated, unpleasantly serpentine. The red light glinted on huge eyes like plates; he had a moment's stab of relief as he realized they were lenses, then felt a renewed horror because the head they were set into was snouty, sleek-skulled. *Just a mask, a hood, biohazard gear.* But some primal part of him knew it wasn't. Then a small hand appeared, holding an instrument that looked like a torturer's Swiss Army Knife. The hand had clawed nails and two thumbs, one where he'd prefer to see a little finger. It was pallid and wrinkled as though it had never felt the sun. Craning his neck, he saw the suggestion of big ears, cast back from the low skull and rolled into sharp points.

The instrument clicked through several vicious permutations, ending with a pointed tube like a hypodermic for elephants. When his shadowy persecutor rammed it into his upper arm, Lucas screamed and tried to jerk away.

The figure—the *creature*—paused, and then it said something, or at least Lucas thought it did. He heard a chittering and screeching at the very edge of his hearing, as though a bat was lambasting him.

"I don't know what your game is," he told the thing, "but my employer is a very powerful man. He'll cut a deal with you." He desperately hoped that was true. "You need to speak to Daniel Rove. You know that name?" Although why the hell would ET's vivisectionist cousin know Daniel Rove?

He heard another patter of shrill fluting and wondered if his own voice had similarly gone completely under the thing's auditory radar.

It went away, though not far because there simply wasn't much *away* in the room. The upped lighting showed a cramped compartment lined with complex instruments that seemed to be almost entirely without labels or screens, only vastly complex tactile interfaces. The ceiling was close enough that if Lucas had sat up suddenly he'd have brained himself. He wondered numbly if he was on a submarine, or even a spaceship, where room was at a premium.

The creature pulled a cord or wire from one of the

machines, and for a moment Lucas thought it was for insertion into humans. Instead it connected the lead to its headgear, and he saw flickering at the edges of its lenses, as if from images being transmitted within.

"Lucas, I understand you're awake."

The voice came from several speakers simultaneously. It was Rove's, and Lucas had never been so glad to hear it.

"Sir, I'm being held prisoner," he said quickly, in case his captor took steps to shut him up. "I've been...I may have been experimented on. They've done something to my arm—"

Rove laughed, and Lucas went cold. Perhaps he'd been sold to aliens as a guinea pig or something. Later on, he would examine that thought and ponder on what it said about his relationship with his employer. But then his boss was speaking again, vouchsafing at least some reassurance.

"You're not a prisoner. You're actually in a very exclusive hospital, if you can believe it. When we got to you, you were in bad shape. How much do you remember?"

"I..." He hadn't remembered anything, because the pain and his surroundings had driven it from his mind, but the question conjured the answer. He had been in a cold place, a forest. There had been some big lump in a robe. There had been a...

"Fuck," he said, because there had been a dinosaur, a great big shaggy dinosaur. Then they'd been chasing the stupid Pryor girl, and he'd ended up in the river, and then...

He remembered Dominic getting attacked. The trees had been alive with fucking *things*, cackling and cawing like monstrous crows with spears and stone blades. Some of them were wearing hides painted with bright patterns.

"I..." Something had caught his left arm. He had a blurred

memory of claws, teeth and a gleaming, hooked blade of bronze. There had been a spray of bright blue feathers tied through a hole punched in the metal. The image stuck in his mind with absurd clarity. "I fell." Going backwards down a stony slope into the icy river waiting to receive him. "Holy fuck."

"Quite," remarked Rove drily.

"What about the others, sir?"

Rove sighed. "Mr. Hinton has the dubious distinction of being the first human being in sixty-five million years to be killed by a dinosaur. The other two... fared less well. They went with Pryor, somewhere we couldn't follow, or not quickly enough to save them. You're a lucky man, Lucas."

The restraints were abruptly retracted into the cot, and he sat up, minding his head. Everything still hurt, and he really didn't like the way his left hand felt. It was in some sort of flexible cast, smarting like hell whilst being weirdly numb. *Hospital*, he reminded himself, despite all the evidence. *Medical procedure. At least you've still got your arm.*

He looked around for the creature, but it had vanished. Maybe there were a dozen trapdoors for slinking little monsters to escape through. Maybe it had been... a specially designed doctor's assistant or... something.

"You'll see a door opening shortly," Rove said. "It's an elevator. Get in, enjoy the ride. It'll bring you to me."

The door was practically at waist height, and the compartment he crawled into felt more like a coffin than a room. Then it took off, not up but sideways, shuttling Lucas away at breakneck pace. It changed direction with abrupt jolts that made him glad the walls were so close, because he hit them before he had the chance to build up momentum.

Then the capsule shuddered to a halt, the hatch sliding open so fast that it clipped his knees painfully. Thankfully, the chamber he tumbled into was at least worthy of the name. The top of his head brushed the ceiling, but the walls were smooth, banded light and dark grey like the worst public-sector wallpaper. And there were *windows*. Lucas took a few steps forwards, feasting his eyes on the view. From one he could look down on a forest canopy—it looked as though it might be somewhere tropical. The other window showed London, a high view onto what might be Canary Wharf. But both windows were next to each other. Screens, then. He was still in the...machine? Space station? Subterranean complex? He had no idea. For a moment he stood there, swaying, feeling his joints creak and complain.

"Finally." Rove's voice behind him made him jump. There the man was, slender and immaculate in his bespoke suit, smiling slightly at Lucas's discomfort. At a gesture, a shelf telescoped out of one wall, clothes stacked on it. Only then did Lucas register that he was naked. The air seemed uncomfortably warm and humid. Lucas decided that if his boss wanted to play weird dominance games, then that was entirely the man's prerogative. He just stomped over and dressed without shame or modesty. The clothes were folded weirdly. It was a small detail, disproportionately upsetting. Whoever had laid them out had possessed definite ideas of economy of space without really understanding clothing. Everything was practically origamied. They weren't his clothes, either. Someone had tried to replicate his ruined outfit, but nothing fit right. He could feel various seams strain as though perfectly normal human arcs of movement had been imperfectly understood by the tailor.

"How long's this on for?" he asked, waving his left hand. The cast, the sheath, whatever it was, was a mottled black-grey, shiny and rubbery to the touch, as though he had a triple-thick condom on up to the elbow. When he prodded it, he could feel the sensation only dimly.

Rove was watching him keenly when he turned round.

"You have that for the duration, Lucas."

"Sir?"

"It's your arm. They couldn't salvage what was left of the original after the beasties got their teeth into it. You left most of it behind."

Lucas blinked. "Sir?" he said again.

"The medical technology here is very good, though," Rove said. "It's why I came. After all, sooner or later something's going to get you, or those you care about. Cancer, injury, dementia...But you don't need to worry about most of that, here. If you're at the top you can have a very long and healthy life indeed. And you know the joke? A long life for them is maybe seventy years at the utmost. That's Methuselah territory for them. I'll probably see out my two hundredth birthday hale and hearty."

Lucas was still staring at the arm—he couldn't quite process it as *his*—and Rove tutted. "Oh, stop scowling. Your nervous system will mesh with it over the next week or so. It'll be better than the original. Though you'll want to invest in some gloves. I doubt it'll look any prettier. Just be glad they were able to make something that human. Or would you rather have a stump?" His voice had become sharper. "Or would you rather we talked about your recent poor performance? I don't usually need to hold employee assessment sessions, Lucas."

Lucas blinked at him. "What was I expected to do?"

"Hold on to the Pryor girl. She knew something. I saw the readings from the App. She was lousy with asynchronous resonance. She'd been *elsewhere*, or been in close contact with someone who had, likely her friend Mallory. Oh, you nod now, do you? As if you have the first idea what I'm talking about." Rove walked over pugnaciously, heedless of the fact that Lucas could have broken him in half. "We're *elsewhere*, Lucas. Right now. You won't be able to use the App in the future because you're contaminated yourself. The dust of another Earth is on you, not to mention in every atom in your new arm. It's all from *here*, and it has the signature of *here* on it. That's how it was explained to me. That also means we can track down anyone back home who's had that contact. Not our actual enemies, you understand, because they can run countermeasures, but idiot naifs like Pryor. My friends seem to think that *she's* still alive and home, even if your cohorts didn't survive the trip." He looked brightly up at Lucas. "You're ready to go home, I take it? To grab another team and get her?"

Lucas nodded slowly. The words *go home* were a powerful incentive.

"And you'll have help, this time," Rove added, not pleasantly. "My friends are just *bursting* to see other places, stretch their legs. You won't realize it, but most of them would kill, actually murder each other with their teeth, to have this much space." He waved his hands at the room, which was on a par with a decent-sized suburban living room. "You might find them upsetting," Rove said, his urbane smile becoming less pleasant with every word. "Your team certainly will. That's why you're still on the payroll, Lucas. You're in it up to your neck, now. You've seen what's on the other side of the mirror."

Lucas filled in the implication Rove didn't feel it necessary to say. *And there's no going back from that.*

III

Alison was on a tea break when it happened again. She had spent all morning and then two solid hours after lunch going through more old case files for Mouser, to trawl for other occurrences of the Plug-uglies. So far she'd rejected almost everything that had turned up. After a frustrating day, she had one tentative addition to the rogue's gallery, in the shape of a report from the early nineties. A surveillance operation on a suspected terrorist cell in Birmingham had ended up watching the wrong house for a week. A young field agent had written up the business in great detail, possibly trying to avoid the inevitable repercussions of screwing up. And he'd found something odd: a house where the people who went in the door didn't seem to map to the people who went out, where several were described as weirdly, similarly ugly: broad noses and heavy brows. No photographs, apparently. Or they'd mysteriously vanished, leaving no trace they ever existed, but Alison couldn't afford to think like that.

She sat on the couch and stroked Simms, trying to work out where this was going. She felt as though her head was full of pieces from different jigsaws and she had the job of making them into a seamless whole.

Movement tugged at her attention. *On the monitor...most likely an update starting, or...*

A new window had popped up on the leftmost screen, where she had been looking into the history of the Birmingham property. It had been held by a shell company for three decades, and other searches suggested it was mostly derelict. It was a former mill, converted into flats by a developer who'd gone into liquidation so hard they were probably still finding the splash marks. But now there was an image there. She turfed Simms off and rushed over.

It was a photograph, showing the front of a building that might be the Birmingham property. Three people stood outside it, wearing heavy coats against a Brum winter: two men, one woman. The woman was holding up... something. It looked like a rod with something affixed to the top end. A fan? Or maybe it was some odd kind of aerial. There was a strange sense of ritual in the way the three stood. They were all Plug-uglies, without a doubt. Seeing them together, she was even more struck by the idea that they represented an ethnicity she had never met before, the people of a remote island or mountain range.

She moved the mouse to drag the image and it was gone instantly. A quick search showed no trace of it ever having been there. Alison stared murderously at the screens, checking the documents saved on the case file. Needless to say, no such image.

She swore for the benefit of Simms and the empty room, then drained her tea genteelly and went to make another cup. When she returned the image was back. No, this was another one: same building, different angle. Now there were two figures under the pall of evening, by a lit streetlamp. The two figures were...

They had just been standing there, maybe conversing. Now

they were embracing. Two big Plug-ugly men, one with an Old Testament-looking beard and a balding head that showed his sloping brow, the other younger, wearing a flat cap, jowls dark with stubble.

Her hand inched for the mouse, then pulled back. The image stepped forwards a handful of frames, the two men parting.

It moved again, becoming video without transition. The older man was at the door of the house, looking back. The younger was walking away, and away, and away. Alison stared at it, knowing you could do this with video trickery or CGI. Hell, Georges Méliès could probably have done it with double exposure and a little patience. But the young man was walking away in a direction that did not involve any of the usual ones. Then he was gone, as though he'd suddenly understood he was within a two-dimensional image and could take a third dimension out of there.

"Where?" she demanded out loud. She moved the cursor into the suddenly vacated space, clicking furiously as though she could dig through all her nested documents and catch up with the Plug-ugly.

She was getting a headache, but she reckoned this was about par for the course given how the universe was messing her around right then.

Her screen moved. Or, no, it didn't, but she had the sense that the corners of the screen were flying away in all directions. Her unfocused gaze was opening it up, *letting* her get past the mundane nonsense of Official Copies and lists of creditors to reach something...architectural, a complex network that fell away into a profound depth that her screen couldn't hold. It had to be a hallucination brought on by tiredness, overwork and the frankly freakish direction that Mouser was going. Or it was a simulation, the distance and perspective she was seeing merely an illusory trick of the screen. But she knew, at some level, that it was real.

Her breath plumed in the sudden cold, and Simms complained bitterly. He bolted up onto the kitchenette counter, where the just-boiled kettle maintained a ring of warmth, fending off the feathery frost that crept out everywhere else.

Her headache intensified but she couldn't look away. She was moving through a virtual space, finding information unspooling away from her in all directions. It could take the form of nested windows or file directories if she wanted, but if she didn't try to make it that, then it was its own thing, a landscape, a topography. She twitched the mouse and the cursor leapt to the other screens, the ones unconquered by the hypnotic virus currently raging through the leftmost one. Connections were sprouting up like weeds, training angular roots from her open documents into the great abyss of data that she had discovered. Hertzelectric, Moraybleak, Glassknife, all of them becoming mere points of data on a great frozen wave of it that receded back through the decades. There were more and more data points the closer the wave came to the present day, gathering speed and magnitude as it rushed towards the *now*.

She saw a Plug-ugly woman before a Russian firing squad; a man's body fished from the Seine; robust, heavy bones in a shallow grave outside Nairobi. She saw objects changing hands, stolen from collections, from museums, from the desk drawers of cranks and conspiracy theorists. She saw shells and pieces of machine and Escher-like geometrical figures made impossible reality. They were the fingerprints of some huge and terrible force, and the Plug-uglies were its vanguard.

She had before her a map, reaching back into history and other directions she could not name. In that moment, she understood that it was a map of interstices, of spaces *between*, where in a sane world there would have been walls. For where there was a space *between*, things could cross from *there* to *here*. She pushed harder, aware that all this data was pouring into her mind and falling out the back, impossible to retain because her brain was never intended to have this godlike perspective, to be the extradimensional eye onto her own flat world. In that moment she saw everything, including—most terrifyingly—that there was an entity *showing* it all to her. She finally understood what Charen Volkovska had found.

She'd thought there might have been an AI at work at Schoen Fayre Invested, flexing its mind against the constraints of its stockbrokerage algorithms. They'd sold off the computer to Rove Denton, so were they behind all of this? Hadn't she *seen* them in that endlessly branching map, nodes marked with their corporate logo for ease of her human comprehension?

There was a depth in the air before her eyes, the physical space extending away from her into grand archives of information. She saw nothing, but she touched it, connected with it. She wasn't even looking at her computer. The pain in her head was like a cold knife, but she rode it, feeling herself on the brink of that omniscient perspective. Her thoughts turned to Rove Denton and she began to see connections: images, glimpses of accounts, transactions, fragmentary email chains. She swayed, face screwed up against the freezing agony of it: not an attack on her, but simply a connection to something bitterly unsuited to liaising with a human mind. And it was doing its best, she realized. It was bending over backwards to help her, to make itself compatible with her own cerebral operating system, and yet the gap between them was vast. But it could look over her brain as though she was a plan spread out on a table. It was learning her, interpreting her desires, so when she thought *Where is Rove Denton in all this?* it understood and was almost able to show her. *So who's behind it all?* And perhaps it tried, but from her perspective the data landscape was just pulling out and pulling out, a grander and grander perspective until the individual connections became meaningless. She was looking at something that simply had more elements than she could comprehend.

This wasn't the SFI stockbroking computer, but it was whatever that system had inadvertently drawn upon to make its miraculous and fallible predictions. It wasn't even an AI, she decided. It was a really big computer existing outside physical space, everywhere and nowhere.

As explanations went, it wasn't much better than magic, but it was something she could accept.

Show me, she thought, and then it *noticed* her.

She remembered going to an aquarium as a child, staring into a tank and seeing nothing. Her dad told her that maybe they'd taken the fish out for cleaning. But even then she'd been a determined searcher for truth, and she'd looked for the fish behind stones and dead coral chunks. Then one of those stones had opened its bulbous eye and stared right back at her, and she'd shrieked—six years old, after all. The sudden transition had given her nightmares for weeks. It was like that. She had been gazing into the abyss, fishing for secrets, and now the abyss gazed right back at her, this insignificant speck that had dared to dangle her tiny hook into its depths.

Alison fell back onto the sofa with a yell, the connection gone, a vice of pain still clamped about her brows. Her breath came fast and ragged. Her fingers were blueish. There was a patch of frozen carpet where she'd stood, the fibres limned with ghostly white.

She stood slowly, waiting. *Gone, it's gone*, she thought. *Or never there.* But that ship had sailed. No telling herself it wasn't real, not now. She had seen...so much. An analyst's dream. If there was some way of taming this thing, then what couldn't she know? Know, and be unable to prove to anyone's satisfaction, but *know*. She would be like the Oracle at Delphi, and the security services would approach her with gifts and sacrifices begging for her guidance.

And that was a queasy thought, because she was remembering that great landscape that stretched into the depths of time. There had been moments of contact going way back into history, a thinning scatter pattern of them. *Did the Pythia have a connection to this same system, to make her prophecies? What other predictions came true?*

Then the pragmatic part of her took over. *Why is it getting...worse? Why are there so many more interstices now?* The data had definitely had that kind of shape, plotting a phenomenon growing over time. *Cracks*, she thought. *What if there have always been a few cracks between* there *and* here, *but now there are more and more, so many more.*

What the hell am I going to tell Julian? And for a brief, happy moment she thought that was what weighed on her. She often had this problem with big emotions: the feeling and the cause of it became severed in her head. Her annoyance at A became stapled to B, much to innocent B's misfortune. Right now the feeling she was dealing with was a wave of impending doom, yet for a moment it might have just represented worries about work–life balance, or the knowledge that she was almost out of dishwasher tablets.

But no, nothing could account for this. She could feel her anxiety levels spiking, and her heart was faster now than when she'd been in communion with the alien supercomputer. *But I'm out of it now.*

What if I'm not? The cold and the visual influx had gone, but did that mean she was entirely divorced from whatever it had been? The sense of something terrible about to happen was gathering like a storm cloud in the room, and she would love to believe that it was only an anxiety attack.

You're an analyst, so analyse! To which the analyst in her replied, *Inadequate data from unverified sources.*

She called Derek. He sounded annoyed when he answered the phone, and she wasn't going to make him any happier.

"I'm really sorry," she said, "I can't take the girls tonight. Don't bring them round, sorry, sorry."

"Well *I* can't take them, it's bowling," he told her.

"I'm really sorry"—*something's about to happen, something bad, it's not safe*—"a work thing's come up, you know how it is." She was trying to keep her voice steady; thank God Derek had never really picked up on subtext. "All-hands-to-the-pumps urgent. They're old enough to look after themselves—or I'll pay for a minder if you want"—*but something terrible is rushing towards me from 4D space and you can't bring them anywhere near me*—"sorry, can't be helped. I'll make it up to you, to them, sorry, bye."

She cut the call and dialled Julian, even though she'd say . . . what? That she had a bad feeling? She had gone beyond, to a place she couldn't even tell her closest friend about without convincing him she was mad.

"Matchbox?" he said.

"Spiker, I may have a problem."

"Tell me."

"I...may have come to the attention of a hostile foreign power," she said, admirably steady. And true, save that she was pushing the definition of *foreign*.

Julian digested this, then said, "Come to the office. Bring a bag. You can tell me the whole business and we'll sort it out."

"Yes, good idea. Be with you in..." Her voice trailed off. One of the Plug-uglies was standing *inside* her flat, and she hadn't heard the door go. He looked destitute, wearing stained, torn clothes, a big coat and a woollen beanie. She recognized him abruptly. His profile had been in the camera footage, next to Elsinore Mallory.

"Julian," she whispered, but what she heard from the phone's speaker might have been static or the reverberation of some vast space where the cold wind moaned distantly and forever.

The Plug-ugly stepped forwards, and Alison bolted into the kitchenette to grab a knife, four inches of serrated steel. The man was still just standing there. He was huge, no taller than she was but with massive shoulders, a keg of a body and slightly bandy legs. His brute visage was...smiling. Under other circumstances, and possibly on an entirely different face, it might even have been a pleasant smile.

"You won't be harmed," he said, with the careful diction of someone speaking a second language. His accent was weird, adding extra consonants and glottal stops where they didn't belong. "But you will come with us."

She jabbed the knife at him to make it clear that getting too close was going to be a mutual problem. Then: *Wait, "us"?*

She had the sense of movement from her left, which was impossible, as there was just a wall there. Someone was approaching, from no direction. Alison stumbled away, seeing a woman in a hoodie and a long skirt walk into her flat from . . . *there*, like someone stepping through a mirror. Alison heard her own cracked whimper and hated it. But it gave her the strength to move, and she lashed out at the woman with the blade. The Plug-ugly woman just gently tapped her wrist, which was enough to send the knife clattering to the floor.

She looked into the broad, cheerily hideous face of the woman who'd once been a Belgian importer. Someone from another country, another people. An inhabitant of *there*. Knowing what she did, Alison thought, *How do they walk unseen amongst us, when they're not human at all?* But then she met the woman's eyes and could read genuine sympathy there, agent to agent, spy to spy.

Soon after, Simms was roaming the floor of Alison's flat, crying unhappily at being left alone.

Interlude: The Utopians

Excerpt from *Other Edens:
Speculative Evolution and Intelligence* by
Professor Ruth Emerson of the
University of California

You're quiet, now, subdued by what we've shown you. How many times can you watch the world end, after all, even if it's not your world?

Perhaps a happy ending now. But I cannot guarantee you'll take much joy in it.

How long, after all, does it take for life to generate sentience, for sentience to generate a civilization that can command its world enough to be proof against disaster? Each branching timeline that we've followed is set into motion later than the last. In each new timeline, the previous lords of Earth are suppressed in favour of a new might-have-been, for otherwise the new hopes would be precluded by the old rulers' presence.

This one diverges in what you might know as the Carboniferous era. Because for some reason palaeontologists ceased naming geological periods after obscure Welsh tribes and holiday regions on the English coast and became ruthlessly pragmatic about things. Carboniferous: coal-forming. In your world these forests give you your industrial revolution. You will burn their bones in three hundred and sixty million years' time, choking on your own technological advancement. But you'll be grinning through black teeth because of all it allows you to accomplish.

But not here. Nobody will ever burn the compressed carbon of these trees.

In the Carboniferous of this Earth, as in yours, the land goes mad for forests. This is a land of giants: millipedes six feet long, dragonflies with three-feet wingspans, armoured amphibians that rut and fight and bellow like water buffalo along the riverbanks. But the megafauna is not our focus.

There was an experiment in your timeline: the effect of high oxygen concentrations on insects. Even modern dragonflies get bigger, given that bracing atmosphere. Cockroaches don't. Roaches grow more *efficient* instead, able to devote less of their biology to the quotidian graft of transporting O_2 to their tissues. They find room for bigger muscles, more efficient guts, a higher energy metabolism, more complex behaviour.

I told you you wouldn't like it.

In these Carboniferous forests, one species of cockroach happens on the evolutionary advantages of communal living. First it influences just mothers and their broods, linked by a chemical communion. This proves sufficiently advantageous that each generation improves upon the recipe, and populations explode over a few million years into super-colonies. These contain hundreds of thousands of insects that, regrettably, already look a great deal like the roaches you so dislike. If you were minded to look closer, you'd see that they are already morphing into distinct castes. There are workers with specialized mouthparts, and guardians whose form suggests that cockroach cousin the praying mantis. In this timeline, they are filing patents on behaviour patterns that ants adopt two hundred million years later in your world. They are cultivating fungus gardens, growing antibiotics and forming partnerships with plants where they fight off predators in exchange for a packed lunch. They build enormous air-conditioned nests that put termites in the shade. The most successful lineage soon goes global, able to tailor its behaviours to the precise climate, temperature and biome that it finds. And then it tailors the biome to fit its preferences.

So when does intelligence arise, precisely? At what point does all this complex but mechanistic behaviour approximate thought? There is no *I* anywhere in this world-spanning colony, yet as time races on, they shape the world to their wishes without any individual unit being aware of it. And when the Permian dying times come for *them*, they are ready for it. Each change in the Earth's temperature and climate and chemical balance is noted, as Death tries to play Grandmother's Footsteps with them. A worldwide chain of experimentation and decision-making is set in motion, a system that feeds information in and gets action out. This species stays on top of environmental changes without falling off the path, neither too much nor too little. It guides the Earth through the Permian deathtrap, without getting a scratch on the paintwork.

Except, of course, this Earth's biodiversity was already colossally reduced before tragedy was averted. The global colony doesn't know much about the environment, but it knows what it likes. The roaches approach the wilderness of the world like a rich old landowner might landscape his estates. Everything seems to show the wondrous order of nature and yet nothing is truly natural. Not even the bacterial content of the soil is left to chance. These insects are the perfect gardeners, and gardeners are the great tyrants of nature. Every species either fits into the million-piece jigsaw that the roach colony mandates, or else it is destroyed without conscience or remorse. They build a perfect world—perfect for them—and they maintain it perfectly, without error or chance mutation. There are no dinosaurs here, but around the time the first Coelophysis lifts its scaly head in our own past, the world of the roaches has found its final balance. Even a meteor landing will only be a tiresome error in need of correction.

But intelligence? Yes, we concede there is an intelligence at work here, but one that we would never be able to reach out to, fingertip to antennae. The world this colony has built for itself is a closed system that cannot process things from outside, save to excise them. We would be quarantined and done away with, should we ever walk this Earth. And then we would be erased from memory, not fit to be part of the eternal *now* that has gripped this world for two hundred million years. So, a happy ending, but not one that admits us. A Garden of Eden from which we are forever excluded.

7.

I

Dr. Kay Amal Khan was delightedly incredulous when she heard what had got Lee into this mess.

"A girl?" she crowed. "Really, love?"

They'd been cooped up together for a day. Khan divided her time between working feverishly through dense fields of numbers with a pen and paper, smoking as much out of the window as she could and asking questions. Lee had already gone through her history with Mal, including both the past and the crumbs of the present.

"I envy you,.I really do," said Khan, shaking her head and tapping a cigarette packet that turned out to be empty. "Fuck."

"I'll try to grab some when I go get food," Lee said. She wasn't entirely sure what her role was in this shabby hotel by King's Cross. Khan seemed important, though, and doing the fetching and carrying felt like a good way of working off whatever she owed for being rescued.

"I saw someone, when I was... escaping," she threw in. She hadn't explained what transformations had been involved in her protracted escape. She was waiting for Khan to broach the impossible first. "Like a big woman in a robe, very broad.

And before, there was this guy with Mal, looked like some street-corner preacher into extreme weightlifting. Scary-looking."

"I've not met anyone like that," Khan said thoughtfully. "Didn't even see who brought you in. I got a call to warn me you were on your way, and then I came out of the loo later and you were just...there. I was shown a picture of a couple of them, before, though. One girl and her Ogg. The girl, I'd met. Supposed to be the same people who were at my flat, defending my honour from the fascists."

"The...?"

"When you were there, after the break-in, I'd just had visitors. A pack of small-minded little shits were going to... punish me, for being me, you know." She rattled the empty cigarette packet on the room's little desk. "I locked myself in the loo, darling. Determined to sell my honour dearly, you know. But someone else got in ahead of them and...made quite a mess. You saw the bodies brought out, and they didn't just all feel faint at the same time. I've...never seen anything like it. My flat was trashed." She shuddered. "And you were looking for your Mal, and your Mal was in fact there, with this weird friend of hers. You'd recognize them from that photo they showed me, wouldn't you?"

Lee thought about Mal's new friend, the ogre, with fresh stains on his coat. She nodded mutely. "So what happened?"

"Oh, some old friends of mine, former employers actually, took an interest," Khan said airily. "Put me up, made sure nobody else was coming to get me. They suspected your friend—and her friend—were trying to grab me as well, and the fascists had been competition. Not that you ever really need an excuse to slap a fascist."

"They thought Mal wanted to kidnap you?"

"They're suspicious sorts. Also, I'd been approached by this girl who was probably your friend, wanting me to go work for *her* friends, and my former employers are possessive." Her face split in a grin at Lee's baffled expression, and in a terrible stage whisper she added, "I was a *spy*."

"What?"

"Well, not a spy as such. This is all Official Secrets Act territory, but I think we're a bit beyond that now. I used to do very hard sums for the government. Hard enough sums that they don't really want me checking anyone else's working. So, yes, not the first time someone got in touch, actually, but..."

"But they got in touch and then there was no trace that they had?" Lee asked.

Khan looked at her sharply. "No. She approached me in a club, actually. But why do you say that?"

"It happened to me." *I think it happened.* "Mal called, but there was no sign of it. No trace on my phone."

Khan was nodding slowly. "When I was in the safe house, after the break-in, they got in touch again. Went straight to my laptop without needing any kind of connection. I wonder if they'd have been able to do it without the thing even being *on*. And okay, they had something to show me, but the contact in itself was like a proof of concept, you know? Saying, 'We can do this.'"

"Proof of what concept?" Lee asked.

"Cryptic Informational Transformation Space," Kay told her brightly. "And if I'd been naming it now I'd have found a word with an *L* to stick in after 'Cryptic,' but I was more of a shrinking violet in those days. It's my field. Theoretical physics. Or it was supposed to be theoretical. We could never actually generate a manifestation of it in the lab."

After that, she insisted Lee go out for supplies, which she did with her hair combed halfway over her face like an emo teenager in case surveillance cameras identified her. The way she saw it, Khan might be the important one, but she was being chased by at least two groups of people, some of whom were probably the real police. She spent the brief walk back trying to work out what "Cryptic Informational Transformation Space" was, and returned with a somewhat underwhelming conclusion.

"We've both spent our lives hunting something 'cryptic,'" she told Khan weakly. "Does that count as a link?"

"You're thinking your *monsters* might be real too?" Khan asked.

"Maybe they exist in Cryptic Transformer Space?" Lee managed a smile.

Khan opened her mouth to dismiss that, then shrugged. "Fuck it, maybe they do, love. Since whoever-the-fuck proved to me that it actually exists, I don't feel I'm the expert I used to be on the fucking subject." She spat the expletives out with relish and lit up, tokenly near the window. To be honest, the whole room smelled of smoke.

"So who booked this place?" Lee asked.

"They just told me it'd been done." Khan nodded. "And you'd think super-secret Russians or whoever they are would have something a bit glitzier. Keep me in the manner to which I've become accustomed, don't you know? But it's this shithole instead. I haven't met any of them since probably-your-friend said hi to me in that club."

"But they proved this cryptic theorem thing and then

they...showed you the world was going to end? I mean, if you *are* going over to the Russians, or whoever, I guess you're taking them seriously." *Not the Russians*, Lee thought. *Not unless the Russians have dinosaurs. It's got to be aliens.*

The snark died on Khan's lips. "Yes, well," she said, deflated. "It sounds dreadfully treasonous when you say it like that. I'll have to assume that if GCHQ was fully able to appreciate the facts they'd probably want me to save the world. Or indeed the universe. If it can be saved."

Lee still couldn't get her head round it, but the other woman's sober manner chilled her. "How?" she asked.

"Saved? Fuck knows. I think they want a meeting of the minds, but I hope to buggery they have more than just mine."

"No, how will it end?" *Fire, zombies, pestilence, war?*

"Maths," Khan spat dourly. "I mean, it's the universe—it's not like you can push it under a bus, love. But one thing CITS postulates is that there are certain parameters and dimensions that feed into the nature of the universe—above and beyond the basic forces we take for granted. The whole theory came about as an attempt to explain where most of the universe *was*. All that matter and energy we can't lay our hands on. But by the time I got in the game, the focus had shifted to whether this space existed, the space where matter might be hiding, and what you could do with it. Or at least, we were all for investigating the first question, and the people paying us were more after the second." At Lee's look, she shook her head and rolled her eyes. "Spy stuff, love. Cracking codes, accessing encrypted data. Theoretically, if you can move your enemy's data into CITS, you can do what the fuck you like with it. There's no regular encryption that would confer any protection or have any meaning there. Except we could never get the idea to work in practice, or figure out how to protect our data if anyone else did crack it. Then there was a shift of personnel, and suddenly nobody wanted to keep us in fast cars and martinis any more." She raised an eyebrow. "When this is done and we've saved the universe, I'll tell them I could do it now, given six months and a decent stipend. I've seen how it can work. Fucking *simple*. If only I'd sat down and thought about it in what is a completely unintuitive and, may I say, frankly inhuman way, I'd be right back at GCHQ asking for my old job back about now. However, my new contacts also showed me something utterly terrifying. A very cogent and succinct proof that the various key parameters of the universe—the ones that CITS proposes— are not only real but are going south. And this is happening in such a way that everything, *everything*, is going to go out like a candle in the appallingly near future."

Lee stared at her. *Maybe she's the crazy one. Or she's wrong. Because it's not reasonable to expect me to have this conversation, not about something on this scale.* For a moment she thought she was going to walk out, give up on this whole episode as a bad job. Then she was going to cry. In the end she laughed.

"This isn't fair," she told Khan's raised eyebrow. "I saw a dinosaur. That should mean I'm the one with the big news."

Khan grinned, red lips against white teeth. Then there was the muted trill of a phone. The doctor frowned and retrieved it from the tangled sheets of the bed.

"Hmm?" she said, then eyed Lee. "She did, yes. You'll have to tell me how you did it, though, cos I can't see the strings." She nodded and held the phone out. "It's for you, love."

Lee took the phone tentatively. It was an old model, just a number pad and a tiny screen. "Hello?"

"Lee?" Mal's voice, tinny and static-laced, from far, far away. "Are you all right?"

"I...I'm very confused, Mal. I'd really...appreciate being able to understand what's going on right now." She heard her voice shake, when she'd kept it level all through being told about the end of the universe.

"I'll tell you. When I can reach you, I'll tell you everything I know. But listen to me, Lee. You need to move on, you and Dr. Khan. We need you to get out of there. They've tracked you down."

II

The new team was underwhelming, put together at short notice from whoever they had sitting on their hands in London. Lucas was already missing Dominic, Michael and Becca. Who no longer existed, apparently. There was no record of them on the Rove Denton system, no sign of anything they'd touched or owned back at the office. Lucas felt that this was an object lesson specifically for him about how Daniel Rove treated failure.

Amin seemed competent, another ex-forces lad, young but steady. Josef was a great beast of a man, not that fragile weight-lifter fitness that was all push and no endurance but someone who could hunt all day. Terrence came last in Lucas's eyes; he had the feel of someone who was very keen to advance his position in the company but less keen to actually put in the work.

Still, beggars can't be choosers. The four of them were outside the cheapest hotel Lucas had ever seen, a converted Georgian on the wrong side of the Euston Road. Their targets had been tracked here, and Lucas had no idea how that worked. *Something to do with Rove's App.* He knew, now, that the boss was coordinating things from *over there*, using bizarre technology to detect anomalies: people and things that had been touched by that other world. Or other worlds. He wasn't convinced the cold forest and the dinosaurs existed alongside Rove's cramped submarine.

He was resolutely not thinking through the implications of anything he'd seen.

There was a claustrophobic enclosed yard at the building's rear, opening onto a narrow alley. Lucas sent Amin that way and left Terrence on the street in case anybody tried bolting from a window. That left him and big Josef to go in the front. He showed his fake ID to the old woman at reception as Josef went up the stairs with his phone, letting the App guide him. Lucas had to stay back for that to work, given he'd set the goddamn thing off himself now. He was touched by the otherworld, like he was radioactive. *Cheery thought.*

"Got a reading." Josef's voice was low, Slavic intonations bleeding through.

"Coming." Lucas nodded at the receptionist and then went up the stairs as quietly as he could, telling Amin and Terrence to be ready. When he hit the second floor he gave Josef the thumbs-up and pulled out his gun.

One kick from the big man almost took the door out of the frame entirely. The room beyond could not have hidden anyone, but Josef upended the bed and ripped down the shower curtain anyway.

There was a litter of cigarette butts on the windowsill.

Lucas brushed his right hand, the hand that could still feel properly, over the ash, sensing a residual warmth.

Moments later he was outside with the others, phones hunting out any trace of disruption. If his quarry had left a trail of otherworldliness, then they were goddamn going to find it.

"Mr. Rove," he reported. "They're gone."

Rove was silent for a few heartbeats, and Lucas waited. Was he sufficiently disappointed to delete Lucas from the company records as well? At last, though, the man's voice came to him, across who knew what kind of intervening space.

"My associates believe they can locate them, but this is not an exact science. Look at your phone."

Lucas pulled the device from his ear. A map of London's surrounding streets had sprung up, featuring a...cloud of red dots. It was as though a plague of blood-filled mosquitos was descending on Clerkenwell. There were denser patches and thinner ones, swirling about a nebulous centre.

"Do you understand?" Rove demanded. "It shows best guesses, probabilities based on the tracking machines here. Pathetic, really. Machines as big as a house trying to penetrate the interdimensional membranes, and this is the best they can give us. Find them, Lucas. We need the doctor unharmed. Use Pryor as leverage against her allies. They seem to be very keen on keeping her alive."

"Understood," Lucas said. He stared at the bewildering scatter of data. *Sheep, and we're the dogs.* Their focus was southeast from their location, a chaotic swirl of probability covering two or three streets.

He barked out orders to the other three. He and Amin

would follow behind, Terrence east, Josef west. It would be like old times, when all that expensive technology could take you only so far and no further. It would be down to using their eyes, dragging those faces out of a crowd and looking for body language that said "fugitive," for people trying not to be seen.

Hanging back was the worst part: necessary because he'd screw with the App, because Pryor knew his face. And he was looking forward to seeing *her* face again; three good people were dead because she hadn't sat still. Just because Rove wanted her as a bargaining chip didn't mean he couldn't slap some sense into her. Or he could stamp on a knee, teach her a valuable lesson about what a privilege running away can be. Lucas wasn't an angry man by nature, but he had a keen sense of when he'd been wronged, requiring due compensation from the guilty parties.

On his phone, the dots were coalescing into something more concrete: from a scatter of streets to a couple. Lucas watched and gave his people instructions as they closed in.

Abruptly the display on the screen jumped, everything imploding so that for a moment he thought they'd lost the trail entirely. But no: there was a dot left over: a single possibility, which meant it was a certainty.

He had someone right there, but his heart sank when he saw who it was. "Terrence, what's your position?"

"Heathcote Street, sir, waiting for your word." Sounding super-extra earnest and vigilant.

"You don't see them anywhere near you?" On Lucas's phone the dot was beginning to expand again, to fuzz from indisputable fact into vague rumour.

"No-o." But there was a slight hesitancy in Terrence's voice.

Lucas signalled Josef to close the trap on Terrence's location and diverted Amin to come round from the other side.

"What?" he demanded, making double-quick time himself.

"Nothing," Terrence said defensively. "Saw a girl who might have been Pryor, but she was with another woman, not the doc."

Lucas's mind went blank for precisely three-quarters of a second, before flaring into life. "You fuckwit, you didn't read the brief, did you? *Go after them!*"

"I read it!" Lucas could hear Terrence scrambling to obey, for all that it was probably too late.

"Not past the *first fucking page*, you didn't." There'd been a photo of a young Khan there, from when he was with some government think tank or other: a slight, unassuming Indian guy, glasses, moustache. Of course, three pages in there were more current photos that showed him in a very different light, but apparently Terrence hadn't felt that reading the brief was a priority. *All eagerness, no diligence.* Lucas was going to take pleasure in shopping the bastard to Rove's HR people, but only once they had their mark. If they didn't get that, he suspected he wouldn't be taking much pleasure in anything.

For a moment he thought they'd lost their chance. The dots exploded outwards, fizzing across the screen as though Pryor and Khan were dust that might end up anywhere from here to Azerbaijan. Then everything was coalescing towards Crowne Plaza. He wondered if they had left something in that crappy hotel, or were maybe trying to get to King's Cross Station. He dropped a request to the office for someone to watch the trains, just in case.

"I see them." Terrence sounded out of breath on the phone. "I've got them, I'm going to—"

"Fucking watch and wait and don't do anything suspicious." Lucas broke into a run. "Everyone converge on his position. Get ahead of them. Where are they going?"

"Sir, I can—"

"You will *not*," Lucas said, because one criminally over-enthusiastic agent trying to capture two people was never going to work out. Even ignoring the possibility that either might be able to call on something *unnatural* at a moment's notice.

"Sir," said Terrence in a mutinous tone, "they're heading to a Post Office."

"The fuck?" Lucas demanded. He scrolled his phone map as best he could. "Is that...Mount Pleasant?" His map was showing a huge postal sorting centre taking up a city block. "Terrence, what's that in the background?" Not just interference: a high-pitched, irregular sound.

"There's a load of people out on the street," Terrence said. "I think our targets are trying to lose themselves—no, wait, they're going round them."

"What am I hearing?" Louder now, past Terrence's breathing and the murmur of second-hand traffic.

"Fire alarm," Terrence said.

Josef added, "I see them too."

Amin was two streets away, lagging behind Lucas. Lucas had the police ID, though: if they were going to make it look like an arrest, he'd rather lead it. "Amin, go back, bring the car up." Not that it had helped last time, but he wanted their quarry off the streets and somewhere secure, preferably with a gun shoved discreetly into someone's ribs, as soon as possible.

"They've gone into the Post Office's vehicle yard," Josef said. "Heading for the main building. Pursue?"

"Pursue. Stop them, hold them, tell anyone you're police. I'm a minute away at most." And then Lucas put on speed, traffic blarting at him as he dashed between cars.

"Got you," said Josef, and then, "Who the fuck—"

A sound like a gunshot.

"Josef?" Lucas pressed, still running. "Speak to me, Joe."

"Holy shit." All of Terrence's keen had just evaporated. "Holy *shit.*"

"Report, man," Lucas snapped.

"This big guy, he just . . . stepped out from behind a van . . ."

Lucas was in sight of the place now: there was a forecourt of cheery red Post Office vehicles. He caught sight of Terrence first: the man had his gun out, right there in the open, but was backing off. If he were a dog his tail would be well and truly between his legs. A half-dozen pounding steps closer and Lucas saw Josef, or his body: his six feet, four inches were stretched out, utterly motionless.

There was a big man standing over him, wearing a long dark coat that somehow made a shadow of him despite the bright daylight. He had a woollen hat pulled down low to his beetling brows, and he was broader than Josef had been. He was the same clown who'd made such a mess of Billy White's boys, Lucas was sure of it.

"He just hit him," Terrence breathed in Lucas's ear. "He stepped out and straight-armed Joe, right in the chest. I heard his fucking ribs break, man. Nobody can do that."

Fuck it, Lucas thought. He stepped past Terrence and shot the clown in the chest. The fire alarm was still screeching and the staff of Mount Pleasant were spilling onto the street. The sound of the shot dissolved in the chaos, and Lucas was more worried about failing Rove than attracting the police.

His hand was steady. He hit his target dead centre of that broad torso, slamming the man into the happy red of a postie's van.

Terrence was running towards the postal centre, past Lucas's target, but as he tried to dodge the fallen man, he caught an open-handed slap hard enough to actually spin him head over heels.

For a moment Lucas stared at the big man, who was levering himself off the dented van. His dark coat hung open and there was a hole in his grimy T-shirt. Lucas saw something lead grey underneath the gleaming metal circle that was his flattened bullet. A sudden stab of unfairness hit him, because some of that formidable bulk was streamlined body armour.

But as he was trying to sight on the thug's unprotected face, the man moved shockingly fast for such a bulky figure. He dodged between the vehicles and vanished into the sorting centre without giving Lucas a clear shot.

Amin finally arrived in the car, and Lucas told him to get Josef and Terrence into the back before anyone started asking questions. Amin was wise enough to have no questions of his own.

"Mr. Rove," Lucas reported, and gave a concise summary of just how everything had gone to shit, his voice flat.

"I see." Rove sounded more distracted than anything else, to Lucas's relief. "I'd hoped to avoid this, but I'll send the other team in."

Lucas just nodded. Of course there was another team.

"You stay put. Have your man keep the App up, in case they get flushed out"—and Rove chuckled unexpectedly—"like rats."

III

Lee had followed Mal's voice in her ear all the way from the hotel, seeing no sign of pursuit but assured at every step that it was there.

The phone was a new one Khan had found in the hotel room. It came with earphones and a mic, and Lee had conducted a sporadic conversation all the way, whilst trying to appear casual.

"What's the plan, Mal?" she asked.

"Working on it," came that familiar, achingly distant voice. "We need to get you and the doctor out. But we need to open a door, you get me?"

"Not to the cold place, please."

Mal's reply, tinnily amused: "Well, you have a choice of cold places, Lee. Not to the *very* cold place, no. That...that was my mistake. Sorry about that."

"No more dinosaurs, please."

"Can't promise anything on that front. They're lovely when you get to know them, honest." Mal sounded harried. Lee tried to imagine her, but the situation was so shorn of context she couldn't. Was this new Mal, of the long dark hair and the lean, muscled body, standing in a snow-swept forest clearing? Was she sitting in a supervillain room full of monitors, seeing twenty variations of the same scene around her?

"Mal," she said wretchedly. "What's going on?"

"Complicated."

"I know it's complicated, Mal. It got so complicated I almost froze to death." She was fighting hard to keep her voice composed and, from Khan's expression, not doing so well. "Why am I...why am I important, Mal? I get that Doc Kay is a maths whizz who can save the universe, and the bad guys want to stop that happening for 'reasons,' but..." Her voice wobbled. "And I will help, right? I mean, it's my universe too. I will fetch and carry for her, and I'll do whatever you ask me, you know I will—but why do they want *me*?"

Mal was quiet for long enough that Lee thought she'd lost contact, hearing only the ghostly tides of static like waves on a beach, wind moaning through lightless chasms deep within the Earth.

"You're almost there," said Mal at last. "But they're almost on you. Move, Lee. Just run."

"Mal—"

"I can't..." Mal's voice cracked, and Lee's perspective on the conversation swung wildly as she realized how upset Mal was. She'd been bottling up just like she used to, with everyone except Lee. "Straight ahead, through the car park. Inside."

"Mal..." But immediate concerns steamrollered her personal ones. "This is a Post Office."

"In, Lee, in! *Run!*"

And she did. Khan had been looking over her shoulder, eyes wide, and she almost went over as Lee yanked her arm. Then the two of them dashed towards the Mount Pleasant Mail Centre, pelting down the ranks of parked vehicles. Briefly Lee saw someone waiting there: a big, hairy man in a filthy coat, a broad face, half child, half murderer. He didn't react as they ran past him, but seemed to be bracing himself for action.

"No, not the main building. Fire exit, left, *left!*" Mal yelled at her from the phone.

An unassuming door was flung open ahead of her. A handful of people were spilling from it, and she registered

214

the keening of a fire alarm. Their invasion of the building played out like clockwork: a gaggle of tourists scattered into the sunlight, blinking, followed by a smartly dressed pair with name tags who must be staff. Lee and the doctor slipped inside behind them.

They pelted down a stairway into the almost solid shriek of the alarm, with Mal exhorting them to keep going.

"Can we stop running about like headless chickens, love? I'm fucking bushed," Khan said in her other ear. "No, wait, fuck, someone's after us!"

"Run!" Lee said, but "No, wait!" came from Mal.

And then there was an agonizing pause as the alarm scraped at their ears. And at any moment a gunman might burst in, and maybe this time they'd have given up on keeping anyone alive.

"Help is coming," said Mal.

Someone bounded down the stairs towards them: not a lean thug like Gym Bro Cop but the man from outside, who'd been with Mal in Camden.

"Bloody hell." Khan stepped back, staring.

"It's cool, it's cool." Lee had the phone pressed to her ear because the alarm was eating up all available sound—and the static on the line was reaching some kind of high-tide mark. She just made out Mal saying, "He's my friend."

"Really your friend?" Lee was backing off, too. The man had stopped three steps up and had his hands out, a big smile on his big face showing massive teeth. He reminded her of someone trying to get close to a skittish animal, maybe to help—maybe to finish it off.

"Lee, this is Stig—say hello to Stig," came Mal's failing voice.

"Stig?" she demanded.

"Well, it's kind of something like Urstegranokut," Mal said over the alarm's monotonous howl. "But I..." She was gone, the noise overwhelming the signal.

"Hello, Stig," Lee said.

Her earlier thoughts came back to her, how Gym Bro had been something modern, sleek, dangerous like a gun or a fast car, whereas this man...was a Stig.

She thought about dinosaurs, and other, more human things that might not be so lost to time as they were supposed to be.

"She told you, come with me?" Stig asked. "She told you, do what I say?" His voice was accented, a citizen of nowhere Lee had ever heard of. A nice voice, taken in isolation, rich and resonant like a classically trained actor's.

"She didn't," Lee said, seeing his brow wrinkle: an expression that was identifiable as frustration, yet not quite the way a normal human face would have expressed it. "But she said you were her friend."

"Hrm," said Stig, as though he wasn't necessarily convinced of that himself. "They are outside. Keep going down. We are going down. We are going out."

"Down? Into the cellar? Where's out from there?" Khan demanded, obviously liking none of this.

"There is a door. There will be a door. We are making one now. Please." He smiled again; it transformed his face from horror movie to broad comedy, but Lee could see that he was desperate to get them moving.

He could just go for us, she thought. He was obviously strong enough. And yet he didn't, and that went the final step to convincing her.

"Lead on, Stig," she said.

He grinned and ducked out of the room, leading them down—leading them, hopefully, out.

She thought down had meant cellars, but Mount Pleasant was hiding more than that. They came out at a platform, a girderwork-vaulted tunnel stretching off into the darkness.

"What the hell?" Lee said.

"Mail tunnels, love," Khan said from behind her. "Used to shunt the post across London with these." At Lee's bewildered look, she added, "Had a soirée here once, all posh gov types and Tory party donors. Fucking awful black tie thing. They let us ride the little trains, though, so there was that."

"Come," Stig insisted, already down by the rails and at the mouth of a tunnel. At the brink of that ersatz cave with darkness at his back, he looked even more like a Stig. Then there was someone else with him, and Lee skidded to a halt before realizing it was another Stig.

She wore a similar mismatch of shabby used clothes, in this case a mauve woollen cardigan straining at the shoulders, a paisley blouse with missing buttons and a pair of dreadfully stained tracksuit trousers. The two of them together were disconcerting in the way that Stig alone wasn't, no longer an anomaly but a people.

"Come!" Stig said.

Mrs. Stig was speaking softly to him, sounds that weren't words Lee knew, and not from any language group she'd ever encountered. Her hand came up, a slab as big as both of Lee's. When her fingers moved in the air, though, it was with the delicacy of a magician.

And the air did magic. Lee saw it for a moment: glimmering lines, depths and glints of icy light, and the temperature dropped several degrees for just a second. She thought she heard great hollow slabs grinding against each other, from a distance not contained within the darkness of the tunnel.

Khan had heard it too; Lee could see it in her expression. More, Khan had perhaps *understood* it, in some small way. Her face was abruptly ashen.

"Where are we going?" she asked.

"Out, away," Stig told her. "Come."

"I am not going into any dark tunnels with you, Stig, love, until you tell me where we'll end up."

Lee waited for Stig to get pushy with them, for all that raw physicality to overflow into action. Instead he seemed to pull in on himself, abruptly abandoning the venture and sloping off into the darkness.

"Kay'malkan," the woman said, intoning "Kay Amal Khan" as though the name belonged to a mysterious deity. "You came because we sent you truths you could understand. We sent to you because you could understand." Her voice was more strongly accented than Stig's, even though her speech was more confident. "We need your understanding. We need all the understanding there is. Please."

Khan had stepped past Lee, still out of reach should the big woman try to grab her. "And where are we going, love? Because I don't think we're just riding the train."

"We will open a door through the boundary that separates this branch from our branch, from where you are to where we are. The potential for such a door exists here, you understand?"

From her expression, Khan did understand; then movement caught Lee's eye from the far end of the platform.

She thought it was an optical illusion at first. Nothing

there, but a nothing of a different quality, a nothing that funnelled into some vast unseen space like water spiralling down a plug. Even as the image came to her, she started thinking about things that might be coming the other way, bristling things, thronging things, pushing their bodies up through the plumbing of the universe and squeezing into places they shouldn't be. Like here, like now. She saw them; they were coming.

She registered a congealed mass of movement at first, something flowing from *elsewhere* to *here*. A writhing mass of discrete long bodies, twisting and serpentine. She saw heads blindly questing, thin limbs that reached out with weirdly twisted hands, long, whiplike tails.

Lee Pryor did not scream at monsters. Monsters were her business, she had jokingly said at more than one crypto-zoology convention. She laughed in the faces of cryptids, and ideally took a few blurry pictures for others to dismiss as sandhill cranes and barn owls.

No cranes here, no owls: only monsters.

They were separating, squirming away from one another across the tracks. The light seemed to hurt them. They made sounds that keened into the very last five per cent of her high-frequency hearing. Abruptly, Lee was six years old again, facing the most terrifying memory of her childhood.

It was goddamn *Wind in the Willows* all over again.

Her parents had taken the whole family. It had been a touring production, only the aesthetic for the masks and make-up had been right out of some Russian folk tale about Baba Yaga. Badger's louring, vacant-eyed face had been bad enough, with its clacking lower jaw snapping out of time with the actor's words. Then the weasels had come in en masse, and Lee had had to be taken squalling from the theatre by her embarrassed father.

Twenty years later and the weasels had finally come for her. The monsters had the same long bodies, huge, glassy eyes and nasty little hands. It didn't matter that they were half Lee's size—they were sheer nightmare fuel from start to finish.

The Stig woman was in motion instantly, covering the distant between her and Khan far too fast. She grabbed the scientist by the shoulder and pitched her into the dark after Stig. She was reaching for Lee, too, but Lee shrank back, because anything that touched her now might be connected with the writhing ball of weasels that had just been vomited into the world.

And then her cryptozoologist's eye came into its own, overriding even her panic. Because the thing about cryptids was that they were beasts, animals that time and the world had forgotten. They weren't supposed to turn up kitted out for expeditions. But those big, glassy eyes were lenses in hoods, and she could see cables or hoses connecting their blunt muzzles with bulky apparatus strapped on their bodies where their hind limbs jutted out. The springy whiskers that jutted eighteen inches from their snouts glinted like metal in the artificial light. Most showed greasy pelts of black or brown or mottled grey, but only where they weren't wearing rubbery ponchos or sheath-like tunics. They were weaving about as if drunk, clawlike hands raking the air, and she guessed the transition from *there* hadn't been kind on them.

One of them, the weasel that had come through first, had absurdly big ears like fuzzy satellite dishes—tufted with elaborately coiffed plumes of hair dyed in stripes. That killed

Lee's fear, switching the creature from terror to cartoon character even as she thought of military officers and rank insignia.

It pointed something at her, a squat implement it gripped with both twisted hands, connected to a spool held by another weasel.

Almost like a gun, Lee thought, and then the creature shot her.

The Stig woman got between it and her. The scatter of sharp metal flechettes thudded into her heavy body, though a couple tore long scratches in Lee's cheek. Mrs. Stig didn't seem to be hurt, and she had her own weapon, which looked more like a knuckleduster than a gun.

"Go!"

She shoved Lee hard enough to knock her down. Then she pointed her armed fist at the weasels and Lee went momentarily deaf. She heard no sound from the weapon. Her head ached instantly, though, and her eyes flashed with dark spots as though a migraine had risen through her brain and was clawing at the inside of her skull. Three of the weasels dropped, either killed or knocked cold by the discharge, and the rest were reeling, scattering, but getting their senses back nonetheless. Mrs. Stig was backing off, pointing her weapon at them. The tunnel thundered silently, an echo without a sound. Metal slivers were flying back at her companion, and then something else struck the woman hard, knocking her over.

Lee didn't wait to see any more. She ran.

She fell onto the rails three times, bloodying shins and palms. Then, without warning, there was a light, a green-white flare that dazzled her.

"What's going on?" Dr. Khan said.

Lee blurted idiotically, "They're coming! They're coming!"

Blinking, she saw Khan, a stiletto silhouette against the light. Caught in its uncompromising glare were Stig and another woman of his general stamp, crouching down near the impossible light. Her hands made deft, elegant moves in the air, like a conductor, or a magician. She had a heavier face and body than the Mrs. Stig Lee had just left, and she wore a robe of pale grey that was definitely not standard Londoner issue. It looked seamless, filmy, stretched over the woman's sagging breasts and paunch, flowing over her broad, sloped shoulders.

Her hands moved. The air glinted where they had gone, revealing shining depths where the ice fell away in uncountable frozen fathoms. She saw intricate crystalline circuits that existed in the *here* for only as long as they were needed, before being banished like obedient demons back *there* where they had come from.

"What's coming, love?" Khan asked.

The world beyond the light flexed and rippled like a pool disturbed by a stone. The darkness of the tunnel fell away into forever, and Lee was looking into the distorted mirror of another place. It was vast, that place, and it was cramped, a warren of interconnecting galleries, pipes and low-ceilinged rooms that were swarming with motion. To look upon it almost broke her eyes, because she was seeing too much of it at once. She was looking simultaneously upon multiple vistas intended by the organization of their geometry to be sequential. The view was focusing, though, narrowing the perspectives, reining in the multiplying spaces until she could see just one: a room crowded with masked, rubber-armoured weasel-rat monsters.

Dozens of them were crammed so close together that they were practically on top of one another. There seemed to be a clear barrier in the air, between Lee and them. But they were armed, gripping a selection of nasty shotgun-looking devices. They were very still too, save for twitches of their artificial whiskers and their lashing, naked tails. She saw sharpened incisors bared, saw them braced as *there* and *here* were shunted unceremoniously closer. They were a boarding party, she saw. They were about to board her reality.

Bizarrely, her chief impression of them, past the horror and her Kenneth Grahame-related phobia, was that they looked terrified. She'd had a friend at university who kept rats, and she remembered the same frozen stillness when their cage had been knocked or a car had backfired outside.

The robed Mrs. Stig said something to Stig-the-original that sounded like "Umunmallinainungamnugulunuh-uh," too fast and fluid to divide into words.

Stig clearly didn't like that and argued back, while retrieving a knuckleduster gun from his filthy coat. Meanwhile, Dr. Khan was staring at the massed rodents. Or perhaps she was watching the clear meniscus that shuddered and clenched between them and the rodents, clearly working its way towards drawing back like a curtain for the main event.

"The space..." Khan said, and maybe what she saw wasn't the monsters at all, but the equations that must be governing this intrusion. "It's true," she choked out. "Fuck me sideways, it really is true. This is the way the world ends."

From a purely personal viewpoint, that would seem to be true. But robed Mrs. Stig stood up suddenly, obviously in charge and cutting off original Stig with a snarled "Unugramung!" She had a weapon of her own too, a stubby rod almost lost in her big hands. And for a moment Lee thought the pair of them were just going to sell their lives dear against the weasel host.

Then she twisted the rod decisively. Stig pushed past Lee, knocking her onto her backside, and his weapon barked out murderous silence into the darkness—because of course there had been a vermin problem back that way as well.

And the shuddering vista was utterly gone, as though it had never been. No host of armed stoats, no labyrinth of crowded spaces and no impossible darkness—just the mail tracks in the pale, cold light.

Robed Mrs. Stig sagged, and although she had plainly just saved them all, she looked very, very tired and old. Her long hair was grey streaked with white, Lee noticed. She looked like she might be fifty or might be a hundred.

"You must go now," she said.

"I thought that was the point," Lee put in.

"Go. With your feet. No door here. No way out but walking." Mrs. Stig sat on her heels, holding her knees. "I have isolated the branch for now."

"Nothing comes in, nothing comes out," Khan said, and the woman nodded tiredly.

"You..." Lee blinked. "You barricaded us off from them...?"

"I have isolated this place and time, maybe two days, there are no usable..."

"Interstitial fractures," Khan filled in. "You let off a fucking reality grenade."

Lee stared at the pair of them: barely a common language, certainly no shared scientific notation, but they understood each other.

"A fucking reality grenade," Mrs. Stig echoed, without enjoyment. "Just so. Not good, for anything, for reality."

At that point, Stig came back. He had a deep cut across one cheek, below the eye. It didn't seem to bother him.

"Done," he said.

He mumbled a collection of syllables to his fellow, who replied in kind.

Stig turned to them. "I will lead you. There are other ways out. Ways into your city."

"And then what, love?" Khan asked. "What if they send the rat squad? Or just, you know, people, with guns?"

"You will keep moving. We will keep moving you." He glowered at Lee as though it was all her fault up to and including the end of the universe. "And when we have more doors, we will bring you."

Mrs. Stig muttered something, and Stig gave her a maniclooking grin, eyes wide. It was an expression Lee had no frame of reference for, but likely didn't mean anything good.

Interlude: The Dead

Excerpt from *Other Edens:
Speculative Evolution and Intelligence* by
Professor Ruth Emerson of the
University of California

There has been a shadow over all these timelines. Earth's oldest children have all had to face the reaper, as life loses its gamble against geology and continental drift. Two hundred and fifty million years ago, on every timeline, across every Earth, the great dying came. This was the End-Permian Extinction Event.

In our past, the Permian was a time of great reptiles and reptile cousins. Not dinosaurs though; the vacuum left by their deaths will be one of the opportunities the terrible lizards exploit to start their long dominance over the globe. This Permian world is one of fin-backed pelycosaurs, crocodile ancestors, armoured and predatory amphibians. Not to mention reptiles already well on the road to becoming mammals, our own forebears.

The Earths I have described all faced the great dying: some suffered more than others, some controlled it, some were spectacular in the failure of their control. But on all of them, one species had the chance to understand what was happening to their world, for good or ill. When death came calling they were at least in a position to try and bar the door.

What is this grand dying, though? It is a long, slow convulsion of the Earth, like the coils of a constrictor. It is the continents of the world coming together to make a single mass of land, the interior of which dries into a desert that expands and expands. It is two million square kilometres of lava flow, in a place that will be Siberia, which raises dust clouds that block the sun. A stifling-hot age of darkness that lays waste to all plant life on Earth. It is acid rain that falls in such toxic abundance that the shells of molluscs dissolve in the waves. Hot algal blooms scour the oceans of oxygen, before dying and becoming bloated mats of decay a hundred kilometres across. It is global warming on a colossal scale—as the volcanos pump out carbon dioxide and the seas vomit forth still more killer gases. The Earth tried to kill us in our cradle, but the timelines you have seen survived it, or at least bequeathed a relic of themselves to the future.

But there are dead Earths out there, withered branches on the tree of life. There are also worlds where life recovered but never became sentient again. Here, dumb beasts move through the ruins of civilizations that were just becoming self-aware. Then the world turned and ground them beneath its wheels like a juggernaut.

There was a world where giant snail-like molluscs were the winners in the Carboniferous swamps and shallow seas. Their glistening paths through ferns and horsetails formed strange sigils of occult significance. Occult, because we can never truly know what they meant. The acid of the seas and the rains devoured their shells and they died in agony, intelligent enough to understand the magnitude of what was happening to them. And after the dying times, no other mind arose to look up into their sky—as they had with their stalked eyes—and wonder about the patterns of the stars.

There was a world where awareness came to the treetops. Small reptilian thinkers, somewhat like gliding monkeys, built complex nest villages in the high canopies. They traded jewel-shelled beetles and kept records of their dealings by stringing beads on vines. They painted themselves in gaudy colours and left votive offerings and ritual diagrams in deep caves. Here they braved huge centipedes and spiders to find a spiritual connection to the Earth. And yet the Earth betrayed them, and only their paintings and beads are left. In their case, chance factors intensified the hostile conditions of the dying times. Nothing larger than plankton was left in the sea, nothing but bacterial colonies were left on the land. It is a blow from which their Earth is still recovering, two hundred and fifty million years later.

And, because we are most affected by those most like ourselves, I will tell you of a timeline where our ancestors had their chance. Even as the world was turning to heat and poison, proto-mammals were evolving bigger brains and a bipedal posture, with only a stump of a tail left. They had hands more dextrous even than our own. They made tools from stone. They lived in nomadic troupes that bellowed and postured at one another when they met, and sometimes traded individuals or food. They were on the very cusp of intellect. Then the dying times crushed all their potential and left them in the dirt, and in the past. And though life went on for their Earth, they would never return.

The lesson here is that the Earth doesn't care; that bad things happen; that it could so easily have been us. I have been describing worlds branching sequentially out of the earliest reaches of Earth's history, but every timeline from here on in will diverge with one key advantage. The dying times are already behind them, as they are behind us.

8.

I

It took four police officers fifteen minutes' hard work, even with a ram, to get into Alison's apartment. Julian found this perversely reassuring, despite the situation. Had Alison been required to destroy evidence in her possession—if they had been the enemy, instead of the cavalry—the intruders would have broken in to find trashed computers and a bonfire of documents.

The difficult entrance also dispelled any hints from Royce and his people that Julian had suddenly turned hysterical about the disappearance of a colleague. Because the door had been thoroughly, almost absurdly, locked from the inside—and Alison was no longer in residence.

They stood in the entrance hall, looking through the empty doorway into the living room and kitchenette space. Taking every precaution, officers went into the bedroom in pairs. Julian heard them opening the wardrobe. And doubtless they were looking under the bed, too, into any space that might hide a human body, living or otherwise.

Julian clenched his fists, reaching the middle of the living room before a wave of helpless frustration brought him to a standstill. Where, after all, was he going?

He had done a lot of hard talking to even be here. The aborted call from Alison had been a very real indication of trouble to him, but had been difficult to parlay into hard currency for anyone else. If Royce hadn't been a friend, if Julian hadn't banked a fair amount of goodwill in the office, this might all have taken longer—not that haste had helped. He'd known Alison's phone was still in the apartment—at her insistence, they'd arranged to be able to track each other if necessary. There it was, on the floor at the kitchenette's edge. It was still perfectly intact, because she kept it in an armoured case intended for construction workers.

There was a startled yell from one of Royce's people, and Simms bolted from the bathroom to claw at Julian's legs, complaining bitterly. Julian felt more of a kindred spirit with the animal right then than ever before. *What the hell, basically?*

Royce was looking at where Alison's locks and chains had been battered away from the frame by their actions, a gouged and splintered woodscape. "Bloody hell, no half measures, isn't it?" he complained. "The windows are all double locked too, you know. From the inside. If this wasn't on the third floor, I'd be looking for hidden cellars and attics. Secret bloody doors."

Julian nodded. The impossibility of the whole business should have been getting to him, but it couldn't make any headway. The cold knife blade of *Something's happened to Alison* dominated everything. He wanted to grab hold of the very air and tear it open in case she was hiding there, just out of reach.

"We'll get the forensics boys in," Royce said. "And we'll get out, to avoid trampling anything else." He shook his head.

"I'm sorry, Jules. I don't understand it. Someone's playing games, is all I can think, right? Someone in your line of work?"

Julian nodded absently. "Thank you, Kier. Look, I better arrange for someone to look after the…the goddamned *cat*. She'd, she'd want that."

"I'll leave Hendry here with you, in case you need anything," Royce said diplomatically.

He and his fellows snuck out, leaving one woman on the door and Julian alone inside. Royce doubtless wrote this off as some Secret Service business, operating at a pay grade over regular police work. What Julian actually felt like doing was not act like a security professional but rage and weep and curse the skies like a Shakespearean tragic hero. Instead, he looked up catteries within a reasonable radius of the place, like a sane and non-distraught person, and arranged for them to pick up Simms on his tab. He would have them liaise with Royce and forensics so there could be a handover at the threshold without anyone *else* contaminating the crime scene. There, all done, all that sensible adult stuff.

He thanked PC Hendry, who would remain to keep an eye on the place until the next phase of police involvement arrived. Royce would keep him posted; Julian knew he would. He phoned the office to update them. He was already braced for someone to suggest that Alison had orchestrated this herself. Her personal file didn't paint the most stable picture, after all. Had she found out something, dropped off the radar and gone under cover as though she was a spy in hostile territory?

Julian wanted to smash his fists against the wall. *Something* had happened to Alison, and whatever the hell it was, he was powerless to fix it.

Instead, he went home, because that was what people did. He wasn't going to tell Josie anything, but in the end he was so bad at covering his upset—which leaked out as irritation and sarcasm despite his best efforts—that she insisted on it. He expected a fight, then, but she stared at him, said quietly that she was sorry, and went to tell John that he shouldn't bother Dad for a bit.

Julian ended up in the garden, looking up at the night sky that was ninety per cent streetlamp-stained clouds. The summer heatwave was dragging on, and the louring cover above seemed like nothing more than the weather taunting people below. Rain would have been welcome, just for the sense of something breaking.

His phone rang. He glanced at the display and answered it without thinking.

"Matchbox?" And then, "Who is this?," because he knew her phone was in a police evidence bag.

For a moment he heard only static and distant retorts, like something vast breaking or fissuring a long way away. He was about to speak when he caught her voice. "Spiker...? You hear me? Spiker, you won't believe what...—iker, it's... Listen to me, they..." Then nothing, and even the groan and crack that had underscored her words was fading.

"Matchbox?" he demanded once, and then again. The first time he heard an echo of his own voice shuddering back to his ear. The second, nothing, and then the very definite silence of a call having ended.

He needed to trace the call, fumbled his phone round, looking for the precise time. There was nothing in his call log. There was no indication the call had taken place at all, as though his own phone was gaslighting him. Even so, he called the office and had a long, heated and entirely unsatisfactory discussion with the technical team, who were patently left with the impression that Julian Sabreur was overdue a holiday. After that, he stood with the phone in his hand, waiting, but it didn't ring again.

II

There had been a metal door separating the more touristy areas of Mount Pleasant's postal rail line from the disused reaches beyond. There was no handle, but Stig had got it open. Probably he'd used some high-tech tool he'd plucked out of the air like these people seemed to do, but also possibly he'd forced it with his prodigious strength. Both he and Mrs. Stig seemed to be built on a different scale or be made of denser molecules than regular people. Their mere presence felt exhausting, as though they were using up all the air, all the energy.

And they could really *run*. They would plainly have preferred it if Khan and Lee could have kept up with them, loping wolf-like through the abandoned tunnels. Except Lee had already run more today than she would normally in a week, and she reckoned the same went double for Dr. Khan.

Stig and Mrs. Stig had a free and frank exchange of views on that quandary, views Lee reckoned were not complimentary to the fitness of either herself or Kay Amal Khan. "We will carry you," Stig offered.

"The fuck you will," Khan said.

"Carry you," he repeated. He didn't loom threateningly. In fact, he seemed to shrink from the doctor a little, faced with her refusal.

"I will walk, love," Khan said. "This is not my day for being swept off my feet. And if the rats or those goons up top aren't *right behind us*, then walk it is, because I have already turned my ankle once, capisce?"

Stig looked hurt, and he glanced sidelong at Mrs. Stig.

"Walking is good," Mrs. Stig agreed wearily. "Long walk though. It is no shame to want help. You find it hard to accept it."

"*I* do?" Khan demanded, but Lee murmured, "I think she means us, both of us...all of us."

Khan glanced at her, frowning, but asked no questions, perhaps divining she wouldn't like the answers. Lee had come to the conclusion that she had finally hit the jackpot in the cryptid game, only in a way she'd never be able to publish. She tried the phone then, because her instinctive thought, even after all this time, was to share the revelation with Mal. Except the phone was dead. Wherever Mal had been calling from was as severed from them as the world of the weasels.

They walked for what felt like the rest of the day, through a low, domed tunnel intended only for the automated transit of the mail, past closed-off stations heavy with dust and darkness. The Stigs were close-mouthed, seldom uttering a word, even in their own mumbled language. They were untiring, too. In the end, Lee asked them to stop, to give their wards a chance to rest. Mrs. Stig had water, cold and clear with a metallic tang to it. Stig had some kind of dried meat, tough as shoe leather and entirely proof against Lee's teeth.

When they ventured above ground again, it was to break against the surging tide of the rush-hour exodus. They met

237

a flood of people shunting along the pavements into the grand Victorian train station that their service hatch led into. They ended up huddled on the street, filthy and cobweb-strewn. Lee and Khan looked like they'd been mugged, but the Stigs could have been any two destitutes abandoned on the streets of London.

"Where is this?" Lee asked.

The pushy, bustling roar of London seemed like another world after so long below. Lee found herself trying to look beyond it, in case there were dinosaurs out there, in case there were militaristic rodent soldiers in the shadows, in case, in case...

She shuddered and sat down. Abruptly it was all too much. She felt like she had after Mal disappeared, when she had been waiting for the world to tilt and decant her *elsewhere* at any moment, just like it had on Bodmin.

"Why are we at Paddington Station?" Khan asked wonderingly.

"Where it comes out. Far from where we were," Stig explained, almost apologetically.

"What now? Your plan got screwed arse-backwards, I take it?"

"There will be another door," he said defensively. "Until then, we move on." His face screwed up, and he added, "Capisce?" with ponderously careful diction.

"Comedian," Khan said, deadpan.

"But can't you just..." Lee reached for the words. "Move us into...another world? Last time I just fell into that cold place—the whole car did."

"Your friend Mal found a door. Not one we would have used. You almost died. These worlds, there are worse out there. Not to be travelled, not safe. Now, Kay'malkan, we go."

Kay shrugged and glanced at Lee. "Come then on, love, let's move."

"No," said Mrs. Stig. "Not her. You."

Lee stared at her. "But...what?"

"They are hunting her," the woman said heavily. "The doctor must stay with us. We need her."

"They're hunting me, too," Lee said.

Mrs. Stig grunted an affirmative and turned away, no longer interested. Stig squatted on his haunches, gesturing for her to join him. It seemed a position he was infinitely comfortable in, but she sat down hard when she tried it, too tired to keep her balance.

"There is a place we are working at, where our engines will gather many doors so we can close them all. Sew the world's wounds." The brief poetry of that startled Lee, unless of course he meant it literally. "Dr. Khan must be with us there. We need her thoughts."

"Right," Lee agreed. "But look—"

"We thought she would be safe with you," Stig said, not ungently. "It is not so. She is not safe anywhere, but you they can track."

Lee blinked at him. His smile was engaging, friendly, utterly merciless.

"You are touched by other places. We cannot hide you from them because of this. We thought we could use you, but the..." He cocked an eye at Mrs. Stig, who filled in "Molecular resonance frequencies" like someone reading off a card. "Yes, that," he agreed. "You and us together, we are too much. Like a beacon for them to find. Scent of too many places all together. The doctor is better off on her own. So you must go."

239

"Go where?" Lee said. "They know where I live."

"Do not go there," Stig advised. "Lose yourself in this place, this city, if you can. If they find you, you cannot say where we are if you do not know." He looked sad then, eyes as mournful as a spaniel's. "Most likely they will find us anyway, but we will hide until the doors are ready to open, then we break and run. Perhaps we get out."

"And me...?" Lee whispered.

Stig stared at her, and she realized that was her answer. Nothing for her.

"Now wait a minute," Dr. Khan said, plucking at Mrs. Stig's voluminous sleeve. "You can't just cut her loose, love. Not now we've seen the fuckery that's out there."

"You, we must keep close," Stig said carefully. "Mughushuper died, for you. I will die for you, if that is what time requires. Every world under this sky will collapse. Every mind like yours must be brought, to find the answer. Or no more minds, no more worlds, no more skies."

"No," Khan said.

But Lee shook her head. "Go, and I'll...I know people I can hide with. Or I'll get on a train and keep moving, maybe. And when you're gone to...wherever, they won't care about me."

"Oh, love." Khan hugged her impulsively. Stig was already making vague gestures to get her moving, and Lee decided she had to expedite matters, backing away from the unlikely trio.

I will just keep moving, she told herself. *I'm at Paddington Station. Circle Line, here I come.*

The Circle Line was a mistake.

At first, there were plenty of people. She rode the rails

beneath London, watching the bright partygoers, the late shoppers, the tourists get on and off. It was wonderfully mundane. She could be assured that in the midst of this regular human activity nothing bad could burst out and assault her, not men with guns, not monsters.

Later, her carriage was half empty, everyone out having fun and not yet ready to come home. The screech of the brakes, the chimes and trills of the doors, the rising electric pitch of the motor as the train moved off—all seemed to fall into a grand void waiting somewhere beneath, each sound increasingly sepulchral. Lee huddled in her seat, sole occupant of her row. At the far end of the carriage, half a dozen suited men were on their way to or from business drinks, but when one of them glanced her way she imagined guns in hidden holsters. They didn't look like professional mobsters, but... what did she know?

Maybe the podgy guy was half a dozen weasels in a man suit.

She barked out a horrified laugh, and then they were all staring at her. She wanted to get off, right now, right here. If only the train would stop, she'd force the doors, she'd...

With a squealing metal sound the train lurched to a halt between stations. Maybe they needed to let the train ahead cruise out of Farringdon before they could shunt in. She looked out of the window and there was only a busy darkness, the suggestions of ranked cables and pipes that might be the infrastructure of the Underground, or might lead down to twisting warrens where the rodent-people lived. Their world had that same unfinished, industrial look, made for function and not aesthetics. The dark writhed just beyond her view, full of motion: hairy, sneaking, snaking bodies. The glints could be her carriage's lights reflected in the thick glass, or gleams from the lenses of the rat-weasels' gas masks.

They could be out there. Surely they were out there. This subterfuge with the trains hadn't shaken them from her trail. She'd played right into their hands.

With a tortured groan the train was moving. Lee was rigid in her seat. She'd seen them. She knew she'd seen them. And she also knew they hadn't been there. It was her imagination conjuring things from the dark.

"You all right?"

One of the suited men was leaning over her. She whimpered, deep in her throat. He was probably only trying to be kind. He didn't deserve to be screamed at, kicked. She thought of him later, dumbly watching the crazy girl who'd pelted through the doors the moment they'd opened. Last time he'd try to help someone, probably. On the street outside Farringdon station, she leant against the wall and tried to get her breathing under control.

It had been like this after Mal vanished. It hadn't been the underground dark, though. Instead, she'd avoided parks, open spaces, trees. She hadn't wanted to leave her room. Post-traumatic stress disorder, they'd said: a perfectly normal response to a harrowing experience. And she really had been fighting PTSD, but the harrowing experience had been anything but normal. And now she had seen a world of seething rodents overflowing from their cramped tunnels into her own world. And where was safe, if things like that could happen?

Lee hurried away from the station, wondering where the hell she could go.

She toyed with the idea of a hostel. But if she used her

card, her pursuers might trace her. They could trace her by magic super-detectors anyway, but would using her card speed things up? Make things easier? Maybe they had a deal with her credit card company too. Selling her personal data to the rat-men sounded like something that banks did all the time. In the end, a night off the dark streets seemed worth the risk. She took out all the cash she could, a depressingly small amount, then threw the card away—just sent it sailing off onto the road, as though that would make any difference.

She found a hostel in King's Cross and was starving by then. The receptionist sold her coffee and a packet of cheese and onion crisps. Her smile almost had Lee breaking down in tears, just at that little human contact and kindness.

When she collapsed on the bed, she was physically shaking, unable to stop. Everyone else in the dormitory was there with coats, backpacks, luggage: students and travellers on the cheap, come to explore the jewel of British cities. None of them had come to see squirming hordes of weasel soldiers with razorblade guns or dinosaurs in ice-age forests. Or even the weird, broad-faced men and women who made magic out of thin air and were trying to save the universe.

Her panic was a boat in a swelling sea. It kept her afloat as long as it could, but at last sleep dragged her down so that dreams could take up where real life had left off.

Later, she jolted awake when a weight hit the mattress at her feet. Lee froze, her mind a collection of jumbled fragments, reality and fantasy understandably difficult to separate. Someone was sitting on the bed in the dark. Someone had found her.

"Please." The word escaped her lips in a whisper. She wasn't even sure what she was begging for.

"Hey." A light sprang up, the glowing screen of a phone. It flashed in Lee's eyes, illuminating a pale, pointed face.

"Come on," Mal said. "It's time to go."

III

They'd kept Alison in a rather nice apartment at first. Some rich family's city pad, plainly not currently occupied by the owners. The furniture was covered with dust sheets the squatters hadn't bothered to take off, though now they were rucked and snagged with being sat or lain on. Maybe the family were off on a month-long Caribbean cruise. Or maybe they'd come back early and been murdered by the intruders. That the squatters were capable of murder was something Alison well knew.

She had seen them before, of course, in photographs, video and images scattered across otherwise unconnected case files. There were half a dozen of them here. At first they'd all looked alike, but a few hours' familiarity let her tell them apart by their faces, expressions, voices. Men and women, all squat, heavily built, no six-packs or thigh gaps amongst them, living in the space between other people's lives.

They could do impossible things too, like spirit her out of her apartment into a dry, dead-looking place. She'd seen badlands and canyons where only grey-white lichen relieved the orange of the rock. One of them had lumped her over his shoulder and then they'd run with her, leaving her with a view of the barren horizon, of a bronze sky where no birds flew. The heat beat at her, a true, dry-desert heat, not just London's midsummer burn. Her mouth turned into sandpaper within minutes, and nobody was talking to her. She passed in and out as they ran, constantly jolted back and forth across the line of consciousness. At one point, she felt a connection, a sudden space where the invisible walls of the world had been. Had she spoken to Julian? Was she about to wake and find herself back at home with Simms? But the next jolt found her still over the shoulder of her abductor, seeing their line of tracks stretching across the dust, crossed only by things like centipedes and roaches bigger than her hand.

Just when she felt her stomach was so bruised from the jolting that something would rupture, they stopped and the woman carrying her did…something. And Alison felt the shift, the connection to *elsewhere*. Not opening a door, but finding a hairline fracture and then applying the metaphysical crowbar until there was enough space to step through.

They stepped through. They had been high on a jumble of rocks, and Alison tried to brace for a fall; instead they came out on someone's shrouded sofa like clowns out of a car. There were broad, coarse faces on all sides, low voices murmuring greetings. She saw big square fingers reach out to touch one another—shoulder, arm, face. They were all tense, all tired-looking. She was dumped into an armchair, braced for flight before she saw that escape would have to wait: the window was shuttered, the door closed, and the apartment was packed full of the stoic physicality of its occupants. The least of them could have ripped her in half.

The woman who had taken her loomed, her face unreadable because it was designed for a different language of expression, one with few loan words from human.

"You will not be harmed." A voice deep as a man's, deeper.

245

"You were searching for us. We must not be found. When we are done here, you will be left. Try to leave us and we will have to kill you."

Alison glowered at her. "Who are you? What are you even *doing*?" she demanded.

A tall Pakistani woman came in from the next room, swathed in a towel, her hair up. Her make-up was incongruously immaculate, as though she'd repainted her face the moment she got out of the shower. Alison goggled at her.

"Kay Amal Khan," she choked out.

"Oh, hello, love," the fugitive scientist said awkwardly. "Who're you then?"

"MI-bloody-five," Alison snapped. "What in God's name is going on?"

"You've kidnapped the government?" Khan demanded. "What are you people *doing*? They'll be looking for her."

One of them grunted, something like a laugh. "Already they are looking for you. More than anyone looks for her."

"But *she* was looking for us," the woman standing over Alison added. "She had a resonant connection. The Ice recognized her and gave her access. She would have found us for your 'government' first. So, she is here, with us. Until we can move you from this place to where you need to be."

"Which is where?" said Khan. "Look, love, you said come, and I came. But this is getting out of fucking hand!"

"Tonight," the woman promised. "We get out tonight." She glared at the others and added something in her muttering language, which Alison interpreted as, "You clowns get ready to move out."

Alison watched them. They weren't feverishly making bombs or taking photographs of secret documents. Most of them were just sitting about on the plushly carpeted floor. But she had the sense of intense preparation nonetheless, a mindfulness, a mental discipline as obvious as if they were stepping through the graceful poses of tai chi.

Alison was well aware that her hierarchy of needs was some way off Maslow's, and at the top of it was *information*. She angled for Khan's eye until the scientist wandered over.

"Listen," she hissed, "I don't know who these people are, or what they've offered you, but they are not your friends." She was aware that everyone there could doubtless hear every word. It was ridiculous, but she persisted. "They're enemies of the state."

Khan sat on the arm of the sofa and brought out a half-empty pack of cigarettes. "Oh, love, I don't think they care about 'the state.'" She made a joke of it, but there was a hollowness to her manner, a fragility that spoke of having seen too many things.

"Doctor—Kay, please. They're dangerous people, you don't know—"

"I've seen them kill someone already," Khan said with almost desperate cheer. "Or at least punch the bastard hard enough to do the job. And they did for Billy White and his friends. Would it help to say they've only brutally murdered people in my defence? People and...things."

"Kay, my name is Alison Matchell. I'm a colleague of Julian Sabreur. He's trying to find you. If you get the chance, call him. He'll keep you safe." Khan had lit up by then—and Alison couldn't fight an instinctive flinch as the woman turned her head and exhaled a plume of smoke.

Khan saw it. "Don't worry, love," she said, deadpan. "Most likely none of us'll live long enough to regret it."

"So much for their assurances that I'll be safe," Alison said, trying to match her bantering tone.

"Oh, not them. It's just the universe is going to end. And I'd like to laugh that off but they showed me a proof. Elegant, it was, working from first principles. Must have given them a real headache to put it into a notation I'm familiar with, but they did a good job. Whole universe, falling in on itself like a broken ice sculpture." Her non-smoking hand made a crushing gesture to demonstrate.

"That's mad," Alison said flatly.

"We're all mad here," Khan rejoined archly. "Your life has been eminently sane recently, has it?"

Alison opened her mouth, thinking, *Carried across a red rock ruin, through the wall of my kitchenette; touching some frozen bloody invisible supercomputer with my mind*, and shut it again.

"You know what I was working on, Alice?" Khan leant on the sofa back and crossed her legs primly, shades of moll to Alison's gangster. "Cryptic Informational Transformation Space. Codebreaking, actually. We wondered if you could take computations out of regular space and put this data into a purely theoretical, extradimensional space. If you could see and work with that data in this space, you could basically waltz past any security. There would be no barrier between you and the information you wanted to get your grubby little mitts on. Government very interested, obviously, threw lots of money at it, paid off my mortgage and then some, believe me, love. Only it didn't fucking work and then they cut funding. Which was frustrating because I *know* I could have got it to work. However, my peers said it couldn't be done, and the review board listened to them.

Except it can be done, because that's how these jokers called me—straight to my phone without a network or anything, using CIT-Space. No passwords, no barriers. It turns out the space isn't so *theoretical*. Those extra dimensions exist, at ninety degrees to everything else. And I can see I'm losing you."

"Dimensions," Alison prompted gamely.

"Height, breadth, depth—forget time for a second, because that's the screwy one. But there's another direction of travel involved here, or *from* here to *there*. There are other worlds, but they are still versions of this one. Branches, this lot call them. Very big on nature imagery, real murder-hippies."

"Parallel worlds?"

"Other Earths," Khan confirmed. "Always have been, maybe, separate, inviolate. Except that's the problem. There are fissures, they say—there are spaces between the worlds that can be used for CITS-style fuckery. And there are also... collisions. Intrusions, basically. The different worlds are now leaking into one another through these fissures, and it's getting worse. This lot have a way better understanding of all this—it's basically National Curriculum over there, they do GCSEs in it probably. So they're trying to work out if there's a cause—and whether it can be stopped. And for that they recruited me. I was probably easier to get hold of here than Xian or Ravichandra, who are the only other people in the field who might get their heads around it. Or maybe they have them as well."

"Or maybe they want to control whatever it is. Capturing the only people who could stop them could be a good prelude to interdimensional invasion," Alison pointed out.

"My, you are a suspicious one," Khan said.

One of the men abruptly slapped his hands together, standing and shaking his shoulders. His breath plumed, and Alison saw a rime of frost on the seams of his torn shirt.

"That—what is that?" she hissed urgently. "The cold, the... What are they doing?"

"Ah, well, love." Khan snagged a coffee cup off a nearby table and deposited a knuckle of ash into it. "That is why they're not here with a room full of high-tech nonsense, isn't it? Apparently there's—"

"A computer," Alison said. Khan stared at her, and she went on, "I'm right, aren't I? An... interdimensional computer. That's what they're using to communicate. But it's not reliable, is it? It comes and goes, and so do these cracks, these doors." She thought of the stockbroker computer. It had been using CIT-Space to read the entire market, as though it was laid out conveniently on a map. "They're going to open these fissures of yours to kidnap you back to wherever the hell they come from. Does that sound like they're interested in fixing the problem?"

Khan regarded her for a stretched moment, one eyebrow cocked. "Well..." she started, and then everyone around them stood up, dusting themselves off. For a moment Alison thought she'd found the secret of secrets, and now they were going to kill her. But instead there had been some silent, independent signal, and now it was time to go.

There weren't any handy interdimensional portals this time, so they took a minicab, making Alison feel she'd been consigned to some kind of death by bathos. The vehicle that pulled up outside their swanky apartment block at what must have been past midnight was a big people carrier. Only four of her captors could fit in, along with her and Khan. She tried to catch the attention of the driver, to silently communicate that a kidnapping was ongoing, but the man didn't seem to use his rear-view mirror, alarming in itself.

So they could walk into and out of my flat, but it's by road across London? She had a ready answer to that, if she thought about it. *Because I found the cracks and pried at them, didn't I. I helped make a space.* She had been contributing to her own downfall all the way.

When the minicab stopped, she fumbled a card from her pocket and left it on the seat, hoping that someone would call the office. When they were outside on the pavement, though, one of the big men just tucked the card judiciously back into her hand with a disappointed expression.

She heard Khan make a surprised noise. "Wasn't expecting this. You here to look up some relatives?" They were standing outside the grounds of the Natural History Museum in Kensington. *Not so bloody far from my flat, for God's sake.*

They were bundled down the steps into the garden, towards the main entrance, and Alison realized that this was *it*. Whatever piece of grand theft, espionage or ritual sacrifice they meant, it was to happen in this ludicrously grandiose setting. She tried to shout, then. It was surprisingly hard to, because it felt so very un-British. Yes, she was being abducted by murderous brutes, but was that really any reason to compromise her dignity? And yet she got a yell out as they hustled her down the stairs. She shouted for help at the top of her voice. Cried out until the echo came back to her from the ornate walls of the huge building. There must be security, police—*someone*.

There was a distant jeering cry, her only response: some late-night partygoer who'd interpreted her yells as drunken revelry. Beyond that, nothing, and a hand like a lead weight on her shoulder.

"No more of that." The big man looked embarrassed for her.

"I will not cooperate with you," she told his broad, brutal face. "You're going to have to kill me."

If anything, the prospect seemed to depress him.

"All be over soon," he promised, which probably wasn't the reassurance he intended.

Then they were up the grand steps and through the front doors, held open by another of the same ilk, this one wearing a uniform jacket over his shoulders like a short cape. *Museum security, only I can't see him getting past the interview stage.* She felt sick, and hoped the jacket's original owner was all right somehow.

There was another pair already in the entrance hall, beneath the arching blue whale skeleton suspended above. A third was stationed up the stairs by Darwin's statue, as though she had a critique to give about *On the Origin of Species*. The team who had brought in Alison and Khan started touching fingers and faces again, something between a catch-up and a business handshake.

"Stay here. Don't make trouble, please," Alison's captor said. "Then we are gone, and you can be home, with your pet." His wide face contorted itself, burlesquing sincerity. "This is all for the good. We are not your enemies. We will not hurt you. Kay'mal Khan has told you what this is. Do not interfere or it is dangerous. Please."

The hairs on her arms and the back of her neck goose-bumped, and she believed him about the danger. She could feel the volumes, the spaces all around her. Not the alcoves and exhibits, the vaulted ceiling overhead, the vacancy of the whale's ribcage, but *space*. She could sense it, through and within the walls and all around. Her captors, all of them, were taking stations around the chamber, reaching out for... nothing, heavy brows furrowed in concentration. But she felt it, the icy pinprick of contact within her mind. The computer, whatever it truly was, was here, or not-quite-here. Just as her captors were connecting to it, so could she, and she had the sudden revelation that it wasn't *theirs*. They were parasites, as she was. Either an unimaginable third party controlled it or the thing was its own master.

She felt she had the whole universe at her beck and call, then, although it would cost her soul. Instead she fell back on her instincts. She was an agent of the Crown, a defender of the state. She reached out to Julian.

IV

It wasn't the first urgent work-related call he'd taken past midnight. He kept the phone by his bed for a reason. Julian's job didn't keep social hours. Still, *If this is just some goddamn telemarketer I'm going to...*

He'd got one syllable into "Hello," as Josie shifted irritably beside him, when a familiar voice jolted him awake.

"Spiker, listen to me, not got much time." Alison sounded as though she was speaking from far away, from some vast chamber.

"Matchbox?" He yelped the nickname out, and Josie was abruptly still, awake and listening.

"Spiker, I'm at the Natural History Museum, in the front

hall. Khan is here too, and about...eight, maybe ten hostiles. Plug-uglies. Almost certainly armed. Spiker..." He could hear her thoughts click into place as she looked ahead to what was going to happen. "Look, wait—no," she said, as he fought to get dressed one-handed. "Call it in, Spiker. Don't do anything stupid, not for me. I'm not in immediate danger." But the tremor in her voice belied that, or he thought it did.

"I'm coming," he said. "With whatever help I can get."

She was telling him not to; he could hear how appalled she was at what she'd set in motion. But he couldn't not go, not for Matchbox. She was like a part of him.

He got as far as the bedroom door before Josie turned on the lamp. She'd heard his part of the conversation, and she could make a solid stab at the rest. She stared at him—there in a dark cardigan and his work trousers, belt missing a loop because he'd fumbled it in the dark. He couldn't imagine what his face looked like.

"Julian," she said softly, as though about to talk him down off a ledge.

"I'm sorry," he said.

"This can't go on."

He felt the threshold keenly, the one he'd always lived on. The life of home and family on one side, the taut wire of security and country on the other, an invisible space always just an arm's reach away that could rip him from normality at any moment. The world Alison belonged to, as though she was his fairy paramour.

"It's not—" he tried, but found himself unwilling or unable even to say what it wasn't.

"Just let me in," Josie said softly. "You never have. Tell me.

Be honest with yourself, even. Have you even done that? Looked in the mirror and admitted what's going on in your head?"

The very idea had him shrinking away, and for a vile moment he was pathetically grateful there was a real emergency, something he had to act on *now, immediately.* Just so he didn't have to deal with or think about things.

"I'm sorry," again, utterly inadequate, an admission of failure, and then he was pelting down the stairs, out the door, jabbing at the car fob to unlock it. He hated driving in London, but he couldn't wait around for a taxi at this hour. He needed to be moving, to have even the illusion of progress.

On the way he called the emergency line at work and reported that Alison had called and what she'd said. They had a lot of questions; he had no answers. He'd already seen there was no record of the call on his phone. He then cut them off before they could put him through to someone with the authority to stop him.

He called the police next, regular 999. He reported seeing suspicious activity at the Natural History Museum. Fake suspicions came effortlessly to his lips, anything to get the closest beat officer over there. He felt a cold stone in his stomach with the knowledge that he might have sent good people in on false pretences to get killed by foreign agents. *But Alison.* She would hate him for it, but he could only drive so fast and get so far. She'd said "not in immediate danger," but he remembered Billy White, beaten to death.

He put in a call to Royce, got no answer and left a message. He called the office again, telling them he had reason to believe a terrorist act was taking place at the museum, with hostages. He was en route, he told them, and needed any support they could give. After he hung up, his phone rang again, heavy with official forbiddance. He didn't answer it.

He was going to be disciplined for this, he knew. Possibly he'd lose his job, get kicked out of the Service; probably he'd lose his current position. If he got Alison back it would be worth it.

Illegal parking was the least of his problems, when he reached the museum. That done, he faced the great edifice of the building, louring over the floodlit gardens, the butterfly tent, all quiet as they awaited the next day's tourists and schoolchildren. If memory served, from when he'd brought John here two years before, the main hall was through those heavy front doors. Which simultaneously made it the most obvious and therefore risky entrance. He cursed indecisively.

Then the high windows over the paired entrance doors flashed with an unreal light, a radiance that put him in mind of sunlight through ice or deep water, of dead things phosphorescing as they decayed. Whatever it was, it was happening.

He remembered the side entrance—he'd gone in with John that way, to dodge the queue at the main doors, and so they'd missed the proper grand vista you were supposed to get when you visited. Well, this time whoever was keeping watch from that vista would miss him.

Sprinting round the corner up Exhibition Road, he also missed the pair who arrived ten seconds later at the main doors.

Interlude: The Aeronauts

Excerpt from *Other Edens:
Speculative Evolution and Intelligence* by
Professor Ruth Emerson of the
University of California

This branch deviates from the trunk of time in a barren world, ripe for the taking. A reptile world, where a dozen lineages of scaly beasts bellow and trumpet and roar. Crocodiles, lizards, even gracile runners whose lineages will explode into the great dinosaur dynasties.

But the terrible lizards will only ever be livestock in this world. Sentience will arise without them.

There is still a great deal of desert, as this Earth claws its way out of the Permian. While the coasts lengthen as the continents peel apart, much of the global real estate is barren. There is an archipelago of life scattered across a sea of dust: oases, rivers, the wind-shadows of mountains where meagre rain falls all at once and in one season. Nothing can grow too large or too numerous lest it starve or parch. Communities spring up where the resources pool, wither away when they are spent. Lives like tumbleweeds, constantly drifting. Slim pickings for an emergent civilization, surely. And yet...

This is truly the age of reptiles. They take to the seas, and test the land's limits on speed, size and savagery. And the air, which represents a bounty of protein if you can only get to it. Insects remain plentiful, and a nimble airborne predator can eat its fill with a little aerobatics.

Here, the aviators are reptiles too. They begin as little

flapping things the size of a mouse, barely larger than the insects they so gamely attack on the wing. Nesting sites are few and far, and so they form jostling, screeching colonies wherever they can lay their eggs safely. Like many bird species in other branches, they are shoehorned into socialization by the sheer necessity of putting up with the neighbours. Defending their eggs from predators and peers who want their land leads to strong pair bonding and egalitarian parental care. Each generation spends longer in the nest and learns more from their parents. They learn flight, what to eat, how to interact with others. They learn that this sound means danger, that sound is a challenge, this other is an entreaty. Soon enough, a language.

Fortune favours bigger brains and bigger wings. To a human eye the creatures they become are goblinish: stick-thin limbs wrapped in leathery cloaks of patagia, one long finger swept back behind them like a gentleman's sword even as the other clever digits are at work building nests or working stone. Their heads are outlandish, too large for the rest of them—pushing the physics of flight to the limit to allow for more thought.

In this parched world, the desert is a riot of thermals to aid them in expeditions, and below are a thousand ecosystems that can never breed a predator to threaten them. They skewer swimmers with barbed sticks, winkle burrowers from holes. They bring larger animals down with rocks dropped from a height and butcher them with sharp stones.

In our own far more recent history, a clever kind of upright ape broke nodules of flint apart—creating keen, serrated edges to take apart the world. It was a fundamental building block of our success, and yet for a long time there was no more to it than that. When our handy ape ancestors had finished with the task, they finished with the tool, discarded it into the brush. Next time they would knap a new one from whatever was at hand. There is a place in our minds now that tools—made things, things of value—occupy, and there was a time when our ancestors' minds had no such place. Nothing was ever for keeps, and there was no tomorrow for the tool-makers.

The pterosaurs have the same limitation, but ruthlessly imposed by physics. They can make things quickly, envisage what tool they need for what task, but they cannot carry a toolkit around. If they hunt, then their little capacity must be saved for the prize, not the means of getting it. They are trapped in a cycle of transience, and their technology is limited by what they can make *here* and *now*. Perhaps one of them thinks, every so often, *Did I not have a better stone last time I did this? If only I had that stone today...*

Their civilization is supreme for a long time across the dry areas. They are constantly visiting each other's colonies, inter-breeding, enacting raucous diplomacy, feasting on fermented fruit stolen from the wetlands (where the prey gets too big to hunt, where their hero-cycles and myths come from). Their lives are too brief and impermanent to see change coming.

It is a grand and good change, from any long-term perspective, although there will be no eyes to look back, ten million years on, to make such a judgement. The world is healing its wounds from the great dying time, and the deserts shrink before the determined advance of green life. From the point of view of global biodiversity, it is a triumph. But for those species that form the crisis ecosystem, adapted to the post-Permian paucity, it is a death sentence. The pterosaurs' mastery of their world shrinks and shrinks again as the time of land giants comes.

Along with the re-establishment of more varied and complex biomes, the continental shifts bring wild changes in weather. There are years—even decades—without rain, and then decades where the rain never ceases from year to year, the storm winds dashing any fragile leather-winged creature out of the skies. Perhaps they prayed, the poor pterosaurs. Perhaps they moved on and moved on, leaving their roosts and eggs and offspring too young to fly. There was no single event to undo them, just a stacked tower of stressors and adverse circumstances that obliterated their culture and civilization. They leave only a few caves etched with their beautiful, elegant drawings, a few bones, a few discarded pieces of sharp flint.

9.

I

"So you met the Nissa!"

It was hard to hear Mal over the rush of the wind and the hairdryer whine of the moped's engine. A moped Mal had stolen, apparently, and when Lee had stared at her—Mal had always talked a good revolution but seldom acted on it—she'd just shrugged.

"What?" she'd asked, standing by the purloined vehicle with her weight on one hip. "Possibly I used an ancient supercomputer from another dimension to hotwire a Vespa. So?"

Lee had paused then, still in the hostel doorway. Mal was a skinny silhouette, wearing a torn leather jacket, stained T-shirt and wrinkled jeans, with big bovver boots. Hair too long and the wrong colour, face too thin even for her, body too muscled. She was like someone else, a stranger.

She grinned, and *that* had survived all the intervening years and the dinosaurs. Lee felt her heart kick.

"No helmets?" she noted, approaching Mal with caution.

"Forgot to steal any," Mal said. "I'd promise to go careful, but I was only reintroduced to the internal combustion engine about four weeks ago. Not used to having a passenger, either." She hooked a leg over the seat. "Get on, and hold tight."

"Where are we going?" But Lee was already behind her.

She hesitated slightly before putting her arms about Mal's waist, feeling the new hardness of four years of exercise, the breadth of her shoulders now they'd filled out. Forty-nine per cent of her brain insisted she get off the moped and demand answers. But the rest was just shrieking out its excitement and didn't care when Mal revved the moped and cut across the nose of a taxi.

So you met the Nissa. "Is that what Stig is?" Lee shouted above the slipstream.

"Right," Mal yelled back. "They found me. Recruited me because they had work to do here. Regretting it, I reckon."

"Four weeks?" Lee shouted.

"What?"

"You've been back four weeks?"

There was a change in the set of Mal's shoulders, achingly familiar: the girl who couldn't quite close the gap between herself and her emotions.

"I wanted to call earlier, but..." And there was no end to that sentence.

"It's okay," Lee said. And though surely this wasn't the time or the place, she added, "I slept with other people." Only two in four years, only one of them more than once. It had felt like cheating, even with Mal consigned to "presumed dead."

"Don't care!" Mal shot back. "And I'm sorry!"

"Not your fault. You didn't go on purpose!" *Did you?* But Lee felt that any ill-feeling, guilt or worry she could generate was being left behind in their wake.

"No, sorry for the trouble, now. Sorry for bringing this to you. My fault!"

Lee leant against her, cheek to Mal's hard shoulder, and if

there were tears of sadness or joy, their breakneck progress whirled those away as well.

She'd had no idea where Mal was going, but she was guessing at some secret den, a speakeasy, a criminal dive, or perhaps out of London altogether. Just out until there was no city penning them in, somewhere where there were trees, open space, rolling fields. Not the august frontage of the Natural History Museum, in short.

"Um, what?" she asked, when Mal had brought the over-stressed moped to a shuddering stop. "Seriously?"

"That's where the show's at," Mal said, and grinned. It was a strained one, though. That pallor was not just life in a cold climate. "They're in there, right now, the Nissa. They're doing their thing, trying to save the world. Worlds."

"And old Richard Owen just happened to build the museum on a... magical portal?" Lee demanded.

"Course not," Mal said. She hopped onto the back of a convenient bench and went up the railings with the casual ease of a squirrel, crouching atop the forked cast iron to reach down for Lee.

Where has she been that she can do that? Lee's own ascent was markedly less graceful, but then they were over and hurrying for the cathedral-like gothic of the building itself. "Thing is," Mal cast back at her as they hurried towards the gothic entrance, "why here, in particular, is a bit of a misunderstanding, really. Bit embarrassing. The Nissa *thought* the same as you, see? Took one look at all that concentrated junk from the past and assumed, yes, this is where the people of this world access the wider universe, or some such."

"They didn't understand what the word 'museum' meant over the door?" Lee said.

"Not from round 'ere, are they, guv?" Even after all this time, Mal's fake cockney was still terrible. "Anyway." They pushed at the door and were greeted by none other than Kay Amal Khan, wearing a grey uniform jacket and carrying a torch.

"I told you—" she started. "Oh, it's you, love. I just saw off a policeman. Told him we were all fine, burglars fled. I'm 'security,' see. Get inside before they come back and arrest you."

She trotted them past the desk and into the great hall, beneath the whale exhibit and flanked by a miscellany of dead relics from the past hundred million years. There were a fair number of Stigs there. Lee watched as they went through the motions of setting something up, striding between invisible workstations, reaching into the air as though trying to shape their dreams into reality. And there *was* reality beneath their hands, she saw. There was a blue-white depth to the air that fell away into chasms uncharted. Their breath plumed; the air was icy, though they didn't seem to care.

A Mrs. Stig stomped up to stare at Mal; Lee thought it might have been the woman from the rail tunnels.

"So, you brought her," she said, not pleased.

"I said I would. It's my price. It was always my price," Mal told her rebelliously. "We're getting out with you, when it all lights up in here."

"And if she doesn't want to stay, on the far side?" Mrs. Stig said, with a glower at Lee.

"Then I'll speak to the Fishnet and it'll find a door back, sooner or later. Only, if the universe is going to pop like a soap bubble, what does it matter which world we're on? Or

you save them all and we have all the time in all the worlds."
She was speaking rapidly, angrily. *Defensively*, Lee recognized.
This was the Mal of old, caught with her hand in the cookie
jar, aggressively trying to talk her way out of trouble.

But apparently it worked, because Mrs. Stig looked pointedly elsewhere. She went to help with the ephemeral set-up,
dismissing both of them.

"Do you...not get on with these Nissa?" Lee said.

"I was useful to them. I could go places without people
staring and pointing. So when they found me, they recruited
me, honorary Nissa agent, right?" Mal said. "Only they don't
own me, and they can't control me. I can make things work
too, now. And they don't like conflict, either. So I bloody get
away with it." Another taut grin, which Lee tried to match.
Her hand crept towards Mal's, feeling as though she was
reaching across more than mere physical distance. The return
grip was strong, calloused, unbelievably welcome. *The Girl
Who Came Back.*

She looked about the room, feeling the invisible machinery
as though it towered over them, past the suspended ocean
giant to the twin row of skylights in the ceiling. There was
one other non-Stig, besides themselves and Khan: a white
woman with fair hair. She was sitting on the ground and
hugging her knees, plainly not wanting to be there. The
nearest Stig was keeping an eye on her.

"Who—?" she asked.

"No idea," Mal said. "Not security or staff. Last I heard—"

The room shivered and Mal stopped speaking. There was
a drop in temperature that had frost sparkling on the columns
and glass cases.

"Mal," Lee whispered. "What are they *doing* here?"

"Great experiment. Trying to seal a load of fractures between the worlds, all at once, then see if it sticks. This mob here, and probably another lot on their side. Close the doors between the parallels, hopefully with everyone on the 'right' side of them. Heal the universe, right? Or fuck it up some more. Although from what I hear, there's not much more *up* left to fuck."

II

Julian had anticipated having to break into the museum's side entrance, but someone had already crowbarred the lock, with enough twisted damage to suggest they hadn't been subtle about it.

He coaxed the door open, ready for any sudden movement, but the hall beyond was still as the grave. Slipping in, he took cover by the security desk, glancing at the exhibits leering from their shadowy nooks: here a Pteranodon skeleton spread out as though for autopsy, there a sand-blasted baby rhinoceros tipped on its back, withered stumpy legs in the air.

The side entrance lacked the grand hall and immediate access to the dinosaur wing, but the place's interior designers had done their best to impress. Beyond the poised skeleton of a Stegosaurus, bony tail raised high in threat, a stilled escalator led into a globe of jagged metal plates. An Earth, Julian thought grimly, either coalescing or shattering into pieces.

The corpse on the floor probably wasn't a regular exhibit.

He approached cautiously, in case the big man was playing possum. Dead was dead, though: a hefty, big-boned sprawl, one cheek pressed to the ground, eyes wide open. Julian recognized one of the Plug-uglies, though by his best guess not one he'd seen before. Not one he'd see again, either, outside the morgue. Someone had shot the luckless man in the back of the head with something small enough not to leave an exit wound.

The body was warm, loose-joined: recent. That complicated things, because, sure, the Plug-uglies might have had a falling-out amongst themselves, but everything about this body and the forced door said aggressive intrusion rather than internecine struggle.

Julian had trained with handguns as part of his job, and for a while he'd kept up membership of a pistol shooting range. He did not, however, own a gun, a forbearance someone else nearby plainly lacked.

There was a stack of maps at the desk, and he took one, turning it about until the layout clicked in his mind. *In the big front hall*, Alison had said. He slipped between the Stegosaurus and the base of the elevator, cutting a path past the silent cafe and a few rooms of rocks, coming out into a long, narrow hall lined with the flattened bones of sea monsters. From ahead, he thought he heard the scuff of footsteps, and a hooked shadow reached into his peripheral vision, a monstrous claw curling for him.

He jerked back, almost falling into a plesiosaur. The looming threat behind him turned out to be just the skeleton of a ground sloth, huge and sad, motionless as it reached for a branch forever denied it. Julian cursed himself silently. For a moment then, he just saw the ranked sea monsters on the wall: the bones of ancient deep-dwelling dead with their huge, bone-ringed eyes. Then they seemed to ripple across the wall, as though testing the strength of the rock that imprisoned them, as though the long-lost currents of Jurassic seas were turning them in their graves. Julian was suddenly ten years old and terrified, just for a moment, waiting for it all to come to life—just like he'd *known* everything did in museums after the visitors were shooed out.

He took a step back and went ankle-deep into a puddle. With a yelp he stumbled away, seeing past—*through*—the wall of sea monsters to a mounded, muddy vista, stubbly with phallic fungi that grew in the shadow of enormous ragged ferns. And there were ruins: mazes of broken walls made of no substance he could name, shattered like eggshells by some unthinkable detonation. The air was abruptly sulphurous. And past where the ceiling should be, he saw a sky strung with rotten-looking clouds lit by a waning moon.

He fell to his knees. His lament for lack of a gun became one for lack of a religion. Because surely nothing short of *God* could defend him from whatever the hell *this* was.

But then even that terrifying vista faded, as though he was seeing films in multiple exposure, one past the next. The muddy, broken landscape he'd glimpsed bowed beneath the weight of what lay beyond *that*, until it gave up and tore. A vast weight of water descended on him, a rolling tidal wave ten feet high, eclipsing everything in its path. Yet it never landed.

Hands up to shield his head, he stumbled down where the gallery had been. The ichthyosaur skeletons were still visible, faded pencil sketches across the face of the rushing waters. Sometimes there was stone beneath his feet, sometimes mud, or rough ice, or the mounded fallen needles of unreal pines.

He couldn't process it, but some part of his mind didn't

need to. He was still going in the same way. He was going to find Alison, even if the map in his hand had suddenly become useless—because the entire edifice it described was coming apart like newspaper in the rain. He didn't need to know if the huge beetle ahead was part of an exhibit or an insect invader from somewhere else. He barrelled on through. And if he had to push through dense foliage that left waxy smears of sap on his hands, if he had to wade through knee-deep channels of salt-smelling water, none of it mattered. It was go forwards or go mad.

It put his worries about being fired into perspective, anyway. Although a ludicrous little voice in his head was saying, *This is why we wait for backup*, and the incredulous answering thought, *Really, this? Because we have protocols in place, do we?*

He reached the main hall, somehow, through both hell and high water. And the Plug-uglies were there, at least six of them, all doing some weird mime or ritual...except then they *were* doing something. They were making adjustments to an icy blue-black interface that existed only so long as they reached for it, and they raised actual instruments towards various side galleries and alcoves. He watched reality come and go, while they shuffled worlds as he might flick through TV channels. There were snow-swept estuaries and crevasses between unscalable walls of ice; there were oceans and tropical forests, and somehow it was all the same landscape in fancy dress. They were all versions of Londons on top of Londons, Londons where London had never been raised. He saw ruins again, lifted up and torn down by an aesthetic he could never appreciate. He saw a hamlet of low, pale buildings clustered about a castle that Mad King Ludwig would have baulked at. He saw cramped chambers within a metropolis that extended above and to all sides, seething with thousands of great rats forced together cheek by whiskery jowl, gnawing at one another and clawing for space, for air.

But past all of these horrors and wonders, he saw Alison, crouched beside one of the Plug-uglies. He saw Khan, too, looking tight-faced but apparently far more comfortable with what was going on than he was. He saw Lisa Pryor, for God's sake, and the girl from the security footage, Elsinore Mallory. The whole gang was together.

Then he saw the other intruders. They stood at the head of the grand stone steps at the hall's back, past Darwin's benevolent gaze. Julian saw half a dozen men who had probably looked tough and nasty at the beginning of tonight's escapade but now seemed rattled to the point of losing it. The one exception was their leader, a big military type wearing one black glove. He was shoving his followers forwards, leaving a couple by the rail with guns levelled as the rest headed down the stairs.

The Plug-uglies hadn't seen them, and Julian frankly had no allegiance to either side, but their leader had been pointing at Khan, and that made them Julian's business.

III

Alison sat back and let the universe come to her. That was what it felt like, and she found she could ignore the burn of the stone beneath her as it grew colder and colder. Frost spread from her in a glittering nimbus, air twinkling with motes of rime. She was going to regret it: hypothermia or

272

frostbite loomed big in her future, but she was *understanding*.

The Plug-uglies were interacting with the same system, she could tell, and it was something far vaster than they were. Something with its own agency, that granted them access to its vast depth of computational power—the same permissions that it granted her. What she touched was only a fraction of its profundity, just as the end finger joint was to the whole human body, but she felt awed and dwarfed by it nonetheless. Not only by its reach and power, but by its ability to read her and create an interface she could comprehend.

She could see worlds stacked sideways, extending out in a direction human beings had never needed a name for until now. Not just worlds but *Earths*—each radically different… catastrophes, prodigies, monsters. The system-entity she was touching originated in one Earth, the Plug-uglies in another. And at her unspoken request she saw a model in her mind's eye: not quite the branches of a tree, because there was no central trunk, but a series of forks, showing each Earth diverging from its next neighbour. Should she ever have time to reflect, the implications would swamp her. But right now, she was lost in the adrenaline high of *knowing*, and that left her proof against the crash of revelation.

She analysed what the Plug-uglies were doing. At first she thought they were inviting all these other Earths into hers, that they were agents of chaos and that this was a terrorist attack by hitherto unthinkable means. But she could follow something of their method, now. They were exploiting pre-existing weaknesses between the worlds, interconnections which had spread like fractures through the interstitial spaces. These had once, she was shown, been hard barriers. Her kidnappers were trying to order and master them, not to exacerbate the problem but to *mend*. True, that mastery was something that could become a weapon, and who was to say that wasn't their long-term goal? Right now, though, they were trying to categorize and enumerate these breaches. They were trying to incorporate them into a schema or system which would allow them to solve all the equations with a single transformation. By this means, they could patch the wounds between their worlds. It was an experiment, she understood. Using their own science and the great icy computer she was losing herself in, these interlopers could gain purchase on the slippery faces of reality. Would that allow them to sew up each rent and tear by hand, technology being their needle and mathematics their thread?

She had just come to the bleak realization—as they had—that the answer was "no" when Julian's yell snapped her out of her reverie.

There were shots right after, and one of the Plug-uglies, a woman, was slapped off her feet, head snapping back. A couple of men were up on the stairs, shooting. Another handful were running down, heading for Dr. Khan. Even as she registered them, the man at the back seemed to miss his footing and fell...away, into that other direction. She had a sense of a great swell, a tidal wave from an Earth with radically higher sea levels, where England had been devoured by the ocean—and then he was gone. The Plug-uglies had brought all the wounds to the surface in their repair work, and Alison's own reality was just a thin skin over them.

Julian pelted out from a side gallery, missing the armed intruders' leader but bundling another man to the ground, fighting him for his pistol. The leader thundered a punch into the gut of a Plug-ugly who got in his way, which should have hit like a truck but barely staggered its victim. He followed with a gun butt to the face, though, and that was enough to get him to Khan.

Something else was coming. She felt it ramming through interdimensional space. It was an intrusion, forced through the fragmenting numberscape between worlds: a conscious effort from another Earth. She had a sense of vast, filthy machinery, of infinite maze-like warrens and massed chittering hordes.

She fell into the abyss too, feeling the ice enclose her. For a moment she saw it all, laid out like the most perfect case file—every connection annotated in such detail that one could lose a lifetime unravelling it. Dreamlike, she reached out and diverted the invading reality, sending it down a thousand blind alleys. She increased the effective distance between *here* and *there* without anything truly moving. Julian was wrestling, grabbing the other man's gun. Another intruder stood over him, lining up for a shot. But if she encouraged the ice system to turn its attention to *this* fault line... Julian never saw the space expand behind him, the hapless gunman suddenly stranded on the desert bank of a Thames that had been dry for a thousand years. And she left him there, because she was not in the mood to mess about. In that moment she was the queen of all creation and she understood everything.

The attackers' leader, the man with one black glove—save that she saw the specifications: not a glove, a prosthesis from another world—was by Khan now. He had grabbed her wrist, cuffing her savagely when she fought. He was yelling for backup, but his colleagues were terrified. The world was going mad around them and their shots were going wide. Alison decided to make their fears justified: here was a crack she could widen until it bit into the world she knew. And—

there!—one shooter vanished into a place of claw-bristling crawling things and radioactive ruins. That was enough for the other aggressor, who ran off into the museum. Probably one of the exhibits would eat the fucker, but she really didn't care about that right now.

Julian took two steps towards Khan's captor, newfound pistol levelled. He shouted a warning; of course he did. Julian Sabreur was nothing if not law-abiding, even here in this mess. He was shouting at the man to surrender.

The man with the artificial hand shot him even as he was speaking. The bullet ploughed into Julian's gut and he sat down hard, his own gun spinning away across the floor. And Alison felt her connection to the great Icenet snap shut as she screamed. She lunged for her friend. He had a baffled expression on his face, as though he couldn't remember where he'd put his keys.

The rats she had delayed arrived then: abruptly the corners of the room were seething with them. They coursed within the substance of the walls, a wave of them washing back and forth. They were hunched, half the size of a man, wearing rubbery black uniforms with gas masks and goggles and wielding ugly-looking weapons designed for use up close against crowds, because that was their entire life where they came from. They pressed and fought the bounds of reality until something tore and they spilled out into Alison's world. They seemed desperate and shaking, some of them dead from the shock. The Plug-uglies were on them quickly, utilizing weapons that unleashed silent shockwaves of sound and vibration to pulp the rodent bodies. They were all monsters, Alison decided. None of them should be here.

Julian shuddered, and she was telling him something.

Words were spilling out of her mouth in a futile attempt to patch this one wound that she cared about—sod the universe, frankly. The man who'd shot Julian glanced her way and clearly wrote her off as a threat. He was still holding Khan and shouting something about extraction, evac... A woman attacked him—Mallory, who'd been with the Plug-ugly at Khan's place before. He backhanded her contemptuously. Then the Pryor girl slammed into him. Alison felt the shift even as she saw its effects. Whatever force had brought the overspill of frantic rodent-people here now rose up like a fish through deep water, jaws agape. It opened about Khan and Pryor and the gunman, snapping shut to drag them out of this Earth and back to its own.

She felt Julian convulse, and for a sickeningly awful moment thought she'd lost him. However, he'd been watching the same thing, and she realized it was the loss of Khan that had moved him. He was trying to go after them, even though wounded, in agony. The Mallory woman was plainly of the same opinion, shouting her rage at the empty space.

But the Icenet remembered their route: Alison felt its freezing touch at her temples, as it helpfully stabbed an informational migraine into her mind. *Here* was the fracture point where that force had intersected her own reality, *here* was the crooked path that had been opened, *here*... was where they had gone.

She hugged Julian to her. He was saying something, and she hated herself for not being able to listen. She had her job, though, and she had the tools—right now in this moment and perhaps never again. Everything was so close to the surface: she could just reach out and touch it.

She reached out and touched Mallory, or asked the Ice to

open a link between them. It was a tiny stress fracture in the already mauled fabric of reality. She stabbed the information she'd been given into Mallory's mind, sharp-edged and raw. It left the woman with a map on the inside of her skull, a snapshot of reality and all its broken channels.

Go get them, she thought. And in the next instant Mallory was gone, swallowed by the world, swallowed by *a* world, and Alison could only hope it was the right one.

Then she was yelling for help, because Julian's chest was awash with blood and he was dying.

IV

When the world lurched sideways, Lee closed her eyes, holding Khan with one hand and Gym Bro Cop with the other. She was braced against the cold, but instead the world tilted and tipped her into muggy, rancid-smelling humidity. Then Gym Bro shook her hand away, like a dog with a rat, before dumping her on the hard metal floor.

She had her eyes open by then, and wished she didn't. Up until that point, the nastiest thing this whole misadventure had brought her had been the weasels as they squirmed their way from their reality into hers.

Now she'd taken the reverse trip.

She was in a claustrophobic room, the ceiling low enough that Gym Bro was stooped almost double. Dr. Khan sat at his feet, looking dazed, and Lee reached for her, trying to snag her hand again. It wasn't a rescue attempt; it was a bid for human contact. The weasel-rodent-people were all around them in the cramped gloom.

Most were in constant motion, scurrying into and out of the chamber through doorways barely a foot high, pattering along on four feet quite naturally. Others crouched at instruments that were a vast maze of buttons, levers and sliders. She saw no screens, but several operators wore whole-head masks. She had a sudden realization about the lack of space: there was no point in having big-screen TVs in this place; you'd never have the vantage point to look at the picture. Instead, everything was reduced to the invasive and immediate. The rodents were over and under each other, at everyone's elbow, under everyone's feet. They didn't look healthy either. Most of their ears had been cropped close to their skulls. Many were tailless and didn't look as though they could stand upright without something to hang on to. They wore grey, simple smocks, and the fur she saw was mangy and skewbald.

"Fuck," Gym Bro said. He looked less than delighted himself. Then he seemed to see Lee for the first time and pointed his gun at her. "If you give me any of your dinosaur shit," he spat, "I will shoot you in the head, you got that?"

Lee wished she had some dinosaur shit to give him, but she didn't see how one would fit in here.

Then the stormtroopers arrived. That was the only way she could process what she was seeing. A dozen rats in that rubbery black armour turned up, like the invaders in the museum or those under Mount Pleasant. There, the creatures had been disoriented and in pain from being shunted between realities. Now they were all brutal efficiency, shoving through the eddying throng of weasels and not sparing the rod when the menials didn't get out of their way. Lee saw flashes of dagger-sharp incisors in the dim light, the bludgeoning fall of gun barrels and truncheons. Gym Bro brought the gun round as they approached, not pointing it at them but not quite *not* pointing it at them either. Lee heard a chittering demand from the lead rat, which raked the air at them with a demanding paw.

"Sure," Gym Bro muttered. "You better be taking me to your boss, right?" He spoke loudly, as though the creatures were deaf and not inhuman. *"Mr. Rove*, you hear me?"

The rat captain screeched and yattered back at him angrily, but then gaped its jaws wide and shrilled something that did sound a lot like "Rove." So maybe Gym Bro knew what he was doing after all.

He grabbed at Lee's wrist, before hauling Khan to her feet. He shoved the pair of them before him, and the military rats eddied back to give them room. She had a sudden, disconcerting idea of what the encounter might be like for *them*: three gigantic, stooping hominids thrust into their close quarters—every footstep shaking the ground, every careless gesture enough to knock them off their skittery little feet.

Then Gym Bro shoved her forwards with the pistol butt. Lee reckoned that he was emphasizing the difference in status between him and his prisoners. The soldier rats formed a close escort, their clammy armour and bristling fur pressing against Lee's knee and hip, unpleasantly intimate.

She had to drop to her hands and knees to leave the gallery, even though they were trooping through the largest door in the place. The room beyond was even dimmer and lower, and she crawled onwards besides Khan, feeling that she'd reached some hitherto undescribed circle of Dante's hell. Right in the corner of her eye was the bleak mask of one of her captors, so close that when she turned her head her eyelash brushed the flat plane of its goggle lens. Snaking rodent bodies pressed against her, big as dogs, jabbing her with their sharp elbows and their brutal-looking weapons. Her breath was coming fast and ragged, and there were sobs mixed up in it. She'd have broken down if it hadn't been for Gym Bro, to whom she wouldn't give the bloody satisfaction.

Abruptly there was a ceiling high enough that she could stand upright, and the rodent guards spread out into clumps of two or three, as though even with space around them they couldn't bear to be alone.

"You took your time, Lucas. Any longer and we'd have to discuss it at your next performance review." It was a human voice, and Lee instantly disliked it; it dripped with smug satisfaction.

There was a little more illumination here: three long skylights in the ceiling revealed a gloomy sky of umber and gunmetal that lent the scene a bleak, funereal radiance. Seated beneath them were three figures, one of whom was a thin-faced man in a grey suit. He had an actual porcelain teacup in his hand, a saucer in the other, and there was a stooped rodent at his elbow holding a tray. She was only surprised there wasn't a towel folded over its arm, a waiter's pad tucked into a pocket.

He was on the right, and the civilized veneer was cracked somewhat by the lowness of his seat, which had his knees almost at chin height. Centre and left were a pair of rat-weasels, reclining in similar contrivances—the effect was as though they were slouching in beanbag chairs, although for rat-weasels this presumably indicated elegant luxury. The one on the left was smaller, sleek and wearing a robe of hatched black and grey. A great spray of knotted plumes sprang from the robe's neckline, arranged behind the creature's head like an opened fan. The rodent-in-chief was clearly the central one of the group, a swag-bellied creature twice the girth of its peers, topped by an elaborate coiffure or headdress that doubled its height. Its robe was arranged for several square feet around it in careful, intricate folds, decorated with eye-wandering arabesques and geometric patterns in a dozen different greys. Briefly, Lee interpreted this all as "barbaric splendour," but then her critical eye kicked in and she understood. Every aspect of the chief rat's costuming was simply to do with taking up space: what greater luxury could there be than to sprawl, in this warren of a world?

The chief rat-weasel hunched forwards. Despite its paunch, it was flexible enough to lean in to stare at Lee and Khan. It chittered and burped conversationally, and she was startled to hear a flat human voice come from a device near the reclining man. "Which is the scientist?"

The man—and Lee was sure she'd seen him before on TV somewhere—languidly pointed. "Dr. Khurram Amir Khan." He smiled urbanely. "I really must apologize for the disruption attendant on your arrival here. It's an inexact science, especially when we have to work against chaotic elements such as your former captors."

"I know you," Khan said. "You're...Rove, the venture capitalist."

The thin man nodded, still all charm. "And I'm recruiting you to save the universe, or whatever small part of it we may be able to wall off from the coming disaster. I'd ask you not to take against my allies, by the way. They need a bit of getting used to, but they at least have a functioning technology capable of the task, as well as many other things."

Khan's retort died on her lips as her eyes slid over to the windows. The air had darkened—showing not evening, Lee realized, but smog. There was a horizon out there now: a dense bristle of spires and mounds—no, lightless buildings, ziggurats and towers, all interconnected with covered bridges, cables and ducts. No sign of the Thames, but the tight-packed constructions extended as far as the dim light permitted. Doubtless the river was buried somewhere beneath, nothing more than an underground sewer for the rats.

"Lucas, you appear to have brought a spare. Is this another scientist of note?" Rove drawled.

"She got in the way," said Lucas. "She's involved with the others."

The chief rat leant forwards again. It had enormous whiskers, Lee saw; no, it had whisker *extensions*, more gratuitous taking up of space. She almost laughed. And then it yattered something, and the unseen translator stated, "Kill her then."

"What?" Khan exclaimed. "Don't you dare, you fuckers!"

Rove's lip curled at the language, as though mere murder was nothing compared to being *rude*. "We could keep her as leverage...?"

"She's trouble, sir," Lucas pronounced. "I recommend getting rid of her."

Rove spared Lee a direct glance for the first time, and in that moment she knew him: a man born *above*, silver spoon and all, for whom the world had always been *his* by right of inheritance.

"Do it, then," he agreed.

Lucas took out his gun.

There was a shrill alarm even as the pistol made its

reappearance, and the air was briefly full of nickering voices. Gravity seemed to shift, and Lee's stomach yawed one way and then the other. Mal, from nowhere, cannoned into her as she was clutching for balance. The pair of them pitched out from under the barrel of Lucas's gun, bowling over a couple of rat-weasel soldiers. Lee had half a second of watching Mal take in what was going on, bunched into a knot of muscle and ready to explode in every direction. Her eyes sought Dr. Khan—out of reach and with Lucas in between. And as gravity twisted again, she mouthed the word *sorry*.

Then they fell, not down but in a sidelong direction to *elsewhere*, leaving the stale air and the rat stink and the gun behind them.

Interlude: The Hunters

Excerpt from *Other Edens: Speculative Evolution and Intelligence* by Professor Ruth Emerson of the University of California

Out of the blizzard they come. You'd hear their voices first, if you were there, because when they are not on the hunt they talk all the time. It makes for a raucous babble of sounds, the building blocks of a language with a vocal range exceeding every human tongue put together. You'd hear them, and imagine they were complaining to one another, bitching that they should have stayed home until this blew over, and they're hungry, and their feet are sore. And "Are We Nearly There Yet"—because there are children with them and the children never shut up either. You'd hear the bellow and grunt of their pack animals too, who also complain about the cold, but with brute sounds that indicate how very hard done by they feel about this domestication business... But mostly you'd hear the rhythms of language within the beast-tamers' yammering, and you'd apply human meanings. As often as not you'd be right to, because they are like us, these hunters. Despite all the differences, they are our close cousins, within the skull.

You'd first see those huge, lumbering shadows through the driving snow, for the beasts of burden are far larger than their masters, and even more so once they're fully laden. Carrying loads is something the hunters are not built for, but they are endlessly inventive with rope and hides, playing Buckaroo to the nth degree to pack up their whole lives onto these monsters.

There are three types of beast in this caravan, besides the handlers themselves. The first are huge and slow, plodding on elephant legs, their heavy bodies bulked out further by a coat of something part feather, part hair, part scale. Reptile genetics driven to new extremes by evolution, to withstand a long series of glaciations. They have swaying, curved necks, small heads with almost prehensile lips, and long tails. At first they seem like a bizarre cross-breeding of camel and elephant, save that the hump is only mounded baggage, a tottering tower of rolled tents, bundles and slings. Beside them, and only marginally fleeter, come beasts that seem more familiar— a patchwork formed from the animals you know. Body of a reindeer, head of a warthog, high-stepping their way over the snowbound, stony ground with surprising delicacy. Some are laden, others carry passengers who perch along their spines in rows, squabbling and occasionally unseating one another. The third tame species is a kind of hook-beaked ostrich. Two of them run the edges of the caravan, their riders keeping a keen watch through the snow for trouble, either bestial or intelligent. It has been a hard winter; there are plenty of hungry mouths out there. The riders hold long, goad-like switches in their teeth and jab at their mounts to steer them; they have no reins. The third bird-beast draws a travois upon which an injured hunter reclines, one leg torn open by a misstep amongst the rocks but already poulticed and healing.

But then they are closer, the whole swaggering, shambling parade of them, and that conversational babble of croaks and quacks and clicks, chirps and cackles, would start to seem more alien to you as you took them in.

It could be a convenient shorthand to suggest this was a

timeline where the meteorite never struck and the long reign of the dinosaurs simply continued beyond the traditional boundaries of the Cretaceous, never knowing the narrow escape it had. Convenient, but untrue. That asteroid is out there in every timeline, set in motion at the start of all things. Barring a powerful presence in space when this rock reaches Earth, no efforts by this species or that will deflect it. But— although I might see some dinosaurs at the back begging to differ—that impact is no great dying time. Of the Earths we have seen who survived the Permian extinction, all weather the Chicxulub impact, to various degrees. It is a time of tragedy and loss, on a scale impossible for us to conceive. However, we are looking at these timelines from the privileged viewpoint of sixty-five million years later. That gives us a certain hard perspective. In this timeline, most of the dinosaurs on this Earth died, it's true, as did an awful lot of other things, yet a handful of dinosaur species lived. A few small therapod carnivores, ones that ferreted mammals from their burrows to snack on through the long dark years of dust and cold; a dwarf sauropod whose island habitat had already forced it to live on moss and lichen and for whom the impact made a virtue of former necessity; the odd maverick species whose hard pasts had led them to evolve the capacity to hibernate through the bad years. The iron hold of the terrible lizards was pried from the throat of the world in the wake of the impact, but they clung on. And when the skies cleared, there they were, ready to take up their mantle.

In this timeline, the Earth hosts a diverse biosphere by now. Mammals have prospered and grown large, scurrying gleefully into the various niches vacated by vanished lineages of saurians. The nimble birds have diversified into a variety of airborne and flightless forms. But alongside these are the hunters we have met, and a scattering of other dinosaur descendants making the best of a more egalitarian world.

This hunter species has come a long way. They are an offshoot of the line that led from reptiles to birds. And they were already clever, as birds are clever, before the impact. Their forelimbs are like fumbling clawed mittens, but they are dextrous with beak and toes. Their lean, whipcord bodies would be the terror of your filmgoers, if not for the dense feathery coats that fluff them out to twice their true size. These were evolved for display and now do sterling service as insulation. They work with leather, wood and stone, and some groups have a little metallurgy. We are in Britain now too, though a Britain currently shackled to Europe by a vast, exposed mass of land. Bronze tools and ornaments are traded from here all the way to the Siberian steppes, to the warm belt of the world where the glacial cold cannot reach, and past that to the frozen southern horn of Africa.

The ice ages we remember as gone these ten thousand years are in resurgence here. Perhaps it's because these hunters never started burning the fossil wealth of their world for industry. Or maybe it's some butterfly-wing foible of climate change, now come into its own. The sea levels are low enough to separate the Mediterranean from the Atlantic, and to virtually abolish the North Sea. All that water is locked in the glaciers that march forwards and back across the northern and southern latitudes of the world. It is a harsh Earth, but the crucible that forged our ancestors was no less so.

Except here there are no ape descendants, and the role of quick, big-brained maker, dreamer and talker belongs to the dinosaurs' heirs. They hunt fish and game with spears and fire, and with tamed birds like savage archaeopteryx—simultaneously hawk and hound for them. They are masters of domestication, with a hundred different species of animal pressed into service for work, meat or raw materials. They paint representations of themselves and the important things of their world—on stones that they erect, on the walls of caves, on rolled canvases of hide. They love ornaments and shiny things; a human could tell instantly which members of any group were high status, chiefs and mystics. The latter's role is to mediate between the *known*—in this harsh place of ice and blood and stone—and the *unknown* that dwells on the far side of sleep and stories.

And here is this tribe, new hunting grounds found, and everyone so quarrelsome and footsore that they decide to camp. They must replenish their supplies and calm their tempers before continuing their odyssey. They know this place from their past wanderings too. The hunting should be good despite the time of year, despite the weather. And there are certain expected rituals they should perform that help the tribe restate its identity and unity in the face of a harsh season. A delegation of hunters and mystics will go to the place they know as the Clutch of Six, despite there only being three stones there.

This year will be different. Though not unprecedented, perhaps. Who knows what the truth of their stories is, because they change in the telling, no hard lines between them and the actual events of the past. Their tales wheel like birds in the skies of an eternal now, where the passing of seasons is important but the passing of years is not. Except the name, the Clutch of Six, suggests that similar events happened a long time before...

This time, there are again six stones, three showing last year's faded votive images, three bare. And if the bold hunters walk a certain way, their heads cocked as though trying to stalk the nature of reality itself, they can find a warm place. A place of odd scents, where the snow melts and the familiar bones of the moor are rendered strange, overwritten by the dream of another world. There is meat, too: savoury, fleecy meat standing about as though it has never been hunted.

The first hunters and mystics who passed from their Earth to yours returned as heroes. They birthed a new myth cycle, given all the wonders they saw. Garbled versions of their deeds, renamed for local familiarity, race around the world. The trappings of your world, distorted and mythologized, will be incorporated into the dreams of theirs.

And something else will enter their world. Some*one* else. A human named Elsinore Mallory, familiarly known as Mal.

10.

Cold, but not the killing kind of cold. Not that place of ice and fissures, but still damned cold for July. They were in the forest again, or at its verge, looking out towards the River Thames, which took up the moonlight like a length of silver cloth. Above them, the stars were fierce and brave, standing proud in the dark fabric of the sky without the glower of the city to obscure them. Lee sat down heavily.

Looking seawards down the length of the river, she could see the bowl of the Thames Valley turned the colour of ash by the moon, with the darkness of the forest looming above it, a barbarian invader never quite arriving to plunder. Here and there were what seemed to be clumps of bushes. But then her eyes picked up restless movement, and she realized there were big animals out there, some kneeling, some standing.

"I'm sorry."

Lee jerked around to see Mal sitting behind her, separated by a few inches of space that she made no attempt to bridge.

"Why?"

Mal's pale face was unreadable. "I...was trying to follow the fault line back to...Earth, human Earth. I thought that was where we'd go. But we're here. I guess this is 'home' to me. I was here too long."

"It's okay," Lee heard herself say. "We can just...wait for the next..."

Mal stared at her. Then she grinned, though it was forced. "It's okay here, though." She was desperately cheerful. "I mean, it's better than the rats, right?"

Lee nodded vigorously, shuddering at the thought. The sheer open space here seemed almost indecent, after those cramped and populous crawlspaces. She rose to her feet and took a few steps downhill in the direction of the river. A hundred yards away something she'd taken for a rock lurched to its feet and *yuffed* in irritation. She had the sense of a big hippo on gangling, knock-kneed legs. For a moment she eyed it, but it neither charged her nor lumbered off, just folded back down into the grass.

"So where's this?" Lee asked. "Also...can you make a fire, or something? It's parky out here."

"I can do better than that. I can take us to a friendly village. I can't guarantee a tavern or an old man giving out quests, but they'll have food and warmth and a roof of sorts," Mal said. "Only...you've got to be cool, right?"

Lee eyed her. "Is this going to be like when you introduced me to your Oxford friends? Because that was awkward as fuck."

Mal just stood there for a moment. Her shoulders shook, and Lee thought she was laughing, because if there was one thing Elsinore Mallory hadn't done since the third year of secondary school, it was cry in public.

"Mal...?"

And then Mal had swept her up in a tight hug with all the

unaccustomed strength granted by her lost years. She wouldn't let go, and Lee could feel her hard body shudder.

"I've missed you," she whispered. "You can't imagine... Four years, and every day I...I'm sorry, Lee, I'm so sorry."

Then they broke apart, and a distance was between them again that only Mal seemed to be able to cross. She was looking about herself, almost theatrically getting her bearings, all but sniffing the air.

"What is it, girl? Little Timmy trapped down the well?" Lee prompted. The hoped-for smile came, a brief flash of teeth in the moonlight. Then Mal was off, heading on a course parallel to the river and the treeline, seawards. She seemed careless of the big grazers, who in turn ignored the pair of them utterly, motes of life entirely irrelevant to their ponderous vegetarian lives. Once or twice, though, Mal took a detour without explanation. Lee could only guess at what hazard or predator had been there, invisible to her tourist eyes but clear to the born-again barbarian her friend had become.

"Mal..." she said, after they'd been trekking for maybe an hour. "Look, I remember you weren't even in the Girl Guides. You hated when we had to pitch a tent, and you made damn sure we had a butane stove with us—or better yet, a local delicatessen we could get brekkie at. How..."

"How did I not just starve to death looking for a coffee shop?" Mal said.

"Well, yes. With a side order of 'How is the same not going to happen to me?'" Lee could feel a very real sense of panic. But Mal was here, after all. Mal was confident, and even if that didn't mean she actually knew what to do, it was a contagious confidence. If she'd been a man in another century, Lee reckoned Mal would have been really good at leading her underlings on desperately romantic but suicidal charges against enemy guns. She'd always been able to make something up on the spur of the moment and be credible enough to convince herself as well as others. She wasn't a hypocrite but a dreamer. In other circumstances it had been endearing.

And yet she *was* still alive, despite that. So maybe sometimes she could even convince the universe to cut her some slack.

"Thumbs," Mal said, concise but not informative.

"What?"

"Imagine life without thumbs."

"Mal, I don't have the faintest idea what you're talking about. Also, could we slow down or maybe stop? My legs are killing me."

"Not far now—look, there it is."

The sky had been lightening in their direction of travel. No fiery industrial sunrise but a grey-whitening that crept in from the east by imperceptible degrees until the first bright edge of the sun was eating up the residue of mist over the river. What Lee had written off as "just more geography" was touched by that light and transformed into something quite different. A village, as promised. She felt as if she was caught in one of those TV shows where popular archaeologists showed you computer images of a Bronze Age landscape before tearing up some farmer's field with a JCB. She saw a mound of earth which was too regular, and too close to the river, to be a natural hill. Atop it were a handful of rough domes that looked like they'd been woven from sticks, like bowerbird nests brought down to the ground. Around the mound, another thirty or so dwellings of various sizes were scattered about. Initially, the grouping seemed random. However, the more Lee stared, the more the whole seemed arranged to some plan beyond her human comprehension. There were pens here and there, and she could make out the huddled forms of livestock within. And there was smoke rising in thin serpentine trails from at least half the huts: fire, warmth, cooking.

"Welcome," Mal said, "to New Goldblum."

They were spotted soon after, and a rider veered out towards them, cutting a curving path over the tall grass. Lee stared, but somehow she was ready for this: a puffball-feathery dinosaur wearing a leather cape and a feather headdress, both patterned in the full spectrum of the rainbow. It was crouched on a wooden-block saddle atop a murder-ostrich, which was itself barded with a saddlecloth of red and white bars. Looking past, she saw at least two dozen of the reptiles gathered between the huts. They'd been called away from their morning ablutions, no doubt, by the arrival of creatures from another world.

There were three javelins sheathed beside the thing's saddle, and for a moment Lee thought: *So this is how I die.* The dinosaur's jaws were gaping, enough to show her a hundred or so curved teeth. Yet she also caught a voice on the wind: at first just bird squawks and whistles, but then, "Mal! Mal!"

Mal waved at it. "Hi! Hola! Hi!"

"Hi, Mal! Clever Girl!" Within ten feet of them, it leant in the saddle and its mount trotted to a halt, shaking its axeblade beak at them disapprovingly. The rider cocked its head, bright gaze flicking from one to the other. "Mal-Mal," it noted, and then uttered a gabble of clucking sounds.

"You speak their language?" Lee asked.

"Don't think it's possible, for humans," Mal replied from the corner of her mouth. "But they can make all kinds of noises, natural mimics, and they pick things up really quick. This one's Wakkatsy, or that's what its name sounds like. Except that's only the root, because they add all sorts of qualifiers, build up words like Lego. I do understand some of their words, some of the time, but a dozen of them picked up English within my first year here. Not conversational, exactly. But given it's a language from a species that doesn't even exist in this timeline, it's pretty damn impressive." And as she spoke she was approaching Wakkatsy, holding her hands out with the thumbs up. This prompted a ferocious hissing display, as though the creature was about to tear her limb from limb.

Or it was laughing, Lee suddenly thought. *Mal has an in-joke that excludes me. It's the Oxford lot all over again.* A weirdly petty thought, but it helped to ground her psychologically, keeping the terror and disjunction at bay. She had Mal, at least, and an alien world with Mal felt at least equal to her own world without.

Under the massed regard of thirty noisy archosaurs, they walked into the territory notionally claimed by the huts. The sound of conversation was as deafening as an aviary. And Lee took it on faith that there was complex meaning in every whistle and chirp, yet she could pick nothing out of it, save the name "Mal"—which she assumed applied to them both equally. Or, she realized, there was "Mal-Mal," perhaps the plural. After all, they wouldn't have needed to distinguish between Mal and other humans until now.

She tried to cast them as aggressive, threatening, even

alarmed. Instead she couldn't see them as anything other than glad to see their visitors, perhaps due to Mal's calm and her cheery thumbs-up gestures.

Then the "villagers" were quieting, and parted to make way for a delegation. If most of the dinosaurs were brightly cloaked and adorned, these were even more splendid: she saw polished stone and metal about throats, chests and backs. One even had a wooden framework of wings on its back, like a Polish cavalryman. They did not have the formal pomp of the rodent lords she had seen, though. Indeed, the other dinosaurs were jostling the group, and one was still having its seashell crown hastily set in place about the back of its skull.

"Return, Mal," said the lead dinosaur, who was a hand's breadth taller than the rest. It had a bronze sickle strung around its neck that looked functionally sharp and heavy. "Mal-Mal."

"I've returned with a friend," Mal agreed. "This is Lee. We're here for all the seasons, maybe. If you will have us."

A fresh wave of croaking and cawing eddied across the crowd, perhaps the more anglophone of them translating for the rest. The lead dinosaur's head cocked at an angle. "Yes-yes," it said simply. "Good-good. All-seasons-and-skies Mal-welcome." Then it was addressing its people, punctuating its rapid chatter with corkscrewing twists of its neck and occasional gestures from one taloned foot or fluttering displays from its arms.

"'All seasons?' You think we'll be here for a year?" Lee murmured. "Is this... winter for them? Or does it get colder?"

Mal blinked rapidly. "I... All the seasons means... just, time, Lee. As much time as there is, as anything takes. It's...

Their language and their thinking gets really weird with time. There's now and next season, and then there's all the seasons."

Lee moistened dry lips. "Do you mean...forever?"

Mal nodded once, birdlike as the dinosaurs.

"Mal, we can't be here forever." She laughed shakily. "Mal, this is...We're in a forest in the Cretaceous or something. We're in *Walking with Dinosaurs*. This is...incredible, Mal. This is amazing. To visit. But we're not living here. We need the Nissa or whoever they are to send a Stig to pick us up... right?"

Mal said nothing.

"Right?" And abruptly all that panic, which Lee was absolutely not going to give in to, was yammering in her head. "I mean, we were just in *London*, Mal. We had coffee and cars and Star Trek and books and washing machines and takeaways. Look at them, they've just about got...bronze."

"Actually that's another lot, over France-ways I think," Mal said in a small voice. "But they trade for it. I went once." She sent Lee an almost angry look. "I lived, Lee. I was here four years. The same four years where you had your coffee and washing machines."

Lee gaped at her. "Are you saying this...that I've *earned* this? Is this fucking *revenge*?"

"No!" Mal snapped, but Lee was backing away.

She broke into a run, the dinosaurs flurrying apart before her as she cut between the huts, looking for magic doors, for caves that might lead to other worlds, for lamp posts and wardrobes. Looking for anything she might recognize.

When Mal found her, she was by the smallest of the livestock pens, the one furthest out. A couple of the bolder hatchlings had followed her out there to gawp, but Mal shooed them away. She stopped a couple of metres away, hesitating.

"Lee—"

"Look," Lee said dully. "They've got sheep. There's parallel evolution for you."

"They're stolen," Mal said. "Rustled. A whole flock, including lambs. Got dragged all the way from Bodmin in our world to Bodmin in their world, to here on the migration route— traded for bronze, amber and feathers. Like me."

Lee stared at her. "They sold you?"

"Maybe. But I wanted to go, too, because I was sick of moving around and this tribe stay here all year. And I wasn't able to talk with them back then, so I didn't really know what the deal was. Fill in the blanks with whatever you prefer."

"And you were here for four years."

"Just about."

"And then the...Nissa found you," Lee added slowly.

"There was still enough of our Earth in me that I lit all the lights on their detectors. Didn't belong, right? Just like always."

Lee was not going to let that "just like always" blunt her ire. She stood suddenly, sending Mal skittering back a few steps. "So what happened then, Mal? I mean, you're like a superhero now. You've got dimension-hopping powers that can save the universe or some fucking thing."

Mal regarded her sadly for a long while, and Lee thought she might walk away, and that would be it. She felt the connection between the two of them stretch taut, ripe for severing.

"I was on the Nissa's Earth, briefly," Mal said at last. "They have an engine that can exploit a fault—enough to send people from one timeline to another. It's not far from where CERN is in our Earth, actually. It's fucking huge, Lee. It has to be, to manage all those calculations, and the energy needed. And even then, they can't just jump about wherever. They need a fault line to follow. So amazingly, no, they have not been able to distil this tech into nanobots or a wearable accessory."

"But what they were doing at the museum, all that reaching into the air stuff..."

"That was the Fishnet."

Lee blinked. Apparently four years in the wilderness hadn't cured Mal of making up jokey names for serious things and she really wasn't up to it. "Mal, I swear, just *tell* me what's going on. Tell me why we're here, why you've...just... *why?*"

Mal let out a long breath. "Because I fucked up, Lee. I fucked it up for you. I am one hundred per cent to blame. I'm so sorry."

A stab of emotion shot through Lee, a twisted-together combination of anger and grief and frustration. But also, maddeningly, she felt bad that Mal felt bad—like she always had. Lee was scrabbling to make things better even though these *things* had been done to her. "That's not," she said tightly, "an explanation."

"The Nissa came and found me. They knew our Earth, and they picked me up a mile off as having gotten displaced from it. They were running an operation in our dimension and they're not the most inconspicuous types, so they recruited me. So I got to go *home*. They had me running errands, mostly to do with Doc Khan, but all sorts. They really *are* trying to save the universe, if it helps." She read Lee's expression correctly. "Okay, doesn't help, right. Look, I..." But she choked up, and it seemed she had no more words, no more excuses.

"You..." Lee wanted to storm off again, except she'd already stormed off and had nowhere to storm further off to. "Mal, please."

"I knew I wasn't to contact you. The Nissa have enemies. Dangerous people. I mean, you know that now, right? And I understood I'd lead them to you, probably. Even me being involved was bad enough. Because if they could recognize me, maybe they'd follow that to you, to my folks, to anyone who'd known me. So I knew it would be an absolutely stupid, *stupid* risk for me to actually get in touch with you direct, and arrange to meet while on a job. Totally unacceptable, right?"

"Yeah, sure, spy malarkey rule number one," Lee said help-lessly. "And...?"

Mal swallowed, and then said in a very small voice, "I couldn't leave it, Lee. I couldn't be in the right world, the right *city*, knowing the whole universe was cracking like an egg, and just...not call, not see you, not...be with you. Lee, I was here for *four years*, and sometimes it was horrible and I wanted you there because you always helped. And sometimes it was beautiful and I wanted you there because— who else could I ever share that stuff with? And I wanted TV and pizza and...washing machines, if you fucking insist, but I wanted *you* most of all. So I went off-script and got you to Camden. Then that business went south and I was delayed. But I met you anyway, and I told myself that would be *it*. No more messing about until the job was done, and then maybe we'd have saved the universe by then. But I did check in on you again, and the bad guys had already found you. So

I got onto the Fishnet and tried to save you. I brought you here—down a fault the Nissa had already used—but you ran off. Then I took you..."

"Somewhere really, really cold."

"I didn't mean to," Mal said. "I don't even know if that was me, or if that was the Fishnet itself. Cos that's where you went—to its home world. The Findus dimension, where the frozen fish are."

"Mal, you're not making any sense." But the whole story had filed away her anger, for now. Lee just wanted to understand.

"Look, let's sit down, okay?" And Mal did so, putting her back to the woven wicker of the sheep pen. Cautiously, Lee joined her.

"Nissa science is better than ours, right? As evidenced by the fact that they come to visit us and not the other way round. But it's not *that* good. They have some suburb-sized hardware at their end, and it's hit and miss. But the Fishnet is different...Okay, look, there's another Earth where it all froze, and these fish guys all died. But beforehand, some uploaded themselves to a massive computer...or no, it's more like...the ice, all the ice on their iced-over world, is their computer. They therefore have a world-sized computer, which makes Nissa tech look like stone axes. The Nissa reached some kind of understanding with it too. All that groping about in the air is when the Fishnet gives them some temporary interface. It brings it close enough to grant them access, letting them do all sorts of impressive magic."

"And you...?"

"I have no access. It was only while on Nissa business that I got to play with the AI super-toys. I only rescued you before because the Nissa helped... and I'm not sure what happened when I was dropped out of the museum, into the rat world, to get you. I didn't do that. And when I tried to get *back* to our Earth, through the fault I thought was still there, we ended up here. Maybe my molecules resonate with this world now. So, yeah, my fault again, and now we're both stuck here unless the Nissa come to find us. Which, as I left Dr. Khan in the clutches of the bad guys, may never happen. We haven't been seeing eye to eye for a while anyway, before this. On account of how I was screwing up their work in my quest to ruin your life."

Lee found she was blinking back tears. "Four years," she said flatly. "How did you live here for four years?"

"The dinos, they're all right. They like me. I have thumbs. I mean, they're really clever with their feet and beaks, but I am a goddamn demon with knots, Lee. They really like me to tie things to other things. And we can talk a bit. I know what berries will give you the trots and what to gather to avoid scurvy—because the local diet is pretty damn palaeo, right? Protein heavy."

Lee reached out tentatively, found Mal's hand and squeezed it. "We're fearless cryptid-hunters, aren't we?" she said. She was astounded at how calm she was feeling. But her own last four years had been a kind of free fall, and now she'd landed. "You lived. We'll live." A sudden thought hit her, simultaneously banal and utterly urgent. "Mal, what do you do when it's your...time of the month? I mean, there aren't any dino chemists to get pads from, right?"

"Oh, right." Mal nodded vigorously. "Leaves and feathers and fucking boil *everything*. Other urgent questions?"

"Just one—who the crap are the Nissa, anyway?"

Mal laughed. "Oh, well, that's my name for 'em."

"Of course it is."

"It's short for Neanderthal Security Agency."

They spent the night in one of the domed huts, warmed by stones taken from a central fire, and by the bodies of a family of dinosaurs. Mal tucked in quite naturally against the feathery flank of one, and Lee spooned against her. The four hatchlings were only still for what seemed brief moments before waking and clambering about, croaking to one another. However, she was worn out and slept anyway, cushioned by a stack of furs.

Daylight pierced the woven substance of the hut like a thousand angry spears, no alarm clock needed. The space beside her was cold and empty by then, but Lee just lay there. Her body was telling her: get up, then shower, teeth, coffee, toast—but if she wanted any of these things she'd somehow have to reinvent them from first principles.

Hunger had her on her feet soon enough. The sky was clear and the dinosaurs had a big central fire going, every family contributing some fuel. There were skins stretched over racks to one side, and meat being dried. A great bustle of dinosaur-bird-people were stalking back and forth, screeching at each other—noises ranging from guttural croaks to piercing whistles and everything in between. It sounded as though each one of them was narrating an audio play featuring a hundred different characters. When they saw her, several of them called out, "Mal! Eat food Mal!" And then one of them, a big individual swaddled in a poncho by the fire, belched out "Lee!" in a reproving tone of voice.

"Food" looked like shoe leather soaked in brine, and also

306

tasted mostly of brine. There was plenty of water on hand, and Mal explained that they boiled it all too.

"You got them to do that?" Lee asked as Mal sat down, chewing on her own strip of meat.

Mal laughed. "They already did it. Maybe it's the health benefits, but I don't think that's why they'd say they do it. They...Four years, and we see eye to eye on a whole load of practical stuff—making, living, even how they settle arguments. But their internal life is still out of reach. I've listened to their stories about the world and their ancestors and... every time I think I understand how they *think*, along comes something that makes me realize I got it completely wrong. You don't know how much you take for granted, how much of your world view is subjective."

"But you've...taught them things," Lee hazarded. "You know, nudged them along with technology—all that time traveller stuff?"

Mal obviously had a dignified answer to that, but instead she smirked. "Seriously, what do I know how to do, Lee? I was going to teach them, at the start. Weaving, metalsmithing, all those next-step-up things. Except they know some of that already, and anything else...I suddenly realized I don't actually *know* weaving or smithing or even *knitting*. I know absolutely fuck all that's of any use. I remember some of the guys we LARPed with were those living history freaks. They used to live in a re-enactment village making pots and stuff for months at a time. Goddamn, but they'd be useful around now." The grin she turned on Lee was bittersweet, infinitely familiar. "There was a time, 1700, 1800, when, if you were a Serious Man Of Learning, you could know the sum total of human knowledge, they said. Philosophy, religion, natural history, classics, whatever they thought there was to know, you could know it. And then, they complained, we discovered too much and you couldn't be an expert on everything. Except, you know what? It's all BS. I am willing to bet my warm spot next to the fire that those Serious Men Of Learning did not know how to make a horseshoe or weave a basket or when to plant turnips. They just knew the useless stuff that their posh Enlightenment-bro peers reckoned Serious Men were supposed to know. Stick them here, now, and they'd crap out just like I did. While Farmer Bob would probably have the winter wheat ready for harvest in a month's time."

"But couldn't you...?"

"I reinvented the wheel!" Mal declared loudly, which the assembled Birdmen seemed to find hilarious, passing the word back and forth between them. "I mean, you can't go wrong with the wheel, right? And they don't have it here. But it turns out that when you don't have any roads or useful flat land, and the ground turns into a bog after every rain and thaw, the wheel is fucking useless. But it gave them a good laugh. That's actually one way they're like us: sense of humour. They love pratfalls and stories where characters build themselves up and get knocked down. Anyway, want to come hunting?"

"What...now?" Lee goggled at her.

"They're low on meat—this dried stuff is their fallback, and they don't like it much. We're actually better at eating this than they are, because we've got molars. You may get asked to chew meat for someone—full disclosure, right?"

"Oh. Right. Okay."

"But they're about to hunt, and they want me—us—to come along."

Lee looked at her doubtfully. "I bet they can run as fast as a horse and they've got...great big pointy teeth and all that. And spears. So my role in this would be...?"

Mal's grin broadened. "You'll see. And there's some furs for you, too. Not going to get much warmer than this until mid-afternoon, by my reckoning."

Lee's mental images of crashing through a snowbound forest at breakneck speed, in pursuit of a sabre-toothed tiger, were considerably short of the mark. Firstly, although there was the occasional flurry of snow, the morning was crisp and clear and the ground was slightly soft. It was, after all, as Mal pointed out, midsummer, albeit in a timeline where the global climate had gone in quite a different direction.

They were hunting on the open ground that led down towards the river, and their prey was a herd of two-legged, long-tailed feathery creatures. They were the same size as Lee and Mal, a little larger than the Birdmen themselves. The animals were grazing, scything at the grass with their beaks, heads crooked like flamingos. They looked dismayingly fast, but Mal explained that the locals didn't much care for chasing down prey when they didn't have to. Elsewhere, other tribes drove herds off high places with fire and noise, or ran them into canyons or artificial choke points. Here on the flatlands, the technique was nets.

"Thing is, the beasties aren't completely stupid, and they are very, very aware of our hosts as top predator," Mal explained. "That's where we come in. Firstly, I make excellent nets, if I say so myself. Thumbs, right? Secondly, none of these poor dumb sods associate my smell with trouble. You and I are going to saunter up there with the nets and a bunch of stakes and set up the trap, and then the others will drive them into it. Easy as that, and nobody has to break into a sweat."

In practice it was a bit more hectic. The birdlike prey could not only run but also jump, and a fair number managed to vault the nets. The whole stretch of ground was frantic with Birdmen on murder-ostriches hunting down bird-beasts and trying to steer them back into the trap. The business ended up something like an accelerated cavalry battle for parrot historians to argue over. The noise and chaos was indescribable, and then the actual business of bird-on-bird slaughter turned her stomach. Doubtless the locals were being efficient and professional, but it was a bloodbath.

It was also a grand success, or so Mal assured her. There was enough meat to keep everyone fed, and to salt some, and to trade some when visitors came. As if conjured by her words, a quartet of new Birdmen rode up. They sat two to a saddle, on a pair of long-legged beasts that looked like hippos that had been stretched and starved until they resembled greyhounds. Even from a distance they were splendid, with feathers and ornaments, in striped ochre and white and black. Seeing this, the lead hunter in Mal's party hurriedly retrieved a proud feather headdress from somewhere, gleaming all the colours of the rainbow. Lee looked suspiciously from one group to the other.

"I can't help but notice the, ah, *livery* of our hosts," she murmured to Mal.

"Uh-huh."

"Mal, did you start off some kind of dinosaur *pride* march?"

Mal's grin was back. "Actually, no, this mob just have some really good dyeing techniques. Their headdresses must look even better to them too, because I think their eyes are better for colours than ours. Bright is really important. Dyed stuff is mainly what this lot trade. But yeah, it was one big reason why I decided I wanted to stick with this tribe. I was pretty desperate for anything familiar."

The newcomers trotted their animals back and forth, and some sort of formal exchange was shouted between them. Lee saw her own band start off tense, ready for trouble, then generally relax. The body language was human-approximate enough for her to grasp broad strokes. Soon after, one of the stretch-hippos and its riders accompanied them to the village while the other galloped off in an alarmingly knock-kneed fashion. There would be guests at the fire tonight, Mal explained. This meant new products and new stories, and retellings of the old ones. When times were good, it seemed there was nothing the Birdmen liked more than throwing a party.

On the way back, Lee had plenty of time to think. She was still experiencing a honeymoon period in this world. Except that wasn't *life*, was it? Life here would be a cold, hard graft, with no medicine, no mod cons, and there would be times when the game was scarce. Maybe she or Mal would get on the wrong side of the dinosaurs, whose customs even Mal didn't really understand. And if all that worked out, there would still be age, infirmity, and no other humans, ever.

The cold wind that came off the river met its counterpart within her, telling her, *It can't work, and you will die a cold, lonely death here.* But what choice did she have?

Then the wan sun brought at least a touch of warmth to her cheek, and all about her the energetic, noisy locals were gabbling at one another for the sheer pleasure of the banter— as far as she could make out. And if they weren't human, they seemed close enough to permit anthropomorphization. Parallel evolution had produced something that could know joy and tell stories. These creatures could meet a thing as alien as a human on their home turf and be curious, not murderous.

Lee reached out and took Mal's hand, feeling the callouses that four years in the saurian Stone Age had layered there.

It will do, she decided. *I can work with this for as long as we have.*

Interlude: The City-Builders

Excerpt from *Other Edens:
Speculative Evolution and Intelligence* by
Professor Ruth Emerson of the
University of California

Of course, none of the narratives I am presenting in these interludes are necessarily true. We do not, after all, have a time machine to visit the many "Thens" I have described. So we interpret the timelines we encounter using what we find in their "Now." We see the rusting war debris of the Silurian eurypterids or the bones of a lost Permian culture—still curled about their patinaed stone tools—and we extrapolate as best we can. We tell stories; all sentient life tells stories. In such a way, we make sense of profoundly alien things—other Earths filled with other thoughts. And sometimes what we find is close enough to us that we can learn its histories first-hand, visit its museums, view its curated artefacts. Or we might meet something advanced enough to communicate with us primates, crafting an interface we can look in the fabricated eye.

Looking back on some Earths, we've been forced to condense their tales so their story is easier to follow. We didn't have time to tell you about the generation of global peace in the midst of the eurypterids' terrible wars, or the death cults that riddled the early centuries of the immortal trilobites, or . . . a thousand million things. All we can do, in the end, is tell you stories. And all of them can be further reduced to a convenient cautionary tale that you—and we—may understand.

And we are closing in on our present, now. Not only is the guillotine shadow of the Permian epoch behind us, but the impact that terminated the Cretaceous period, too. These are events so cataclysmic that there is a reason they mark the end of those otherwise arbitrary geological periods. The life in the timeline I'm about to describe weathered those challenges exactly as ours did. The selfsame grab bag of species crept out to stare at that Cretaceous meteorite's smoking crater. Birds, mammals, reptiles, insects, fish, plus an awkward gap next to the avians where the rest of their less flighty complement should be. In this timeline there are no dinosauroid survivors, no bold therapod hunters stalking the cold wastes of Bodmin Moor.

In the resulting Paleogene era, birds and mammals shove and elbow for terrestrial dominance. The birds will determinedly fatten up and make a bid for their dinosaur relatives' lost crown. However, the mammals will prove to have better megafaunal elbows in the long run. Here in the Paleogene, across two continents you can already recognize as the Americas, this timeline branches away from the trunk perhaps forty million years ago. For the first time it's the mammals' turn at self-awareness, and they're going to have a solid run at it.

Mammals have been diversifying rapidly by this point, sets of teeth flicking through new fashions like a time traveller's fast-forward shop window. The big battalions begin to make their presence known: dog-forms, cat-forms, bear-forms. Early whales too, who took a look at the extinct mosasaurs and decided they wanted a piece of that murderous action. There are the first elephants, the first tiny dawn-horses, even our own primate ancestors. Which of these majestic contenders will feel evolutionary pressure to develop a greater intellect, more complex interactions with its peers?

None, as it turns out. On northern America's first prairies, under the newly evolved hooves of the herds, a hidden revolution occurs. It happens to an omnivorous rodent species, whose formidable gnawing teeth are not averse to a little predation, a little scavenging, the cracking of small bones. They live in vast colonies, whole subterranean cities, and breed at a remarkable rate to overcome their own mortality, bringing litters of up to two dozen into a harsh, rodent-devouring world every month.

They live cheek pouch by jowl, hundreds, thousands even, crammed into their constantly expanding polities. This is a narrative we've seen before, of course. The demands of so many neighbours can't be ignored, applying powerful leverage when it comes to the crank handle of intelligence. The rodent's awkward position between eater and eaten is a significant factor too. These creatures are omnivores, yet also delicious to any passing predator with a yearning for a snack. Early on, snakes and proto-mustelids are a terror for them. Give this species a few million years, and it will fortify its homes to keep such threats outside, where they belong. Later these rodents go out mob-handed, wearing coats of thorns like impromptu hedgehogs. Any incautious predator properly rues the day it tried to chow down on them. They leave home with spiny branches smeared with faeces and the juice of poisonous berries, and later with crude atlatls, which can launch envenomed spears into the faces of their enemies.

Give them a few more million years, and predatory species have learned to stay well away. The predators' range also retreats and retreats—because the rodents never stop breeding, even though their infant mortality rate is far lower now. They are mammals, after all; a love for their young is rooted deep within them. As they develop their high-pitched language, they begin weaving mythologies about themselves and their significance in the world. The number of an individual's offspring is a measure of worth, in that prehistoric rodent culture. It is their purpose and their pride, and it drives their every advancement.

So, throughout stops, starts, reversals and recoveries, they spread across the world. They move by land bridge when the cold comes, then by way of bustling houseboat armadas when the seas are high. Their species settles every continent except Antarctica, and everywhere their approach is a pragmatic one. They possess an iron-clad drive to survive and increase their number, eliminating countless species that might threaten their communities and their kits. Their societies are clannish: enormous blood families splintering into subfamilies under the weight of time. Hosts of brides and grooms are exchanged with distant polities to keep their genetics healthy, building a culture with similar values across the globe. These rat cities become ever more elaborate, extending above and below ground, made of earth and wood and stone and concrete. The inhabitants grow larger than their ancestors, but stabilize at around half the size of a grown human. And while their brains are smaller than ours, they are highly organized— complexity making up for volume. If it is true that a human mind can maintain relationships with perhaps three hundred individuals, for the rodents, three thousand is nearer the mark. Most of those are close relatives. You have to get very smart, very fast, to juggle so many in-laws.

However, despite their earlier start, their technological development is only a little ahead of your own. Their close-packed living conditions lead to several cataclysmic, civilization-ending epidemics. They always recover fast, though, because even a handful can breed a society of thousands in a short period of time.

While you had your Renaissance, they had their leap into industry. This included the joys of fossil fuels, mechanized agriculture and factory-line mass production. For them, far more than for you, it was a desperate necessity. There were already seven billion of them, and starvation was whetting its knife in every major city. By the time you had your coal boom, your railroads, your first telecommunications, they were reaping the result of centuries of burned prehistory. Colossal cities had turned grey under clouds of sulphurous pollution—and the deep chambers of their underground metropoli were overflowing with choking bodies and sifting ash.

And now? Now the rodents' Earth supports almost a hundred billion souls. Despite the poisoned air and the failing harvests, they still breed faster than their world can kill them. However, they have no space at all—their cities touching, their borders merge with one another. Only the keen edge of their science has kept them from collapse, but that science is very keen indeed. It's been honed by absolute necessity and their enduring love for their vast multitude of children. Those with sufficient wealth would deny their children nothing. Even as their population continues to explode, they have also devised methods to stave off death for decades. Technology has enabled these rodents to extend their brief natural lives until they live as long as we do. They have cured every cancer, subjugated every bacterium or virus. Over time the poorest families die, but the richest only multiply. The poorest of the rich then become the new poor, and the cycle continues. Their rat scientists scrabble desperately for some way out of the maze. They need an escape that would give them room to live, air to breathe, food to eat.

Sometime around your 1880s, these creatures had their first inkling that there was, indeed, somewhere else they could go. An otherworld sufficiently vast that even their incredible numbers might be dwarfed by it—for some small time. They were laughed at, those early scientists, in high, squeaky voices. They were ridiculed and cast out. Yet within each fleeting generation, some brilliant rodent mind would come back to the theory and gnaw at it a little more. These pioneers fleshed out the madness with numbers and experimentation. Until one day, they chewed right through the boundaries of accepted science and out the other side. Into *our* side.

11.

I

Daniel Rove's stateroom on the airship had been several other rooms once, but the lords of the rat empire were happy to indulge their honoured guest and ally. Lucas wondered idly how many little squeaker mandarins had been unhoused so that Rove could have this spacious cabin. As it was located along the outside edge of the airship, they'd even had a big window put in so Rove could gaze down on the cluttered, smoky, filthy ground below. It was, he gathered, a rare honour, usually reserved only for the rat kings.

The rat kings preferred to lord it over their minions from on high. From airships, explosive chastisement could be dispatched from above, should any large part of their domain decide to stop taking their calls. Lucas hadn't seen the vessel from outside, but even with most of the interior spaces being vermin-sized the thing must have been huge. It definitely relied on something other than gas to keep it in the sky.

And here was Rove, dining at one end of a long table he'd had them build. The rats were good at making things to his order. They'd had enough access to Earth media that Rove could pick products as though ordering them bespoke. The rats were giving him every luxury. More than that, in fact.

Lucas had been told that if a rat worked in the factories, the hydroponics vats or the reclamation plants, its life expectancy was very poor indeed. They had just enough time to pop out some offspring then work themselves to toxic death. One upshot was that Rat-Earth medicine was, Rove informed him, nothing short of miraculous by human standards. They had gene therapy, blanket cures for cancer, rapid screen-and-clean treatments for your blood, spinal fluid and every other damn part of you. It wasn't as though they were backwards, scientifically, was the point here. It wasn't like they weren't trying. And yet it wasn't enough to stop 99.999 per cent of the population dying from pollution, malnutrition or frustration-bred violence before they had a chance to see the grandkids.

The rat kings themselves lived for three times the length of a rat's natural life. They hadn't quite defeated Death, but they'd thrown enough obstacles under his bony feet to earn them that much. *That* was the prize Rove coveted. He'd already repaired his ageing genetic material, cleaned up his cells, all that biotech stuff. He was now looking forward to a few centuries of hale heartiness with which to dominate the multiverse. With his rodent allies, for now, but Lucas imagined they wouldn't share a throne comfortably for long. Still, big world out there. Big *worlds*. Room for more than one god-king, surely.

It had taken him a while to work out what the rats were getting out of it. Eventually he discovered that Rove had given them *Earth*, human Earth, with all its prime real estate. Not exactly something Rove had the right to sign away. However, the rat kings lived at the pinnacle of a vast, interlocking machine of social interactions. Perhaps they valued the appearance of legitimacy as much as the information

Rove was trading about humanity's defences. And Lucas reckoned the locals who sold Manhattan Island to the Dutch probably hadn't had the right to do that either. That was how this sort of thing went down.

Beyond that, though, and despite the limitations of human tech, Rove had brought new things to the rats' table. For example, a stock market venture—featuring an interdimensional computer—was how he'd made contact with the rat kings. It remained his best bargaining counter, his ante for the big game.

As for Lucas himself, he was...still alive, still here, which put him in the black as far as his personal accounts went. Rove's allocation of space and resources extended to staff, and Lucas found that the food was all right, and the new hand was holding up. When Rove set himself up as the techno-duke of some otherworld, or whatever, presumably Lucas would get to be chief of police or something. That would, at least, look good on the CV. Although he'd been told all worlds were facing extinction, so whatever ambitions Lucas harboured were probably moot. Rove had a plan to protect a small corner of infinity, and Lucas knew which side of that divide he needed to be on.

Right now, self-interest also involved playing serving staff, as Rove was dining with a guest. Perhaps being waited on by rats felt too ridiculous. Lucas's own feeling was that Rove was the only one who was going to derive any satisfaction from the evening, and that thought was compounded when Dr. Khan entered the room with a pair of armed rodents.

Lucas had examined his opposite numbers here on Rat-Earth. He'd labelled them "BDSM troopers" due to their black rubbery uniforms, although he didn't recall them being overly effective in the museum. Lucas had seen enough action to know the difference between an army and a repressive police force, and the latter weren't soldiers, just bullies. Certainly they were pushy with Khan, shoving him into the chair despite him being halfway to sitting.

Him. Lucas stared at Khan, keeping his own expression neutral as a good butler should. Rove had given Khan new clothes, stolen from Earth or run up by rat tailors. There was a shirt, a tie, a jacket, trousers—all of it saying "beta male" to Lucas's eyes. The difference was fascinating. Khan had been a loud, angry woman, full of expletives. The man before Lucas looked three inches shorter and a hundred decibels less pugnacious, too small for the made-to-measure clothes, shrunken in on himself.

Lucas felt that he should get a kick of satisfaction out of that, restoring the proper order of things and all. Except, seeing just how much had been ripped away from Khan—by new clothes and the scrubbing away of the make-up—he found he didn't like it after all. It was a weird time for empathy to come calling, but he looked at Rove's slight, polite smile and thought, *Well, this is fucking pointless dickery, isn't it.* Oh, Rove would say it was to establish who was in charge, which would at least have been dickery with a point. But Lucas thought the dickery was its own point, here and now. It seemed Rove had a few Good Old-Fashioned Values he wanted to wave around, and who was going to say no to him?

Certainly not Lucas, because Rove, dick or not, was still his boss. And his boss was planning to choose who survived the apocalypse. Lucas swallowed his empathy and stepped forwards to serve the wine.

Rove gave Khan his best smile as Lucas poured, and signalled to the rat escorts to leave. Rove had done his time as man of the people, when it had been politically expedient. His direct line to folk like Billy White wasn't accidental; he'd made sure to keep that crowd sweet for when he had a use for them. He'd worn the same smile holding pint glasses next to nationalist soap-boxers as he had beside upper-crust heirs out of the Home Counties.

"Mr. Khan," he said crisply, that friendly expression still on his face. "Or, I should call you Khurram, really? We are, after all, going to be working closely together." A remarkable thing, that smile, Lucas considered. Despite all his practice, Rove could never entirely escape a hint of piranha in the curve of his lips.

"My name," Khan muttered, "is Kay. I want my clothes back."

The smile widened. "As you have been made aware," Rove said pleasantly, watching Lucas fill the scientist's glass, "the universe is imploding upon itself. We don't really have time to indulge that kind of foolishness. When our work is done, I suppose you can pretend whatever you like."

A little of the old fire flickered in Khan's eyes like far-off lightning, but then he—*she*—hunched her shoulders and stared at the wine before knocking back half the glass with an expression that suggested she'd rather it was Scotch. Lucas went out to get the food the rats had brought up. He hoped it wasn't roast rump of rat.

Rove hadn't been just another over-privileged profiteer with an inheritance and a few cousins in the House of Lords. Rove was a genuinely smart guy. He invested in computers and data before the world saw that was where the future was.

He also invested in vastly complex webs of corporate ownership. So when a pension fund collapsed or personal data was
sold en masse, the dirt never splashed high enough to soil
the immaculate uppers of his bespoke shoes. He'd cruised
through polite society like a shark. You could see the fin and
the wake, and it was obvious that Rove was working towards
something—but it was never clear what. Lucas knew, of
course. Daniel Rove was going to take what he wanted from
the sinking ship that was Britain, the whole world and possibly
the universe. And... well, this was what he was expounding
on when Lucas carried in the steaming tray.

"It's all maths, Khurram," Rove explained easily. "Which is
providential, because you are one of our premier mathematicians, after all. I need you to work on the equations, find a
solution to the mess we're in now."

Khan looked as though she was going to ask why in hell
she should help Rove. But she was smart too, and the sentiment remained buried. Instead she spat out, "As though there
is a way out. You're right. I've seen the figures." She snapped
her fingers suddenly. "Get me a fucking cigarette, you bastards."

Rove nodded, so Lucas obliged, and had one himself for
good measure.

"I have every faith in you, Khurram," Rove said. "After all,
our thuggish friends wouldn't be so interested in you if there
wasn't *something* you could do. They probably wanted you
to save their home. Yet why should they survive rather than
us?"

Khan gave him a level look. "You're saying you want me
to save the world, our world? That's what all this cloak and
fucking dagger is for?"

"Well, that would be grand, wouldn't it? Saving the world.

Or even *a* world," Rove said. "I've looked at our hosts' theories, run the figures past my own expert. Turns out saving *all* the worlds is likely to be problematic. I think we're going to have to be a bit ruthless. And you can see this world out of the window: not much to save, and ours isn't much better. Used up, poisoned, overheating and filled with a great surplus of people." That smile again, like a snake loosening its jaw to swallow something. "But there is a way. Somewhere out there, behind these collapsing worlds, is an engine. Something has *made* all this, a god or a machine. I don't believe these branching worlds just *happen*. And if we can find the origin point, perhaps we can save...something. Perhaps we can save what's important, the things of value in creation. Let the monsters and the other nonsense fall in upon itself. We can start with a new Jerusalem, sans competition, survival of the fittest and all that. Green and pleasant land." He laughed without really opening his mouth much. "Every faith in you, like I say. We have cigarettes, and whatever other luxuries you might want to earn. Even a change of wardrobe, if you want to play dress-up again. We have an army of sapient rats, and we have Lucas here with a length of rubber hose or just that nice new hand of his, but I'm sure such encouragements won't be necessary. Because you want to live, Khurram Amir Khan, and maths will set you free."

That smile, still, so terribly pleased with itself, and Lucas found he couldn't look at it. The rats were more human, in that moment, than the man whose glass he refilled. He wondered at what point Rove intended to double-cross his rodent allies and remove them, and most likely their entire branch of reality, from the picture. He wondered the same about himself.

II

Kay Amal Khan, born Khurram Amir, allowed herself to be led to her new quarters.

"Luxury," said the big man who was Rove's cyborg right hand. "Believe me, the squeakers go home to dorms filled with fucking hundreds of the little bastards. Bunking up here is better." His shiny black prosthesis had been tight about her arm all the way here, and two black-uniformed rats had scuffled along behind. She found the rodent soldiers nightmarish, not for their inhumanity but for the very human images they conjured up. Their helmets resembled Great War gas masks and their get-up signalled *fascist* to human eyes. She'd like to imagine valiant rat resistance movements and that the forces of authority were on the point of being overthrown at any given moment. She wouldn't put money on it, though. Not that these jumped-up rodent Nazis didn't have plenty of human counterparts, ready to put the boot in. She'd been on the trans scene for long enough to know that.

"Your lab. Done up for real people at this end, for rats that end," the big man told her. She saw a desk, a chair and something that looked like a computer from the front and a plumber's nightmare from the back. The bed was a coffin-sized space set into the wall. Dully, she realized minuscule storage was being pointed out to her. Apparently there were various built-in gadgets for hygiene and the like too. Her attention kept slipping.

Her eyes slid unwillingly to the other end of the workspace. No chairs there, no screens, just a low table like a footstool and a host of connections. Apparently the rat-creatures believed in a clean-desk policy. "I'm supposed to work with the . . . them?"

The big man grunted in agreement. "They've been talking to the chief long enough to translate their jabber into English. You get one of their top scientists, kind of like the 'you' of this world."

"I can't work like this." The forthright words came straight from the scientist within her, and she waited for the slap or the put-down. The big man shrugged though, and shuffled awkwardly.

"Anyway," he added. "Supposed to be all set up for you, got all the squeaker scientists' work loaded up."

"He's mad, you know," she tried, in a whisper. "Your chief."

"Nope." He turned away, leaving her under the glassy gaze of the soldiers. "Just really, really sane and knows what he wants." He paused, and she thought he might venture some other assessment, less complimentary, perhaps a four-letter word. Yet that would have crossed a line, and so he kept it to himself and walked off.

Stripped of other options, feeling acutely miserable in her own skin, Kay sat at the computer. It was just as she'd been told: all their data was there for her, with an interface that was close enough to Windows and controlled by a touch screen. The translation had a few rough edges; that was all. The rodents had been reaching for language to describe universal phenomena, as alien to them as to her, but the numbers came through loud and clear.

I had no idea. Not quite true, but an idea was all she'd had. The rats were a step ahead. Their scientists had gone on to develop their idea into a reality: that their Earth was part of a sequence of parallels, each one branching from the next.

And now the principles that had maintained the separate existences of these worlds were failing. Soap-bubble universes threatening to merge into one another and, eventually, pop. Even Kay had to stretch her mind to believe it.

This entire universe of parallels was complex, held together by inviolable laws and irresistible forces, composed of an unimaginable amount of energy. Yet, at the same time, these were just tiny particles that existed on reality's knife edge. It was all numbers, when you came down to it.

The universe had sprung into being due to an imbalance between matter and antimatter—which gave rise to All That Was. The energy this took was like a huge debt borrowed from the future. And now being called in? *One minus one is zero.*

As far as causes for despair went, there wasn't much to beat the end of everything. On the other hand, Kay knew numbers. Numbers were her business. She wasn't going to save the world on Rove's say-so... but she could still save the world.

Several hours of deep perusal later, she had visitors, as the soldiers at the door let in another pair of rat-creatures. Thankfully these ones weren't in uniform. The foremost of the two wore what looked like several layers of jackets, each one pulled out into starched points at its lower corners. The overall impression was something like a tiered pagoda, or a spiny segmented pyramid. Its posture switched rapidly: sometimes a tall stretch that would have brought the top of its head to around Kay's breast level; at others a hunched, low stance, monkey-like hands clutched before it like a pantomime villain. Its companion was... Kay frowned. Its companion was a full-on cyborg super-rodent. The creature's head was shaved, giving it a horribly cadaverous appearance. And a metal implant extended over the left rear quadrant of its skull, bristling with stubby antennae. It wore decidedly less ostentatious clothing, just a loose smock—and its ears and tail had been cropped or injured at some point. Its posture was entirely hunched and low, and Kay retranslated that stance from "plotting" to "placatory."

"Please adopt an appropriately abasing attitude within yourself!" The voice issued from the metal of the cyborg. Yet a moment after she'd heard it, she realized it had been preceded by a battery of squeaks from the more grandly dressed rodent. "We await your confirmation that you are the hominid expert—assigned to further our grandiloquent oversight, for the purposes of mastering the universe." The voice itself resembled a mobile phone personal assistant, calm and vaguely female, never human enough to be threatening, entirely at odds with what was being translated.

"My name is Dr. Kay Amal Khan. I am a mathematician." She almost added "from Earth," except they were all from one Earth or another. Most likely this jumped-up pagoda of a creature had been given her old name, but she would make damn sure that they called her by her real one.

"You have the honour of addressing me as Dr. Rat," the creature's translator rat announced, as it drew itself up to its full height. "Kindly adopt an appropriate stance, if you would be pleased to."

Kay shifted, and abruptly it fell into that hand-wringing, shrinking posture, cowering in her shadow before remembering itself and straining for height and space again. *Good, little fucker, remember I can stamp your tail flat . . .* But the need to bully left as quickly as it came, shooed out by common sense, which reminded her who held the cards now. She could put herself in the creature's place too, imagining how she might approach some alien monster twice her size, given into her care.

Carefully, she let herself down until she was sitting on the hard metal floor. "Hello, Dr. Rat," she managed. She imagined its real name was a series of inaudible squeaks or contortions, or maybe just the smell it made when pissing on things. But seriously, was its name Rove's *joke* or something? "It's your work I've been looking at, right?"

"Mine is the genius to draw together the weft of many minds," the translator said, the artificial voice's lack of enthusiasm sounding like sarcasm.

Abruptly a memory surfaced from when Kay'd been working for the UK government. Her head of department had been very full of himself too. He'd been desperate for the various scientists under his care to understand just how important he was, how indispensable, whilst simultaneously never really understanding any of the research. This Dr. Rat was probably a better scientist than that, but she had the same sense of someone puffing themselves up as much as possible—lest they be forgotten and left behind. *And from what Rove was saying, that fear could be very real, if the chosen few are about to evacuate to a virgin New World.* She had loathed that browbeating supervisor for two years. Then, after she'd left, she'd run into the man in a gay bar in Leeds. He'd been a completely different person, as, in a very real sense, had she.

Maybe we can build bridges and I can cadge a fag off you too— or perhaps reconstruct the molecular sequence for nicotine from first principles, because I am gagging for it. But first things first.

"One thing, Doctor," she said. "Just so there's no misunderstanding, I'm a woman, okay? Female. I don't know what that really means to you, but it's important to me."

There was a pause. Perhaps it was accessing files or remembering instructions from Rove. But Dr. Rat only twitched its whiskers. "That is acceptable," the translator explained, probably quite mystified, but Kay was surprised how much better the concession made her feel. *I can work with you*, she decided. Or at least she could try.

III

In the third interview Julian's bosses had put him through, Alison was in the room when they brought him in. That was when he started to think it might be all right. Or at least that everything else might be sufficiently screwed that firing him for breaches of protocol was no longer anyone's priority.

"Matchbox." He nodded to her.

"Spiker." She looked tense, pale, likely operating on the same cocktail of stress and adrenaline that he was. He hadn't had access to a mirror any time recently, but probably he looked worse, on account of how he'd been fatally shot two days ago. Tended to put a crimp in your day, that.

Using those very words inside his head, he allowed himself a small smile at just how goddamned *British* he was being about this.

He took a seat two chairs from Alison—no point in seeming in cahoots, after all. Their respective minders took up places at an angle, leaving the head end of the big table expectantly vacant. They wore impeccable suits, what Julian would have worn had their positions been reversed. Neither was armed, but he knew damn well there was a police officer with a Heckler & Koch MP5 down the hall if anything kicked off. Knowing as he did that things might indeed kick off without warning, via parties who didn't require conventional means of ingress, he was glad of it. Their minders were theoretically bussed in from elsewhere in the country, to avoid even a hint of collusion, but Alison's was named Dave something-or-other. Julian had met him at a Christmas do two years ago. He recalled only that the man was a monomaniac about minor distinctions between small-batch artisanal fruit gins. Not something it would be easy to shoehorn into conversation to generate rapport. The other man, greyer and broader, kept glancing at his phone in a precise manner. Julian reckoned he was checking some kind of sports results.

His superiors had debriefed him alone in the last two interviews, and he'd been doing his best not to enjoy himself. Yes, he was neck deep in a Very Serious Security Matter and so forth. Except he kept being tempted to replay an exercise he'd been on, some training malarkey, where they'd taken it in turns to play the uncooperative prisoner for each other. It struck him as ridiculous that the department had accidentally trained him to be an awkward sod in exactly this situation. He had conquered the instinct, though. He had told his interviewers everything. For one, the parts of the story that were career suicide couldn't be obfuscated. For two, he had a duty to his nation. And the nation was apparently under threat of...some damn thing. Having seen what he'd seen in the shadow of the skeletal whale, he honestly didn't know what it was, except a threat.

What Alison had told them, he had no idea, but his best guess was that she'd be frank with them as well.

They'd given him one phone call, and Josie had been simultaneously frantic and angry. She'd demanded to know details he couldn't give her, including when she and John might actually see him again. She wanted to know why people with official search warrants and stony expressions were searching the goddamn *house*. He had only allayed her fears to the very small degree that spousal honesty permitted, and hadn't mentioned anything about getting shot. He reckoned it was a forgivable omission in the circumstances.

The silence in the interview room was growing taut, and he guessed their watchers were waiting to see what he and Alison would say to one another. He turned to her to smile, and found her staring right at him, all the words bottled up in her face.

"Could we get coffee or something?" he drawled for the benefit of their minders, testing the boundaries. To his surprise, Dave Whoever stuck his head out of the door to ask, and yes, this would be a Meeting With Coffee. This incrementally improved his best guess at how much shit he was in. And it would be *him*, after all. Alison had been a prisoner of hostile operatives.

"Spiker..." Her voice came out with all the emotion bound up and sealed in triplicate. "How are you feeling?"

He frowned at her, because it was the sort of question someone asked when they meant *You're falling down drunk, maybe you should go home*, or *I hear your wife left you*. Then he clicked and managed a smile.

"Pretty much good as new." He was in fact bruised from

collarbone to groin, but he'd take that as an alternative to dying in gutshot agony.

He had some surprisingly sharp memories from when that had been going on. He remembered the gunman seizing Khan and Pryor and somehow walking away—very fast—to somewhere not on the Natural History Museum's tourist map. The other woman, from the security footage that started all this, had gone after them. And, although he'd been too middle-class polite to mention an embarrassing faux pas like being *shot*, Alison had made quite a fuss about getting help for him. Which he was grateful for, all things considered.

The Plug-uglies had been dealing with their wounded. One heavyset woman had loped over, though. She had long, greying hair and her broad face was human enough to be hideous, yet shorn of any empathy. He half expected her to go away, or get out a jar of leeches or finish him off. He had been in a great deal of pain, shivering with cold, aware that the metrics of his life were skiing rapidly down that slope from which there was no return.

Then she had reached out and torn open his shirt with one effortless motion, so that he was aware of her sheer physical power, like a bear in human skin. If she decided to make his last minutes that much more painful, there would be nothing he could do to stop her. But the Plug-ugly never touched him. Her hands hovered over his blood-slick abdomen, and he saw glints and structures in the air, blue-white, seeming to arrive from a great distance without ever travelling. Then the cold came, and he screamed and screamed, thrashing as Alison tried to hold him down. The Plug-ugly woman put one massive hand on his chest and crushed him to the hard stone of the museum floor. He looked up at the hanging whale ribcage above, big enough to hold a dinner party in, and fought with all the accumulated instincts of his ancestors, sure he was being killed.

In the end—surely no longer than a minute, although it had felt like ninety-seven years—he had a whorled, cancerous-looking blemish where the bullet had gone in. His insides felt like they were full of broken glass, but the real pain had ebbed away. And, most importantly, he wasn't dying any more.

Armed police had kicked in the door then. Simultaneously, they'd appeared at the head of the stairs, under the benign gaze of the stone Darwin. He had expected the Plug-uglies to vanish, one more conjuring trick in the interminable string of scarves this night had been pulling from its sleeve. They had stood there instead, lumpen and awkward—never putting their hands up, nor getting on the floor, nor making any sudden moves.

The police had put handcuffs on everyone, read rights and recoiled from the rodent bodies. They'd gathered briefly to examine the other dead: the gunmen, the Plug-uglies who had fallen. It had been a bloodbath. The museum wasn't going to be open to the public come morning. Twenty minutes into this, a trio of half-undressed security men burst in like extras in a farce, having been released from a broom cupboard. Julian had viewed their arrival with a disproportionate stab of relief. Nice that someone had come out of that night unexpectedly well.

The door opened, snapping Julian from his recollections. In strode his boss, Leslie Hind, with a face like iced-over thunder. Being summarily fired and possibly detained went right back on the table. In response to a gesture, their minders left without a word. There was one of those weird pauses then, as Hind's secretary entered to pour them coffee from the department's cheap plastic cafetière.

"I'd say you have a lot of explaining to do," Hind said brightly when the door had closed. "But you've been explaining yourselves ever since you were recovered and nobody's any the wiser."

She sipped her coffee thoughtfully, somehow managing to stare at them both without dividing her focus. Her secretary opened up a file and began laying out photographs, making a mosaic of bleak images across the tabletop. Mostly they were corpses, and not all the corpses were human. He saw several of the human gunmen though, both in situ on the museum floor and later, on slabs at the morgue. There were four Plug-uglies, and one at least was not from the museum, to judge from the ground she'd died on.

The uniformed rat-weasel creatures were also in the ranks of the dead. With their masks off, they inhabited some uncanny territory between hideous and cartoon cute, with big round eyes and short, whiskery muzzles. Julian could entirely have seen them teaching children about the alphabet with a bouncy, catchy theme song. As it was, they were dead and ghastly.

"In the tunnels beneath the Mount Pleasant sorting office," Hind recounted, "this woman, and seven of these creatures, were found dead. Her thin finger picked out more images. "In the main hall of the *Natural History Museum*, for God's sake, three dead men. Also three more of these individuals who, I think we can agree, are not necessarily *people*. Plus five of those same...entities." She indicated various post-mortem close-ups of rodent physiology: their jaws, their weird two-thumbed little hands, the head of one with callipers measuring the braincase. Numbers written on a piece of paper had been nudged into shot. Julian wondered who the hell you went to for that kind of autopsy work.

"These three." Hind moved the three human casualties to the fore. "Two of them could be professionals, as they took care to carry no identification. The third, one Dane Vellotti, has been placed as an Italian national with a somewhat aged criminal record. He's not been on anyone's radar for the last eight years. We're talking to Interpol and the AISI, but nothing useful as yet. However, *this* gentleman's face is known to us." They saw a photograph of a clean-shaven man with a receding hairline, looking in death less like a gunman and more like a bank manager about to refuse someone a loan. "I doubt he's officially on any books, but he was working for Rove Denton two years ago. He wasn't guilty of anything that we could definitely pass to the police, certainly nothing I was allowed to investigate. But I kept a note. I always do." There was a slight quirk at the corner of her mouth, and Julian wondered just how much dirt on Rove she had.

"There is, of course, no formal link between these remarkable events and Rove Denton. Were I to openly suggest one, I'm not sure I'd retain my position in the department. I've already had something just shy of a direct instruction from the Home Office that these matters—including your ongoing interrogations—be placed in the hands of certain private contractors. These contractors are also, if you follow a trail of ownership, shareholdings and shell companies, within the control of Rove Denton subsidiaries..." Hind steepled her fingers and sat back in her chair. "I can stall these requests for the time being. And I don't think the Home Secretary will quite dare to order the extraordinary rendition of two of my own staff. Especially as Daniel Rove himself seems to be unavailable for direct comment. But that is how matters stand. You may both thank me, now."

Julian gabbled a few words and Alison nodded, watching warily over the lip of her coffee mug.

"Now the others," Hind said, and more photos were laid out precisely across the table. Many were black and white; some were of poor quality. They showed...

There was a thing on an operating table—a great, segmented beast like a man-sized lobster, curled on its side in death. A thin lab-coated man with a face mask was using a cane to point past the rags the thing wore, indicating the clutch of pouches belted under its smaller limbs. There was a shot of a beach where *something* had washed up. A dozen men with rifles were standing around it, their uniforms dating the scene to before the Second World War. The stranded monster's shell was half in the water still, and the body that projected from the wide end was a scavenger-stripped ruin of tentacle stumps. It must have been thirty feet long. There were more rat-weasels, pitiful, starved things in cages alongside mangy tigers and a moulting eagle. There was also the photo Alison had already seen, the Plug-ugly woman posing as a Belgian smuggler.

"It's been going on for a while," Hind said quietly. "It's getting worse too. Some of these are from operations I oversaw. Others were obtained by less standard means, and often via the back door from sources associated with Daniel Rove or his companies. I won a couple in a blackjack game with a Luxembourg embassy clerk." There was no way to know if she was joking. God knew her expression was deadpan enough to murder a dozen comedians. "For a long time I didn't realize there was a *'this'*—a wave of related events. It was Rove who showed me the truth, ironically. He was recruiting or, in some cases, disappearing people who had any link to it. He was buying artefacts, both biological and otherwise. And with such secrecy it couldn't but raise alarms when you saw the pattern. If he'd played the clueless tycoon buying gauche souvenirs, it might have escaped my notice, to be honest." There was the slightest fragility about her as she regarded them, and Julian suddenly realized that Hind was worried they'd denounce her as mad. *Monsters, really? Someone call the men in white coats, old Hind's gone off her trolley!* But he'd seen enough not to bat an eyelid, and Alison had likely seen twice that. At any rate, whatever Hind saw in their faces reassured her.

"Heads of this department have inherited files, passed down from hand to hand...never mentioned openly, like a dirty secret. We've not known what to do with them. And any attempt to properly investigate, well..." Hind shrugged. "The whole Service would become a laughing stock. So we sat on it. And then, on my watch, the pace seemed to accelerate. I thought we were just better at picking this nonsense up, but no." She sighed. "Apparently it really is getting worse. We won't be able to keep hiding it away in these files any longer. And this freak show is just the trimmings, unfortunately. There's also a worrying up-tick in cyber-intrusions into government systems, into major corporate systems, which is somehow linked. Intrusions that walk through our protections as though they're not there. And again, we only see the fingerprints, not the hand. The true scale of the problem is unknowable. The best technical minds of our generation tell me *someone* must have cracked some magic piece of virtual legerdemain. Apparently we abandoned our attempt at it—and the only person still saying it could be done has been taken."

"Dr. Khan? This is her project?" Julian asked.

"*They* have her?" Alison asked, pointing to the Plug-ugly morgue photos.

"They say not," Hind replied grimly. "They say Rove and those verminous monsters do."

"Why? What's this to him?" Julian asked. *What is so tempting that he'll send armed thugs and monsters to get what he wants?*

Leslie Hind looked profoundly dissatisfied. "That is where we reach the hard limits of our knowledge, Julian. I'd like to believe he's short-selling the country for personal gain, the usual thing for a man in his position, but I'm sure it's something even worse." She closed her eyes briefly, and Julian wondered how long she'd been awake. "We're outside all rational borders now. The reason we're having this conversation is that you are, for better or worse, already part of this. The transcript," she directed, and the secretary handed out slim, wire-bound documents.

"Page fourteen, line eight onwards," Hind instructed. They had hauled the Plug-uglies up for questioning too, and here were the results. He would have expected the prisoners to be surly and reticent, but this one had been weirdly verbose, albeit in halting English. He read over it, and exchanged glances with Alison.

Dr. Khan hadn't been kidnapped but recruited, apparently. Not as an act of hostile espionage, or even for her security-breaking physics research. Because the universe was breaking.

"This is...insane." He waved a hand, words insufficient.

But Alison made a thoughtful sound, and he glared at her, feeling abruptly undercut. "Really?"

"I'm not saying that alternate worlds makes sense of what I've seen," Hind said slowly. "But I'm not saying they don't. And it's all we were told by the prisoners, the *foreign agents* we took at the museum. None of whom remain in our custody, which I doubt will surprise you."

"What's our official position?" Julian asked. *Help me know what to think, please.*

Hind closed her eyes briefly. "We're dealing with an actor that apparently employs a technology we cannot understand. And I would far rather there was some other explanation to this multiple-worlds business, but the impossible things keep mounting up. I don't think we can have an official position. But the unofficial one, between ourselves and these four walls, is that we proceed on the basis that there is a very real threat to national security, and possibly everything else as well. And if there are any possible steps that we can take to avert it, then we will."

PART 3
RED QUEEN HYPOTHESIS

12.

I

Three weeks after the events at the museum, there was a raid on one of Rove Denton's facilities, an industrial unit near Edmonton. Home Office interference was still preventing Hind from going in mob-handed on her own ticket, but it turned out HM Revenue and Customs had a longstanding investigation into Rove under way. Hind co-opted it seamlessly, using the pretext of looking for accounting records to get her people through the door. Her firearms team request was a prescient step, because the occupants weren't human.

The morning after, Julian read through the preliminary report with a growing sense of dread. Alison came in as he crossed the boundary between espressos two and three, and waited for him to finish reading. She had already digested it, of course.

Rove Denton had long abandoned the facility, but other things had moved in. Julian looked at a skewed photo showing seventeen corpses twisted in attitudes of death. The rat-creatures looked pathetic and scrawny, and these hadn't been uniformed or armed. The reporting agent had been vague about how the shooting started, but Julian suspected it might have been a knee-jerk reaction to the alien. Everyone involved had been practically tattooed with the Official Secrets Act. Julian's natural instinct was to thoroughly approve of this approach. Obviously it must be kept secret from the general public. That was what the Secret Service was *for*: to worry so the masses didn't have to. Except...he knew, then and now, that what they'd seen so far was the tip of the iceberg. They were dealing with powers that made Russia and the U.S. and the nuclear arms race look like Tinkertoys, and it was getting *worse*. At what point did "trying to keep it secret" become both impossible and less than creditable?

Now the two of them were sharing a sandwich, although not in the canteen because they couldn't talk there. Their colleagues, overhearing even half a dozen words, would think they were insane. Alison was coping, or that was his take. She took this business home every evening and worked through the latest intrusion reports. She did that...other thing, the thing only she could do right now, that gave her such an insight into what was going on. She was starting to predict the intrusion sites ahead of time. And every day Julian looked into her face for the strain he knew must be there. Or perhaps for something else, for signs of the abyss that must be gazing into her every time she tapped it for information.

Julian was not coping.

It was a slow thing. It surfaced in snapping responses to colleagues, exasperation with Josie. He was being put under too much strain at a fundamental level, and he wasn't dealing with it. It was ruining him as a person.

It was almost a month now since he'd been shot. Since Hind had co-opted him onto her secret task force, not because he was suited to it but because he was there. Every day he was waiting for the barriers to break, for his work to be front and centre, *News at Six*. And somehow it never happened. The rest of the country and the world were spared the horrible understanding that was eating him alive.

"At the museum, I saw creatures," he told Alison. They were in his office, despite the fact that he had always fastidiously refused to eat so much as a biscuit at his desk because of crumbs. He wanted to get the words out, but his nerve failed. "I cannot account for anything I've seen, Matchbox. The rats, that thing on the Dorset coast, those machines they found in Morocco. It's so much past anything I understand that my mind isn't even trying. I'm going on with my life as though it'll be ironed out by next week and then I can forget it ever happened."

"Instead of...?"

"Instead of everything being changed forever. Which is how it is." He gave her an almost pugnacious look. "How are you still holding up, Matchbox?"

"You ever watch old horror monster movies? I mean ones from the sixties, mostly. They're still trotting out the same old monster tropes from the thirties, except now it's science everything. Films like *The Quatermass Experiment*, *Frankenstein*, that kind of thing. So we still have vampires, werewolves or some silly rubber monster—but now the hero's a scientist and everything can be explained away, scienced away. We learn a rational explanation conquers all, explains even the inexplicable."

"You know *Frankenstein* was a book before—"

"Spiker, pedantry is your least attractive personality trait." But she was smiling, and that was good, at least, one small light in the darkness. "And you know what? That's how I'm seeing all this. 'Sufficiently advanced technology is indistinguishable from magic,' right? So there *is* an explanation, we just can't see it yet. That's what I'm getting, from my contact." He shuddered at the thought of her reaching across an unthinkable gulf, to something cold and vast and yet compliant. An operating system that gave her fragmentary backdoor access to the mind of God.

She must have seen his less than convinced look, because she grinned again. "When the Plug-uglies grabbed me, I got to watch them work. They wizarded me out of my bloody kitchenette, but they didn't blindfold me. They were like any covert team working under adverse circumstances, rather than mad wizards. Except they bitched at each other less. And that made me think 'rational explanation' too."

He felt a keen stab of envy—that she could skate so easily over the morass that was dragging him down. It must have shown, because she grabbed his hand.

"Spiker, we'll have it, soon enough. Sometimes I can almost see...It's like I could just draw a map of the whole thing, with Earth marked as 'you are here.' And I can see where the other places are rubbing against ours, breaking through."

II

Alison was quite proud of how she'd handled that. She'd seen Julian take solace from it, at any rate, which had been the point. And it was true she was dealing with things better than he was, but not because she was hauling all the Weird down to ground level. Instead, she felt that her own feet were leaving the ground, that she was floating off at the insistent tug of an infinite bunch of balloons.

The ice interface wasn't always there, but she was finding it more and more reliably. She could reach out and touch it, feel it through the gossamer substance of reality. It told her things, sometimes when she asked, sometimes without even that formality. In her mind it unfolded its dendritic map. *You are here.* And she could see the cracks spreading, each one a fissure between her world and another. Dead worlds, drowned worlds, worlds bustling with life. Alien worlds that were also Earth.

She could tell when others were walking the same roads, sometimes. She could feel the creeping encroachments of the rats, the Plug-uglies as they exerted their minds to part the seas between the worlds and walk across. The terrifying thing was how quickly Hind had come to believe her. All Alison needed to do was file a prediction and there would be a team on the way, racing to find whoever had been skulking through the shadows. She had lived her professional life constructing intricately designed castles of evidence, and now she felt like a fraud.

They had interrupted three bands of Plug-uglies and another two rats' nests. She was a fraud who got results.

Sometimes, when her forehead crackled with frost and the ice cream headache had its fingers gripping the inside of her skull—when the architecture of the interface opened up to her like a multidimensional flower—she felt godlike, all of creation within her reach. She felt that all she had seen was a drop in the ocean compared to all that there was, but it could be hers if she reached just a little further. Better than any drug, better than sex, was the lure of infinite understanding.

Sometimes it was less sanguine.

She woke thrashing, fighting the bedcovers, that icy trance already on her. She could feel reality give way, cracks splintering inwards through the walls of the world like bullets aimed at her. They were coming through, right here, right now. She scrabbled, flung a pillow across the room, kicked her blankets off. There were figures in the darkness of her bedroom, standing at the very edge of her bed, waiting patiently.

And she was dreaming, of course she was. Her nightmares had been shot through with recollected contact with the interface and the mind-twisting sensation of all that other space. The frozen complexity existing next door.

She sat up, panting, the sweat she was drenched in chill on her skin.

Just a dream, after all.

She took a deep breath and looked up into the eyes of the heavyset woman at the foot of her bed.

There was a man sleeping on her sofa, courtesy of the department. He had a gun. One yell would suffice to bring him stumbling in. And then what? The woman, the Plug-ugly, could probably break him in half. The close confines of her small bedroom were no fit environment for gunplay.

And still there was just the one, and she stood there, not meeting Alison's stare—shuffling slightly as though embarrassed.

"What are you here for?" Her voice sounded admirably composed.

The Plug-ugly risked a moment's eye contact, then stared fiercely into the corner of the room. She mumbled something Alison couldn't make out. She was wearing some kind of shapeless robe. *Like a muumuu.* It didn't look like anyone's idea of Earth-casual camouflage, not even like the mismatched tramp outfits the others had sported.

"Say again?" she prompted.

The woman sighed hugely and said, "We want your help."

From the standpoint of their respective technological developments and their own past history, that seemed unlikely. However, Alison caught herself thinking: *But they did help Julian.* That was a real debt, owed by Alison to the enemy and separate to her obligations to state or Hind. So she listened. Then she called Hind on the twenty-four-hour emergency number she'd been given, requesting emergency debrief facilities for a non-human agent.

Julian had obviously got wind of what was going on before he pitched up for work the next morning. Alison had half expected him to get hauled out of bed at three in the morning for the interrogation. But apparently the conspiracy was already broadening and Hind had other people for that. Having already gone through two complete caffeine cycles, Alison was feeling ragged, exhausted but still strung out on excitement and anticipation. Julian seemed brighter, too, and she guessed that whatever happened now, at least something had *happened*. Living day to day under the Sword of Damocles was exhausting. Sometimes you needed a change, even if it meant the blade was going to drop.

Hind called them both in shortly afterwards, their chief's office seeming too small for Hind, her secretary, four armed security men and their new guest. The latter, particularly, seemed to simultaneously take up too much space and be trying to shrink in on herself. Alison was well aware of how physically *solid* the Plug-uglies were. Standing there, the woman seemed to stress the floor beneath her. Her quiet stillness seemed an implicit threat.

Alison could not have pointed to any one feature that, seen

in isolation, would have marked the woman as something *other*. Each element of her face was within tolerance for human, but perhaps there were too many differences in aggregate not to notice if you passed her in the street. Or maybe essential British reserve would have kicked in; you don't stare at a stranger, after all, no matter how odd they look. This Plug-ugly had wild, bushy eyebrows and long red hair streaked with dirty grey. She looked fifty, perhaps. Her face sagged from her huge brow down to an almost absent chin, her eyes bird-bright and quick.

"Julian, Alison." Hind was perhaps overdoing the aura of icy calmness. "This is Musmursumbrer. Or something like that. She's come to us because her people are trying to retrieve Kay Amal Khan from... where she's gone. They are offering to work with us to accomplish this." And nothing was said about who would end up with Khan after all that, of course. Diplomacy, as the saying went, was the art of shaking someone's hand with your right until your left found the knife.

There was a proper internal briefing later. They weren't quite getting into bed with the Plug-uglies, after all. However, even if the bid to spring Khan failed, this was an invaluable intelligence-gathering exercise. They were still playing catch-up in a game they had only just realized existed. Hind was plainly willing to take all manner of off-the-books liberties right now.

The Plug-ugly had done her best to explain, but between her accent, her tendency to mumble and the fact that she was talking extremely high-level physics, Alison thought she'd lost almost all of her audience very quickly. Alison herself had...

Not understood, exactly. Probably you'd have had to be

on Dr. Khan's level for that. But she'd found archives opening before her, within her. When she'd repeated some mystifying phrase of the Plug-ugly, something had unfolded in her mind's eye. Images and models had danced there like the cold fire of deep-water fish. She had been skating over the abyss, constantly in danger of being drowned by data, but a tenuous comprehension had glittered into being in her mind.

There was a frequency scale, or something like it. Every alternate Earth could be identified by its specific resonance. The Plug-uglies made use of it, but so did the rat-creatures who had Khan. The rats and the Plug-uglies were now in some kind of cold war, and the rats were able to shield sensitive sites from intrusion by the Uglies. *And I bet Hind would give a lot to duplicate that feat.* It wasn't that the Plug-uglies could just walk in and out of wherever they wanted—there were fault lines and weaknesses between worlds that they had to exploit. Yet where those faults existed, they could walk, and there wasn't a blind thing human security forces could do to stop them. If a crack opened into Number 10 Downing Street, then the PM might find unexpected guests at the breakfast table.

Those faults, in and of themselves, were a symptom of the wider problem, of course: that the boundaries between worlds were falling. The problem the Uglies wanted Khan's help in solving, or so they said.

Musmursumbrer had explained haltingly that the rats were not taking steps to protect themselves from intrusions by humans, because humans didn't have the capability to intrude on their spaces. Hence the Plug-uglies needed a human-resonant task force to go get Khan, and they would provide the means.

Everyone, Hind included, had assumed this meant an MI5 team. Julian had begun making plans there and then. The Plug-ugly woman had broken in immediately, apologetically. Apparently there had been a misunderstanding. They had chosen who they were sending in already. What they needed the department's help with was the extraction.

When the team came out with Khan, the rats would likely be in hot pursuit. The Uglies needed a rearguard, someone to take the flak. Not the most enviable part of the plan, but Alison had seen the calculations in Hind's mind. A plan that put Khan and a concentration of human armed forces in the same place gave them the best chance of hanging on to the scientist, post-rescue.

After the briefing, Alison ended up in Julian's office again, and he said, "I suppose we have to stop calling them Plug-uglies, now we're working with them."

She laughed, and it lit him up in a way she'd missed. "To their faces, certainly. I was thinking—based on what they are, what they *say* they are—we could call them Cousins."

"Nice. Just the right connotation of inbreeding." Julian shook his head. "Who the hell is on their rescue team, anyway? Who else are they working with? The Americans, you think?"

Alison blinked. "I thought..." But of course it hadn't been said. She'd just *known*, through the mainframe shared by herself and the Pl—the Cousins. "It's those two they were working with before." Because Alison bet the Cousins didn't trust MI5, any more than Hind trusted them. They weren't about to put Khan into the hands of Her Majesty's Government if they didn't have to. "Mallory and Pryor."

III

The Birdmen travelled, towards the end of their brief summer. Or at least about half their village did, and Lee and Mal went with them. The stay-behinds would be doing their best to gather food for the winter, so perhaps fewer mouths to feed was useful. The travellers would doubtless bring back a bounty when they returned too, and Lee thought she understood that the return would coincide with the start of true winter. Nobody in their right mind would be abroad then. It was all part of a cycle of life, perhaps originating before anyone could articulate why they did it.

Yet the practice obviously meant far more to the Birdmen than subsistence. The travelling party was in raucous high spirits at the prospect. The elders were trying out ever more resplendent combinations of feathers and paint, strutting before the village with heads cocked back and stiff-plumed tails lifted high. The youngsters—and it seemed that every adolescent in the village was going—were in a frenzy, leaping on each other in fake ambushes and generally making a nuisance of themselves.

"Sex," Mal explained.

Lee gave her the side-eye.

"They're going to be meeting other groups of Birdmen in a big get-together. Youngsters go there and perform, and maybe they'll end up married off to another tribe. It's a big thing, highlight of the year. You're a fancy Birdboy and you get chosen by another village or some nomads, that's a big honour. You're a village like ours and your young stud gets farmed out, that's good for you because now you've got a link, another bunch of people you can call on if times are hard."

"Seems to me times are always hard." Lee shivered. They were both swathed in furs, clumsily tailored to fit a human frame, and she was still shocked at how far the climate was from the London she knew.

"There was one winter, my second, when the hunting had been really bad. You'd not believe the lengths they went to, to find food. They've got a whole library of desperation measures you've not had to see. The sheep were a godsend for them." She shook her head. "There was this one hunter—I couldn't understand much of what they said then, so I got this in retrospect—but she went to this hill every day, sat out there and starved, and the rest obviously thought she was mad, or whatever passes for mad with them. But she was remembering—they have their stories, and the stories are often tied to places. So one day in midwinter, she comes back dragging this carcass. And it was a cow, an actual cow. Somehow she'd got through to our side and came back, like some fucking mythic hero stealing fire from the gods. They still tell the story of it."

They set off with great ceremony, a cacophony of squawking and keening seeing them off. The pace was easy and their path took them downriver, towards a sea which was considerably further off in this world. Bands of hunters would break off from the party, coming back with game or fish. Mal showed Lee edibles to look out for along the way. "Idyllic" wasn't quite the word for it: Lee felt that she'd never been fitter and leaner, but at the same time she was cold and hungry almost all the time, footsore, and she was dreading catching a winter cold.

In the evenings she would lean into Mal's embrace by the fire and try to feel grateful for what they had. But in the back of her mind would be the thought, *I can't see how you lasted for four years.*

Seven days downriver there was something like a carnival, a spread of hides, tents and lean-tos arranged about a collection of stick-mound dwellings, which was presumably the village of their hosts. Birdmen were everywhere in riotous profusion. Lee found herself pushed to the front with Mal, and they entered the gathering in the midst of an eddying crowd, as every Birdman came to eye them and chatter to each other. *We're here as trophies*, she thought.

"They're not going to sell us or something, are they?" Lee managed as she was jostled and pricked by claws, menaced by beaks filled with curved teeth. They all seemed friendly, but at the same time infinitely ferocious.

"Hope not," was Mal's less than reassuring answer. "Get used to being stared at, though."

Except there was something off in the crowd's body language. A month amongst the Birdmen, and Lee was starting to follow the currents of their interactions. Right now, something was different, and one of their own group was trying to tell Mal something she couldn't understand, lots of repetition of "Mal, Mal!" and "Clever Girl" and "Lee" too.

"New Mal new!" They were being shepherded along through the jostle and feathery fluff of the crowd. Then a space opened up, and there was a shape there that went on two legs and yet was not Birdman at all.

Lee stopped dead. Not a human, not quite. A man, though, big and burly and robed in sheer grey like a . . . *space druid— go on, say it.*

"Stig?" Mal asked.

There was a shake in her voice that made Lee realize that, all this time, she'd been hiding how hard it had been for her to be stuck back here. That the hospitality of the Birdmen hadn't, after all, been something she'd hankered for every day since she'd left. That she'd been putting a brave face on for her friend.

Stig stared at them. Mal stared back. Lee felt it should have been a grand reunion, people throwing themselves into other people's arms, Gandalf the White returned from the dead, all that. Except there was very clearly a subtext going on that she wasn't quite getting, and not a happy one. Eventually Stig jerked his head towards the domed hut behind him. He ducked inside, leaving them to follow.

The floor was covered with overlapping hides, Birdman style. The place smelled strongly of musty decomposition and the acrid scent of the Birdmen themselves. Stig was sitting on the floor within, as she'd seen his people do before, and there was a fire lit in the hut's centre. It gave his heavy features a sinister, ruddy caste and threw dancing shadows around walls caked with hard-baked mud and decorated with intricate pictures. These didn't resemble the usual Birdman art, which could be powerful and evocative but in ways that told her that a human mind and eye would never entirely appreciate the thought behind it. These images were much smaller, packed in one after another, and she had a jolt of misplaced revelation, thinking they were writing. A second glance suggested they were more like ... sequential art, panels of sparse lines. Some clearly depicted Birdmen; others were incomprehensible but seemed too abstract to be script.

Then she saw one string of panels, halfway down a wall,

which dragged at her eyes. There were other figures there amongst the Birdmen: recognizably bipedal and tailless. However, they weren't depicted in any way she'd have thought to draw a human being. Was that Mal? Or perhaps one of Stig's people? Abruptly she wondered whether this hut was special. A place devoted to recording events—not just of a mystic past, but of recent living history. Perhaps a proto-historian's attempt to shoehorn in a category of time between "now" and "all seasons."

"So." Mal loomed aggressively over the visitor for a while, making a point before she sat down. Stig didn't seem keen to start talking. He looked everywhere but at Mal, poking at the fire, picking at his big square fingernails.

"You need us, I'm guessing," Mal filled in when he wouldn't say anything. "You're not here for a rescue. But you need us."

Stig grunted, still apparently absorbed by the dirt beneath his nails. He could have broken the pair of them like a bundle of dry sticks, but instead he was flinching from the brow-beating like a child. Lee realized how easy it must be for them to harm one another, with those absurdly heavy, muscular frames. Maybe that had made them averse to any serious confrontation, always looking for another way.

"Say something," Mal challenged. Stig sighed hugely and rolled his shoulders, as though about to attempt some great feat of strength.

"We have been hunting Kay'mal Khan," he muttered. "We have been...fighting the builders. Our machines are better, but the city-builders are many and do not care about how many they lose attacking us. They keep us out of their world. They know to scent for us with their clever noses. You, touched by your world and this one, they do not expect. So

361

yes. We need you. And, after Kay'mal Khan is returned—if any of us live and if any world still remains—we will bring you where we can that you want to be. Here, there, wherever." He held his hands out, palms up, as though carrying or offering an invisible burden. "You do not do as you are told, and you are trouble. But of all those who are not us, you we trust most to do this thing."

"High praise," Mal said. Though Lee knew that particular tone was "Mal trying to be cool and distant while actually being deeply touched and/or impressed." "You can take Lee home—" she started, but Lee wasn't having any of that.

"Both of us," she said. "No more four-year gaps. It has to be both of us."

*

Lee was disappointed. She'd wondered aloud whether they were going to where the Nissa lived, which might be somewhere worth seeing. Instead, they ended up in a vacant lot on the outskirts of London. The space was edged with barriers and barbed wire, but the vivid incursions of graffiti showed how little of an impediment these were. And the lot's current occupants had just stepped in out of thin air, Lee included, which was over the pay grade of most security contractors. A handful of Stig's relatives had already been waiting for them.

"Our home is no good for you," Stig explained shortly. He was tugging open the neck of his filthy shirt, dressed in shabby human clothes again. Similar garb for Lee and Mal. Striding out of thin air was one thing, but striding out dressed for the Palaeolithic was plainly beyond the pale. The London summer was shocking after the Birdmen's winter world, and Lee was sweating already, but they kept handing her more layers, even suggesting she bundle up over her dinosaur hides.

"No good?" She had thoughts of disease, poison, the Nissa hailing from a radioactive wasteland, but then Stig said, "Those who have Kay'mal Khan know we want her. They have used a machine, where she is, that works against the frequency of us and our place." He sagged, as though the effort involved in translating was exhausting. "We are steeped in our world. You are not." He nodded at Mal. "So, we open a door for you, you meet Kay'mal Khan, and we open another door to bring you all back."

Lee nodded, nodded some more, and then said, "You know we're not superheroes, right? I mean, Mal, maybe a little, but I'm just someone who writes blogs on animals that don't really exist for a living."

"It will work or it won't," Stig said, shrugging and looking away. If it was a Nissa figure of speech, it was an uninspiring one. "There is someone there you will meet. He will help you. He too works to save the universe." At that, he looked her in the eye for once. "And it's your universe, too. You have the right to help."

The right to help. Perhaps that was a Nissa thing, too. It suggested a fundamentally different approach to civic responsibility than Lee was used to.

"I mean, yes," she heard herself say. "I really want to rescue Dr. Khan from the rats, but ... you say the universe is ending. All our branches are breaking into each other, because something's gone fundamentally wrong, right?"

Stig gave a little upward nod.

"Well, how can even the smartest person in our world help,

when you're obviously so much more advanced than us? How can we possibly add anything?"

Stig touched her arm gently, although his latent strength could have crushed her bicep to jelly.

"We cannot know what we do not know. We cannot see what we do not see," he said, the words coming slowly, heavy with thought. "Dr. Khan understands the numbers behind the branches and the worlds, although that is not what she thought she was studying. She can help because, when we take her to where the problem is, she will have different thoughts to us. She will have ideas that come from places our history has closed the doors to. And it will not just be her and us. There will be other minds, all working. Only one needs to find the answer, but difference is strength. To save everything, we need as much difference as possible. Everywhere we have found those who can understand, looked for the brightest minds to take with us on the journey." He took a deep breath, plainly embarrassed at having talked so much, all in one go.

One of his relatives said something brisk at that point and began moving her hands in mystic passes. A cold light glittered in trails where she'd touched, so that Lee could almost make out the shape of the vast invisible machine she was interacting with.

"We're going now?" she asked, but then there was a screech of metal. Another Nissa man was shouldering his way between the lot's barriers, carrying a bin bag over his shoulder. Something about his pantomime clearly communicated "Sorry I'm late" without any words needing to be said.

He dumped out the contents of another bag, revealing yet more clothes: fake furs, scarves, mittens, woollen jumpers. Just looking at them made Lee sweat.

"Oh, fuck," Mal said. "We're going *there*, are we?"

Stig nodded impassively.

"Narnia...?" Lee asked helplessly, and then she understood. *The cold place—the really cold place.*

If it was Narnia, it was a Narnia where the White Witch had won. Always winter, forever and forever, in a world that had died a hundred million years before lions might have evolved.

From the dull, surly heat of London summer to... this. Ice as far as the eye could see, a crystalline field of it beneath a sky ragged with torn strips of cloud. They raced along in a wind that seemed entirely divorced from the weather down at ground level. Here snow skirled and flurried in bands and tatters, seeming to form fleeting images against the clarity of the ice. And there were lights in that ice: Lee could look down and see vast, translucent depths where cold, clear radiances winked and moved like deep-sea fish. Patterns, patterns always shifting, but never anything that spoke meaning to her human eyes.

Lee felt a shock of recognition as she looked from those lights to the snow, to the clouds, to the frozen horizon. Her breath was pluming, the cold burning the exposed skin about her eyes. It was all patterns. It was all one pattern. She almost saw it, just for an instant. The world around her was frozen dead, yet animate. Even the weather was part of a vast and sentient system.

Then she lost the sense of it, left only with an overpowering sense of awe.

Stig was already moving, not looking back to see if his fragile human wards were following. He trekked out into the endless antarctic waste, without even the courtesy of an "I may be some time."

"This is London too, is it?" Lee demanded.

"London in high summer!" Mal called back, muffled by two layers of scarf. "I was here once before."

"Me too, remember. Almost killed me."

They hurried after Stig, and Lee wondered whether this was it, a death march to a parallel world's gulag across this killing wasteland. Her feet were already numb as they marched to a destination invisible beyond the horizon.

Her next step was uphill.

She stopped, but that was fine because Stig had stopped too, standing there like Moses parting the sea. Except it was not the landscape ahead which moved, but the ground beneath their feet. Lee felt the temperature rise abruptly, a wash of mere cool where before there had been sub-zero cold. From deep within the ice came a long, tormented groan, and she and Mal clung together as the world lurched, shuddered and lifted them all up.

"What the hell?" she demanded. A tower was growing beneath them, the ice flowing like liquid to force it upwards, one storey, five storeys, higher and higher. Not straight up, either, but rushing forwards, rising at a steep angle—like a building-sized serpent striking. All round them the icy plain was fracturing and cracking. Again she almost grasped the pattern, like code written across the landscape in letters large enough to be seen from space.

"The masters of this place"—Stig had to raise his voice over the suddenly rushing wind—"are very powerful, very wise. And dead, very dead a long time. This world is their corpse, and they inhabit it still."

But Lee was staring down at the ice as it surged forwards— *on, Donner; on, Blitzen!*—hurling them across the landscape and, simultaneously, high into the sky.

"But why are they doing *this*?" she asked, not that she was complaining—it was perhaps the most magnificent thing she had ever experienced—but still...

"We travel from branch to branch, but it is easiest if we match place and velocity!" Stig told her. "Now, you are ready." Not a question but a statement.

"Velocity?" she said. "Wait, where are we—?"

The door in the air opened for them so suddenly it cut the question in two.

Interlude: The Hedonists

Excerpt from *Other Edens: Speculative Evolution and Intelligence* by Professor Ruth Emerson of the University of California

We're getting close to home now. It's been a long voyage to reach our timeline, half a billion years over multiple Earths. But the branch point of this particular Earth diverges from our own only around ten million years ago. It is almost modern. Great swathes of grassland are beating back the forests of the world; herds of grazing animals drift across them, practically familiar from nature documentaries. There are oreodonts like waddling hippo-sized pigs; elephant relatives (with long lower lips, functioning as a thumb alongside the grasping finger of their short trunk); camels, deer, hornless rhinos. Everything seems larger than life, ruminating bellies crammed with bales of tough, nourishment-poor grass.

And there are primates. If you could look back millions of years, you might see a troupe of cunning apes. These fall somewhere between the baboon and the bonobo, and are staking out a waterhole with what seems like optimistically predatory intent. They have no tools more dangerous than a stick to winkle out termites, but their gaze is intent on the elephant relatives. They hoot and bellow in a frenzy of furious noise, jabbering, leaping on a wretched herbivore's back and off again, throwing faeces like the filthy beasts they are. Their victim, a young male, lashes at them with his trunk, bellowing angrily, trampling after them as they flee into the grass. So much for the hunting efforts of our might-have-been-ancestors.

What takes the elephant is a cat built like a bear. It's armed with curved teeth that it uses to carve open the luckless herbivore's flanks before applying these daggers like pitons— staking one haunch. Another two of its kin leap a moment later, tearing open thick grey hide. They work at hamstringing, climbing claw over claw up their prey's side to bite at the back of its neck. Between them, they bring the lumbering pachyderm to its knees and hold it there until blood loss drops it, keeping out of reach of trunk and tusks. The primates look on cautiously, their work done.

The three cats cough and mutter at one another, spraying a little scent for emphasis. They begin to dismember the carcass, sitting on their haunches like bears, or perhaps huge and murderous hamsters. One frees a rib from the corpse and cracks the bone at an angle with her carnassials before using the sharp edge like a crude blade to flense away at the meat. They have thumbs, not as nimble as yours or mine but enough for tools of convenience.

There is a lot of meat on a dead elephant, more than even these monster cats can eat. However, they leave precious little on the bones for the vultures and hyenas that keep hungry watch. The cats grumble and cough at each other throughout. Teeth, claws and makeshift tools make short work of all that flesh.

The primates approach the cats deferentially, body language loud with tones of submission. The hunters flick ears at them, growl a little. Then all three stand, four-legged, thumbs held upwards to keep clear of the ground. When they amble off, the primates are following them, semi-bipedal, carrying the joints and slabs of meat like paid porters. You know the drill now: not your Earth and not your story. This world belongs to the cats.

These creatures are not what you'd call sabre-toothed tigers, but teeth like those turn up like a bad penny throughout the fossil record. Their ancestors in our histories are called barbourofelids: husky killers that terrorized the world for ten million years or so. They then died out before they could trouble the dreams of the earliest humans.

This species lives in prides and hunts a wide range of prey. The thumbs are lucky happenstance, a freak mutation. Over the next few million years these Miocene felids will languorously expand into a variety of habitats; prides will draw territorial lines that become diplomatic boundaries. Toolmaking will be improved on, and in this the cats will be assisted by domesticated breeds of smaller animals. Various creatures come to live in their shadow and treat them with slavish deference. Ten million years back they had primates to pick fleas off them and fetch water in rolled leaves, look after kittens and bury the cats' excrement. And sometimes to serve as a light snack. Yet they stayed, subservient to a fault. Meerkats and mongooses were their cleaners, honey badgers their guard dogs and monkeys their valets and artisans— weaving wicker, shaping stone, crafting bright masks or creating false manes of bone and feather.

Perhaps the primates are receiving protection from the association, though nothing that protects them from the cats, but this is not the symbiosis at work. The cats are only half the masters of the world. Their partners in crime are single-celled amoebae that infest both the cats and a wide variety of animals sharing a habitat with them. Far more than the disputed effects of *Toxoplasma gondii* in your domestic pets, this infection burrows into the brains of its non-feline victims. It instils in them a deep adulation for the cats, their scent, the sight of them, their needs. Tribes of primates, far from becoming world-striding hominids, are merely the servants, and the cats have evolved to make use of them.

Over time the cats develop a culture of leisured aristocrats. They rule, preen, confabulate about the nature of the universe as they lie about in the shelters their creatures build for them. They develop their minds, and their aim is always to do less work than the generation before them. The most successful communities are those where not only the cats but also the parasites have evolved, bringing more species into the fold to queue up their throats for the knife, or settle at the cats' feet to make and serve and work. The cats eventually become aware of their invisible ally as their vicarious technology advances. At the height of their sophistication, perhaps half a million years ago, the cats held sway over a global empire, countless small polities getting on because wars are too much like hard work. Meanwhile, feline scholars earn their credentials through the extended erudition of their scurrying packs of monkey minions. Their microbial science is exceptional, and they work hard at honing the efficiency of the little passenger—engineering it through trial and error until it can leap to just about any species they choose and stay ahead of any resistance it might encounter. Rather indolently, the great cats secure their hold on the world by having all of nature love and worship them. In ten million years they pass from being at the mercy of the elements to inhabiting a genuine Eden, where every beast is placed on the Earth for their convenience.

They are there still, unchallenged rulers of everything they survey. There are no scientists as such any more, though some still while away lazy hours in idle speculation. They make nothing, because anything they might conceive of is made for them. And at the first presentiment of privation there is a world of species ready to give up comfort, time and life so the cats can continue to prosper. Not a world you'd want to visit, in case you ended up at their feet, grooming their luxurious coats and hoping you were too small a morsel to prove appetizing.

13.

I

Every few days, Rove made an inspection. Dr. Rat fawned on him, and so did the dozen other rat-creature scientists and mathematicians who were in and out of the lab at any given time. Kay had already worked out that hierarchy amongst them was something of all-consuming importance as far as they were concerned. Dr. Rat was very definitely in charge, and didn't let any of them forget it, but below him there were constant confrontations and escalations as various underlings tried to pull rank on their fellows. It was almost entirely done with body language. Kay imagined that there might be a scent element to it as well, but they were all so universally pungent, and her poor human nose was incapable of picking up any of the subtext. For a long while she had decided the rat-creatures just stank, but then she'd caught one of the more junior scientists applying a reeking cologne and realized they were all "dressing for success" in the nose department. They were drenching themselves with the olfactory equivalent of the elaborately impractical clothes their superiors wore.

She, as a giant alien from a parallel Earth, was excused from having to play games. She intimidated them because she had unwittingly been born with the biggest signifier of superiority in their world: taking up a huge amount of space. They practically tied themselves into knots around her, trying to suppress their own instinct to cower and defer. Only Dr. Rat was comfortable enough in his post to get past it, and he was more than happy to poke her and shoo her out of the way when he wanted to look over her figures. He ignored the human-style keyboard and screen, instead plugging his techno-monocle into her terminal and viewing things there.

She had seen a lot of their kind, by now. Not just in the lab, either. She had made some advances in the field of counter-surveillance, in fact, and had smuggled in a steady stream of images from the world below the airship. She'd seen rooms of ratlings, crop-eared and lop-tailed, crammed in like battery hens. They'd seemed intent on whatever their goggles showed them, double-thumbed hands busy with their spindly interfaces. These were classrooms, she'd understood at last. This packed throng was learning, because learning gave you status and a chance at a job that might give you space for a family, for a brood of your own. These were the lucky ones. She had been looking at a rat-creature private school for the offspring of the affluent middle class, or what-ever their equivalent was. The poorer echelons—meaning the vast majority of their gridlocked global civilization—lived and died without education or prospects, choking on fumes and pollution, victims of violence caused by overpopulation and stress, starving, suffocating...

Kay very badly wanted to see the rat-creatures as a plague that sought to unleash itself on the rest of the universe, her Earth included. Yet after a month of clandestinely spying on her captors, she characterized them more as their own primary victims. Oh, she could certainly despise their leadership caste, with its monopolization of the world's assets and free space. But even the considerable luxury they lived in would seem cramped to a reasonably prosperous human.

Rove always spoke with Dr. Rat about her, pointedly asking how "he" was doing. Kay tried to anticipate his visits, so she could wear one of the dowdy suits he'd sourced for her. She generally stood looking miserable as Dr. Rat bragged about the great strides she was making under his erudite guidance. The creature strutted back and forth before Rove and his thuggish bodyguard, body twisting and undulating. His little hands made grand gestures like a dictator before a rally, only for him to collapse back into cowering when either of the men shifted position.

Then it was Kay's turn. Daniel Rove strode over, hands behind his back. "The little *dottori* seem quite taken with you," he noted on one visit. "Of course, they're always very keen to impress on me how much they've achieved with the tools at hand. Perhaps you'd like to comment."

Kay was well aware that the translator was feeding all that back to Dr. Rat, but Rove plainly didn't care. Besides, the rats did seem to be profoundly rude to anyone they considered beneath them, so maybe that was just basic etiquette this side of the looking glass.

"We have a good mathematical model of the declining forces that form the structure of the branching universes," she confirmed. "We've attempted to isolate some of the matter, energy or particles involved—using the bigger accelerators down below—but so far that's still—" She bit off "up in the air," because the last thing she wanted was Rove's derisive laugh at anything resembling a joke. "Inconclusive," she finished awkwardly.

"And can you affect the decline?"

"Using our equations, one of the practical labs was able to reverse the degradation measurably for five one-hundredths of a second. The results appear to be replicable. However, as matters stand, there is insufficient energy to achieve a greater result."

Rove raised an eyebrow. "We want to preserve a part of the universe, a lifeboat when the ship goes down. I think we'll find the energy. What are we saving it for, after all? One Earth, two...We can burn quite a lot to get what we want." He gave her his brisk, soulless smile and would obviously have left at that point. Yet Khan's professional pride was pricking her, and she added, "There are other ways. I think it's a question of leverage."

Rove regarded her. "Explain."

"We are...not best placed to affect these forces, here. It's like we're pushing on the short end of a lever."

"I'm aware what 'leverage' means, Dr. Khan."

"There is a gradient in the changes we have modelled. The disintegration within the universe is *coming* from somewhere...Or to put it another way, the disintegration is a symptom of a collapsing core structure, originating somewhere else. Like ripples—so when it gets to us, the wavefront is so broad we can't do anything to stop it. But if we were at the source..."

"What source?" Rove demanded.

"Well..." Kay shrugged. "That's the question."

"Answer it," Rove said. "And find out how much energy you need to move the lever from this end, otherwise." With that,

379

and a stern glower at the shrinking rodents, he was gone with his man at his heels.

"Fuck you, mate," Kay said when he was safely out of earshot. Then the chief scientist drew himself up and screeched at his underlings to get back to work. *Not good enough*, Kay could almost hear. *Results! Results! Results!*

Later, when the workforce had been dismissed—sent to their tiny beds or banished to sift data in lesser labs—Dr. Rat approached her. With great ceremony, he took out a bottle. It wasn't exactly Scotch, but the rats had alcohol and it was potent stuff. The translator had fished out her vapes, too. Back home she wouldn't have touched the things, but the smell of cigarettes violently offended the rats. When she was in rodent company she was reduced to inhaling a nicotinous mist. It stopped her climbing the walls with withdrawal pangs, at least.

"Show me what he's been up to, Doctor," she suggested.

"With eminent pleasure, my fellow doctor," the translator interpreted, and Dr. Rat began pulling up images on her screen.

Spying went two ways, and maybe Rove would look in on them. However, Dr. Rat had already set the surveillance gear in the lab to provide fake images, culled from other days, all nicely set to the correct time stamp. Rove was a suspicious bastard, no doubt, but he was also used to being in control of the situation, the top dog whom everyone was afraid of. It bred a certain complacency, Kay suspected.

In their spare time, she and Dr. Rat had been feeling out the extent of Rove's plans, none of which looked good. She had seen recordings from this Earth and her own, which had been instructive. She now knew that, over in her Earth, Rove kept a whole training ground of what she thought of as Rovetroopers—a uniformed youth corps keen on drills and combat training and survivalist exercises. They were all clean-jawed and nouveau Blackshirt. She wasn't sure where he'd got them from, but likely Billy White's mob hadn't been the only pack of neo-Nazis on the clandestine payroll. Doubtless they would be the pioneer corps for Rove's brave new world. He had them hunting rats back home too, she'd seen, luckless rat-weasels released onto the Scottish Highlands. Rove's people were rewarded for every tail they brought back. A couple had died, but he wasn't exactly pitting his men against the rat kings' special forces, just the starving poor and desti-tute. It made for easy victories and bloodlust to bind them together and to him. And anyone who got cold feet about killing rat-things that cringed and begged at their feet got cut from the programme, and probably from existence. Besides the Rovetroopers, Rove had stockpiled food, tools, petrol, vehicles: a man prepping for an apocalypse he certainly had no intention of averting.

She had wondered about that, because what if it really *couldn't* be averted. Surely Rove and his goose-steppers surviving in some fascist paradise was better than *nothing* surviving? There was a rational case to be made, but she couldn't bring herself to accept it. *And besides, who says we can't save everything?*

The figures, she suspected unhappily, didn't support her hopes, but she wasn't giving up yet.

Dr. Rat partook of another glass with her. The rodent liquor was potent, and she dreaded to think what it was made from. But the receptacles were little more than thimble-sized, enough to take the edge off with no danger of getting her indiscreetly drunk. She took the chance to change, too, out of the drab suit and into clothes that she and Dr. Rat had arranged to be fabricated. They let Kay feel like herself again for a bit.

"Fuck the lot of them," she tried experimentally. She heard the discrete chitter of the translator and wondered if what Dr. Rat heard preserved the sense or was bewilderingly literal.

It helped that she got on roaringly well with the little doctor. He seemed to be exactly that kind of death-by-ulcer, anxious supervisor type she'd met back when she was amongst humans—save that he could also walk the walk, science-wise. And he was a quisling, of course, which also helped. Rove wasn't to know his star performing rodent was already booked into someone else's circus.

Right about then, something lit up in Dr. Rat's monocle, folded partway up but still in view. He slipped it back in place and then went very still, holding up a little manicured hand for quiet.

"Fortuitous times are upon us," the calm voice of the translator informed her. "We have witnessed the much-awaited transpiration of our allies."

Kay's heart leapt. "They're here, now?"

"All measurements suggest so," agreed Dr. Rat. "There is now required a time of risk and preparation. Remain here and endeavour to be prepared for all eventualities. I must gather necessary and valuable things."

She imagined Dr. Rat with a suitcase of diamonds and jewellery, lengths of gold chain caught in the hinges and dragging behind him. She admitted to herself she had no idea what one of the rat-creatures would consider so valuable that it couldn't be left behind.

"And then?" she asked.

"I shall retrieve the agents of our emancipation and bring you to them, or them to you, or a combination of both options," Dr. Rat confirmed. "And there will be a multitude of leaving this midden behind."

II

It was almost pitch-dark.

Lee had been braced for their headlong rushing momentum to stop without warning. But instead she was momentarily completely still, with all that inertia somehow perfectly taken care of. A moment later she sat down heavily, overcompensating for the jolting shift that hadn't happened.

"Ow. What?" she demanded vaguely of the darkness. "Mal?"

Mal's hand groped for hers and found the top of her head instead, giving her a proprietorial pat. "We're in an aircraft, I think?" she said. "I feel engines."

Once she'd given herself a moment to adjust, Lee agreed. Wherever they were, there was a constant rumbling thrum from somewhere, seeming to come from a fair distance. A *big* aircraft, then.

She stood, leaning on Mal, and stamped experimentally. The metal floor was concave and felt none too thick, with space beneath it. It was cold, too; draughty. The outside air getting in? "We're at the bottom of it, maybe, in the belly. Cargo hold?"

"Could be." Mal sounded slightly further off. There was a clatter as she ran into something. "Goddamn Nissa could have given us a torch."

"They are completely mad, you realize," Lee said mournfully. "I mean, sending *us*?"

"We're here and they trust us." Mal chuckled. "It's a million-to-one long shot, and only these two desperate lesbians can save the world. Perfect action movie material."

Trust us not to screw them over, maybe, Lee considered. *Not necessarily trust us not to screw up.* "What have you found?"

"Chandelier...?" Mal said uncertainly. Lee groped towards her and found a spiral arrangement of can-shaped objects hanging from a ceiling that turned out to be only six inches over her head. The things, whatever they were, came away in her hand, then clanked back into place with a magnetic tug. She could now perceive a little light, and she realized that it was coming from below—a dim silvery luminance glimmering from a strip that ran the length of the chamber. Feeling down, Lee found a crack in the floor, from whence the light came. For a moment she was terrified, sure the structure was unsound. Then she spotted that they were kneeling on the very faint outline of two double doors. Of course! Cargo had to come in somehow.

When she pressed an eye to the gap, she could just see that they were passing over a city spread out below them. It extended as far as her limited vantage showed her, a complex range of lit areas surrounded by darkness, linked by thoroughfares. It looked dull, as though someone had taken a human city and turned down the dimmer switch. There was movement on the broad roads between the various centres, though, and that meant the vehicles must be monolithically huge, given how high up they were.

There was nothing human in the organization of the lights though. She saw no sign of streets, grids or anything like that: the lit areas seemed to have sprung up as randomly as fungus. And, just as the dark between stars held only fainter stars, the more she looked, the more dim lamps she saw, until she realized there was nothing beneath her that was not city. Their conveyance coursed smoothly over a metropolis that showed no sign of ending or even changing, more splotches of light creeping into view in an endless urban progress.

"I don't think we're going fast enough to be in a plane," she said slowly. "Could this be something else—their version of an airship?"

Mal might have shrugged. "Maybe."

"Only...this might be paranoia, but what might you keep in a compartment like this? With doors that could flap open when you're going over a city? And you've stored a whole load of magnetic objects, which would simply drop when you turned the magnets off..."

Mal digested that. "You're saying the Nissa ported us into a bomb bay?"

"Just a thought." Lee stood up and jangled another of the hanging assemblages, wincing. "Can we get out of here?"

"Dunno," Mal said.

Without warning, a hatch opened in the ceiling further down the bay, letting in a harsh square of reddish light. It gleamed on three more spiral arrangements of what Lee was now certain were bombs. A head appeared at the end of a flexible neck. It was a rat-weasel, all arrowhead skull and big, tufted ears, with a technical-looking monocle over one bulging eye. It saw them and withdrew instantly in what Lee parsed as alarm.

"That's torn it. Mal, this was a stupid idea. What was the *plan*?"

"The Nissa have a contact here. They said the Fishnet would alert their contact to come find us. Then all we have to do is get to Khan, and the Nissa will drag us out. Hey presto."

"They didn't bother to tell *me* any of that."

"Lucky I asked, then. Frankly, they're crap at explanations." Mal was at her side again, squeezing her arm. "They assume you know stuff, a lot of the time. They're big on self-sufficiency, where they come from."

Lee was watching the hatch, waiting for a rodent death squad to drop down. "You saw where they come from, you said."

"When they took me from the dinosaur place, the first time," Mal confirmed. "Peaceful, underpopulated. All green and natural. Nice retirement option, right?"

"Except the universe is ending, so it doesn't matter."

"Except that, right."

"Visitors from the distance, undertake no aggression."

There was just enough light for Lee to exchange glances with Mal. The voice had been artificial, human, almost-female.

"Also, conduct yourselves with a minimum of confusion, as on the detection of your presence woeful consequences would transpire."

"You had better be our contact," Mal grated.

"Your surmise is accurate." And it was tempting to poke fun at its broken English, except it meant the creature was impressively streets ahead of either Lee or Mal linguistically. "I now intend to enter the bombardment chamber and entreat no violence from you." The calm, flatly melodious tones jarred with what was actually being said.

A moment later, the head reappeared, and then the rest of the creature plus a friend, slipping through the hatch with a fluid agility. The foremost of the rat-weasels was wearing what Lee uncharitably decided resembled someone's show-offy wedding cake—complete with layers and way too much icing. At its back was another of the creatures, like a Terminator-style death cyborg. She only revised her opinion when it became clear the creature's function was to translate.

For a moment they were monsters: inhuman without being animals, the Beasts from the Uncanny Valley. Lee felt a spike of some emotion that had no precise name but partook equally of fear, revulsion and existential dread.

When the silence on both sides had ticked on a handful of seconds more, she started to recast them. For one thing, they were so much smaller than human. And while that didn't necessarily make them less fearsome or hideous, it would skew the odds in her favour if it came down to fisticuffs. For another, there was enough commonality of body language between the hominid and the rodent that she could tell they were terrified. And why not? This was their world; they were the poor natives confronted by gigantic alien monsters.

"Hi," she said. "I'm Lee, this is Mal. We're here on a mission to get our scientist back."

The leading rodent drew itself up and spoke, or at least made a lot of chittering and squeaking sounds, many of which were on the very edge of Lee's hearing. The calm false voice came from the other, or specifically from its implant.

"Your surmise is accurate," it repeated. "Communiques have been received detailing your requirements and a plan of action has been draw up to be effected. Details of the reciprocal arrangement must now vary—and progress may not be attained without your verification."

"Repeat, please," Mal prompted. "What do you mean, 'reciprocal arrangement'?"

"I now require the accelerated extraction of myself and precious accoutrements owing to worsening conditions and increased security threat," the implant, or its owner, translated. Lee was beginning to get a sense of urgent agitation in the lead rodent that the translation was not conveying.

"Perhaps escape was its price for helping... I don't suppose the Nissa said anything about this, when you were briefed?" she murmured to Mal, who shook her head.

"What is your job here?" Lee asked.

The creature listened to its end of the translation and then adopted a grandiose posture—and it was such a *pose* that Lee virtually crammed her fist into her mouth to stop herself laughing. To human eyes the only descriptor for it would be "fabulous." The ratty head went up, muzzle angled towards the ceiling, and the creature stood tall so that all the spiky tiers of its peculiar outfit splayed out. They prodded the interpreter in the side, making it shift over irritably. The calm translation relayed its chittering as, "I am the great scientist Dr. Rat."

The name was the last straw, and the best Lee could do was turn the laugh into a bleating sound which, fortunately, the translator didn't do anything with. Possibly it sounded like an awed exclamation if you were a rat-weasel.

"Matey here is their Dr. Khan, maybe?" Mal murmured. She'd meant it for Lee, but the translator chittered its own version; of course those rodent ears were more sensitive than humans'. "The Nissa wanted different viewpoints, and the weas... welcoming party here obviously have the science to understand what's going on. But we were here for the doc..."

"All plans require urgent acceleration, including full provision for the extraction of valuables," said the translator's voice, and some kind of switch had been thrown to give it a lower, ominous tone. Dr. Rat had relaxed its extraordinary posture but was still standing tall—*defiant*, Lee read. And, behind that, *frightened*.

"You want out now, and you want to bring your stuff," she summarized.

"Your surmise is admirably accurate," came the translated sentiments of Dr. Rat.

"We can do that," Mal said confidently. Lee badly wanted to qualify her friend's words. This was high-stakes poker, and Mal was bluffing on a hand of utter junk. Still, Dr. Rat seemed to accept the promise without question. It bunched itself, the layered clothes concertinaing about its lithe body, and then bolted almost straight up through the hatch in the ceiling.

The translator cowered when Lee approached. There was intelligence in its eyes and manner, rather than it being some lobotomized cyborg. In the reddish light from the opening above, its shaved head looked blotchy and misshapen. The edges where its flesh met the metal implant were ragged and badly healed.

"Does that hurt?" Lee asked. The creature seemed to understand, although it flinched back from her voice. Perhaps the relatively low voice of a human sounded unpleasant and threatening to its cropped ears. Then it said—no, *recited*—"We are all in pain together." The phrase sounded like a piece of folk wisdom or a politician's campaign slogan. She remembered the rodents who'd been reclining in luxury when they'd jumped through with Dr. Khan. They hadn't looked like they were in pain, but she could imagine them mouthing the words to the suffering masses below. Or perhaps she was inventing all that out of whole cloth and the cultural fine print was too small for her human eyes. It left her with a queasy feeling, nonetheless.

Then a cable dropped down, and both she and the translator twitched. It was segmented with regular nodules and, before its end had stopped swinging, rats began crawling down it, nose first. Nose to tail, nose to rump, a grimly determined procession until Mal and Lee were surrounded by a host of scrawny, hairy bodies.

There were about thirty of them, but many had little ratlings clinging to their pelts or garment loops. Most wore shapeless grey or dun smocks, but a few looked as though they had basked in the great Dr. Rat's reflected glory, their elaborate clothes tricked out in stiff and pointlessly space-filling pleats and folds. They were all festooned with sling bags and packs, each of them carrying their own body weight in bric-a-brac and nonsense, as though they were setting up an impromptu car boot sale in the bomb bay. Lee wanted to laugh, and then something flipped in her mind and she felt disgusted by her own anthropocentrism. The comical posturing of Dr. Rat, the hilariously overladen rodents turning up like a bad cliché in a farce...except it was none of it funny. Dr. Rat was desperate. His "precious valuables" were his family, whom he needed to get out of danger, and who knew what persecutions and horrors went on in this place? They were refugees—and they were willing to throw themselves on the mercy of a different species, from another world, on the wager that it was better than whatever life they had here.

"We have to help them," she said to Mal, who gave her a somewhat wild look.

"Good luck with that," was her answer, but she nodded. Lee squeezed her hand, knowing her friend would do whatever was in her power. "But first," Mal declared, "Dr. Rat, we need to retrieve Dr. Khan, in a way that's not going to get us caught and dissected."

Dr. Rat seemed to find no hyperbole in that statement. "Vivisection is by far the more probable outcome," the translator noted crisply; and Lee could have done without the candour. "Owing to superior planning, measures are in place for extraction of your co-specific. This onerous task falls to the pre-eminent Dr. Rat—to abstract fellow scholar Dr. Kay from her location and convey her herewith."

"Uh," Mal said, "any chance of conveying her somewhere that isn't filled with explosives? Only..."

"No hostilities are anticipated in the immediate future, absent unheralded unrest in the conurbation beneath," the translator failed to reassure them. "Sufficient difficulty will be encountered in the conveyance of my learned colleague, Dr. Khan. The transport of two additional giant extradimensionals would interpose a needless logistical barrier. Also, the majority of locales within this vessel do not readily admit organisms of your proportions."

They turned the words over until the meaning fell out.

"I guess we're lucky we turned up without our heads stuck in the ceiling," Lee said soberly.

"Fishnet knows its business," Mal said. "Okay, Dr. Rat, go get Doc Khan ASAP. We'll wait here with your folks and hope nobody starts a war." She was clearly frustrated that she couldn't go herself and sort it out with her two hominid hands. However, this was one enemy base they weren't going to be able to sneak through by dressing up as guards.

"Admirable correctness in all particulars," the translator confirmed.

Dr. Rat made a piping speech to the huddle of other rat-creatures, all of whom had been eyeing Mal and Lee with no small concern. Hopefully, they were being reassured that these ogreish outlanders had no taste for rodent flesh.

III

Waiting for Dr. Rat's reappearance was one of the hardest things Kay had ever done. She had no doubt that Rove would be a vindictive fucker if she was caught trying to get out from under his prim thumb. She had already backed up her work as discreetly as possible. Dr. Rat had given her portable storage in the form of a thumbnail-sized wedge of plastic, and it all fitted onto there somehow. She'd have liked to take the whole lab's results, but her human-enabled system had only limited permissions within the rats' wider network.

Dr. Rat and his cyborg shadow returned at last, and she knew them well enough to see that the creatures were frantic with worry. *We're committed, then. No turning back.* "The rescue team—they're here?"

"Indubitably present, indeed." The doctor was skittering about the laboratory, connecting his monocle to one terminal after another, making adjustments. "Measures are in place for great mendacity insofar as laboratory surveillance is concerned," the translator explained. "However, beyond these environs sufficient control of systems is not possible. Hence you will require carriage."

"You what, now?" Kay asked, imagining a straining sedan chair with a score of rodents labouring to cart her about.

Dr. Rat dashed across the lab, practically on all fours, which she knew was a sign of extreme nervous agitation. He slid open a screen to reveal a plastic crate, its sides marked with a succession of symbols in dull reddish colours. She knew these would be vibrant to the rodents' eyes, and probably backed with various warning scents and textures too. *Hazardous contents.*

He hauled it out, and it glided frictionlessly over the metal floor. The plan unfolded away from her in directions she didn't much like.

"I won't fit in there," she said.

"It is imperative you do," was all Dr. Rat had to say about that.

"Look, Doctor, if this goes wrong I'm going to be a fucking fish in a barrel." Not a helpful metaphor. "I'll be stuck in there for Rove or one of your guys to shoot me."

"My honoured colleague, if matters fail to transpire as we wish, then we are both entirely fucked," the translator said crisply. Kay did a double take, wondering where that vernacular had come from and whether some of this over-elaborate language wasn't an artefact of translation at all but a very clever rodent having fun.

"Sod it," she said, and got into the crate, folding herself up knees to chin, already feeling her muscles trembling. "Be quick."

"With all appropriate celerity," Dr. Rat agreed, and then he and his assistant had closed the lid, leaving her in utter darkness.

The container started to move after that, periods of weird gliding contrasting with sudden stops and changes of direction. Kay's right foot was cramping, but when she tried to twist it she jogged the lid, leading to a sudden stillness outside before their progress resumed. She gritted her teeth and pressed her nails into her calves to try and distract herself. Her neck and shoulders were starting to twinge.

Then they stopped, and she realized there was some full-blown debate or argument going on, with more than two rodent voices. She imagined a patrol of rat troopers halting Dr. Rat and demanding to know what was in the box.

Utterly helpless, all she could do was wait. Even when she heard their sharp-nailed hands at the latch, she kept the screaming inside.

There was a renewed shrilling, probably Dr. Rat again. She wondered if he was pointing at the danger markings, telling them they'd be fatally irradiated the moment they opened up. Holding her breath, Kay waited. Every muscle in her body seemed to be spasming, adrenaline building up in her tissues with no possible outlet. *Oh fuck oh fuck oh fuck.*

And then, without warning, they were off again. For a long while she wasn't even sure who still had her—maybe the rat troopers had confiscated the crate for disposal or examination—but at last they stopped again and the lid was levered off, revealing the only two rodent faces she wanted to see.

"It is not suitable for disembarkation," the translator cautioned her. "However rejoice, for delivery is nigh."

"I am bloody glad to hear it," Kay hissed back.

"Your patience is appreciated," she was told, which was so much like being put on hold by customer services that she mustered a chuckle. Then the lid was back on and they were under way once more. There was more smooth gliding, and then what her stomach suggested was probably a lift going down. She had no idea how big the airship was, but it patently dwarfed anything human engineering had put in the air, a flying behemoth sufficient to make Jules Verne weep.

Now the movements were more hurried, so the container scraped walls and jolted over uneven plates in the floor. She imagined the lower levels of the ship, the less salubrious maintenance ways.

And then the challenge came that she'd been waiting for all this time. A voice snapping out for them to halt, in English. They kept moving until he called again: not Rove but his thug.

"What've you got in the box?" came the voice. "You, Brainiac, I know you can translate. No point playing dumb with me."

Then the calm, feminine voice of the translator's implant. "This is hazardous waste requiring disposal with the utmost of delicacy."

"Sure it is," said Rove's man. "And not a human scientist at all, then. Only, I've just been by the lab, Squeaker. On account of how I saw Doc Khan was working late, and how I'd got hold of a dozen packs of Benson & Hedges and was up for sharing. So imagine my surprise when the cameras showed Dr. Khan but my eyes didn't agree. Open the box."

"Hazardous and dangerous to the utmost extent," the translator noted calmly, though Kay could hear Dr. Rat's fevered chittering over it. "Inadvisable in any degree to access the containment. I raise all manner of protests!"

"Can it," said the thug.

Then something impacted the top edge of the crate—the man's boot, she realized. The crate tipped sideways, the lid came off, and she spilled out across the metal floor. For a brief moment her uppermost emotion was sheer relief that she wasn't crunched in any more.

Then she looked up and saw the man and his gun—levelled

steadily even though he was bent under the low ceiling. There were half a dozen rat troopers behind him, all with their nasty flechette shooters that would doubtless turn her and the other fugitives to jam. She crouched behind the upended crate, not that it would help.

"Dr. Khan," the thug said. "Over here, now."

Dr. Rat yattered something, but instead of the translator paraphrasing it, the creature's spindly hand grabbed Khan's wrist and dragged at her, trying to get her further down the low passageway.

"Not going to help," she said, but it was still tugging, its nails sharp in her skin.

"Dr. K," the thug said, and his hench-rats were muscling past his legs, screeching their own warnings.

Dr. Rat cast a look back. She saw the dim light glitter on his monocle before he leapt onto the toppled crate and went for what she had assumed was a decorative broach on his outlandish outfit.

The translator beside her shuddered. It clung to her arm, twitching and spasming. The rat troopers had the same reaction, dropping their weapons as they writhed, clawing at their rubbery masks. Kay could hear a high, tinny sound, like the whine of something electrical. Dr. Rat brandished the broach triumphantly.

"Know that I consider you something akin to a niece or distant cousin!" the translator passed on, to Kay's absolute bafflement.

Then the floor suddenly dropped beneath her like a hangman's trapdoor, and she and the translator were dumped into a hold full of dangling spirals of cannisters.

"What did he say?" she demanded. "You got that wrong."

But the translator was staring up, shaking, still clinging to her. A shot rang out. Just one shot, but Dr. Rat had been almost nose to muzzle with the thug's pistol, and a bullet meant to kill a human would tear a rat in half.

"Merciful God," Khan whispered.

The two of them were still in the pool of light from above. She made to move, and then realized there were bodies all around her. She shrieked, seeing heavily laden rodents pressing in like diminutive zombies. And humans, too: Lee Pryor, of all bloody people, and that lanky white girl, her friend.

"Everyone get in close!" Pryor was shouting, and Kay felt a score of clutching hands scrabbling at her.

"What the fuck's going on?" she said shrilly.

Mal grabbed Pryor's arm and lunged for Kay's shoulder.

"Boom," she declared.

Nothing happened.

Pryor glanced from her to Khan. "I thought this was it. I thought we just had to touch."

"Yeah."

"Oh, this is all very nice, but you little turds all better come up here right now." The thug was leaning through the hatch, upside down, gun levelled. Kay tried not to see the way he was spattered with blood. *Oh God, oh merciful God, I don't know if you care for poor, brave rat-creatures, but...* The gun seemed to have a magnetic presence, drawing her gaze to its brutal lines.

"I'm going to count to three," Rove's man said.

Kay watched the translator, at her feet, take a lead from its implant and connect it to a socket in the floor. Perhaps it said something, because the other rats were clustering even closer to her, clinging to her clothes, her ankles, anything they could reach.

"Two," said the thug.

For the second time the floor opened up beneath her. Only now there was no more airship beneath them, just the vastness of the sky and the bowl of an alien Earth.

Interlude: The Purists

Excerpt from *Other Edens:*
Speculative Evolution and Intelligence by
Professor Ruth Emerson of the
University of California

Two and a half million years ago, give or take, and a familiar world. Perhaps a few more varieties of macrofauna, a surplus of shapes of elephant. But there are apes that look like our ancestors to be found across Africa, ready to make their great leap forwards to seize the reins of evolutionary destiny.

This branch leads to a world gone awry, ever so slightly. For many ages, it is another cold Earth. The delicate inter-actions of orbit and albedo, the tugs of near-miss asteroids, the fluctuations of the sun itself introduce a variability that plays out somewhat differently every time.

In this Earth, the ice awoke a couple of million years ahead of schedule, piling on the weight of glaciers in the northern hemisphere, stressing the world with their grinding weight. Where the ice wasn't present, that pressure forced its way out as volcanic activity across all the fault lines of the world, filling the air with ash and poison. Each time the ice came, it squeezed this Earth tighter in its grip, each interglacial period flipping the world into a harsher, more barren climate. This passes, but it is the crucible that forged our players here.

In Africa there were many primate varieties, big-brained, social, omnivorous. We could look for our near cousins and find the huge and powerful gorilla-forms, along with bands of predatory chimpanzee kin. The latter combine speed and wits with a taste for meat, and have the mental capacity to reap entertainment from ripping a monkey apart. There are monkeys too, and it's not their story either. Instead, while this Earth was being crushed by the ice and sickened by its own inner fires, there was a species of lemur just smart enough to know it was having a hard time.

The big lemurs are just shy of the chimps in size but in no way able to go toe to toe with them. And they're brainy, the harsh conditions spurring their intellects into overdrive. A handful of chance mutations also start a cascade of evolutionary advances in communication and social organization. The lemurs come to an awareness of themselves as threatened on all sides and inheritors of a world that's trying to kill them.

What saves them is community, and an emergent culture that draws very definite lines on the world. They build walls and barriers which declare this as *inside* and that *outside*. They learn the scent, fur patterns and facial markings of their kin and declare them *us* and everything else *them*. Even when they have hunted their threats to extinction they remember the big cats, the marauding bands of apes; these become the goblins and ogres of their folk tales. And even as the glacial and interglacial periods alternate in their slow dance, this emergent civilization marks out a hundred small polities in equatorial Africa.

Lemur communities replace the forest with monocultures, trees that grow only what they prefer to feed on. But eventually the soil is exhausted, depleted by its denuded ecosystem, and harvests fail. When cupboards are bare, eyes turn to their neighbours' orchards and plantations. It doesn't take a lemur genius to work out that it's easier to spend four days stealing someone else's harvest than six months growing your own.

So the farmers train devoted bands of orchard guardians to risk their lives against the stone, copper and bronze of their attackers. And, eventually, the elders whose ancestors appointed these valiant defenders find them at their doorstep— with sticks and stones, and a particularly nasty sort of beaked mace fashioned like an eagle's head. They say: *We take the risks, we reap the rewards. We rule now.* After a few generations, any village that isn't run by a military aristocracy has gone the way of the dodo.

Now every surviving city state is a military dictatorship, where warriors are lionized and whose leaders are celebrated in song and story. The martial cities feed themselves on tales of how their ancestors were "destined," and how they are not just more skilled at wielding the beaky mace, but *superior.* Everyone else is fit only to work the fields and clean the dung pits. Or, when you get right down to it, to be driven out of their villages by the bronze-mailed phalanxes of the warriors. It gets to the point where reputation steals a march on reality, but hearts and minds are half the battle. If your enemies keep running away, it's easy to maintain a winning streak.

The leading city states can still be found in a vast fertile basin in Africa. They change over the centuries, but what doesn't change is the creed. Every state is insistent that its bloodline is the purest, that diluting it with *others* would be heresy. Enough generations of this, and each city state's inhabitants develop a distinct look, only accentuating the *us* and *them.*

The lemurs manage to go on for a surprisingly long time, despite the cultural stagnation and inevitable population shrinkage that their isolation brings. They fight, and one city or another becomes the big dog. Sometimes things become particularly fraught and one state goes on a genocidal spree against a neighbour. And always there are less of them, even though the world is milder now and the harsh times exist only in myths.

The real leveller is disease. Every generation sees plagues decimate one city state or another, laying such waste to the population that often there is nobody left to explain to passers-by that here were the chosen of the gods, the anointed bloodline that kept themselves pure. Disease approves of a restricted gene pool, which limits a population's ability to resist infection. And when plague arrives, the lemurs sicken in their thousands, inbred and insular as they are.

Another city state moves in to take the vacant land eventually, sometimes finishing off shrunken tribes living in the ruins. Another proud flag is raised to denote the current claimants to the empty title of master race. But diseases mutate and adapt, while the lemurs continue to reject interlopers who might bolster their failing genetic heritage. They are chosen, after all. They are better than the other lemurs and cannot be seen to mix with their inferiors. So they never grow or progress, and sooner or later they die.

14.

I

The next morning it all kicked off, despite everyone's best efforts. Alison, eating cereal on the couch as she watched the news, was treated to a junior BBC reporter running out of words. They were reporting live from the Florida Keys because...something was happening.

The TV camera had caught it all, even though few knew what they were looking at. Off the coast, past a marina of rich retirees' yachts, was an impossibly stationary tidal wave—as though the sea had suffered a critical error two hundred metres from shore. The camera was looking into an ocean which wasn't our own, where the icecaps had melted and then some, creating a wall of water through which alien sunlight shone. The wave hung there, as though contained by some invisible membrane. It faded in and out, while behind the reporter's stammering form people screamed and car horns blared.

Alison felt it like a knife to the gut, even on the other side of the globe. Two branches had slid into one another and fractured. Two Earths overlapped, a pick-and-mix of realities slopping together. She should get her phone. She should call...someone. Somehow make the situation better, using her inexplicable knowledge, within the remaining half a second before it all...

Then the impossible standing wave collapsed and began to roll in towards the shore. And there was more water behind it, more and more, a vast tsunami doing what water did when confronted with a gradient. Alison heard the reporter whimper as he started to run, but the cameraman was made of sterner stuff and filmed another handful of seconds before understanding what that great onrush of sea meant.

Alison could hear her phone ringing.

Heading into work, her driver—she had a driver now, as well as a bodyguard—had the radio on. Doreen from Croydon was calling in because everyone on her street had seen impossibly large rats scavenging in the bins. Or, in some cases, they'd bodily carted them away, as though hired by the borough council. Doreen was saying that her Patrick had seen one of the giant rats wearing a diving suit and telling the others what to do. And there was an epidemic of missing cats and dogs— was it connected? Alison asked the driver to turn the radio off, before anyone started talking about missing children.

Julian, when she met up with him at the office, had obviously been following the same news. But what he, the BBC and Doreen from Croydon couldn't know was that the intrusions were multiplying. Fractures that could once be numbered in tens and then hundreds were now running into the thousands, as the Ice compliantly quantified for her. Little ones, mostly, often where no one could witness them—in the upper atmosphere a handful of air might appear from another world. In the depths of the sea, a fish might appear that hadn't evolved in any ocean Alison knew. The Florida breach was the largest by some margin, but the world was becoming permeable. The walls were breaking down. Things were coming through. And this wasn't even the active malice of the rats or the border-trotting of the Cousins. This just *was*.

She would be the sole human being, to her knowledge, to witness the end of the universe in real time.

"We've got our marching orders," Julian said. "The Cousins have given us a place and time to recover Khan. Neither clandestine nor convenient, naturally."

If she tried, she could probably pre-empt the information, feeling out where the anticipated breach would fall. Except there was so much noise in the signal now, so many cracks fragmenting the walls of the world. "Tell me."

Ten minutes later they were fighting their way across London through the first swell of morning commuters. They rendezvoused with a baffled Royce and a squad of the Met's finest near London Bridge Station, at the foot of a glass-and-steel tower silhouetted against the early sunlight.

"What the bloody hell's all this, then?" Royce demanded. It wasn't the early emergency call that had him het up, so much as the score of army lads who'd turned up after him. They were armed to the teeth and surly, not having been briefed either. Alison wondered whether Hind had expanded operations to include the military chiefs of staff or whether she was calling in some serious blackmail-level favours.

"We need to clear the building, Kier, quick as possible," Julian told Royce. "Terrorist threat."

Royce, no fool, could see that the military presence wasn't kitted out for bomb disposal so much as urban gunplay. He gave Julian a disbelieving look, but a moment later he was giving orders. Shortly after, the fire alarm could be heard, and the first cleaners, systems admins and precociously keen white-collar types began to shamble out. Julian marched off to tell them all to go home, or at least go get a coffee or something. They weren't getting back into the office any time soon. People stared at the soldiers, who were looking embarrassed at the attention.

"Captain Pete Southall." Alison jumped at the voice, turning to see a stocky, red-faced man with a beret shoved through his epaulette. He had rolled-up sleeves and sunburn, and she pictured him being hauled back from a well-earned beach vacation by Hind's imperious commands. "You're Matchell?"

"That's right."

"I'm told you know what's going on, ma'am."

"Chance would be a fine thing," she said automatically, which probably didn't inspire confidence. A moment later she added, "But more than anyone else. Except her."

The Cousin with the long name was striding over, looking like a bag lady deprived of her baggage. Musumbermber, or something like that, Alison recalled; she and Julian had ended up referring to her as "Jane."

"We must go in," the Cousin said, even as she was marching up. "Now, there is no time."

"We're still clearing the building," Alison objected, but Jane actually looked her in the eye with a shock of challenge.

"Now, up high, near the top. Get those out who must be out, get those in who must be in." She nodded at the wide-eyed Southall and his men. "Now, immediately, *now*."

They argued the building's management into switching on the lifts again, because nobody wanted to take the stairs up to level eighty. Alison shared an elevator with the Cousin and Julian, who wanted to know: "So why the top floors? Why this place at all?"

"To minimize the vertical distance for re-entry," Jane said flatly. Her face looked tight and tense—and Alison realized the Cousins usually looked tired and vaguely depressed. It was as though being here and dealing with regular human people was just so much work. Now the bones of Jane's purpose were showing through; she was at the edge of her personal resources.

"The…re-entry?" Julian demanded. "And then…what? The rats come through after Khan and company, and we're stuck on top of a building? We're going to run down eighty flights of stairs to get out, or be trapped in a lift?"

"Plans have been made," Jane said flatly. "We have done what we can. We are running out of chances. We must recover your scientist now."

"Why now? Because otherwise the rats will kill her, or what?" Julian demanded. Alison said nothing, because she knew with a killing certainty why this urgency and why *now*. This morning's news was the tip of the splintering iceberg. They were running out of time, and so was everything else.

Shortly thereafter Southall reported up to her on the eightieth floor. "All clear to floor ninety, ma'am. We're working up through the last few, just kicked a cleaner off floor eighty-nine." He obviously realized how that sounded and hastily added, "Sent her down the stairs, I mean. We think that's it, but I've got people checking loos and broom cupboards."

Alison nodded, as Julian ended his call and said, "Royce has a cordon about the building now, covering every entrance. Building management have checked everyone against the entry logs and say there shouldn't be anyone left. Oh, and every damn company with offices here is filing complaints and threatening to sue the Met and the Home Office, so this had better be worth it."

Jane made to speak, but Julian turned away, looking only to Alison. "Matchbox?"

She wanted to say she didn't know when Khan was due, but even as the word sat on her tongue she realized this wasn't true. She looked to Cousin Jane and saw the shared knowledge there. Glints of frozen water danced in the suddenly chill air between them, and the temperature kept dropping. She saw Southall's breath plume, and one of the soldiers swore.

"They're coming…" Alison's fingers twitched, and somewhere, a dimension away, an unthinkable interface made itself into a keyboard for her convenience, opening its senses for her.

"Ma'am?" Southall's voice was tight, ragged at the edges.

"Who're coming? Our people or theirs?" Julian asked, and when no immediate answer was forthcoming, "Captain, tell your men not to shoot unless there's a real threat. Tell your men…" She felt his wince, and then he was raising his voice so the entire squad could hear him. "Listen to me. You're going to see…some weird stuff. Some people are going to appear out of bloody thin air, okay? Just…do not shoot them. We're looking at, probably, three women, right? And…if there's more than that…"

"Where from, sir?" Southall asked.

"I…"

Coming now. Right now. Almost here. It was like standing on a midnight road and seeing the oncoming headlamps of an eighteen-wheeler as it bore down on you. Alison pushed past Julian and kicked open a door into an office. "Here!" she said. It was hard to get the word out against the freezing air. She felt that some quality of the room, not anything in regular space, was rushing out through some invisible hole, draining past her. "*Here*, right here!"

Southall gave orders with creditable economy, despite the rime forming on the desktops and crusting the carpet tiles. His soldiers were still taking up posts behind desks when Alison felt the membrane of the world bulge and split. The eighteen-wheeler image suddenly seemed far more apt, because there was more coming through than three people could account for. She bolted into one of the office cubicles, feeling space deform and shudder behind her, hearing the shocked exclamations of the soldiers. *What are they bringing back?*

II

They fell. Below them the lights of the rat city spread to the horizons in their irregular patchwork. The surface extrusions of a buried metropolis she could hardly begin to imagine.

And it would be the last thing she saw. Above them, the airship blotted out the entire sky. It was not receding as quickly as it should have been, either—*Odd, the things you notice when you're going to die*—and she wondered if it was losing altitude too.

Her ears were full of the twittering and shrieking of Dr. Rat's family. She knew that at least one furry body had been hauled off by the wind, but what did it matter? Dead alone or dead all in a heap was still dead.

Dr. Khan's fingers were painfully tight in her hair. Lee had Mal's hand, clenched in hers. Clinging precariously to the last in a chain of desperate ratlings, she saw the translator, agent of their misfortune. Perhaps this was its revenge for a lifetime of slavery and invasive surgery.

She didn't notice the shift in temperature. The wind

whipping past them was already chilling her to the bone. She didn't even notice that the looming airship wasn't there any more. But the dim lamps of the rat city were abruptly replaced by a great radiance from below, a vast plain of ice shining back at the moon.

Goggling downwards, she caught her breath, seeing the frozen Earth beneath. There were depths to that ice. There were structures buried within, like icebound leviathans awaiting the end of the world. Except the end had come and gone, and here they still were.

And one was coming for them. She let out a sound that was neither scream nor whoop, just some mad animal noise. Something shifted deep within the glacial depths as a leviathan arose indeed. A colossal fish-like shape gathered itself from the substance of the plain and leapt up to meet them with gaping jaws.

Khan swore, and the shrilling of the rats reached a new peak.

The monstrous ice-fish was rising for them, vast enough to swallow a house and grounds. Lee tried to brace, but she had nothing to brace against. She heard Mal yell in what sounded suspiciously like exaltation.

The horizon of her world became the rim of the ice-fish's colossal maw, and there was a tongue of frost below her. Then the fish fell back towards the solid plain with them, still falling, in its open jaws. The ice of its substance was falling away, sliding off in great sheets and bergs that whirled off into infinity. Its clutch of fugitives felt their momentum slowing, the speed of their descent bleeding away as they clung to one another. Frost crackled over the rats' fur and Lee's hair.

"God!" Mal shouted, and clutched her tight. Lee drew in a breath that sawed at her lungs like a cold knife. Ice was forming on her face and sealing her eyes shut. She felt her body heat leaching away as swiftly as her momentum. It looked as though she was still going to die; only the executioner had changed.

Then, with shocking suddenness, she struck a hard floor. She'd retained just enough residual velocity to whack the breath out of her body. Rats exploded outwards, as did their possessions, scattering across the floor of—

An office?

Mal was up and waving her hands, because there were guns everywhere. "Don't shoot!" she shouted at the horrified soldiers, making herself target number one. The rats clustered about her legs as though she was a latter-day Saint Francis with poor taste. "Don't shoot!"

Lee tried to speak, but breathing still felt like a privilege. She waited for the bullets.

Instead there was a man giving instructions in the office doorway. Nobody had been shot, but nobody was lowering their rifle either.

"Get those creatures in the corner," their apparent leader barked.

Lee blinked and said, "I know you." He'd turned up at her door with a policewoman—just before Gym Bro had kidnapped her and everything had gone irrevocably to hell.

"Dr. Khan, over here," the man snapped, ignoring Lee entirely.

The scientist was picking herself up unsteadily. "Jules, be cool," she managed, then coughed out a laugh. The cold of where they'd been was probably still in her marrow. A moment later, one of the Nissa shoved effortlessly into the room, her presence demanding attention even before she spoke. She stood between several guns and their targets, and didn't seem to care.

"We must go," she declared.

"Nobody's going anywhere until Dr. Khan's away from those creatures," Not-a-policeman said. "You said nothing about *them* coming through." Some of the soldiers were discreetly shuffling sideways to acquire an angle of fire past the Nissa woman.

She grunted, sending an enquiring look at Mal and Lee, but it was the rat-creature translator who spoke.

"It was necessary to secure his family. A situation much to be lamented." The words came out in its usual melodious, almost-woman's voice. It was as though Dr. Rat was back with them, but it added, "He is now deceased from us."

The Nissa woman's face, never very expressive, closed down completely. Not-a-policeman tried to take charge again, but this time Khan cut him off.

"The translator means the other *me*, Jules," she said. "One of these chaps was their expert—was supposed to come through to save the universe with me and whoever else. But the fuckers shot him. Rove's sonofabitch goon put a bullet in him, because he was trying to get *me* out. If this is Dr. Rat's family, then we will fucking well look after them." She glowered at human and Nissa impartially.

"His research," the Nissa woman croaked. Her hands were crunched into fists like cudgels.

"I have some of it, if that's your bloody priority," Khan said.

"All right now!" Not-a-policeman stepped forwards, carefully. "Kay, you know me, but for the sake of your companions and your…"—he gave a flinching glance at the translator and its entourage—"companions, I'm Julian Sabreur, MI5. And I am asking everyone to stay calm and cooperate. There is transport on its way that will take everyone to where they can be debriefed, and we'll take it from there. You'll appreciate this is something of an unprecedented situation, but—No." This was directed to the Nissa woman, who had taken a step towards Dr. Khan. "Thank you for helping recover Kay from… wherever, but we'll take it from here." Some guns had moved subtly to bring the big woman back into their sights.

Lee knew shifts between worlds could happen without warning, and she kept expecting everyone to vanish off to some Nissa safehouse. Julian "Not-a-policeman" Sabreur could easily be left with an office full of empty air. So either there was no convenient breach to exploit or the Nissa had other plans.

Satisfied that his tenuous authority was holding, Sabreur said, "If you'd all form a line, I'm afraid there are quite a few stairs to the ground floor. And only one lift."

"No," the Nissa woman said. "Up."

He stared at her—everyone did. "Why would we go up?" Sabreur asked.

"They are coming."

Lee went cold all over and grabbed Mal's hand again. Sabreur was in the process of demanding what the hell she meant when someone shouted, "Spiker!" A woman burst in, a woman Lee had last seen at the museum, as the Nissa's prisoner.

"I'm getting intrusions all over," she reported, eyes wide. "I can feel it…coming through, lots of them."

"Let me guess, below us?"

"Must be the bottom eight floors at least. Two dozen separate breaches."

And Lee thought about the rat city they'd seen and how various Earths differed. *Maybe their ground level is our eighth floor... unless something's coming through from the airship.*

"Up," the Nissa woman repeated implacably.

To his credit, Sabreur just nodded. "Get the things moving then," he said. "Head for the roof."

"There will be more," she told him. "Your people should be ready."

His face said eloquently that there was no way in hell any of them could be ready for this, but he just nodded tersely. He answered his phone as the whole mob of them headed through the fire exit door. "Kier? Yes, I...Christ. Get out, get your people out, just...clear everyone away from the building, as far as you can. I don't *know*, Royce. All goddamned bets are off." For a moment he sounded on the point of tears, and Lee felt an unwanted stab of sympathy: the man of authority whose writ has run translucently thin. "Do not engage, just clear out and watch the bloody fireworks from a safe distance." Lee was mounting the stairs, like a sheepdog behind a moving carpet of rat-creatures. Mal and Khan were already around the turn of the next landing. Sabreur was on her heels, and she heard him close with, "Kier, if this goes south, it's been a pleasure," with such desperate English stiff-upper-lippery that she almost liked him.

"How many floors to this fucking place?" Khan called from above.

"I think ninety-five," Sabreur shouted back, jostling Lee to go faster even though she was practically treading on tails.

"Fuck me!"

Sabreur was on his phone again. "Yes, helicopters, as many as you can find. I need immediate air evacuation from the roof. Leslie Hind will give you all the authority you need, but get things in motion *now*. I don't know what sort of time we have—"

The air flexed around them. Lee thought it was an artefact of her own labouring breath, but everyone had stuttered to a halt. The rats clustered into a single mutually supportive mass, the translator at their head.

"Earthquake?" Lee asked, but the shudder hadn't touched the building, hadn't touched anything except the fabric of reality.

"*They are coming!*" the Nissa woman shouted, actually shouted, real alarm breaking through. "Move! Move!"

And they moved, but even as they did, Lee realized it was too late. Somewhere below them, rodent soldiers would be funnelling up the stairwells, a tide of matted hair, black uniforms and murderous weapons. But that wasn't the only place they could come from. The colossal airship must have been packed to the gills with rodent stormtroopers. It had a bomb bay. It was plainly intended for some serious pacification when needed.

"Keep going, Kay!" Sabreur shouted. "Just...up. Oh Christ."

The flex happened again even as Lee reached the next landing, something fundamental about the world abruptly straining to breaking point. She remembered the tunnels beneath Mount Pleasant and turned hastily, so that Sabreur almost slammed into her.

"They're forcing a breach! Do your thing, the reality-bomb thing!"

The Nissa woman already had a device in her hands. She was shaking her head, though. "Too wide, too much." And then some exclamation of disbelief in her own language.

"What's happening to the walls?" Mal called from above. She had stopped, the panicking rodents flooding past her on both sides, while Khan led them upwards like the Pied Piper.

"Walls...?" But there was daylight crawling in ragged tears and cracks through the concrete of the fire escape. Its very substance was attenuating until there was nothing but air, the steps beneath Lee's feet abruptly only a likelihood rather than the hard certainty she would have preferred.

"Up!" cried the Nissa woman despairingly. Mal had Lee's wrist, Sabreur had her other elbow, and they hauled her upwards, towards the higher floors. Here the regular number of dimensions still reigned. Below, soldiers were pushing past the Nissa woman as she stood there trying to make her device work, trying to bar the way. *You shall not pass.*

Oh. Lee knew how that one went.

Three storeys of wall disappeared beside them, and Lee put on a burst of speed, dragging Mal with her. But what should have been open air... was not open. She saw a honey-comb of girderwork, compartments, ducts—a cut-away diagram of the airship's decks as it overlapped impossibly with the tower. Sabreur pulled his friend up, then the lead soldier, then the next. Every space was thronging with uniformed rodent soldiers, waiting to intersect with their reality.

She didn't know if someone gave the order to fire or whether the situation simply accelerated of its own accord. But the soldiers below were now shooting into that impossible, slewing vista, and the rodents were firing back. Lee caught wild glimpses of carnage on both sides, shredded bodies caught point-blank with nowhere to hide as the walls of reality simply ghosted away. She saw buckling infrastructure, shattered concrete. The building and the vessel were fighting over the space, letting shrapnel and shot fly both ways through a breach in reality that a bus could have driven through.

The Nissa woman presented her device like a talisman and a shearing blade of flechettes carved into her, sending her tumbling into—*through*—the wall that should have been behind her. She fell through a cluttered void that couldn't make up its mind about what world it was in.

There was a deep, groaning sound, and Lee abruptly understood that this wasn't just some theoretical duelling of realities. The tower's very structure was under attack. There must be fissures racing through every part of it—and they were heading for the top.

"Southall! Up, man! Keep going up!" Sabreur yelled. Lee saw a flechette strike near him, shattering an emergency light.

The rat-soldiers were leaping from their airship to the tower. Some fell towards the London streets, through shattering concrete, or away—hurtling into an abyss Lee had no name for. A handful of Julian's soldiers were shooting down into them, but there were more flooding over as they left the sinking airship. She turned and ran. The leader of the soldiers was yelling at Sabreur to "Just go! Get up top!"

The fire escape ran all the way to the roof. And by the time Lee arrived, Khan and the translator had the door open and the fugitive rats were spilling out into the wild, chill air. All around, the building was undergoing renewed assault: partly physical collision, partly existential crisis. Space that was tower block in human London was being randomly replaced with empty air from the rats' world. Lee looked out across the morning-lit city with Mal, expecting a fleet of rescue helicopters to power over the capital like something out of *Apocalypse Now*.

But the sky was empty.

"What now?" she shouted, as the tower groaned in torment and listed slightly but noticeably. She imagined cracks spidering through every concrete beam, only the twisted cores of steel holding everything together. "You!" she yelled at Sabreur. "You said there'd be helicopters."

III

Julian looked at Pryor blankly. *I should have bloody well arrested you when I had the chance.* "There will be helicopters. They're on their way," he said, because he still felt it was his job to tell reassuring falsehoods. Past the lip of the roof, he saw the impossible bulk of the rodent flying machine, a vast dreadnaught now fatally entangled with their tower and half a dozen neighbouring spires. It was raining glass onto London's streets, and he hoped to hell that Royce had reached cover—and that his men had made some headway in evacuating the area.

"Christ," he choked. Alison squeezed his arm reassuringly, but it didn't help. There must be tens dead, hundreds. A thousand phone cameras would be recording the architectural carnage. The eyes of the world would already have seen the worst. Julian risked a glance back down the stairwell.

"Southall!" he called.

But to his horror the rat troopers were swarming the stairs, and the humans on the roof hadn't a weapon between them.

"Get back from the door!" he shouted, slamming it shut. The building shuddered and groaned, like a thing in pain. Everyone lurched towards the nearest edge, and he could hear their adopted rat-creatures' high-pitched screaming.

"Kay!" He found her crouched in their midst. He half expected her to be lighting up, or to make a sardonic comment, but her eyes were wild with fear and she just shook her head.

His phone went. Without taking his eyes from the door to the fire escape, he answered.

"Julian, what's your situation?" Hind's voice.

"We're on the roof." He felt he was being creditably calm, under the circumstances.

"Helicopters on their way from RAF Ruislip. Just hold out."

"Not sure that's going to be quick enough." The building listed further. "I suggest you evacuate as much of the area as possible, at your end." A little shake to his tone, but forgivable, he felt.

"Spiker," Alison said, grabbing his shoulder.

"Wait," he said, but the pinch of her fingers was painful. *Is it colder, all of a sudden? Is she doing something again, or is it being done to her?*

"Spiker," she hissed. *"Look."* Even as his breath plumed and floriate outscrollings of ice unravelled across the screen of his phone.

The sky had more depth to it than any sky had a right to display. On a clear day, he discovered, you really could see forever. And from the far side of forever something was approaching.

Then the first rat-soldiers spilled from the doorway, seemingly fighting each other as much as trying to apprehend the humans. The tower took that opportunity to sag again, and three of them just tumbled in a wrestling ball across the rooftop and were lost over the rail. Julian almost went too, saved by Alison's grip.

The thing, the horrible thing on the other side of the sky,

approached from infinitely far away, very quickly. It kept on approaching until he understood that it was far too big to be anything living. And yet it lived, and he felt they all must have shrunk down to the size of creatures that lived within a drop of water. Because abruptly it was *here*, in his sky, in his world, and it covered a score of postcodes with its shadow.

Julian wanted very badly to believe in God, right then. Not some C of E school lip service but a deep and comforting belief in which he could seek refuge.

Instead, he was forced to believe in a spined, segmented thing, kilometres long, hanging in the air as though physics had no more hold on it than reason. It had a head, or fore section, shaped like the crescent moon, and its shelled body was divided along its length into lobes. Protruding from the outer edges of each lobe were twenty-metre thorns which lined its flanks. Its underside bristled with limbs, some large enough to stamp on a double-decker bus, others so fine they could have adjusted a chess piece on a board. *A woodlouse. A flying woodlouse the size of a village...*

It was swinging in the air as though gaining purchase on some other, denser medium, skewing towards the tower top and its pitiful human–rodent refuse. Julian's muscles fought for control of his bones, locking him rigid. He wanted to scream, but part of him—the part still answering to *Julian Sabreur*—refused.

Alison was looking up at the hideous thing in wonder. Ice danced in the air about her brow like a crown.

With exacting gentleness, the monstrous arthropod came to rest against the side of the tower, curling itself slightly so that the listing building leant into its floating bulk, which supported the crumbling edifice's weight without difficulty.

"Tell me that's not our ride," he managed, but his consent was not required.

An articulated forest of limbs reached out, each one hooked and barbed, each pincering towards a target. He saw Alison's lips move, and then she stepped forwards like a somnambulist. He yelled and tried to drag her back, but a whiplike appendage jostled him and he ended up clinging to Alison, caught in a cage of interlaced spines. He could see refugee rodents, the two girls and Dr. Khan—all of them being gathered up. In a couple of minutes, the flurrying limbs had cleared the roof with hungry efficiency.

IV

Lucas expected Rove to be furious, but in this moment of crisis the man was eerily calm. All part of the plan, apparently, despite the fact that their vessel was self-destructing beneath their feet. The structure thrummed like a guitar string, and every so often a piece of wall or ceiling would simply disappear, an unwanted window onto another world entirely, or onto no world. There were rat-creatures rushing everywhere too, great, panicked mobs of them.

"Morons," Rove stated briskly. He had been packing a briefcase with swift economy, a black leather article monogrammed with his initials. "They could have just set up some insertion portals, done this gradually. But they're obsessed with taking all their toys with them."

"Sir?" Lucas asked neutrally. He had his pistol out, and in the back of his mind was the thought that, if worst came to worst, he could make shooting his boss his final act in this or any world. Not an urge he would act on, but it scratched at his thoughts nonetheless.

"Why do you *think* they're so keen for information about Earth?" Rove said, straightening up with briefcase in hand. Another convulsion racked the ship. "They want it for living space, and they only think in terms of invasion via over-whelming military force. They could do it, too. Taken globally, their army is almost as large as our entire population. They're an aggressive pack of vermin, Lucas. But they rush in like this, and now their flagship's being pulled apart between two worlds."

"Sir, we should really—"

"Come with me."

Rove marched past him. He almost managed it with his veneer of upper-class calm intact, but Lucas knew him well now. He reckoned many CEOs had left the office with that slightly hurried tread, the day before everyone discovered the pension fund had been cleaned out.

Striding with dignity down the corridors of power was unfortunately not something Rove could keep up, not with the ceilings as low as they were. Lucas found he rather enjoyed seeing his boss having to crawl for once. Then Rove had him go first, which he enjoyed less. Partly because they kept running into mobs of rats trying to save the ship, or perhaps escape it. Lucas had to roar and threaten to make them give way. And Lucas never quite convinced himself that Rove would still be there if he glanced back. The bastard was certainly equal to deciding there was only one seat in the lifeboat.

If there is a lifeboat. Rove seemed to think there was a way out of this, but every step saw the airship fray further. Sometimes they only saw dimly lit rat warrens. Sometimes

Lucas was looking down onto London streets: showered with broken glass, gusting with flames. It was like all the war zones he'd ever seen, live or on video, except it was his home under the hammer.

Rove climbed into a tiny lift with barely enough room for Lucas to squeeze in beside him. A rat-soldier tried to get in with them, and put the barrel of a weapon in their faces, twittering shrilly.

"Kill it," Rove said flatly, and Lucas shot the creature point-blank. He recognized the same deficiency he had noted previously: the rat kings were used to their threats being respected. Their bully boys were less used to having to pull the trigger.

The force of the impact threw the small creature away from them, and they ascended.

"I don't get it," he said, trying to shift so that Rove's elbow wasn't in his ribs. "How did they fuck up so bad? I mean, they grew me a new *hand*, for Chrissake."

"Poor leadership," Rove said. "Inferior genetic stock. I mean, they're *rats*, Lucas. What did you expect? You saw those ridiculous creatures."

Lucas choked down a number of possible responses. His boss was right about one thing, though: it wasn't a meritocracy around here. The rat kings would pass their fancy robes and spacious chambers on to their little rat princes and princesses. And all their time and effort would go into jockeying with each other and maintaining the status quo. They probably didn't do the hard work of understanding how things worked—they had people to do that for them. But if those experts told them things they didn't like, inbred privilege trumped actual knowledge and they did as they pleased.

Then they were up top, and it looked like the end of the world. They were in London's commercial heart, in a ship that had manifested within a half-dozen separate buildings, all now slanting perilously. He could hear screams, sirens and the basso profundo moan of buildings stressed beyond their tolerances.

"Quickly now." Rove sounded positively ruffled. He had a rat device in his hand, and as Lucas watched, a circle of littered deck was abruptly swept clear. Glass, concrete and rat bodies were vanished away. "Here, Lucas, right on my heels."

Still need me then? But despite his mutinous thoughts, he found he was pathetically grateful. He'd resigned his will to Rove, trusting as a dog that his master had a way out.

Rove adjusted his device and pressed it into Lucas's hand; then they were both holding it up, like the handle of an invisible umbrella. The sky above was thick and busy: glass like a killing rain, chunks of concrete and sheared iron. But it all turned to air within a few feet of the device, vanishing into another place.

"If they could do this...?" Lucas yelled hoarsely.

"The rats? Oh, this is beyond them. It's tech from our rivals, Lucas, who are a bit defter with the dimensions than even our rodent allies. It only works because we're within a breach right now, one the stupid rodents put a crowbar to and widened so they could get their ship through."

"So where's all this shit going?"

"Why should I care?"

Rove was now at the highest point of the wrecked craft, now a twisted clutch of beams and girders. Even as they reached it, the structure dropped and canted further. Rove skidded, clutching for purchase and finding none. Lucas's black artificial hand caught him by the arm and hauled him up again. Apparently, in a pinch he knew where his loyalties lay.

"Now." Rove's face was taut with pain; likely his shoulder was half out of its socket, but he had his phone out and was looking up.

Lucas followed his gaze. Eclipsing the sky like a sign of the end times was a...goddamn gigantic woodlouse thing. Lucas stared and found that it didn't matter. Things were already so sincerely fucked up that adding extra impossible monsters couldn't ruin his day any more than it already was. *I mean, why the hell not?*

It was grappling the top of the nearest building, which was already four-fifths of the way to toppling. But its segments undulated and twisted, and Lucas saw a clutch of jointed limbs moving to support the collapsing tower blocks.

"What...?" But there were no words, because how could he possibly question what was going on. Of course Daniel Rove had an escape route, even from this. He was a better rat than any of the rodents. He always had a way out. And if he brought Lucas along, that was fine.

As a barbed assemblage of claws reached for them too, as the city fell in ruins on all sides, Rove treated Lucas to his best urbane smile.

PART 4
RED KING'S DREAM

15.

I

It ate us.

Except the orifice they had been scooped into had been somewhere mid-rear, which could mean something even worse. Lee had closed her eyes when the creature clutched them to itself. Now she found herself in darkness on a hard floor, other bodies jabbing into her with elbows and knees, scratching her with claws. Rat hair was bristling in her face. She shuddered and sat up, experiencing a wave of dizziness.

"Mal?"

"Here," came her friend's hoarse voice. "Ow. I'm bleeding."

"What?" Lee fumbled over to her, stepping on at least one tail. All around her, other voices were expressing their discontent with the situation. She heard Sabreur, then Khan's eloquent expletives, and over it all the shrill bickering of the rats they'd brought with them.

"I think it stabbed me with its spikes, when it was grabbing us. Nothing serious, but . . . ow." Mal found her arm, squeezed it, then hugged Lee close. "I'm going to say, for the record, I was not expecting that."

"What, a giant centipede thing dropping in over London?

Everyday occurrence, surely." Lee heard her own voice shake, but she was being brave for Mal and that helped her keep it together.

"What…" Mal's own tones quavered and she had to start again, casting out into the dark, "Does anyone know what just happened?"

"You mean you don't?" Sabreur demanded. Then a woman's voice, probably his colleague's, added, "I think I…Hold on…"

"We are to travel." It was a new voice, deep, the words slightly unclear. "There will be light. Probably."

Not the most inspiring way to start a new religion, Lee thought, feeling giddy.

"Stig?" Mal asked in a small voice. "Is that you there, you thickset bastard?"

"No more than me," Stig agreed. His voice seemed closer now, as a dim greenish radiance began to spread across the walls of their…what? Compartment, prison, stomach? The space was rounded, lozenge-shaped, lined with something hard, plasticky and slightly irregular, as though it had been poured out and set almost instantly, whorls and ripple marks baked into the surface.

Mal threw her arms around Stig and gave him a compulsive hug. He returned it gravely.

"Your friend," Lee said. "She got shot by rat-soldiers. I'm sorry."

Stig sighed massively, unsurprised but miserable anyway. "Who are all these?" he asked dourly, as though the presence of so many guests was just more work he could have done without.

"The family of Dr. Rat, the scientist you were working

432

with," Mal explained. "He got shot too. And some government people, who you should probably drop off somewhere."

Stig glanced at Sabreur and friend. "Those we know. Julian Sabreur, Alison Matchell. You weren't supposed to be here."

"Yes, you were going to swipe Dr. Khan from under our noses, no doubt." Sabreur was standing, tensed for a fight as though he'd last three seconds against Stig. "And now you're kidnapping employees of Her Majesty's Gov—"

"Spiker," the woman, Matchell, said, and he bit down on the words "Mr. . . . Stig?" she went on. "Where are we travelling to?"

"To the start of it all, the only way we can," Stig said solemnly. "With our own scientists, and Dr. Khan, and others. Great minds, many minds. We are going to mend the universe, if it can be mended. Or we will watch it die, because someone should."

Lee felt a tremble start up inside her, a sense of incalculable awe. Not that she'd given a thought to religion in the last ten years or more, but she was still thinking, *We're going to visit* God . . . ? "Where?" she managed, plucking at Stig's ragged tramp's sleeve. "Where does it start?"

He eyed her sternly, and she half expected a fierce sermon, an exhortation for poor, ignorant humans to mend their ways. Instead his gaze slid off her. He mumbled something, rolled his shoulders inwards and found something of enormous interest in the substance of the wall.

"What now?" Mal pressed him, and prodded him hard in the arm when he tried to ignore her. His expression, when he turned back, was easily readable as exasperation.

"I don't know, don't ask me. I don't make these decisions. I don't talk to these things. I'm just a . . ."

"Soldier?" Sabreur filled in acidly.

"No. Not a soldier." Stig glowered at him. "I am like you, Julian Sabreur. A servant. I do what I am told, and I do what must be done. There are more clever people than I who understand, and some of them are dead. Others are elsewhere, and we must go where they are—because if it is just me then we are lost. I am not the wisdom of my people. I am just me and I don't understand any of it." By the end of that his voice was shaking, and Lee thought he was going to burst into tears.

"I'm sorry," she offered: inadequate, she knew.

"We have worked hard, lost much, since we began this, since we discovered that everything was collapsing," he ground out, staring fiercely at the wall. "We had used the gaps between worlds for our study and wonder. I liked that. That was a good time. And now we discover they are not a great discovery after all, but the symptom of a sickness that all the universe has. And we go to *your* people"—a single jab of his big, blunt finger at Sabreur—"and to the rodent-people, and you fight us, you kill us, you do all you can do to stop us saving you."

"Maybe if you'd just told us…" Matchell said, her heart not in it.

"So who's at the helm, then?" broke in Dr. Khan. "I thought this was *your* giant scorpion monster."

Stig's eyes swivelled as he continued trying to avoid looking at any of them. "We found others," he said, but then corrected himself. "They found us. When we had made nuisance enough of ourselves, they came to us. The cold place, that is one you know, but this…"

"A living ship," Mal put in. "That's right, isn't it? A spaceship, maybe?"

"Space, and other things." Stig shuffled, evasive.

"So who's captain?"

Lee watched Stig try to form an explanation, and find himself unequal to the task. At last he slumped, and gestured at one of the walls, indistinguishable from the others. "Fine. We'll go. I'll show you. Then you'll know, and you won't like it. You'll wish you hadn't asked." He scowled like a reprimanded child.

Julian started, "If Pryor's going then—"

"All of you that want!" Stig threw a hand in Sabreur's face to forestall the words. "Why not?" And he stomped off towards the wall, moving with enough momentum that Lee expected him to break his nose.

Instead, a seam drew itself from floor to ceiling, with a flurrying, scrabbling bustle of half-seen bodies or limbs. They clawed away the substance of the wall until there was a gap large enough for Stig to step through.

I do hope, she thought timorously, *that it is not ants. I do not want to be stuck in a spaceship full of ants.* Cryptozoology had its limits. When they passed through the newly moulded portal, however, there was no sign of the door-makers. In retrospect, what she'd seen had seemed more like a multitude of busy fingers than individual creatures, and she wasn't sure if that was better or worse.

The corridor they stepped into was still being built. Lee had a sudden moment of vertigo, seeing its end recede as if being tunnelled into the hard, shelly substrate by invisible miners. The resulting passageway was ribbed, unpleasantly organic-looking, and shiny wet where it was freshly cut—but drying to a dull sheen within seconds.

"So where's the crew?" Mal asked.

They were all hanging about the doorway, even the rats, wary of this new space.

Stig just grunted.

"We're in quarantine or something—they don't want to share space with us?" she pressed. They were daring the corridor now, skidding and stepping over the awkwardly ridged floor. "Only," Mal went on, "this making corridors up as needed is grand, but the crew must have their own suite somewhere?"

Stig gave another grunt, hunching his shoulders.

"If we're going to speak over the phone or something," Sabreur said gamely, "why get us to walk somewhere?"

"Command node," Stig muttered into his beard. "Have to be where there's complex functioning."

"Remaking the internal architecture isn't a complex function?" Matchell asked.

Stig shot her a look as if to say "why does everyone think I have the answers?"

The corridor widened out and opened onto a chamber that looked for all the world like the inside of a gourd: a lobed, symmetrical room. Its walls sported ridges which ran up towards the chamber's apex from all sides, joining to form a central rosette. It was devoid of anything resembling either crew or controls.

Stig was saying nothing, so Lee prompted, "Are they... on their way?"

"It is a living ship," Stig stated. His expression was willing her to understand without him having to haul all the words out himself.

"Yes...?" Lee prompted.

"So it doesn't need crew," Mal finished. "It just... is?"

Stig nodded.

"Well, what are we—?" Sabreur started, and then flinched back. "Christ, what is it doing?"

The rosette at the centre of the ceiling was opening out, and through it were coming…

Worms, Lee thought at first, and her stomach lurched. She was wrong, though. They were more like centipedes, articulated and leggy, hundreds of the damned things of all sizes—from as thick as a thigh bone to slender as a hair.

But the cascade of *things* wasn't just pouring out onto the floor. The largest appendages formed a kind of superstructure that the rest twined about and clung to. The more she watched, the more Lee saw an emergent shape within the crawling chaos, a thing that had two legs, two arms, torso, head… The head was the worst, because where a face would be, there was a frenetic business of whiskery feelers and writhing bodies all twining and seething about one another.

She remembered a nature documentary where the grave, mannered commentator had explained how the legs of insects had evolved to perform countless different tasks. That narrator hadn't known the half of it. The limbs twisted together in twitching cables that were nothing much like lips and locked their chitinous joints into the lines of jaw and cheekbone. They dug sockets in which metal-sheened beads flowered like something breaking from a cocoon. Little comb-edged arms clicked over them and back up, and Lee realized it was feigning blinking.

The face that finally formed was androgynous, puppet-like, constantly on the verge of fraying apart into its component pieces. It regarded them blankly, and then animation came to its various parts. They started out of sync, movements staggered, but at last every limb was moving with purpose. It cocked its terrible head slightly and smiled, showing teeth like the pale backs of burrowing beetles.

For a long time nobody spoke. The facsimile's glittering regard played over them as its features settled and resettled, waves of change flurrying across its visage. Alien and hideous precisely because it was trying so hard to look human.

"It's us," Matchell said, and Lee saw she was right. It was a fairground mirror creature, composed of their distorted reflections.

"I think it's trying to put us at our ease," Matchell went on hollowly. "Look, any chance we can get off, round about now?"

"Don't know," Stig told the floor. "We are travelling, I think. Probably it was too late before you even asked." And all the while the composite features gurned and grimaced at them.

"Well this is unsatisfactory, Stig," said Dr. Khan, who had been in a huddle with the rat translator. "Look, this has gone way past what I signed up for. This is well into the realm of fucking alien abduction right now." Lee could see she was scared but wouldn't give that emotion the satisfaction. Probably she'd had a lot of practice, in her life. "Just tell us what you can, love, because you still know more than the rest of us."

Khan might have said more but stopped hurriedly because a noise had started up from the facsimile, as though there were wasps trapped inside it. Its mouth remained in that horrible false smile, but she could see tiny limbs rubbing against one another within its chest like a legion of crickets, until the whole became speech. Speech in Stig's leaden tongue, so Lee couldn't follow it, but words nonetheless. The head cocked further. One hand lifted in a marionette's unsteady gesture.

Stig pointed angrily at humans and rat-creatures alike, and mumbled something that might have been a grudging introduction. The iridescent gaze shifted, ersatz eyeballs turned in their sockets by tiny legs mimicking muscles, the orb rolled between them like a pellet of dung at the mercy of competing scarabs.

It made more sounds, not in Stig's language now, just random noises. Then Sabreur's phone rang twice and Matchell's once. In the startled silence that followed, the busy orchestra within its chest rippled like typewriter keys and Lee heard that not-quite-voice say, *Hello, good evening and welcome.* The words were imprecise, scratchy and pocked with clicking static, but she understood them nonetheless.

"Please," Sabreur said. "Take us back, please. We're not supposed to be here."

You are tolerated.

Sabreur blinked, and the thing blinked back, its face a mockery of his own. The man looked a hair from breaking down and screaming, but Matchell put a hand on his shoulder and he seemed to take strength from that.

"Spiker," she said softly. "Let's not say or do anything that might result in it withdrawing that toleration, hm? Don't want to get shot into space or anything because it decides we're not worth the air we breathe."

"Excuse me," Lee tried. It shifted its facing in a way that reminded her uncomfortably that it was not truly standing at all, but suspended from the ceiling. "We're just...We don't know what's going on."

If a lion could talk we could not understand him, it pronounced.

439

She was absolutely certain it could have no real grasp of what a lion was, but maybe it had found the quote on Sabreur's phone. Or possibly it had just downloaded the entire human datasphere into its unimaginable consciousness, and identified this as the key concept it wanted to convey.

"Does it mean we can't communicate? Is this rigmarole just so it can tell us it *can't* talk to us?" Khan complained.

"We can talk to *it*," Matchell stated. "But this is not the ship. The ship...is alive, it has a mind I can't even...Prop me up, Spiker." Abruptly her knees folded, but Sabreur had her, gathering her to him so she didn't fall. The air in the room had dropped five degrees in as many seconds, and Matchell's breath ghosted white from her lips. "*This* isn't the mind of the creature we're within." She indicated the simulacrum, the words rattling from her in fits and starts. "There is a mind out there, and it's as alien to the Ice Mind as it is to me. It's vast, segmented. It can compartmentalize itself, whereas the Ice, the Ice is a whole planet of thinking engine. They can both...lower themselves, degree by degree. If a lion could talk we could not understand him. But if we had a sequence that ran without break from lion to human then perhaps we could pass words up and down the chain. This isn't the ship entity here, this is...an organ, a specialized limb it has evolved to speak to monkeys like us." Her eyes were screwed shut and sweat sprang up on her brow and instantly froze. Frost crept across Sabreur's light stubble, making him look ten years older. "The entity is barely aware of us as a group, certainly not at all as individuals," Matchell got out. "It can just conceive of Stig's people as a whole, and through them it understands that there is something similar but distinct, which is us. Even the rats are almost identical, to it. But it has a big mind. It understands that we might help. It . . . Damn me, that *hurts!*" She sagged, shaking her head.

We are all children of Earth, the specialized appendage said.

So sayeth the lion, Lee decided, *and we cannot know what it means by it—only load it with our own preconceptions.* She had signed up for an extra philosophy A level once, under her parents' insistence that no university would look at her if she only had four to her name. Now—for the first time—she regretted bunking off most of the lectures.

"Look." It was Sabreur, speaking to Stig because he obviously didn't want to face the ship's avatar again. "Just tell it to let us off. Please." The word obviously cost him a lot.

"I can't make it do anything," Stig told him. Abruptly he placed his palms against the nearest wall. His face was clenched like a fist and he shook with what Lee belatedly realized was sheer rage and frustration, a whole iceberg of it that she had never even guessed at.

The ship's avatar spoke, in Stig's language once more. It was only a few words, but they made him leap round, wide-eyed. He queried it, and the response he received was transformative. Lee watched the burdens slough off his big shoulders.

"We *are* going back," Stig breathed. "Yes, get off, go away, Julian Sabreur. Anyone who wants, go away. And I will not have to make decisions for you. I can go back to being a servant of my people. So many things will be better." His relief was contagious.

"All very well," Khan put in, "but for those of us going all the way to the depot, how backwards compatible is your tech, exactly?" She got perilously close to jabbing the ship's avatar with a finger but clearly decided against it. "Because I have a whole month of data on a ratty thumb drive here. Maybe you could locust me up a terminal I can work with, because if I'm going to be of any use to you, then I'm going to need some kit." When this failed to evince an immediate response she nudged Matchell. "Can you make it understand, or are we back with the fucking talking lions again?"

"Kay—" Sabreur started, but Matchell waved him down weakly.

"Give me a few minutes," she said. "And does anyone have anything for a headache?"

*

The transition caught them unawares, as though someone had taken a wrench to everything around them and violently twisted. It was the action of a moment that left a bruise on the mind. They were mostly all back in their original holding area, and everyone started clamouring again, but Stig pointed downwards. The centre of their chamber was disintegrating, clawed away by busy arms so small Lee could barely see them.

"Kay!" Sabreur yelled. "We're leaving!" For Dr. Khan was still in the gourd-shaped room with the ship's avatar, working on an interface that would let them share notes.

"Go to the ball without me, love," Khan shouted back. "I've got work to do."

"You will come back," Stig said to her. "For now, take this chance to have the Earth beneath your feet. There may not be another one."

Lee could see Sabreur and Matchell exchanging glances. She said nothing though as, one by one, everyone went to the new-formed hatch and was lowered down in a cradle of articulated limbs. She suspected there would be a spirited attempt to grab Khan and get back to MI5 HQ with her, as soon as the two government types had found their bearings. But when it was her turn to leave—she and Mal were last, after the rat-creatures—that turned out not to be an issue.

The world they were shown—past the grey curtains of rain—was a dour green composed of rolling hills and copses. Yes, there was a river, but it didn't follow the course of the Thames. And above all there was no London. She knew her geography. People lived where London was because there was good land there, easy to transport goods in and out, all that schoolroom stuff. The Birdmen had only built a village there because they were carnivores who didn't plant, and they couldn't support the numbers that would add up to a city. She glanced down at Stig, a weight of tension already gone from his wide shoulders.

"You said 'going back,'" she remembered. "You meant back for you, not us, right? This is your home?"

He didn't reply, but she saw the truth of it in his face.

"Nice place you've got here." But she was thinking, *This is where they come from?* Humanity and the Nissa seemed close enough, and the Nissa were clearly technologically advanced. So...she'd thought that, should she ever see this place, there would be a city—as the rat-creatures had a city. She had braced herself for smog and walls and bustle and all that good stuff. Instead she could see...

A few handfuls of buildings, no more than a dozen in any one place. Maybe there were three separate hamlets of domed huts dotting the landscape. Fewer buildings than in the Birdmen village, in fact, as though the Nissa were pastoral remnants reverting back into some more primitive existence. The rain frustrated any attempts to see further, but all she could see was more of the same rural idyll. There were even goats, or at least grazing animals.

"You saw this before, right?" she asked.

Mal nodded. "Couple of times. They got a good deal, the Nissa." She looked down at Stig, waiting below. "Less of them, and they managed better than we ever did."

Sabreur was a dozen paces away, staring at the same vista. Lee decided to avoid him for the time being; he was probably furious to find that Stig hadn't meant his London.

"So what now?" Mal asked Stig.

He jerked his head upwards, indicating the vast trilobite ship—currently acting as their outsize umbrella. "It's working out the trajectory."

"You never told me you had one of those." Mal followed his gaze to the ship's sky-eclipsing segmented underside.

"Not ours. It's its own. Of another world. Older. Oldest world, maybe. Anyway, you are guests, now. So come to the..." He looked at the nearest handful of huts. "Research station? Yes. Come, I'll find someone to look after you. You're hungry, probably. Tired."

"I could do with a break, it's true." Matchell was sitting on the ground, heedless of the damp. "Spiker, let's make a move."

He didn't move, perhaps still absorbing the latest developments, but then he took a deep breath. He looked at Stig, and for once the other man didn't look away.

"Not fools, are you?" he said, just loud enough for Lee to catch. "You know a lot of good people—*our* people—died so you could end up with Kay."

"And ours," Stig said simply. "To save your people, and my

people, and other people who don't even know we exist, and wouldn't understand. *Everything* is at stake, Julian Sabreur. I'm sorry about your people, but it's *everything*."

"God, I hope Kier got out." Sabreur shook his head, finally resigned. "Lead on, then. Take us to your leader."

Stig shambled off, signalling for Lee to join him at the head of the column. "Nice place, you said," he said awkwardly. "Wasn't always like this, you see? Does that help you?"

"Help me?"

"You compare this to your city. We have rebuilt this. Three hundred summers before and this was all poisoned. Our great engines were here, drawing power from the tree."

She was about to frown, uncomprehending. But the answer came before she could get the question out. "The tree... that the worlds all branch from?"

"Good, yes, good. Cheap, clean energy, except the harvesting is never so clean. The building and the making which that energy powers, less clean still. We have been making and building longer than you, a thousand years longer. We poisoned so much. This land was black and dead. Nothing grew, just mud down to the dead river, you see with me?"

"I see," she agreed. "But now it's..."

"We healed, we..." He was short of the word, but then he pronounced carefully, "detoxified. We learned and did better. But this is still made landscape. We can never return it to what it was. The land is never still, and what we've made here cannot change and grow like a land should. It is a garden, but a garden is better than a wasteland."

"Are you telling me we could do this too?"

Stig shrugged and seemed to lose interest, looking at the huts ahead. She had known his people long enough to understand that they didn't confront one another, that they always gave each other space to think and feel. *Easy enough when there aren't a million of you crammed into the same conurbation.* Maybe this was Stig being too polite to say that no, her strain of humanity wasn't capable of regeneration. Still, she put a hand to his arm, feeling him twitch, and said, "Thank you." They seemed to be a very polite people, and she wanted to show them it wasn't purely a Neanderthal trait.

The domed buildings were just outside the rain shadow of the trilobite vessel. They looked fibrous, closer up: grown, and yet not wood or anything Lee could identify. They were bigger than she'd thought, two storeys high. The upper reaches were covered with tessellating transparent sections of irregular shapes, veined like a dragonfly's wing, plenty of light passing through to the interior. A trio of Nissa had come out to watch them approach, a man, a woman, a child of indeterminate gender. They wore hooded robes like druids, yet the garments were of some thin fabric that shrugged the water off like a duck's feathers. Their faces, in the shadows of their cowls, were intimidating in their alien commonality. Seeing them together, kin to Stig, no kin at all to Lee and Mal, brought home just who didn't belong here.

Probably there was a solemn and ritualistic greeting in the works, but it was scuppered when Dr. Khan let out an outraged shriek, pointing back the way they'd come. Lee's stomach lurched to see Daniel Rove and his man, Gym Bro. Lee saw Stig's expression in that moment, entirely legible as someone who had previously spotted this coming and then forgotten about it. He interposed himself between the incandescent Khan and Rove. But the rat translator darted past, shrilling furiously, while the calm voice of its implant intoned "Murderers!" over and over.

Rove's man had a gun out and was pointing it at the little creature, as though about to finish what he'd begun on the airship. Khan physically shoved Stig, trying to shift him, while Mal tried to restrain the translator because Gym Bro's gun was entirely too steady in its aim. The two government types were squaring off—to Lee's surprise—against Rove, apparently with their own grudges. For a moment the whole thing seemed about to kick off in all directions.

A word rang out: one alien syllable, not even shouted, but it cut through the clamour and silenced everyone. The Nissa woman was walking towards them, and there was something in her face that said disappointed mother to a primal part of Lee's mind. Everyone else must have had the same response, save for the translator. It was left complaining vociferously in the silence, before its words—composed of high squeaks and an urbane list of accusations—petered out.

The Cousin spoke again, and Stig translated for her. "You are all our guests." She was old, her hair grey with a few red streaks and her craggy face deeply lined. With her, the lack of eye contact was not self-effacing but imperious, beyond question.

Dr. Khan did not feel the same way. "Why does *he* get to be your guest? He's a murderer; he kidnapped me and..." A moment's flash of pain and vulnerability. "He's a fucker, okay? Translate *that*, Stig."

Stig's put-upon expression intensified, but he certainly translated something.

"I am here, Dr. Khan, for the same reason we all are," Rove said smoothly, with that little smile Lee dearly wanted to punch. "It's my universe too, after all. I have perspective and resources you lack. I have the rodent scientist's research, too. I know you weren't able to take it, only your own work."

Khan looked to the Nissa matriarch desperately, a child seeking the judgement of an adult. The woman simply stared at them. Their squabbles were beneath her, and she had more important things on her mind. Then she turned and went back inside. There was little to do but be pulled along in her wake or stay outside and get wet.

There followed possibly the most awkward meal in history.

It wasn't just that they were eating elbow to elbow with Rove and Gym Bro—or Lucas, as he was apparently called. Rove himself was clearly one of those people who could push buttons without actually saying anything controversial. Khan was fuming from the start. There was also the fact that the Nissa themselves didn't talk at the table. Or rather on the floor, as another thing they didn't do was furniture. There were cushions and rugs on the ground, and they sat wherever they pleased. The matriarch seemed to lose all interest in her guests the moment food appeared. Stig referred to her as "Murther," which was either her name or indicated that their language shared an ancient commonality with most human tongues.

The food had a lot of meat in it, extremely rare, plus some kind of chopped-up something like stuffing. The sticky white stuff was probably cheese of some kind, and there was a sort of pottage which likely wasn't meat but instead featured mushrooms and hazelnuts, as well as a sharp flavouring Lee couldn't identify. Every element jarred with all the rest, by any culinary standard she was familiar with, but the Nissa were tucking in with gusto and she did her best. Khan shared a sympathetic glance with her. "Fucked if you're a vegetarian," she remarked drily.

When everyone had finished, Murther stood, ponderously and with help. She regarded her guests for a brooding moment, and Lee wondered what on Earth they looked like to her, these thin, angular humans and their rodents of unusual size.

"I have spoken with the Wayfarers," Stig announced, translating for her. The woman's gesture, up and out, made it plain she meant the creature-ship that had brought them. "They are ready. When morning comes, they will depart. You and you and you must go with them, as shall we."

The three "you"s were Khan, Rove and the rat translator, and "we" was apparently Stig and Murther, or possibly a wider Nissa delegation.

"And the rest of us?" Sabreur asked sharply. He had been very quiet since they arrived. "For the record, and in the full understanding that it won't matter a damn, you're laying claim to two citizens of the United Kingdom."

"Julian—" Khan started, but he waved her down.

"I said 'for the record,'" he emphasized. "I know that what I want and who I am doesn't mean a damn right now. But I can't just...let it go by without at least registering a complaint."

Stig cocked an ear and then went on with his translation. "For the rest of you, you have a choice. If you choose to journey with us, then the Wayfarers will carry you. If you choose to stay amongst our people, that too is possible. If you wish to return to your own places, this can be achieved, when conditions allow it."

*

Afterwards, Lee and Mal, overfed, short on sleep and apparently safe for the first time in a good while, lay together on the soft synthetic rugs by the hut's inward-sloping wall.

"We could stay here," Lee said thoughtfully. "Learn the language, find a place. They seem friendly, and there's space. We could do what you did, help out with their interdimensional-explorer project, go visit the Birdmen again, or... anything."

"Been there, done that," Mal said dismissively. "And... they're not easy to get on with, these guys. They don't let you in. They're big into self-sufficiency, but at the same time they're all about helping people, and you're supposed to know when people need help cos they don't exactly ask. They've got a million ways of letting you know you're not pulling your weight, too, without even talking to you. And you keep expecting them to be like people, our people, but they're always slightly *not*. I guess you'd get used to it, after a while, but..."

"You want to go travelling," Lee finished.

"I really, really do. I mean, the Cousins reckon there's a process that creates these different Earths, one that's been running for a billion years or a hundred billion or... who even knows? They reckon it's there, it's gone off the rails and, of all things, they can *fix* it. With maths and sufficiently advanced technology. Which is where Doc Khan comes in, and where Doc Rat would have, if that sonofabitch hadn't killed him. There'll be Nissa scientists and that ice thing and the flying bug monsters... They say there are other Earths where there aren't mathematicians or scientists or dimension-crossing engines, but those Earths need saving too. And we can be a part of it, Lee, we..." Her voice trailed off, and she lay there for a while as Lee stroked her hair. "I'm always doing this, aren't I?"

"What?"

"Fucking your life up." She captured Lee's hand and brought it to her cheek, just held it there, skin to skin. "I got you into trouble so many times at school, and never thought twice. I dragged us off to Bodmin and screwed you up with that. Then when I had the chance, I crashed back and derailed everything all over again. You were caught by the bad guys because of me, and nearly killed in two other worlds when I talked the Nissa into saving you. And now..." She stared at the rounded ceiling, her mouth a straight line. "I will stay," she said, slowly. "Ask me, and I'll stay. I'd rather be here, anywhere, with you, than at the ends of the Earth without. I will stay."

Lee took a deep breath, blinking rapidly. It was a moment before she could speak. "We'll go," she said at last. "I mean, this is affecting the whole universe. There isn't exactly a safe place to watch from."

Mal didn't say anything, but she squeezed Lee's hand tightly.

Later on, the rat translator came to join them, mostly because Dr. Khan was elsewhere. It clearly didn't like anyone else, nor did it want to be alone. They were a gregarious people, after all, and this was a big, empty world.

"The precious kin of Dr. Rat have been accommodated," it explained when Lee asked. "Our hosts have rendered duplication of the architecture of my implant. Communication will be feasible, at first through the mediation of your own language."

A strange compromise, that English should be the lingua franca between two separate species, but perhaps Rove's dealings with the rat lords had done some peripheral good.

"I thought you were Dr. Rat's...slave? Experimental subject? When we met you, anyway."

The translator shook itself. "In early years that was approximately the case. He was not good. He was good. He was not bad." The creature considered what it had said. "There are shades of qualities your language does not accommodate. Between us there was not love or love but love. Love is pain sometimes. Sometimes pain is good." It crooked its four thumbs at them, perhaps trying to express its frustration. "Complicated things," it finished, leaving Lee to wonder what gradations of sentiment the rat-creatures knew, that English—or perhaps humans—simply had no words for.

II

The rain had exhausted itself by nightfall. Though the skies were still hung heavy with cloud that promised more before dawn and which swallowed all the stars. Julian had dragged a rug outside and was sitting there, looking down the hilly country to the river that was emphatically not the Thames. Being under the Cousins' roof seemed too much like complicity in what was going on. He was aware he was being ridiculous, but it was *hard*. He'd strayed beyond all the comfortable borders and rules he'd surrounded his life with to date. Above, just below the clouds' blanket, he could just make out the dark shape of their living vessel— the thinking entity—that had brought everyone here. And that wasn't even the maddest thing he was being asked to accept.

"Spiker." Alison dropped down beside him, shoving him over on the rug as if it was her couch back home—and they were about to watch some new thing on Netflix.

"Matchbox." The nickname was something he could still cling to.

"Holding up?"

"Not really."

Alison put an arm around his shoulders, and he was surprised at how comforting that was.

"We left a hell of a mess back home," she said quietly. "They're trying to spin it as a terrorist attack—three separate packs of opportunists have even tried to claim responsibility. But people *saw*. You can't cover up some crazy airship materializing through three tower blocks. You *really* can't cover up a woodlouse the size of a borough, hanging over London. But the world was breaking up before then. Because there really is a bigger problem, and the Cousins really are trying to fix it."

"You got all this from your...woo." He waved a hand in the air in a manner he hoped approximated "ancient alien ice-computer mind."

"The connection here is good," she said, as though it was no more complex than Wi-Fi—a facility that, Julian realized, he also didn't particularly understand. "The Cousins have been working with the Ice Mind for a long time. There are...established diplomatic channels. Just like they have with this Wayfarer, though I think that's more recent and a lot more tentative. The Cousins are on sufferance with that latest lot, just as we are with them. And there's more, other links, other places." She laughed suddenly, and it was a welcome enough sound to warm Julian's heart a little. "A new woman arrived at the hut, by the way, Auruthmer; she flew in to meet us."

"Us? Why would they need to..." He thought about that. "Don't tell me, she's an *anthropologist*."

"She studies us, right. They've been hanging about in our world for a while. I get the impression they have whole symposiums and whatnot about these wacky humans and their junk food and cat memes. But she speaks English better than Stig, or at least she's chattier; speaks about nineteen other human languages too, as far as I can gather. So if you wanted to get answers about all of this, she's your woman."

Julian nodded, finding the idea didn't appeal. "So who's this other Murther character?"

"Mission control, far as I can gather," Alison said. "She's a top scientist, specialist in not letting the universe get destroyed."

"And she lives in a hut in the middle of nowhere." *That should be London*, all his memories screamed to him.

"They have a completely decentralized society. I can...I can't roam around in their data archives, but I can see the shape of things through my Ice Mind link. It's very good at taking an ungodly amount of information and remodelling it in a way I can understand." She took a deep breath. "Spiker, we need to talk."

"We are talking."

"Kay wants to go. We don't have the right—"

"Yes, yes." He cut her off more sharply than he'd intended. "Look, I am way beyond my job description right now. I have no power to go against the Cousins and drag Kay kicking and screaming back to Whitehall. And yes, duty to Queen and Country aside, it's her call. She wants to go, she goes."

454

Alison was quiet for a while. He could practically see her next words in letters of fire over her head, but he was damned if he was going to prompt them.

At last, and with a slightly aggrieved look—because he wasn't making this easy—she said, "I want to go too."

"That would be a terrible idea," he said.

"Really? Because everything is falling apart, and knowing what I do, I don't think I could go home and plod on for another...what? Ten days? A month? A year? Knowing that it was all coming down and that at any moment I could... cease. I'd rather be there, where the work is going on, even if I'd be no earthly use. I want to see it saved, or not saved. Otherwise it's the mother of all swords of Damocles, isn't it?"

Julian thought about that, feeling her arm and her warmth as an anchor, preventing him from flying into the void and being lost forever. He was, he realized, unutterably in love with Alison Matchell. His feelings tipped the hat to sexual attraction, but only on the way to a number of other things that were vastly more significant. Not exactly a grand revelation this late in the game, but somehow he'd never been able to admit it.

He thought he could have lived under that particular sword forever, because he was an expert at throwing up routines and rules and habits until the uncomfortable breadth of the wider world was entirely hidden from him.

Except that, as Alison said, things were screwed up beyond recognition back home. He didn't feel good that the casting vote in his decision was *Don't want to face the mess I made*, but so be it.

"Of course we'll stay." He made a creditable stab at making

455

the words sound sincere, as though they were what he'd always intended to say. "We're HM Government's representatives—they'd want us to look after the national interest."

Alison barked out another laugh, and he saw for a golden moment how glad she was that he was along for the ride. His heart twisted painfully, and then the usual guilt flooded back. "Can you...use your link to communicate with people, back home?"

"Possibly. You want to report to Hind? I don't know what she'd make of it. We're somewhat outside our jurisdiction, to be honest."

"I want to get word to Josie. To tell her...I'm okay. But yes, I should probably do that as well."

"Then you'd better start dictating," Alison invited. "And keep it brief. I'm not sure how much I can smuggle over the borders."

He couldn't say much to either Josie or Hind, in the end. Little more than "still alive, watch this space." Alison herself was mostly concerned with getting a neighbour to look after Simms. Julian had prompted her to message Derek and the girls, but after some reflection she'd simply said, "That ship sailed a long time ago."

Soon after, Alison introduced him to Auruthmer, a relatively small, dark Cousin woman, her ginger hair cut short. Whilst "relatively small" still made her broad and solid by Julian's standards, her features seemed subtly more human than her compatriots'. She had narrower cheekbones, and a knob of chin beneath her broad mouth. He wondered if that difference had led her to her field of study, or if it was the result of camouflaging surgery.

"It's a pleasure to meet you, Mr. Sabreur." To Julian's

surprise, she spoke English with a pronounced American accent. She also made eye contact, albeit slightly too intensely. "So, you've decided to journey with us, is that right? A gesture of solidarity and fraternity between two civilizations?" She gave him an entirely human grin. "For context, Mr. Sabreur: I've been teaching at the University of California for the last two years, and I did three at Buenos Aires before that. I'd still be in your world, but they called for an interspecies liaison— on account of how we'll be riding the Wayfarers' coat-tails together. What can I do for you?"

"I have a favour to ask," Alison said.

"Not to send a message home, I take it. You appear to already have remarkably free access to the Posticthyan network."

Alison blinked, off balance. "The . . . Ice Mind?"

"A good enough name. It likes you. Which is obviously an anthropic generalization. But something about your contact with it has induced it to leave an open channel for you. It doesn't happen with many, either ours or yours. So using it to sneak messages back to your government seems to be using a sledgehammer to crack a nut. We would have passed your messages on, had you asked. But I understand that you'd rather have the agency." The contrast to Stig was marked, Julian noted. With Auruthmer, the challenge wasn't getting words out, but getting a word in edgeways.

"There is one thing you can do, though, if you do want to help," Alison prompted. She and Julian had discussed this, and decided that right now they had one priority, and it was trying to understand. They weren't genius scientists like Khan, and they weren't interdimensional gadabouts like the two girls. Alison herself had access to a remarkable entity without even

457

ADRIAN TCHAIKOVSKY

knowing what it was or whether it had an agenda. If they were to gain any purchase on their circumstances, they needed to understand the big picture.

"Stig kept saying he didn't understand enough to give us an overview, to tell us how all this happened," Julian explained, uncomfortably aware the man's name wasn't actually Stig. "But we were hoping that you, or someone, could tell us. Please."

Auruthmer's expression softened slightly. He hoped that meant she appreciated they weren't primitives to be lied to—rather than being happy the animals had learned a new trick. She glanced up at the sky and the leaden shadow that was the living ship.

"Come inside," she said. "We'll sit in the warmth, and I'll tell you. I'll tell you from the very beginning."

Interlude: The Humans

Excerpt from *Other Edens:
Speculative Evolution and Intelligence* by
Professor Ruth Emerson of the
University of California

So here we are.

I've taken you through all the other spurs that arose from the tree of time and went their own way. Now it's time for me to unveil any final revelations or reversals of fortune. Time to uncover any last surprises this multiplied cosmos might have for you. And once you understand this last twist, you can understand our current dilemma.

In our timeline, this late branch on the tree, there are no hyperintelligent cats. And if the rodents grow as large as capybaras, they only grow as smart as capybaras, which is exactly how smart capybaras need to be. Big brains are expensive, and species must cut their evolutionary cloth to suit their purse. Being clever isn't the universal panacea we'd maybe like it to be.

No dinosaurs, then; no super-intelligent arthropods or molluscs. Just us.

Two and a half million years ago is as good a point to start as any. Our ancestors were apes that had left the forests for the plains. In the tall grass they stood taller, because the plains were full of things that wanted to eat them, and things they wanted to eat. Shorn of a role in locomotion, time found uses for their idle hands. This is where the stone tools start. And for a long, long time our ancestors don't really do much

461

in the way of R&D. They have fire, they have stone axes. They have a détente with the more dangerous predators. Sometimes the leopard gets you, sometimes you get the leopard, and if it's the latter then you have a new blanket and a story to tell. Because they told stories, we're sure, even then. Although perhaps they were just the same stories at first, over and over, the same proto-words and gestures stuck together in the same ways.

Their brains work at a level that contemporaneous apes—and modern apes—can't imitate. They learn more quickly from one another, copying the movements that turn *this* rock into *that* blade. They remember. And they confabulate beyond the dreams of chimps. Or other primates. And yet for a million years our ancestors were happy with what they had.

We don't know what changed, really: was it better brains or harsher environments? Look at us: all the stories we've told with such confidence about inhuman civilizations on other Earths, and we remain absurdly ignorant about our own origins. Those proto-humans had a tool revolution, though. Clearly someone looked at the flint and hammerstone they were holding one day and thought, *What if I did it like this . . . ?*

Perhaps that's where the first group who truly feel like *our ancestors* arise. Half a million years ago, a handful of our world's denizens transformed from some*things* into some*ones*. And we have their bones, their teeth, a few trackways and their tools.

Those trackways took them outwards, away from the grass-lands of their homes. They spread into other continents and changed to meet the demands of climate, diet and experience. They mythologized their journeys and their ancestors; they added a dimension to the mundane world to account for all the things they felt and believed—and needed to believe but could not see. And they died and grieved and loved, just as we do.

At some point they crossed into Europe and met harsh winters and monstrous long-haired beasts. Cut off from their past, they became something different. Privation moulded their interactions, and yesterday's mammoth hunt became tomorrow's pantomimed performance before the fire. The world chipped at them like a flint until they were a sharp enough blade to unseam it and use all its component parts.

Even then, perhaps, they knew that there was *more*. They felt it, at certain places, certain seasons. There were places you did not go casually that could transform you or vanish you away. There were valleys where monsters might brush your elbow, from the other side of a divide incomprehensible to the human mind. There were clawed tracks that led off in directions they had no name for, into impossible distances as though whole worlds were held within the cracks of a cliff. Or foreign seas were folded into the inch-deep waters of a puddle. They sensed these spaces, we suspect, and there was value in knowing what places to avoid, or perhaps what places might offer inexplicable warmth in the hard ice-age winters. So this sense was honed by time and the passage of generations.

And of course there were the others that shared their world, in case all this wasn't uncanny enough.

Our ancestors couldn't have known how unusual their timeline was, to birth two sentient species. Only the isolationist icthyans truly shared their Earth with another thinking species for long—that we know of—and their mental and geographical worlds were so different. There was nothing for them to compete over, no way for them to threaten one another until the bitter end.

But for us, there was always a ghost waiting in the dark places.

When we began to move out of Europe into Asia, there *they* were. When we ventured south to where we'd come from, we found them too. These meetings made a sufficiently keen impression on our Stone Age ancestors that they sank deep roots into our mythologies. It is a profound and troubling thing to realize you are not alone. Like us, yet not like us: we remember the people of the forests and the grasslands, the people of the rich, warm lands to which we returned. They fascinated us. They became our elves, our fair folk. The stories we inherited have changed a thousand ways since, of course: nothing is left that could stand as evidence in any court of palaeontology. But our ancestors were still relatively careful curators of their stories. They passed them from generation to generation, and each pair of hands added only a few new fingerprints. We collect them still now, a hundred thousand years later, from across our world. We distil them, boil them down to discover their common features. In this way we can almost remember what it was like to crest the hill and see the fires of the *other* between the trees.

We speak of them dancing and singing a great deal. That must have been important to them. Or perhaps it was something our own ancestors did not do, until we learned it from the *other*. We speak of them as frail, slender, ethereal almost. *Fragile*. Ghost-like in the bamboo forests of Asia, flurrying in hunting parties at the edge of our kin's fires. Their high, clear voices would lift in chants and choruses after sunset. We remember they were beautiful and fleet and brittle, like glass people, like their music.

We moved south and east, and the *others* were always a step ahead of us, dancing away into the night. There was some trading—there are stories that have become great legends, of the exchange of impossible things between us and the elusive forest folk. We have tales of questing heroes, travelling to reclaim important things that should never have been bartered away. And maybe there were exchanges of another kind. Genetic investigation certainly suggests that there is a little bit of *them* in *us*. Perhaps that tiny germ of code is a key element of what makes us who we are.

We tell ourselves that we didn't drive them away as we inexorably increased our range. As we returned to the warm lands and adapted our ways, hunting *their* animals that didn't know our tricks so well, we used these *others'* resources—to replicate and improve on our existing tools and techniques. Perhaps those mysterious singing people were already in decline when we found them. Perhaps the fact that they are no longer in our world doesn't mean there's blood on our hands. But our ancestors were strong and determined, and our brains were larger than those of the *others*, just a little. And we had been remade on the glacial anvil. How likely was it that our coming and their going was simple coincidence? By the time any of us could ask that question, it was too late. The others were already gone, and all we had were their stories and their bones.

By now you might be saying, "Hold on...," because this doesn't sound right to you, but again—and we promise for just this one more time—this isn't your Earth. This is ours.

After the others had vanished, we were still around, refining our tools. Our development went down a slightly different path to yours because our brains and senses are slightly different. We evolved a sensitivity to certain stimuli, signals that don't come into the world via regular channels. And early in the half million years during which we became *us*, chance mutation and evolutionary pressure bore strange progeny. In our distant past, we told ourselves that we had found doorways to other worlds. And why not? What good would a more precise knowledge have done? No point having a complete mastery of quantum entanglement when you still have to stick a spear in an aurochs for dinner.

However, in our more recent past, our scholars decided that we'd found unstable points in space–time. Here, the underlying fabric of the universe was being deformed by unknown forces, existing upon an axis that had no material analogue in our familiar universe. By then, we had already been exploiting these weak points for our technology. We started with regions where the regular laws of the world were suspended: we'd found water that flowed uphill, patches of localized weather, places where inconsistent objects suddenly appeared as though they'd fallen from the sky. All isolated, random, unreliable. Your species might have dismissed them as hearsay and madness. We, with our particular senses, did not. We *knew* something was there.

You might imagine this produced religions, superstitions, cults and would-be sorcerers. But magic is just another way of trying to understand the observed world. Your historical magicians, who you might scorn for their credulity, were deeply concerned with the rules and mechanics of how things work. In our world as in yours, their studies transformed seamlessly into those of the first scientists. We worked out how to use minute local variances of pressure, we harnessed electricity and the fundamental properties of matter as a source of power.

Exactly one hundred and seven years ago, give or take a few lunar months, our most visionary scientist of the day completed her great work—a unified theory of the substance of space–time. She theorized that in order to account for the phenomena we could perceive and measure, there must be other Earths parallel to our own. The earliest beliefs of our mystical forebears were true; the weak spots really were doorways to other worlds. Practical proof of this came some nineteen years later. We were able to open a door into another timeline for precisely two point eleven seconds.

Research and experiment proceeded at a rapid pace from there on in. Very few of us ever asked why these spots existed—this was the natural order of things, we thought. What we did not realize, at that point, was that other species had begun to test the bars of their cages too. What we did realize was that the branching of timelines was part of a process.

Imagine a tree trunk with many branches—and all the branches, wherever they arise on the stem, all reach up to the same height. That's because they're timelines and that height is the present moment, and that's how time works. And throughout the history of time, as we know it, the tree has put out new branches. These are new timelines, each one growing off the trunk a little higher—thus diverging later in time. And all these worlds share the same roots. There was, we hypothesized, a prime Earth, somewhere far back in time: a point where all the timelines agreed, which formed the stem all these branches arose from. And we turned out to be exactly right.

But before we get to that—before we get to the important bit, really—I need to share something with you. We worked out something else, and to our knowledge no other species ever took this step. We realized that the process whereby timelines branched off from one another was not only scientifically explicable, but replicable.

Our technology, being based on the existence of the parallel Earths, was uniquely suited to such an act of hubris. And our scientists were so buoyed by their understanding of the cosmos that they did not examine the consequences of such an act. Drunk on our wisdom, we simply did it.

We made our own subordinate timeline.

We had it coalesce as a divergence point perhaps one hundred thousand years beforehand. We had little control over precisely what that other Earth might look like. Many thought it would be exactly the same as our own, barring a few names and details, because our mastery of the world was obviously inevitable.

When we opened a gate to that world, though, we were dumbfounded. The world we stepped into had been given a hundred millennia to diverge, and diverge it most certainly had. In this world, the currents of chance had shifted, and our own kind had lived in miserable decline for fifty thousand years after the branch point before shuffling into myth and palaeontology. In their place had come the *others*, spilling out of Africa into Asia and Europe. They brought their own songs and tools, their burial customs and strange ideas. We had created a strange new world, and it had such strange people in it.

In short, we had created you.

16.

I

The previous night, Lee and Mal had come across the two government types talking with a new Nissa arrival. They'd come in midway, but eventually they'd worked out that what they were being given, in Californian-accented English, was *it*. This was the story of the world, insofar as the Nissa understood it. So they'd sat and listened to Auruthmer (or Professor Ruth Emerson, as UCAL records had her). And then they'd gone to bed far too late, shaken and disturbed by what they'd learned.

This morning the sky was busy. Stepping into the glare of dawn, Lee saw multiple broad shadows crossing the rolling landscape. Up above, a dozen colossal trilobites performed a slow-motion circling dance, no two quite the same. Some had vast sweeps of spines, others were smooth and rounded. There were profusions of eyes, single broad bands of facets, stalks or blind-seeming crescents of shell. She understood a little about them, now. They were the Wayfarers, as Auruthmer called them. They were Earth's oldest children, whose self-awareness spanned half a billion years. In that time they had transcended most of what made life *life*—at least by the standards of Lee, student of biology. They seldom produced offspring; they evolved at need; they could build and dismantle molecules and needed almost no sustenance from outside; they lived forever. And yet, godlike though they seemed, they were still children of Earth. These few had therefore returned from their travels in their motherworld's time of need.

The human delegation was gathering, blinking in the dawn light. Mal clasped Lee's hand as they both stared up. Lee considered that, somehow, *this* was what her friend had been looking for all her life: an escape from the ordinary, the door to fairyland. A girl who'd never fit in, searching for a place nobody *could* fit in.

Lee was still somewhat leery of Julian and Alison. Government spooks, after all, though decidedly de-fanged by circumstance. Except that Julian Sabreur was very much not the brooding action man he obviously wanted to be, and Alison Matchell seemed as weird as Mal in her own way. Dr. Khan had become an inadvertent bridge between the two groups because Julian knew her from way back and seemed to like her, rather despite himself, Lee suspected.

And then there were the other two passengers. The fact that Julian plainly *didn't* like Daniel Rove or his man, Lucas, was another point in his favour.

The rat translator was also coming. It had finally tried to reproduce its name, coming out with something like "Ertil."

There were at least a score of Nissa ready to embark. Stig and Auruthmer would be playing human-keepers, she gathered. The others would be on one or more of the other living vessels taxiing ponderously above them.

"Makes you wonder what they've seen, doesn't it?" Mal said. Her eyes were starry, and perhaps she was imagining their freedom to travel, to just *be*. Lee squeezed her hand tighter, to remind her of the human entanglements she might leave behind. From what Auruthmer had said, there was no real trilobite society. They were, each of them, an island. This gathering must be unprecedented within the last hundred million years. "You think they've been to all the other timelines?"

"They have not." It was Auruthmer herself who spoke, with sharper ears than expected. "We've been climbing the other branches of the worlds for generations, most especially yours. The Wayfarers have walked amongst the stars of their own timeline and seen vistas none of us can possibly imagine. Yet they never guessed that theirs was just one universe of many; only when their sense organs began to detect the symptoms of the collapse did they become aware. And because we travel more than any and leave our fingerprints many places, they become aware of us. Since then, they have taken our little science and applied their great leverage to it, to enable us to get to the heart of the problem." She gave her intense smile. At her back, Stig shuffled and stared fiercely at his feet.

"Here," Auruthmer said, but instead of imparting more wisdom she was just pointing up—and it was something the Nissa didn't do, Lee realized. They had a dozen ways of indicating something other than picking it out with the jut of a finger. Probably there was a whole complex subtext there, completely lost on a Western European.

The ship, *their* ship, was descending slowly—as impossible now as it had been when she first saw it. It kept coming, and she kept having to re-evaluate how big it was. She had no idea what force was keeping it airborne, save that there was no downrush of air, no howl of jet engines, just a thousand-ton arthropod drifting ghost-like against the flat, silvery early morning sky.

"What can it think of us?" Lee wondered, almost mournfully.

"I understand the situation has some precedent, for them," Auruthmer said, as casually as if it was nothing. "Do you think they haven't met others, on their journey?"

"You mean—out *there*?"

The Nissa woman raised her shaggy eyebrows, inscrutable.

A cradle of limbs descended from the trilobite, which was thirty feet above them, blotting out the sky. The mode of ascension was still somewhat unnerving, but Lee found she could look on it and think, *It's our monster. It's one of us.*

II

Having travelled freight on the way in, Lucas was relieved to see that the monster had manufactured an entire suite of rooms for its human cargo overnight. Better than sitting in a modified swim bladder or whatever the hell the thing had found for unexpected passengers. The downside was sharing the space with everyone else—and nobody was exactly fond of Lucas or his boss.

"How long's the journey?" he asked the Neanderthal woman who spoke the best English. He was told she didn't know, because nobody had ever made this trip before. Less than reassuring.

Khan straight up hated the pair of them now she was out from under Rove's thumb, and apparently the rat-thing translator was an entity in and of itself, which was news to Lucas. It had retained some of Dr. Rat's research too, which Rove wasn't happy about because it devalued his own offerings. Too late, Lucas suspected, for the cyborg bastard to have an accident. Thankfully the cavemen didn't seem to care, or at least weren't going to let a grudge get in the way of any help that might be on offer.

This was, in Lucas's personal opinion, a mistake. Not that he was going to turn down useful naivety in his enemies, but if he'd been in their shoes, he would have fed Rove to the closest woolly mammoth or let the giant trilobite shit them out into space. Rove was definitely not someone who'd happily play as part of someone else's team. He called the shots, or he dismantled the hierarchy until he was the highest part of what remained. Lucas guessed his boss was already applying his mind to the task.

It wasn't that Rove was a genius-level intellect, but he had a very specific set of skills. Lucas wasn't qualified to diagnose sociopathy, but Rove was capable of telling anyone anything, making utterly convincing promises and being bound by none of it. Rove loved Rove first, things useful to Rove second. And nothing else.

After being hoisted into the creature's interior, Rove glanced around with a proprietary air, grasping the layout of their lozenge-shaped rooms and picking the one he liked most. "We'll make our stand here, I think," he told Lucas, and sure enough that chamber was Rove's from then on because nobody else wanted to be near him.

After the rest had settled, Lucas found his boss sitting comfortably against the rounded wall, making staccato motions at the touch screen of his phone. *Probably not checking social media*, Lucas guessed. He could hear the voices of the others echoing dully from elsewhere, engaged in some kind of tedious get-to-know-you session he felt he was well out of. The cover of their jabbering meant he could at least pump his boss for intel without worrying about being overheard.

"Some clarity on what we're doing here would be appreciated, sir," he said.

Rove looked up brightly. Sitting in this windowless room, there was a slight air of the white-collar convict to him, which Lucas found more amusing than he expected. There was no admission in the man's face that he was anything other than in control, though.

"First order of the day is to gather information, Lucas. Our hosts believe they can find the source of what's going on, and once that is understood, many things may be possible."

"The source of it?"

Rove lifted an eyebrow. "The prevailing school of thought amongst our hosts, based on the amalgamated evidence, is that a *process* has been at work, splitting linear causality into parallel branches. Our immediate interlocutors have even replicated the process, at considerable cost. Charen showed me how that worked a while back. And though I won't pretend to have mastered the mathematics, the implications are eye-opening, in respect of what options it puts on the table."

Lucas frowned. "Options like what?" He was aware that he wasn't talking to his boss with quite his usual deference, and Rove wasn't kicking against it. He was equally aware that Rove would drop him the moment he ceased to be useful. It was a fine line to tread.

"It's a work in progress, Lucas. You know me, I like to look ahead. I've been planning for this for longer than anyone else, except the Neanderthals."

Lucas nodded, took a quick look out into the rest of the suite to make sure nobody had crept away from the party and sidled back. "So who's Charen, precisely?"

"Just another valued employee," Rove explained. "One with her finger on the pulse of all this multidimensional business. She's something of a favourite of another major player here— virtually its high priestess, in her own mind. Don't worry, she's not your replacement. Her services are of a different nature." Rove's plastic smile drifted almost fondly onto his face. "How flexible are you feeling, Lucas, morally?"

"You know me." This was the safest answer for now. Lucas was wary of examining just what he would or wouldn't do in the course of his further employment.

Rove seemed to hear the answer he'd wanted. "We're going to have to think on our feet, I fear. Until they take us to the heart of this business, we're not going to know where we can stand or how big our lever is. But if the opportunity arises for us to sort this mess out, we'll need a firm hand— you understand that? We are, after all, looking to preserve *something* of value for future use, but our conspecifics here may lack the required ruthlessness. You understand me?"

Lucas considered their fellow passengers: the rat, the two annoying girls, the bloody security man and his girlfriend or whatever, and Dr. Khan. Plus the two cavemen who were shacking up with them, the one with the U.S. education and the thug who'd already killed several of Rove's minions. He'd shoot some of them less readily than others. However, if it came down to his future or theirs, he was unhappily certain the trigger was going to get pulled.

Rove saw as much in his face, because he nodded pleasantly. "Good fellow," he said, with that just-add-water instant chumminess the cameras had always loved. "For now, though, feel free to mingle. Just don't get attached."

III

There was some initial jockeying and verbal fencing—especially with Mallory, who was more pugnacious than Julian would have liked, given he was sharing an internal organ with her. Afterwards, he and Alison sloped off to what he tenuously thought of as the "front" compartment, where Kay Amal Khan was. As, regrettably, was their transportation's ghastly humanoid avatar, still dangling from the ceiling like the nastiest marionette in this or any world.

Khan gave them both a quick grin when they ducked in. She'd been up here for most of the night, Julian guessed, and seemed positively energized.

"What's up with you, Jules?" She waggled her eyebrows, looking from him to Alison, but he chose to ignore her.

"I still don't feel happy with the Plu—with our hosts, the Cousins," he confessed. "Too much like hostile foreign agents. And the two girls don't like us. Or don't like me, anyway."

"They're counterculture kids," Khan said. "And you're the authorities. I mean, if I didn't know you, I wouldn't like you either. Full disclosure, love, but I've always felt there was a bit of a tension between you, decent public servant that you are, and the ethos of what you serve."

The nest of tiny limbs that was the avatar's head seethed and rippled. The net effect was that its "face" slid along the outside of its "head" until its fake eyes were directed at Khan. The motion was utterly unlike a human turning to look at something.

"Our calculations are ready for the transition Innerwards, if you would like to examine them." It moved its arms upwards, chitinous muscles sliding and interlocking around articulated bones. The hands were held as though the creature was a film director framing a shot, describing two corners of an invisible rectangular space. More tiny limbs spidered out into that notional plane, locking into place to form script: numbers and mathematical notations. Khan leant forwards, squinting, and the thing obligingly moved its hands up to her eye line and then further apart. Extra limbs and feelers twitched into place to even give her a more legible font.

"It sounds more lucid than it did yesterday," Alison noted.

"Oh, Cam's been learning," Khan confirmed. "Or, no, he's been...evolved into something more fit for purpose. Maybe that's a better way of putting it."

Julian stared at the thing and felt an unwelcome shock of contact from its glittering eyes. He was meeting the gaze of an entity, not just looking at an unappealing object.

"What is it now, then?" Alison seemed happier to peer at the thing, and it mirrored her scrutiny inexactly, the verisimilitude lost. It became just an elaborate animatronic in Julian's mind again, the emergent personhood fled.

"Cam is...a marvel, really." Khan was still squinting at the figures. She delicately took the avatar's hands and moved them yet further out, widening the non-existent screen so that the displayed data obligingly increased in size. If she'd ever had the creeping revulsion Julian was feeling, she'd lost it overnight. "Auruthmer gave you the low-down on them as a whole, right? What they *are*?"

"Somewhat." Julian felt agreeing that he understood would be pushing matters too far.

"In their timeline, sentience first evolved during the Cambrian period—half a *billion* years before now. Hence 'Cam.' Cam is a small one, but it's lived basically forever, travelled through space, can make independent drones to go do stuff, etcetera. It doesn't have kids or anything as gauche as that, doesn't even have anything to do with its own kind much. The others here are just those who could be contacted, when they worked out there was a problem. They probably had to work almost as hard to speak to each other as they're doing to speak with me. Comms is not their strong point, right?" Khan grinned at them, obviously happy to have the chance to lecture. "That's where your friend comes in." She levelled a finger at Alison. "You and I are going to have to have a chat about how you became part of all this, because access to the Posticthyan Ice Mind is patchy even amongst Stig's lot. Anyway, Cam and his Wayfarers have engineered a high-level connection to your chilly friend, and the Ice is *terrific* with comms. So overnight, Cam used that link to go download...the internet."

"Christ," Julian managed, feeling a sudden stab of *but-our-secrets!* He had to forcibly remind himself that a space-going trilobite probably wouldn't care about national security, or ministerial peccadillos.

"Thing is," Khan admitted, "this entity here is just...a limb, a specialized organ informed by its reading of human interactions. Cam itself, the big one, probably can't conceive of us—tiny motes that we are. But being a godlike thing, it's able to make a series of filters, simplifying and contracting to create its puppet here. This"—she indicated the mannequin—"is like the tiniest tip of its pinky finger, force-evolved for the specific purpose of talking to *me*, and by extension, humans in general. Makes you think, doesn't it?"

For a moment Julian felt that he was on the verge of truly appreciating what she was telling him—and that made him feel faint. He actually sagged into Alison, who did her best

478

to prop him up, arm about his waist. He caught Khan's eyebrows jiggling again and scowled at her.

"What? I figured you two were an item. I thought you were finally living a little, Jules," she jibed.

"There's nothing like that." Abruptly both he and Alison had made sure that there was a discrete—and discreet—space between them.

"Well, okay, my cisgender relationship radar was always shonky," Khan admitted. "I am shipping the fuck out of you in my headcanon, though." That grin again, but cutting sufficiently close to home that Julian couldn't return it with any feeling.

"The others concur." Cam's scratchy voice chose that moment to break in. "We are preparing for transit Innerwards."

"Right, yes, I concur too," Khan said hurriedly. "This looks solid." She patted the thing's shell-like shoulder and it retracted its display, letting its arms fall to its sides.

"What's 'Innerwards'?" Alison asked.

"I needed a word for the direction we're going to be trav-elling. I mean, picture an axis that isn't height, depth or breadth but exists at a ninety-degree angle to all three. So, Inner, Outer. And it *is* Inner and Outer because of the way the parallels are organized. That was the big clue, for Cam and for Stig's lot—and even me now I've seen the full maths." Suddenly Khan was serious. "Look, you've had the spiel from Auruthmer. They call it a tree and branches, but if you think about it, there's no tree on Earth that works like that. It's not branches that split into branches that split into twigs, is what I mean. Each branch is singular."

"The Ice Mind has shown me it," said Alison thoughtfully. "Each branch diverges from the previous branch. Our Earth buds from the history of the Cousins after Neanderthals and our ancestors diverged, but before the Cousin civilization arose. Their Earth buds from...those awful lemur things, and so on...? But that's just how things are, isn't it?"

"Well it isn't, or that's what the equations say," Khan explained animatedly, as deadly serious as Julian had ever seen her.

"There is no physical barrier to multiple parallels arising at once from the same instance or world," Cam confirmed precisely. "There is no discernible reason why multiple parallels should not give rise to additional parallels. But this has not happened. It is our hypothesis that, though the potential for engendering parallels is inherent in the structure of the universe, this does not happen spontaneously because of the energy gradient that must be overcome. Such energy must necessarily be directed Outerwards at a very precise trajectory."

"And Stig's lot, the 'Cousins,' confirm this—I mean, they are the only people who actually *did* it, right?" Khan shook her head wonderingly. "So we don't think this process just happens. And if it did, we should be seeing a much more organic pattern of parallels—branches like an actual tree, most likely. So, best guess, there is an artificial instigator that's budding off parallels, each from its previous result. It seems almost like someone trying to refine an experiment, someone searching for something. And now this fantastic, intricate structure of worlds that something *built*—which incorporates everything all our various species have ever known—is coming down like universal fucking Jenga. So we're going Innerwards to try and stop it all folding."

"Innerwards to...?" Alison prompted.

"To the start, to Universe One, to the original Earth and whoever lives there." Khan's voice shook, ever so slightly.

We're going to see God, Julian thought, *and it's a god that even*

480

this godlike monster we're inside accepts is God—the creator of everything, except itself and its own universe. "I feel a sudden need to sit down," he said. Alison gave him a nod, and she was as pale and strained as he felt.

At that point, the rat-creature translator bustled in, pushing past Julian's legs.

"Some change transpires," its bland voice announced, although its body language suggested considerable alarm. Its fur was bristling out as though caught in a strong electrical field.

"We're on our way, love," Khan confirmed. "Buckle in."

IV

There were no words. None of the languages Kay spoke possessed any vocabulary to describe the sense of falling in a new direction. Not vertigo, nor flying, nor plummeting. Having a working grasp of the physics didn't help either. She just knew there was a moment where she was everywhere and nowhere and all places in between.

And then there was stillness; she would have said silence, but everyone else was complaining about what they'd experienced, which rather spoiled the sanctity of the moment. She ignored Julian and Alison, because Ertil was receiving information through his implant from Cam and she wanted to hear what he had to say.

"Are we there yet?" she asked, bending down to him, so when Cam said, "Of course," it was politely addressing the space over her head.

"This is the domain of origination," Ertil's implant confirmed. Kay felt a tremor inside her, because this was *it*. Out there, beyond Cam's exoskeleton, was the *answer*. If there was a god, then this was divinity's home address. If there was a super-civilization of big-headed aliens or a pantheon of squabbling relatives or a huge floating head or the most perfect piece of mathematics, this was *it*.

"The ultimate answer is...forty-two," she quoted softly, and then, "Can we see?" Because the disadvantage of travelling within the bowels of a trilobite was that you were short on windows.

She'd hoped for a screen. What actually happened was that the floor thinned almost to nothing in the centre of the room, prompting much alarm. They all ended up at the chamber's peripheries, then everyone else arrived in response to the noise: Mal and Lee, Rove and his thug, plus Stig and Auruthmer as their Cousin handlers. Cam ended up scooping away at the walls so everyone could fit.

There was still a membrane covering the floor, attenuated to an almost perfect transparency. Probably it would bear an elephant's weight, but Kay wasn't about to experiment. They were some distance up, but the Earth in question was entirely different. It was still morning, and the sun bleached down out of a cloudless sky onto...

"That it?" Rove's man said.

Although he wasn't the mouthpiece Kay would have chosen for the human race, he was saying what they were all surely thinking.

There were no cities, not even a hamlet or a wattle-and-daub hut; no straight lines that might betoken roads, tracks or a sophisticated telecommunications network. There were no forests—no trees at all, in fact, nor bushes, hedgerows or anything resembling any biome Kay might recognize. No dinosaurs lumbered ponderously over the sward, nor could she see mammoths or cattle or any moving thing. Kay called for magnification, and a section of the membrane sharpened and twisted obligingly, throwing the ground below into exaggerated focus. Yet the close view was almost the same as the far, the same details at a different scale.

"What're we looking at? Fractal Park?" Mal asked blankly.

Kay could see her point. There was *something* covering the visible land, and it came in a range of colours and textures. Adjusting her mental scale, she reckoned none of this ground cover would have come past her ankle, but it carpeted every available surface they could see like lichen or moss, or particularly meagre heather. It wasn't like any plant Kay knew, though. In place of the dendritic branching she might have expected, everything was weirdly tessellated. She could make out assemblages of geometrical shapes cast in flat, leathery material, grey and brown and dull russet. As far as the eye could see, the world was like a patchwork quilt made from the corduroy offcuts of a geography teacher's wardrobe.

"Atmospheric oxygen is low, beyond regret," Ertil reported.

"Under two per cent," Kay agreed. "No ozone layer either, so ultraviolet radiation would fry us, although..." She squinted at what Cam was showing her. "Our host can shield us, should anyone want to go hiking."

Kay was about to ask if Cam itself was at risk, but the trilobite ship could endure the vacuum of space, so current conditions were probably balmy for it. She glanced at its avatar: no clues as to what its parent entity was thinking.

Then its "face" rippled around to look at her, and it said, "We have detected the shadow of a field that is distorting the Innerwards–Outerwards axis."

Kay took a moment to translate that. What it chiefly suggested was that they had come to the right place. "A 'shadow'...?" she prompted, because Cam was reaching for human expressions and she wasn't quite sure what it meant.

"The force itself is not detectable to us, although we are refining our senses even now," Cam reported. Kay realized that "we" was not just the royal self-designation of a godlike entity. It meant its fellows: the dozen other living ships that had accompanied them. "However, we can calculate hypothetical attributes of the force from its effect on those measurements we are able to take."

"But there's nothing here," Lee complained. "Where are they? Where are this world's inhabitants, if they're doing all that?"

Their viewpoint had been drifting across the barren, leathery ground, with its weird flowering of organic geometry. *Fungus? But that would mean there would be something to decompose, surely.* Kay was uncomfortably reminded of horror stories she'd read about ships beaching on unexpected islands inhabited by carnivorous seaweed or mushroom monsters. *It's a far fucking cry from "Put out my hand, and touched the face of God."*

A coastline passed smoothly beneath them, a rocky shore engulfed in the same creased and quilted encrustation, which stretched all the way to the waterline and beyond. No flotsam surged in the limp waves and the water itself was inky.

And yet. "It's down there." Kay heard herself say it, but she didn't like it. "Cam, are you seaworthy?"

"Down there," Cam echoed. At first she thought it was echoing her disquiet, but no, it was backing her hypothesis. Her stomach lurched as the trilobite began a steep descent towards the black waves.

Kay did her best to maintain a veneer of scientific unflap-pability, but Cam pitched sideways before it struck the water, perhaps forgetting it had passengers on board with a less cavalier approach to gravity. Everyone slid to one side of the chamber, the avatar swinging overhead. Kay received a sharp elbow to the temple from Rove and reflexively trod on Stig in retaliation. Lee yelped in pain and Julian strangled out, "Bloody hell!"

Cam shuddered tortuously, the waves battering at its cara-pace as it undulated and flexed under the water's pressure. Then it adjusted its limbs, and they were coasting smoothly into deep water on an even keel again.

"Apologies," buzzed the avatar as it swung then settled.

Its human cargo picked themselves up and Kay saw Rove dust off his jumpsuit distastefully, putting some distance between him and everyone else.

"This is less than edifying," said Ertil's implant. The rodent had fared better than everyone else, clinging to the floor with his claws then descending neatly after the heavier mammals had hit the wall. Below them, the transparency gave only onto darkness. Cam had dimmed their chamber's lights to allow them to see outside. The walls now glowed with a greenish luminance, but it only lit up silty, particulate water.

"Strike a match, will you, Cam?" Kay asked.

For a moment nothing changed, and they were left with the benthic dark and the limbic sensation of descent. Then the same bioluminescence that glimmered from the walls of their quarters appeared outside, as Cam unfurled radiant ventral organs along its segmented length.

Only water was visible, at first, dancing with motes that might have been organic or just dirt. But as they moved away from the shore, the living light penetrated further through clearing water. Still no fish came to investigate; no leviathan moved in the depths. Beneath them, the sea floor fell away in steep shelves, and every surface was covered with a grander form of the life they'd seen on land. Grander, but not by much. True, these varieties were not as dried out and gristly as the hardy terrestrial strains, but the patchwork organization was the same. Cam seemed to be gliding over a broken carpet of folds and intricate whorls. The interlocking quilt-plants, if that was what they were, were packed closely now—it was hard to know where the boundary lay between two neighbours—and the occasional weed-like flag curled slowly in the turbulence Cam created. Under the light all was greenish-grey, almost unpigmented.

Then the sea floor levelled out, Cam's lamps grew stronger, and they found themselves staring at...just more of the same.

"Are you sure this is still Earth?" Lee asked in a small voice.

Kay looked on thoughtfully, remembering. She'd been a wide reader, scientifically, back in the day, with a shallow purchase on many fields that had little to do with her own. Before she'd worked out who she really was, it had been her major escape.

"This is familiar," Cam said, and she nodded thoughtfully.

"Have you any records I can look up?" she asked. "Our timeline's records?"

"Of course," it told her, and she rattled off her requirements quickly.

As everyone else goggled down at the organic plain below, Kay scrutinized the information picked out in tiny limbs between Cam's hands. She tapped on individual entries for more information, as though it was her personal touch screen.

Abruptly the avatar changed stance, standing more heavily, its feet spread further and the shoulders rolling forwards. In just a few motions it conveyed the impression of *Homo sapiens neanderthalensis*, one of the Cousins. When it buzzed again, Kay could pick out a creditable impression of Murther's voice speaking their own mumbling language. A transmission from one of the other Wayfarers.

"She says—" Stig started, but Auruthmer tilted her head and he fell silent, acknowledging her greater expertise in the field of speaking down to humans.

"What we are seeing is known to us, Murther says." Auruthmer cocked her head. "This superficially resembles what we know about some very early life on Earth."

"Ediacaran biota," Kay finished for her. "That's our word for it. Very early multicellular life, which came before almost everything else, way before anything like Cam even. Although we could be looking at something entirely independent that only happens to look like it."

"We've gone back in time?" Lee tried.

"Retrograde movement in time is impossible," Auruthmer said. Murther's transmitted voice made an objection which reeked of scholarly pedantry, even across the species barrier, and so she corrected herself: "Save in one very specific circumstance. Even then, *we* can't travel back in time, as in us individuals."

Kay filed that away for further questioning. "So what the fuck is this?"

"It's a world where this form of life never went away," Alison said. She had a faraway look in her eyes, and Kay wasn't sure if she was interfacing with the Posticthyan machine or if this was just general wonder.

Murther said something that sounded disparaging, and Auruthmer translated, probably diplomatically, "Unlikely. That would imply stagnation for half a billion years. In *every* branch that we've visited, a different scenario has played out, evolutionarily. This has resulted in a different biota, differing types of sentience, but still change. The world does not stand still."

The land that time forgot, Kay thought, and then her imagination sank its teeth into the thought and worried it for a while, because there was something in it. "You're right," she said slowly. Murther's sharp reply, untranslated, was probably to confirm that, yes, she knew she was right, but Kay wasn't finished.

"Life succeeds life—that's how evolution goes. And evolution must therefore have produced what we are seeing below—developed it from a microscopic ancestor to the macroscopic. All these weird squiggly shapes, they must have evolved to do a thing, and then they ought to keep evolving to do it better. Because the best thing-doers have more offspring, survival, fittest, all that. That's just nature's way, right?"

She looked from face to face, and at last to Cam's false features—currently a stand-in for Murther, aboard one of the other trilobites.

"But you can put a real spanner in the works of evolution. Take Earth, I mean *our* Earth, right now as an example. You'd see planned monospecific plantations that are a terrible idea ecologically but really useful for the lumber industry. You'd see dumbass little fucking dogs that have no practical use but fit in a handbag. You'd see fields of exactly the same crop as far as the eyes can see. And on *this* Earth, you see this fossil ecosystem alive and well five hundred million years past its use-by date. My hypothesis is, someone *made* this. There's someone here, some bloody I-know-not-what, my loves, and *it* made this. This is its farmland or its plantation, or the grounds of its stately home." She swallowed, the enormity of what she was saying catching up with her. "I mean, all our parallels broke from here, right? So here, Cam's ancestors never evolved, but *something* did. And it evolved before the Cambrian; it evolved so goddamn early there was nothing but this nonsense as far as the eye could see. No plants, no animals, except this brain-looking stuff that isn't either. Something arose from this mess and it made everything else, just started branching out worlds like a fancy candleholder."

"Unless this *is* it," Lee dropped into the following silence. Seeing all eyes on her, she flinched. "I just meant," she clarified, "that what if the sentience we are looking for is *this*. We talk about engines and making things, but Cam's people just *do*, don't they? They don't build things, they *are* things. So if this patchwork has been artificially kept the same way for millions of years, and we consider this evidence of intelligence—what if there isn't a gardener after all? What if the garden is doing it to itself?"

That led to a longer silence. Beneath them, the living seabed continued to flow past, not an inch of it free of alien, quiescent life.

"Further information," Cam said, in its own voice. Perhaps its equivalents were making similar announcements on the other ships. "We have now surveyed approximately nineteen per cent of the planetary surface between us. So far, we have found that this life we are seeing has one hundred per cent coverage, land and sea, poles to equator. These entities, or this composite entity, have or has achieved global coverage.

No examples or traces of other multicellular life have been discovered." It cocked its head to one side as though listening, and Kay wondered from whom it had appropriated this mannerism. "Also, to correct your earlier statement, Lee"—the girl jumped at the thing using her given name—"the organism or organisms we perceive here is or are not alive and well. We have found numerous regions of dead or dying biota. The expanse you are currently viewing beneath us is being actively broken down by bacterial agents."

Kay looked. It seemed the same as everything else they'd seen. Except there was a lot of mottling and discoloration, now she really looked. But then, what was a well-preserved Ediacaran biota *supposed* to look like?

"This patchwork stuff is the source of the…field whose shadow you picked up? Where does it come from, though? Is there a centre, some…emperor brain creature?" she queried.

Cam spread its hands again, populating the space between them with a dense forest of calculations. "We believe the field to be global in scale, from this harvested data," it explained. It spoke so smoothly now that she constantly forgot she was hearing a schoolchild version of its thoughts, watered down for human comprehension. "The homogeneity of this Earth's life leads us to believe it is acting as a single organism on a global scale. It is able to generate forces permitting it to interact with the universe to manipulate Outerward space. This has resulted in alternative timelines, where this life was succeeded by other forms."

"Resulting in *us*," Kay finished, a first-person plural that included humans, Neanderthals, rodents, trilobites and the long-dead creators of the Ice Mind. "And now it's dying."

Interlude: The Ediacaran

Excerpt from *Other Edens:*
Speculative Evolution and Intelligence,
revised second edition, by Professor Ruth
Emerson of the University of California

In this world, long ago, something awoke.

The supine sprawl of the Garden of Ediacara, all that weirdly fractal, quilted life: in our shared history, nothing that followed it was kin to it. It was just a failed experiment in multicellular living, soon to be outstripped by the more active monsters of the Palaeozoic, blown to pieces by the Cambrian explosion. But not in this world. This is the original, and in this world, this is all there ever is. In the beginning, the Ediacaran ecosystem arose and spread, following bacterial herds across the sea floor. It put out its crenulated flowerings— even adapting, after millions of years and with extreme difficulty, to the harshness of the land. It is a weird, undifferentiated life, sans organs, sans neurology, as though evolution had tried to shortcut its way to larger forms without taking any of the prerequisite steps.

As below, so above. If the individual Ediacaran entities represent a ham-fisted creator's attempt at larger life, then something comparable occurs when we look at the leap to sentience. This is a world where hard borders never existed: not between plant and animal, not between single and multicellular, not between species or individuals. It is a frontier town kind of world where the rules don't apply.

Something awoke when these creatures achieved a certain

acreage, and what came to an awareness of itself was *all of it*. The world is a garden and the garden is a brain. Each individual life is a part of the whole, so that a consciousness arose back in the murky depths of time, one no later minds could conceive of. But it was vast and it was alone and it was aware of its loneliness. It became aware that its very presence, as a conglomerate entity, was imposing a status quo on the world that denied a thousand other alternatives. Using senses we cannot guess at, it understood that if it directed its great, slow thoughts like *this*—then it might push in a certain direction until a space was created. And possibility would flood into that space. Nature abhors a vacuum, after all. The appropriate waveforms would collapse into something *different*, a complementary world where events had followed another path entirely. Not cheap or easy to do, but it had the energy of a whole planet and literally nothing else to do with its time.

So, after a hundred million years of lying there, slowly coming to terms with what it was, the Ediacaran decreed: *Let there be . . .* not light, but something new.

And there was.

17.

I

The next step, as far as Julian could see, was for Dr. Khan to put her head together with various other brainy types—some of whom didn't even *have* heads—to apply science to the situation. That was the extent of Julian's personal grasp of the business. He took it on trust that they could fix things, now they had actually arrived here. If "here" was even the appropriate word for the space, or place, where they found themselves. Doubtless once the hard sums were done, they could just throw a celestial switch or apply a cosmic sticking plaster and then go home. The human Earth could continue in magnificent isolation without ever having to see another rat-creature or gigantic floating cockroach. In his fonder moments he was even drafting damage-limitation press releases in his head, to explain what had happened and thereby prevent them from having to know what had *actually* happened. He composed sentences about terrorist attacks and felt a heart-rending nostalgia for such familiar and commonplace threats.

Because he was no fool either, he considered that if they were able to repair the walls of the world, they might all end up stuck on the wrong side. Perhaps they would be marooned on this dying, poisonous world. Or they'd squeak their way back to the Cousins' carefully manicured pastoral idyll, but get no further. He, Julian Sabreur, would have sacrificed himself to the greater good. His own minute contribution towards getting the relevant intelligentsia to this point might result in his never returning home. And he could genuinely live with that, he found. Not his preferred outcome, but he'd trade his own future for a restoration of normality.

The waiting was the problem, though. If there was a switch, then the boffins were still fumbling in the dark for it. It had been three days of being cooped up. Cam was proving to be a good host, under the circumstances. There was a chamber for necessary biological functions—which was a horrible thought given they were *inside* a living creature. Cam had also opened orifices in one of the walls that could dispense food. Moreover, as a side effect of talking shop with Khan, it had apparently picked up something about cuisine. People were still experimenting with asking for particular dishes. The hit rate, in palatability, was about fifty per cent. However, Julian grudgingly admitted that wasn't a bad outcome and tried to forget it was created inside the organs of a bug. All in all, though, if he was going to be swallowed by a monster, he'd rather it had all mod cons. Jonah, as Alison said, never had it so good.

At least she was with him. Often, she was distant, and he could feel the temperature drop when he approached her as she worked her contacts with the "Fishnet." That was also reassuring, in a strange way. The tools were different, but she was still doing what she did best—analysing data. He wondered if that was why the icy artificial mind found her so conducive. Maybe Charen Volkovska, the stock market systems admin, had thought in the same way.

Right now, they were sitting in Cam's forward chamber, trying to ignore the dangling marionette at their back for the sake of the view below. The trilobite was still cruising through the deep ocean, its luminescence picking out the great folded carpet of the Ediacaran. He gathered that it was a composite creature, simultaneously many and one. Auruthmer had done her best to explain, adding to and modifying her earlier account of parallel worlds to include a new first chapter. But she was guessing, as much as anything, simplifying for children.

He stared moodily at the undulating sea floor below them. This was another dead section, he'd been told.

"How can it die, though?" he said out loud. "Why now?"

Alison shrugged. "Time, maybe? Accumulation of infections. A thousand separate stressors combining over half a billion years until it can't keep up. Maybe the whole thing we're trying to preserve, the structure of parallel worlds, is what killed it. The stress of maintaining *us*." She laughed a little. "I bet you've been thinking about God, am I right, Spiker?"

"Hard not to, right now," he admitted.

"Bible God, Genesis God, right? Only, I reckon what we've got here is more like the Trimūrti, the Hindu three-in-one— creator, maintainer, destroyer. Makes you wonder what some old wise guy back in India might have contacted, now we know people have been in and out of the different worlds for thousands of years."

"What, seriously?"

"You should talk to the girls a bit more. They found half a stone circle."

"A stone semicircle?"

She laughed again. "Nope, half a circle, and the other half

was in that dinosaur place they visited. Which means that, a few thousand years ago, some humans and some dinosaur-people got together to mark where the weak spot was. Only they couldn't have known the weak spot was a crack, and that the cracks would keep on getting wider until everything fell apart. All because the force that was holding these worlds in place was on its way out, even then. And eventually, pop goes the universe."

"Not sure I believe it, Matchbox, if I'm honest." Julian did his best to sound blasé, overplaying it because he hoped he'd make her laugh again. "I mean, this is obviously a local Earthly matter. Hardly seems like it could affect the whole universe like everyone says."

She didn't laugh, though, becoming solemn instead. "Well, functionally you're right, I suppose. I thought the same, so I've asked questions, in here." She tapped the side of her head. "The rest of the universe might or might not notice what's happening here, basically. There are the various timelines, and there's a universe in each. And we have no idea if those universes are different to one another, save in what happened on their Earth. But the existence of the timelines is being actively maintained by this...thing, this stuff. All the academics seem to agree about that." She kicked a heel on the membrane below them, making it quiver. "And everything collapses back when it finally dies off, so that we're just left with this one Earth, that's basically a mass grave for a corpse covering the entire planet's surface. The rest of the universe would still be here, but only this timeline's universe. All the other timelines' universes—including ours—would simply be snuffed out. As though we'd never been. The Red King doesn't even wake up, but just dies in his sleep."

"Jesus, that's jolly."

"Isn't it, though?" she agreed.

"And Kay and the rest believe we can actually *do* something about this? Forgive me for saying so, but this seems out of even Cam's league."

Alison shrugged. "This is where I run out of maths, frankly, but they seem to think that a deft enough hand on the scales could result in the timelines becoming independently stable, like putting a keystone into place on an arch. We couldn't have built the arch ourselves, none of us, but the Ediacaran had the scaffolding to do it. Except they *were* the scaffolding. They're holding the whole thing up by hand, so that it topples the moment they stop. Khan reckons there's an equation out there that would let us nudge everything into a stable alignment that just holds itself up. A tiny, precise application of force, something we can achieve at our little level, which would result in the universe..."

"Leaning against itself." Julian had a mental image of John trying to build a proper campfire at scouts, increasingly frustrated as the sticks kept falling down.

"All the timelines distinct and stable. And then we can all get on with our lives." The way Alison said it, he knew that she thought they'd be stuck here, too, locked out by their own success. He put an arm about her shoulder, ostensibly to console her but more to console himself. He needed the luxury of human contact, the infinite reassurance that he didn't have to face the madness alone. Alison leant into him, and the chill of her extradimensional connection ebbed, replaced by the welcome warmth of her body heat.

"Spiker," she said, and then nothing else. He found his arm had slipped down until it was about her waist, and her hip and thigh were pressed against his. Her head was turned slightly, lips an inch from his cheek so that he could feel the flutter of her breath. All terribly genteel and polite. And yet, under the skin, he found that he wanted her in a way that was more powerfully physical and erotic than anything he had allowed himself to feel in a decade. *We are at the end of the world*. And no one would ever know. Right now, there was nothing preventing the two of them finding a chamber within Cam and tearing each other's clothes off.

Julian felt the moment stretch, excruciatingly aware of Alison's own stillness. Knowing that she was exactly *there*, at that same crossroads, waiting to see what path they would take. If he said *yes* then she would most likely say *yes* too. They would have committed themselves to that one thing that had been the elephant in whatever room they shared for years. Despite all the recent lessons he'd had about his infinitesimal place in the cosmos, Julian fancied he could hear the universe holding its breath.

But he was Julian Sabreur, after all, and he was cast from a certain rigid mould, built with more sealed-off compartments than a sinking ship. After a while he just said, "Yes, well..." and the moment passed by, never to return, and propriety was restored.

II

Lucas couldn't avoid noticing that the two lesbians were, frankly, getting it on in one of Cam's side chambers. He wondered vaguely what the creature thought of that, if anything. From what he gathered, Cam hadn't done any sex stuff for a hundred million years or something. It sounded like God's own case of blue balls, frankly, but presumably giant cockroach monsters didn't get that.

The boss was on his phone, of all things. He'd sent Lucas to make sure nobody was eavesdropping. And through some negotiation with their host, he'd arranged to have their chambers burrowed deeper into its structure so the danger of unwanted visitors was lessened. Lucas mulled over that word, *host*—considering it could mean they were guests, but also parasites. Human fluke worms, which seemed about right.

Working for Daniel Rove was dragging him in two directions. On one hand, it was clear the man had his own plans. These would inevitably involve Rove treading all over everyone else's faces to achieve them. And he was busily putting them into action while everyone else—or at least everyone with the correct number of doctorates—was trying to fix things. On the other hand, if Rove was getting out of this on top, Lucas intended to be standing close enough to get out with him.

Drifting closer, Lucas wouldn't have been surprised to hear the man saying, "Sell! Sell!" but Rove's tone was weirdly intimate, leading Lucas to think, *So everyone on board's got someone, except me.*

"That's very good," Rove said consolingly. "Now, you have their schema? Does the machine understand it?" He sounded eerily as though he was talking to a child, or someone socially unaware enough that you could lay it on thick and get them to do anything. "Excellent, well done, my dear. And can you ask it to prepare the calculations for inversion? Splendid, very good." He looked at Lucas and nodded briefly. "Have that ready as soon as possible. And let me know when our friends at this end are nearing a solution. Good girl, well done." He ended the call and turned his razor smile towards Lucas. "Do you think Dr. Khan and his friends can make their dreams into reality, as you've been amongst them?"

Fuck knows. "A bit high level for me, sir. They seem to think they can pull it off."

Rove nodded. There was the faintest tremor about his eyes that told Lucas how long he'd been pushing himself, how tired he was, how tense. His plan was like a steel trap that he was holding open, waiting for the perfect moment. The thought brought an unexpected stab of sympathy for his boss. The path of self-interest wasn't necessarily effort free, after all. Rove was one man pitting himself against the whole of creation.

"Charen seems to think everything is in order," Rove said. "But we may need to move quickly, when the moment arrives, and I have no doubt our fellows here will get in the way."

"I'm ready, sir," Lucas confirmed. "You're happy this Charen can deliver, though?"

"Charen is in deep with the ice-computer that these cavemen use to get from place to place," Rove replied, closing his eyes. If he'd been fresher, he wouldn't have said so much. "She's in so deep that she's in suspended animation at round about zero degrees centigrade in my secure facility back home. She has been for a couple of years now—but that just means she can communicate constantly with the ice- machine. It's what she would have wanted, probably. It gives her unparalleled access, and she's tractable enough in that state. And she's almost like a computer herself. She doesn't have any desires, really, little enough conscious volition. She just does what she's told—because as far as she's concerned she's already achieved her nirvana, the thing she was always chasing. She thinks she's found God, poor deluded soul."

Lucas stared down at him, feeling the shift in his innards brought on by this latest revelation. It was one more sin to add to the ledger of things he was enabling. "So what good is she?"

"Every manner of good, Lucas. Did you never wonder how I ran rings around the rats, for all their lauded technological superiority? Charen was walking in and out of their data systems on the back of the ice-world machine. If you can access a system from elsewhere on the dimensional axis, you can circumvent any kind of security. That was Khurram Khan's original work for the Home Office, you know? A panic about how to keep their state secrets secure. They never realized they had the key to the universe a hair's breadth beyond their fingertips. But by then I'd already snapped up Charen and was using her to talk to the next civilization over that understood the maths. She's already sequestered a store of the rats' technological advances, translated and ready for use. I've bankrupted half my companies ensuring that I have the necessary resources to build their useful toys. All in place, Lucas, all waiting. If only Khan and her menagerie can do their damn job." Rove let out a long breath. For a moment he looked twenty years older, the real man, shorn of the youthful twinkle he always saved for the cameras. "Bugs and monkeys and vermin and queers," he said softly. "What sort of a way is that to run a universe? I'll be glad when we're rid of them."

Lucas stared at him, knowing that *this*, *now* was the moment he could turn back. He wasn't as smart as Rove, and he lacked the man's vast influence and ambition. But he had two strong hands, one of which was superhuman in its capabilities, and Rove's neck was thin. He felt the will to do it rise in him, a sudden surge of violence born as much from personal frustration as from a desire to do the right thing. But an instant of visceral satisfaction would gain him nothing in the long run. And then Rove's eyes snapped open; he was awake and alert again. Lucas ensured his own expression was professionally neutral and servile, as it always had been, and that appeared to be satisfactory.

III

Once, there was a species of fish-like creatures who had been the masters of their Earth. That Earth had become a frozen ball of ice where only microbial life survived, yet the fish-creatures themselves persisted, even though they no longer *lived*. Their last act had been to make their world their greatest work, their archive, their mausoleum.

Alison could sense them, sometimes: the minds of the Posticthyans. They existed at what she thought of as a much deeper level of the Ice Mind than she usually accessed. From their fleeting contacts, she gathered only that they were very alien minds to hers, and had little interest in her. She fancied that at the heart of the Ice Mind was a vast simulated space, a recreation of their civilization in its halcyon days, and that they had no inclination to stir themselves from it. Only very occasionally did she have a sense of them, like ponderous shapes passing in the depths far beneath her.

The Ice Mind itself extended further than that. Partly it was following its deep programming to protect and preserve the minds of its creators—but partly it was a vast computer system of near limitless capability which would roll over and do tricks for just about anyone who asked. The engineers who built it had never considered that they might need to restrict access, because they hadn't thought there was anyone *outside* whom they might need to exclude.

It didn't think and wasn't conscious, or that was her tenuous guess. However, it was also a system of inconceivable complexity, self-organizing and self-improving, with a planet's resources at its disposal. Sometimes she felt she had cast her lot in with a genie or demon, all that power reduced down to something she could petition. Impossible to shake the impression she was dealing with a personality rather than a system, no matter how hard she tried to be distant and professional about things.

She'd had to limit her access, because the ice cream headaches were only getting worse. Possibly she was doing permanent damage to her brain, every time she reached out to it. The headaches only really bit when she cut the connection too, so while that communion endured, she had little feedback on the self-harm she might be inflicting.

It was addictive, though: who wouldn't want to know everything, especially someone in her profession? Sometimes she felt that she could merge with it, become its genius loci, the ghost in the machine and the god out of it. The thought was intoxicating—yet because she was who she was, that was when she cut the link and spent some time being human amongst other living people. There was something to be said about being brought up in a culture of guilt, self-denial and being told you weren't worthy. It meant that when someone offered you all the kingdoms of the Earth, you tended to pass. You went back, of course, after a little abstinence, like a smoker who quits a dozen times each day.

Right now, she was monitoring "local traffic"—the current pipeline the Ice Mind was using to communicate with those around her. It had an automatic algorithm to identify the most efficient breach between timelines, and this would grant it access to wherever or whoever it needed. As those breaches were growing wider and more numerous by the hour, that meant it could channel a lot of information. Much of it was going to the various trilobite ship entities, but Alison knew that the Cousins' science chief, Murther, was tapping the line for her own communications. She was speaking to the body scientific back home. The rat translator, Ertil, was also maintaining contact with someone through his implant. Probably *he* didn't get headaches. Or if he did, they were subsumed into the bigger headaches caused by vastly invasive cybernetic brain surgery.

And then there was Daniel Rove. She hadn't picked up on him initially, with everything else going on, but she was on to him now. He had his own channel to the Ice Mind, using it to communicate with someone or something back on their Earth. When she'd tried to investigate, she'd met access issues for the first time. It wasn't that the Ice Mind stood in her way, but *someone* had more privileges than her and evaded her enquiries effortlessly. Knowing it was someone on Rove's team, Alison had a good idea who that might be. But there was nothing she could do about it, except keep tabs on Rove. She couldn't perceive his exact words, but she could chart the rhythm and shape of his activity, and what sort of analyst would she be if she couldn't make something of that?

She broke the link, bracing herself, and the stab of pain

came right on schedule, skewering her frontal lobes. She went to get painkillers from Cam, who seemed to have taken on a good working knowledge of human pharmaceuticals along with everything else. After that, she found Julian talking to Stig, of all people.

She paused a moment, considering how things stood between them. She had thought, earlier, that he was going to finally breach the wall between them. The one they had never spoken about, because to even acknowledge it might bring it down. She had always known she would carefully rebuff any overtures—saving him from hating himself later. And yet, when she had felt him just a breath away, she'd thought, *To hell with the consequences.* That had shocked her as much as any of the madness they'd been living through.

Alison watched them as Julian gesticulated, talking a little too loudly because, somewhere in his head, Stig was a foreigner, and he needed to help the poor caveman along. He was talking, with surprising frankness, about MI5 operations against the Cousins. Recalling that moment when he and Alison had started to put everything together. For his part Stig just sat, mostly impassive. But his shoulders shifted up and down, and his hands were never quite still. There was a whole bag of Cousin body language that she didn't quite get.

Julian looked up now and smiled, same old Spiker, and she sat beside him chastely enough. Stig slapped the hard, ridgy floor with one palm and said, "Been in your branch, maybe eight years. Forget what it's like to be home, sometimes. Helping study, at the start. With Auruthmer, at first. Don't like it much. Except Finland. Finland was quiet."

"Why do you do it, then?" Alison asked.

"Someone's got to." Stig met her eyes briefly, mouth

downturned in an exaggerated frown. "Me, I'm good at surviving you people, all the many of you. Know your languages, seven or eight. Keep the scholars safe too, hm?"

"Seven or eight languages?" Julian sounded doubtful.

Stig made a dismissive gesture with one hand. "Your languages, pff. Ours are more different. I know twelve, and twenty..." He made a clutching motion, the epitome of someone grasping for a word.

"Dialects?" Alison supplied.

"Just that. But you don't do language like we do. Every child learns three, four. For every part of life, mostly, one language is common—like you had Latin, once, for your science. So you learn birth tongue, neighbour tongues, learning tongues for higher study—then also work tongues, two or three. Me, I was diplomat. I went for my...town? Went and talked to other places about what they needed, what we need."

"You're a diplomat?" Julian's doubt had visibly increased.

Stig sighed at the burden of explanation, but Alison suspected that his "reluctant bruiser" act was just that. He probably found pretending to be simple meant humans wrote him off more easily.

"We don't live like you do. Fifty is a big group, hundred is too much. We like to be spread out. Back in history, when we got together like you, bad things happen. Madness, wrong decisions. But to make big things happen we need more hands than we have. So people like me go to the neighbours, speak their language, say what we need: so they can come and help or give us what they have. Then next time, they come to us and say, and we give what we can."

Alison's knee-jerk reaction was to ask how they ever got

anything done, and what happened if a community decided it didn't want to share, but Stig was describing a system that had evolved over thousands of years. She guessed that in his timeline groups that were selfish today found themselves without helpful neighbours tomorrow, and the scales had tipped in favour of mutualism.

"I don't think we could work like that," Julian said slowly.

"I think we maybe could, if we'd stuck with small groups," Alison suggested.

Stig slapped the floor again, apparently in agreement. "We know everyone. You have your thousands, your millions—how can you know who's around you? No wonder you lock your doors and trust nobody. And also—" He stopped himself, but Alison and Julian were so clearly waiting for the sequel that he sighed and pressed on. "You are gullible. Surrounded by people you don't know, with your leaders even less knowable, and you are gullible. Someone says a thing to you strongly enough, you believe them. You take confidence for truth. We don't do that. Someone says a thing, we tell them to show us how it is true. We are slower than you, because of that. 'Measure twice, cut once,' you say, but you don't do it. We always do. There is a balance, I think." He mimed something teetering left and right about an invisible fulcrum. "Our branch, caution wins out, things take longer but get there more surely. Less dark ages, less collapses, just plod, plod, plod, the way we like it. Foolish daring means your people burn themselves up. Your branch, daring pays off more. But you let people with strong words tell you what the truth is. Kings, emperors, tyrants. You are about the many for the few, for the one. In our branch, you learn what you can do for your family and your neighbours."

"Communist cavemen." Julian shook his head. "There's something to terrify the Home Secretary." Then he looked up sharply: Kay Amal Khan was at the doorway of their chamber, the rat-creature Ertil peering past her legs.

"We need to get everyone together, loves," she said, words tripping over each other in their hurry to get out. "Even Rove. We think we've found a solution."

*

"The timing will be the trickiest aspect," Kay explained. Everyone had gathered and was listening, all their little ex-patriate community.

"We could solve the problem from here, but obviously we'd end up stuck in this timeline if we did. Now, for Cam's lot, that's no big deal, because they fully intend to fuck off back to the stars when we're done, and it doesn't affect them much which universe they're in. But for the rest of us, we'd have a choice between living in a trilobite's gut for the rest of our natural lives or suffocating PDQ outside. So, yes, we're working this to let us all get home in the end, those that want to." She glanced at Ertil, and Alison guessed that the rodent would be after some kind of diplomatic asylum, most probably with the Cousins and Dr. Rat's extended family.

"What about creatures—people—who've already crossed over?" Julian asked. "We took in a load of rat-creatures, for example."

"We don't have time for diplomatic treaties and repatriation, Jules. We'll have to live with it."

"What about the rats, though?" This from Mal. "You've seen how they live, en masse. They're going to be stuck, aren't they?"

Kay blinked. "I don't think you...We're trying to stop the universe collapsing. We can't pause along the way to effect fucking societal change in a non-human culture we know very little about. Priorities, love."

Mal looked mutinous but subsided.

Kay peered out over her audience, a lecturer whose students were probably not going to pass the end-of-year exam. "The problem is that everything we know is being actively maintained by this...Ediacaran sponge-monster thing. And it's finally wearing out. When enough of it dies off—which is going to be really soon, because we cut it very fine indeed—it can't keep the lights on. And then that's all she wrote, okay?" *Dumbed down enough for you?* said her expression, but it wasn't patronizing if people really did need the CliffNotes version to understand it.

"*But*," Kay went on, grinning like a madwoman, "I have a fucking library of equations right now that show that if you balance the field *just so*, then it should stand up on its own. You can whip away the tablecloth and all the plates stay put. At which point every timeline just continues on its own, theoretically indefinitely. Job done." She made it sound simple, but Alison was looking inwards, where the Posticthyan computer was throwing up complex rotating models demonstrating the forces and principles involved. The models were doubtless hopeless simplifications, and even then Alison had difficulty understanding them. But the main thing Kay wasn't saying was how delicate the operation was, how exact any tinkering would have to be.

"How is this to be accomplished, precisely?" Rove broke in. "You're talking blithely about playing with universal forces."

Kay gave him a look loaded with dislike. "This is why we

need to start *here*. This is where we can muster sufficient leverage to alter the field the entity is putting out. And even then it isn't going to be easy. We'll need to get a bunch of resources in at short notice, specialists, engineers. Cam's lot are going to build an engine in orbit, based on principles put together by Stig's and Ertil's people, and the big icy bastard is going to stitch it all together and flick the switch. By which time we all need to be home in bed, loves, all goodbyes said, because that's when the boom goes down." Alison saw this as well: a simple query and her mind was filled with technical specifications, blueprints, designs for machines that existed across multiple timelines simultaneously. Each component was meaningless unless you could perceive the whole. She let out a shuddering breath, seeing it ghost white from her lips. Julian was holding her hand in his, and she knew her fingers must be icy.

She became aware of another then, in that mental space. It was Rove, albeit Rove on the back of someone else. He was using Charen Volkovska, spirited away years ago, now Rove's demon ambassador to the court of the Posticthyans. Alison watched, holding her breath, as Rove's presence moved through the same models and diagrams. She was unhappily aware that he probably grasped it all just a little better than she did.

Khan was pressing on with more layman's explanations, simultaneously reassuring and practically useless. But Alison just watched Rove, waiting to see which way he would jump.

She was practically in the man's mind. He was concentrating so hard that he had no idea he had an audience. She saw him construct his own model, or perhaps Volkovska had built it for him. Alison couldn't quite see how it would work.

512

However, it would be operating upon the same forces that Kay and her peers were marshalling, intervening at a crucial moment to do...something, but she couldn't say what. If it was Rove's plan, though, she was willing to bet it would be catastrophically bad.

Then, even as she watched, she saw him come to a decision, expressed purely through his interaction with the model. Rove looked at the whole tangled structure, Kay's grand plan and his own parasitic addendum, and took a step back. Pragmatically, probably even reluctantly, Rove packed up his own subversions and decided to back the home team—rather than trying to short-sell the universe. Alison wouldn't have credited it, but it seemed that even a man like Rove could decide saving everything was more important than a narrower chance at a more singular victory. Glancing at him, she had the impression of a weird release of pressure, as though his ambitions had cramped him out of shape for years and now he was freed to be someone else.

Lee Pryor held her hand up now, looking profoundly embarrassed to be the focus of attention.

"What about the thing?" she asked. "What does *it* want?"

Kay frowned. "The thing? Oh, the Ediacaran, the pancreator, whatever you want to call the sod. We don't know that it wants anything. We don't know why it's done what it's done, to be honest. I mean, possibly it all just *happened* as a side effect of some other purpose we can't even guess at." Her manic grin was back, wider than ever, and Alison wondered if Cam had been dispensing some pharmaceuticals for her as well. "So, best answer to your question: no fucking idea, love, none at all."

The time it took to save the universe was approximately

a week. This was nonetheless a lot of time to be cooped up inside an arthropod. Three days in, Cam fabricated some breathing gear, allowing for excursions outside. However, Alison found that after the initial strangeness wore off, there was precious little diversion to be found out there. She and Julian went on a hike for hours across the blighted landscape, treading across the folds and convolutions of the planet's brain, as Cam sailed overhead like a vast and ghastly kite. Aside from a faint sighing of wind and the unpleasant squish of their footsteps, there was no sound. Nothing moved in their sight. They were in a world that had been held in stasis for half a billion years by the will of the conglomerate organism that had evolved on it. All its activity was focused elsewhere, unseen, imposing pressure on the universe through a means that owed nothing to limbs or organs as humans might understand them. Even the Posticthyans could offer no insight. It was simultaneously a living and a dead world— and Alison knew the scales were tilting towards the latter.

At last they signalled Cam, which descended gracefully, tilting until they could step onto its upper surface. Lee and Mal were sitting together, masked heads close. They stared out towards a sunset that would be as wan and unspectacular as all the rest here. Alison felt a sudden stab of jealousy from left field, utterly unlike her. She knew the story of the two losing and regaining one another, and of all the humans they seemed to be able to take anything in their stride now they were together. She glanced at Julian, but he was looking elsewhere. Probably he was simply thinking about the mountain of explanations he'd have to deal with when he finally made it home.

Several new trilobites had made the jump over, as Alison

understood it, and there was practically a shuttle service between here and the Cousins' timeline to bring materiel and experts across. Daniel Rove had even been back to the rat world. He seemed to have done some sort of service as ambassador, given that the rodents and the Cousins had been engaged in an old war. Certainly the rats were now contributing to the universal repair effort too. And if Alison wanted, she could speak to Kay Amal Khan and hear her talk endlessly about buttressing, self-perpetuating waveforms and mathematically describing the status quo. None of this was terribly edifying, even with the Ice's pictorial assistance.

She half expected there to be a goodbye when Kay finally approached them aboard Cam. She'd thought the scientist would end up going with the Cousins to their world, one more thing for poor Julian to explain. Apparently not, though— and probably it was for deeper reasons than the Cousins' lack of cigarettes.

Lee and Mal drifted in soon after, then Rove, his lackey trailing on his heels. Rove had been remarkably well behaved, for Alison had been keeping as much of an icy eye on him as possible. He had made no moves to initiate whatever grand project he had been preparing. Instead, she suspected he'd been acquiring as much know-how and tech as he could from more advanced timelines. In the post-healing world, he'd probably turn out to be rather more of a problem than anyone currently realized. But that was tomorrow's issue.

Lee and Mal were looking a little tearful in the face of all this closure, which was fair enough, as they'd been the only ones having even halfway to a good time. "I just...We're losing something huge," Pryor said. "Who knows how much of our past has been influenced by the other Earths just...

being there, a breath away, down the wrong path in the forest, through the stone circle, on the other side of a closed door... and now there won't be any magic, you know?" She caught up with what she was saying and looked instantly ashamed. "Not that it's magic, but...it'll just be us."

"It was always supposed to be that way," Julian said firmly. "Having seen some of *them*, no offence, it's for the best." Alison wasn't entirely sure she agreed, but said nothing.

"The Six Brothers will really only be Three Brothers from now on," Mal added, which obviously meant nothing to anyone save Lee.

Stig and Auruthmer had disembarked, as had Ertil, to board a Wayfarer heading for the Cousins' timeline. There was only one thing left to do.

"Brace yourselves," Kay advised. "Cam? Let's go home."

In the moments before transit, Alison found herself thinking, *I wish I could have seen more.*

Cam's colossal body seemed to clench itself and leap forwards, whilst moving nowhere. The step Outerwards seemed easier than moving in, and Alison saw a fleeting skein of images and explanations about gradients and energy costs in the instant between *there* and *here.*

"Home," Kay said, but she was anything but relaxed, eyes wide. "Now we just have to—"

Something happened, everywhere and all at once. Something stopped, as though a voice Alison had heard all her life had been silenced, and only in that silence did she realize it had ever been there. It was as though the world had always contained an extra dimension or a colour filter, and now everything was flatter, less vibrant, whilst being object-ively exactly the same.

Cam was dropping them off precisely where it had picked them up, the devastated square mile in the heart of the City. Julian was grinding his teeth through sheer embarrassment, because all the emergency services would be on their way, not to mention a thousand cameras. He had only ever wanted to be a faceless man who made things happen behind the scenes. She saw Rove straighten his cuffs and knew he would be calculating how he could best use this development to his advantage. Khan had poked her head through into Cam's avatar chamber and was presumably making her farewells.

The centre of the floor irised open, revealing a clutch of legs ready to lower them to the ground. Alison took Julian's hand and grinned, trying to convey that he wouldn't be alone when he had to face the music.

And stopped.

Something cold touched her mind.

Her grip on Julian's hand tightened until she heard him hiss in pain.

The Posticthyan Ice Mind was abruptly all around her, feeding her far too much information. She was receiving a bewildering flurry of equations and notations she couldn't hope to understand. And it shouldn't be broadcasting anything. The doors of the universe had been nailed shut, because it was that or have the house fall down. She couldn't possibly still be in touch with the...

"Julian," she said, as Cam's legs unfolded. He'd been asking her what the matter was for a while, but she hadn't had the mental space to deal with it. "Julian." She hugged him tight, buried her face in his chest as, in her mind's eye, everything that there ever was collapsed inwards into nothing.

As they descended, she could see forever—through the

glass towers of London, the bird people's snowy wilderness, the rats' busy cities, the Cousins' rural idylls—all the way back to the prolonged Ediacaran period, the true and original state of the world. She could see that singular, static entity that had once dreamt a dream of difference.

She felt, through the Ice Mind, precisely when that dreamer diminished to the point where it could no longer nurture the fruits of its imagination. She felt the complex artificial structures that Kay and her peers had put into place take the strain, and crack, and fail.

Even as Julian instinctively put his arms around her, as though he could shield her from anything, it all came down, and there was nothing more.

17/1.

I

As Kay outlined her plan, Alison became aware of another, in that icy mental space she was plugged into. It was Rove, albeit Rove on the back of someone else. He was using Charen Volkovska, spirited away years ago, now Rove's personal ambassador to the court of the Posticthyans. Alison watched, holding her breath, as Rove's presence moved through the same models and diagrams. She was unhappily aware that he probably grasped it all just a little better than she did.

Even as she watched, she saw him come to a decision, expressed purely through his interaction with the model. Rove looked at the tangled structure, Kay's grand plan and his own parasitic addendum, and sent a single instruction to his agent in the machine.

Proceed.

She refocused, seeing the man with her real eyes. He was looking at his phone while Khan talked, as though the science had burned through his attention span and he was checking his mail. Every input was an order, though. She had the sense of a series of organizational blocks slamming into place, each of them held in readiness for this moment.

And then, without fuss, he tapped his lackey on the arm and they slipped out, unnoticed by anyone save Alison.

She was tempted to break into Kay's lecture with the news that Rove was doing...something. But if there was something amiss, greater minds than her would have spotted it— Kay, or certainly Cam...After all, she was just Alison Matchell, painfully middle class and brought up in the grand tradition of not making a fuss.

Instead, she tugged Julian's sleeve and murmured, "We need to speak to Rove. He's up to something."

Julian raised an eyebrow. "How? He's stuck here with us." He glanced around and saw that Rove had in fact disappeared.

"Spiker, if there's one thing this gadding about has taught us, it's that walls don't make a prison, right? Come on." She gave a half-apologetic wave to Kay then backed out of the room, Julian sloping after her.

She found Rove's man literally packing, gathering up the little they weren't actually wearing. This included what looked like fresh clothes and sealed rations—presumably fabricated to order and without curiosity by Cam. The big man, Lucas, at least had the grace to look up guiltily when discovered, but Rove had only a polite smile.

"Ah, Ms. Matchell, Mr. Sabreur, what can we help you with?"

He's not going to gloat about his diabolical plan, Alison noted. Although she was still watching the shunting slabs of maths move back and forth in the Ice Mind's conceptual spaces. The more she saw, the more she was convinced that *diabolical* was the perfect word for Rove's actions.

"Mr. Rove, I'm going to give you one chance to step back from what you're doing," she said, as firmly as possible. "Or I'll get everyone in here and we'll have Cam open the Ice

Mind to see what you've been up to." She had no idea if it was possible, but likely Rove didn't either.

Rove adopted a creditable frown of puzzlement. "I have no idea what you're talking about." His eyes slid off her to appeal to Julian. "Mr. Sabreur—" he began, as though the man was her keeper and should have kept her on a shorter lease.

A stab of anger ran through her. "Then why the bags, Mr. Rove? Or did you have a golfing holiday you couldn't postpone, not even for the end of the universe."

He was good, she had to give him that. There was nothing whatsoever in his expression that admitted culpability, and in the face of that utter shamelessness she felt her case falling apart. Even Julian, who would back her through most things and didn't like Rove whatsoever, was wavering. He only saw the deceptive outer shell; he couldn't perceive the logical battle going on just a dimension away.

"Rove, where's Charen Volkovska?" she snapped out.

"Who?" But she'd scored a hit. There had been a moment's pause before the bland response, and the profession of ignorance itself was exposing. She *knew* Rove had bought up the corpse of Schoen Fayre, including its revolutionary computer. And—via her employment contract—he'd bought Charen, its votary. Julian knew this too.

"I'm guessing she's still in our world, somewhere very secure indeed," she said. "You've worked with the rats for years—you've known what was going to happen. And you've had your own plans for what to do when the universe breaks down—I'll bet you're not trying to prop it back up again, either."

Rove watched her, and she could feel the tension in his studied pose.

"So what's going on, Mr. Rove?"

He shifted his attention to Julian once again. "Mr. Sabreur, you're a good servant of the Crown, are you not? A loyal man? You've seen the circus they're running here, a zoo where all the cages are open. I can't believe any of this sits well with you."

Julian said nothing, but Rove obviously read something encouraging in his face, because he went on, "We are facing the destruction of everything we know. But even if this ludicrous plan of Khan's succeeds, do you really think the things we truly value will survive? Do you think life can go on as before, with our country riddled with rat-creatures and cavemen and who knows what else? Do you honestly think that once our monstrous host has dropped us back in England it will simply go away? Why should it, when it has all of us to lord over? The Earth was a prehistoric wasteland when it left; now there's a whole planet of slaves for it to play god to. There'll be religions and cults within a week, once we're back. And these cavemen have been infiltrating our society for decades. That woman has a seat at a U.S. university, for God's sake. Do you really think they've not been pulling strings elsewhere, in the Oval Office, at Downing Street? Believe me, I've been opposing their machinations for a long time."

"So what's your alternative?" he demanded.

"Reset the clock, Mr. Sabreur. Burn away the rot that's been degrading our society, this monstrous fifth column. Rebuild something truly human, English, from the ruins. After all, you saw how things were collapsing back home, when we left. What sort of state do you think things are in by now?"

Alison had only been half listening, struggling past her headache to focus on what the Ice Mind had built for Rove. She hoped Julian wasn't wavering, even though Rove had a good idea of what levers and buttons lay beneath old Spiker's skin.

"Enough," Julian snapped. "Save it for the debriefing."

Then Alison suddenly understood the plan, pulling her viewpoint out from under the tangled complexity of details until she could see the broad strokes. All those armies of equations and figures were making up a single vast transformation, an inversion that turned Khan's complex, many-stranded piece of universal engineering into...

Rove's phone buzzed. In her mind's eye, Alison saw the signal from Volkovska: *Ready*.

Possibly some of the Cousins had noticed something odd by now. Or maybe Cam's vast intelligence had already foreseen and neutralized Rove's treachery. Yet ultimately, she couldn't rely on anything but herself. She lunged forwards and slapped Rove's phone out of his hand.

She had the momentary satisfaction of seeing his smiling mask split open to reveal the howling outrage of someone who is *not* to be touched by the hoi polloi under any circumstances. It was mingled with the panic of a man who *really needed his phone* at that exact moment. Then Lucas straightarmed her in the chest and sent her flying across the room to bounce hard against the wall. Julian went for him, and Rove's man slugged him in the temple with his artificial hand, flinging him senseless to the floor.

Rove picked up his phone. The universe held its breath. Her heart plummeted as she saw his crisp smile re-establish itself.

"Kill the bitch," he said, tapping at the screen. Stony-faced, Lucas drew his pistol and, even as Alison drew breath to yell, shot her in the head.

II

In the aftermath Lucas asked, "Do I get Khan or the rat next?" He was talking too loud, his ears ringing after the shot, but that was par for the course.

"We don't need them any more," Rove said. "We don't need any of them. They've done their part." There was something in that smile that made Lucas grab his wrist. But Rove made no protest nor tried to shake him off, so perhaps he hadn't been about to abandon Lucas after all.

There was a lot of shouting, and people would be barging in at any moment. Lucas toyed with the idea of putting a bullet into Sabreur as well, for completeness. They were committed now, after all. Even as he lifted the pistol, though, the air around them rapidly dropped ten degrees, and Rove tapped his phone's frosted screen one more time.

They fell. At first they fell in that other direction, Outerwards. They were travelling away from the dying world, back through the failing timelines that their Ediacaran gardener had cultivated so carefully.

Then they were falling in a far more real, gravitic way. They'd been ripped into a different timeline, exactly where Cam had been floating—materializing over an ocean of riven, jagged ice. Their Wayfarer host was nowhere to be seen. Lucas heard his own scream before something rose to meet them.

It was a boat, rising towards them as the broken plain below swelled into a great stylized wave. It resembled nothing so much as a Hokusai print, the wave lifting the narrow skiff towards them. Lucas's arms and legs were windmilling as he fell, all attempts to retain contact with Rove forgotten. But he and Rove both ended up sprawled inside the boat, caught perfectly as the wave broke and then ebbed.

"Fuck," Lucas got out, lungs filled with icy air.

He clutched the boat's rail with his black hand, which didn't really feel the cold in more than a distantly informational sense. Rove sat up and plucked at his clothing, restoring his dignity before reapplying his smile.

"Bracing," was his only comment.

Rove looked past Lucas towards the stern. There was a pane of ice positioned there, transparent, less than an inch thick but six feet tall and three wide. It seemed impossible that it hadn't shattered, except that *impossible* was a word that held no real meaning now. Staring into it, Lucas saw the mirrored image of his own and Rove's pale faces, and past them, he saw a figure. A reflection with no original. It was a woman, robed and carrying a long staff, poling an ice boat down the side of a frozen wave in defiance of all logic and nautical convention.

"Ah," Rove said with a wan smile. "Charen, my dear. Perhaps an overly artistic manifestation, but who am I to complain?" Calmly he dug into the holdall and began to extract layers of clothing. "We have something of a journey to reach the appropriate coordinates, Lucas. We'll need to conserve warmth. There'll be a little privation, unfortunately, but it will all be worth it in the end."

They passed through that frozen, dead world with

remarkable speed, their boat cutting a wake in the ice that healed slowly behind them. Lucas spent the trip huddled in the bows, wearing every layer he could scrounge and with his hands shoved into his armpits. He wondered idly what was going on back aboard Cam. He replayed the moment when he'd shot Alison Matchell dead. It wasn't his finest hour, and he could have said no. But he was self-aware enough to know that once warm and safe he would justify it to himself as necessary. One more stop along the road to securing Rove's inevitable destiny.

Then, obviously sooner than Rove was expecting, their spectral boatwoman said, "The inversion equations must be enacted now. You will have to transition immediately."

"Of course." Rove stood, even as their reckless headlong progress slowed. "Lucas, on your feet. Time to head home."

As he said it, Lucas saw the world around them superimposed onto another landscape. He saw the ghosts of trees fighting their way clear of the ice, a hillside rising phantomwise from within the all-encompassing glaciers. Ahead, the hard-packed ice was melting into a channel, so that it seemed as if their boat was descending into the bowels of the frozen Earth. *Because the ice layer is higher than the ground layer. This is to stop us coming out in mid-air.* All very well to rationalize the situation, but the feeling of being carried off to hell was inescapable, what with the boat and its ghostly gondolier.

Then the temperature rose and the dense conifer forest leapt from abstract shade to actuality. All that was left of their journey was some meltwater about their feet. They were standing on a rocky, heavily wooded hillside and the sun was beating down, actual summer sun that Lucas hadn't realized how much he'd missed. The air was full of birdsong, and if he didn't recognize the individual sounds, the impression was familiar. The breeze smelled of pine resin.

"Where are we?" he asked. He was on his knees, stripping off layers of now-stifling synthetic fabrics. Rove, a metre away, was doing the same.

"Scotland," Rove said, "approximately."

"*Scotland?*" Lucas demanded. "You mean we're home? We're actually..." He stared at the trees, which were definitely conifers but weren't quite right. The shades of green, the arrangement of branches, the precise shape of the needles looked odd, and the birds sounded...He looked up at the sun, filtering through the criss-crossing network of branches, and it was the same sun. But the squirrel-sized thing up there, crouching on a branch, had a long nose like a trunk. "Not the right Scotland," he finished, surprised at how his heart had leapt when he'd thought he was actually home.

"Nil desperandum, Lucas," Rove said jovially, and then, because he was a patronizing sod, "That means 'do not despair.' All will be well. We're still a little way from base, unfortunately, but that was unavoidable if we wanted to get here at all." Rove smiled up into the sunlight, and for a brief moment it seemed genuine. "It's been quite the trip, hasn't it?"

"Not that I'm sorry to be out of the ice, but why the rush to get here, sir?"

Rove laughed lightly. "Oh, that's just the whole plan, Lucas. Just the fruition of all I've set in motion. I'm sure we could have put it on hold for a few hours though, simply to spare you a walk."

"I don't mind a—What the fuck is *that*?"

Something that had been still since their arrival now decided that two humans were definitely beyond the pale and bolted. He had the impression of a long, scaly tail and a hairless brown body—like a rabbit crossed with a pangolin.

"No idea. You can name it if you want." Rove shrugged easily and pulled his phone out. "Ah, a signal, good. I was worried we wouldn't have the infrastructure in place yet. Score one more for good forward planning."

"Whose signal? The ice guys?"

"Oh no, we're done with that now." Rove's annoying smile was back, but beyond that, he seemed suddenly looser and more congenial than Lucas had ever known him.

"And...let's get up high, out of the trees—keep going upslope." He followed his own advice immediately, leaving Lucas to stumble along in his wake. Rove had never been much of a physical specimen, all angles and stick insect limbs inside his immaculately tailored suits. However, after twenty minutes of uphill walking he hadn't slowed. Lucas, a route-marching veteran, had difficulty keeping up, and Rove cranked that smile up a notch. "Oh, I had quite the tuning-up when I was living with the rats, Lucas. Their medical technology was vastly in advance of ours, remember. And human physiology wasn't too far from their own. I should have a good three centuries in me before I start to slow down."

Lucas conserved his breath for slogging.

Eventually they broke from the trees onto a rocky, scrubby slope, surprising a herd of hyrax-looking things the size of sheep. They mostly ignored the humans, even when Rove and Lucas walked through their midst.

"Where," Lucas demanded, "is this? Why here and not home?"

"It *is* home," Rove said. "Or at least, it's the world where home is now. I'd have preferred to be delivered to the door, but time and tide, as they say." He had his phone out again, tilting it left and right, apparently satisfied with what it showed him.

"Some other Earth, fine," Lucas grunted. "So what lives here? More rats?"

"Nothing sentient," Rove informed him. "Oh, there was once, a prehistory ago, but it died off. Nothing's arisen since with the wit to look itself in the mirror. Apparently there are some marine mammals that are both bigger and brighter than the average fisherman might like, but that will add a bit of spice when we mount our first whaling expedition, hm?"

"Who's 'we'?" Lucas asked. He was looking out over the trees below, which stretched most of the way to the horizon. Maybe it would have been familiar to him if he'd known Scotland, but he'd never spent much time north of the border. Then his ears finally acknowledged a sound. "Is that...a helicopter?"

"Well, I wasn't planning to walk all the way," Rove said.

A big, double-rotored aircraft manoeuvred over the trees, doubtless homing in on Rove's phone signal. The grazing animals took fright and scattered across the hillside as it dipped low towards them, a ladder unravelling from its hatch. A figure in a dark uniform was crouched there, throwing a salute to Rove, who returned it idly. Lucas made damn sure he was firmly on the bottom of the ladder before Rove reached the top, just in case. Adding more people into the mix meant that he was suddenly less indispensable, even if just as an audience for Rove's self-congratulatory speeches.

The helicopter had a crew of three. They were all young

men, no more than twenty-five. Their clear skin, regular features and glowing good health made Lucas feel old and ugly, as did their adulation when they looked at Rove. They all wore the same uniforms, black with silver trim, cut in a fashion that Lucas had hitherto only associated with certain science fiction franchises. Or with people who fetishized entirely the wrong parts of mid-twentieth-century history. A bundle of clothes was shoved into his hands, and he glanced enquiringly at Rove. His boss had already stripped to his vest and was pulling on a clean black shirt. The jacket being held out for him sported plenty of braid at the shoulders. Lucas was only mildly surprised that the man hadn't awarded himself a chestful of medals for his own cleverness.

"You'd better change," Rove shouted at him over the roar of the rotors. "You don't want to stand out, after all."

Looking at these bright young things, Lucas felt that ship had sailed, but he donned the uniform anyway. It was only the outward sign of the inward commitment he'd already made.

After an hour of flying, they came in sight of "home."

Someone had felled a whole load of trees, levelled the earth and enclosed a few acres with a serious amount of barbed wire fencing. They'd obviously miscalculated though, because the buildings inside the compound were squashed right into one corner. And there was an expanse of excess space at the far end. Maybe Rove would turn it into a parade ground for his youth corps.

The buildings looked prefabricated, matching the sort Lucas had experienced during his army career. But every roof here displayed a gleaming expanse of solar panels. There were tents, too, on the spare ground, suggesting that someone's numbers had been off—or some of the staterooms weren't quite ready for human habitation. Lucas ticked off the likely purpose of each hut: barracks, mess, stores, HQ, vehicle pool. He could see a handful of machines already in motion, mostly clearing more ground of trees outside the wire. As the helicopter came down, aiming for a big quad in the centre of the compound, uniformed figures ran up and formed into ranks. There were far more of them than Lucas was expecting. When Rove stepped out with a languid wave, everyone there snapped crisply to attention. It was enough to fuel the wet dreams of a dozen Napoleons.

"Welcome to the new world!" Rove called out as soon as the roar of the helicopter had subsided. "Welcome to *your* new world!" He strode down the line of them, Lucas stomping in his wake and making damn sure every ambitious young bastard saw he was the boss's second. They were all so painfully clean and bright, men and women with barely a patch of acne or an ounce of melanin between them. It was one thing to suspect that one's employer's prejudices ran in a certain monochrome direction, quite another to see it in action.

Rove stopped in the centre of the line and turned smartly towards his soldiers. "You have all been vetted for your heritage and ambition, selected from countless fellows, chosen to carry forwards the flag of our nation under these trying times," he said. "You saw clearly enough to understand that the world we knew had no future. Now you've taken the great step of accompanying me to another world, a world that can accommodate our destiny. A world where we can be strong—without the weak pawing at our ankles and bleating about their rights!"

He was just getting warmed up, so Lucas tuned him out,

standing to attention like everyone else as Rove's rhetoric washed over him. He was aware that his boss wasn't quite the rabble-rouser he probably thought he was. Towards the end of his speech, Lucas could see all the familiar signs of people who were bored but striving not to show it, recognizable to anyone who'd come up through the ranks and had had to listen to one too many long-winded colonels.

Rove handed command back to a boy with perhaps three more hairs on his chin than anyone else there and marched towards one of the storehouses. Lucas made sure he was right on his chief's heels.

Inside it was mostly boxes, each one immaculately labelled. But Rove headed straight towards the dimly lit back of the building, where there was...an eight-foot robot coffin. A dim reddish light glowed under the clear Perspex lid, and within he could see a woman. She was mostly naked, cadaverously thin and pierced by dozens of tubes.

"Of course, we'll have to break it to them gently," Rove said, looking down at the sunken face within.

"What now?" Lucas asked.

"Our troops outside don't know the complete story, of course. It would have muddied the waters to give them full disclosure. They might have had second thoughts. For all that, if they'd changed their minds, they'd not even be dust now."

"Speaking of full disclosure..." Lucas prompted. "This is..." The woman's face was familiar, now he came to look. "This is the woman on the boat?"

"Charen Volkovska," Rove agreed. "Useless to us now, unfortunately. She's done her bit, and I suspect the sudden disconnection was too much for her. We'll see if she can be recovered, but I suspect we'll end up having to switch her off."

"Disconnection from the ice thing?"

"From that and everything else, yes. Hard to go back to being one person when you've had your head spread across multiple worlds for years." He shrugged, and Lucas saw the iota of regret he felt over Charen Volkovska winking out of existence. "In the end, both she and her ice god were... good computers, really. They'd do anything you told them to, irrespective of personal cost."

Lucas took a deep breath. He had to ask, now, to confirm his suspicions, but at the same time he found himself unwilling to take that final step. If he didn't ask, then he could go on pretending he didn't know.

And yet: "So what did she do? What did you get her to do?"

"We took the calculations that our erstwhile fellows, Khan and the rest, cooked up, and adapted them a little. Charen thought they wouldn't have worked anyway, in their original form. What we've done is save the universe, Lucas. Or the bit of the universe that could be saved. Rather than trying to shore up the whole overpopulated mess of it all, we've saved what was important to us, turned those fields and equations inward to shore up this single parallel. Which was easier, believe me, than trying to keep the overstrained edifice standing. This is it, now, Lucas: this one world is all that remains, as of the moment when Charen decanted us into the forest. The rest has gone, save for that dead origin world we were in. Probably Khan and the rest are still floating about in their ridiculous insect boat there, trying to work out what went wrong. But we'll never see them again."

"So Earth, real Earth, our Earth…" Lucas did not trust himself to go on. His imagination kept throwing up things like game shows, bookmakers, lager, street lamps, chips, all of them gone, winking out of existence with the rest of the world.

"All is not lost, Lucas," Rove told him. "In a very real sense, all is not lost. Do you really think I would go to all this trouble just to play frontiersman in some primordial wilderness?"

If the uniforms were crisp enough, yes. But Lucas said nothing. Rove was patently in one of his expansive moods, eager to demonstrate how clever he'd been.

"They should have the helicopter refuelled by now," he said. "Let's go for a jaunt. We'll have to be careful of reserves after that, but I think we can indulge ourselves this once."

They lit out again, and this time Rove and Lucas wore helmets with a radio connection, so his boss could gloat without shouting himself hoarse. They were heading south-east, by Lucas's best estimate, and for a while there really was nothing but darkly shadowed forest below them. And then, beyond it, the snaking mouth of a river widening out onto a silver sea. At its mouth, there was a town.

"I thought you said there was nobody…" Lucas stared. There were roads, though the northwards routes ended abruptly where the trees started. There was movement in the streets, people rushing out to stare up at the helicopter. He saw cars gleam in the sunlight, a train of them heading south down…the A1. "What the—?"

"It's Berwick, Lucas."

"Berwick?"

"Berwick-upon-Tweed, a picturesque holiday destination on the brink of the Scottish border. I chose it as the most northerly point of what I cared to save. All barbarians and picts north of that, eh?"

"You brought..." Lucas couldn't quite grasp what he was being told. "You brought Berwick-upon-Tweed into another world? What the fuck for?" Some of Berwick was on fire, he saw. Other parts had been flooded, because the river feeding in from the north hadn't been following quite the same course as it had back home. Ten metres made a big difference where drainage was concerned.

"Lucas, on this world, before I came, there was a set of islands off the coast of Europe, but it wasn't our Great Britain, it wasn't England. It was a wilderness populated by beasts. When I understood what was happening to the universe, and what forces we could potentially marshal if only we had a few clever brains like Khan's to chew over the maths, I decided I'd save all that was worth saving. We've heard politicians mouthing the words, haven't we? Making hard choices for the good of the nation? Well, I put it into action. I've saved *England*, Lucas. All of it...from Land's End to, well, to Berwick. Because to hell with John o' Groats, frankly. I've brought it all over. You should have seen Charen modelling it, working out how it would swap places with its corresponding map coordinates on this Earth. There was a moment, Lucas, when fifty thousand square miles of forest were dumped where England used to be, and then there was a moment when that world just ceased to be. But England survived. *I* saved it." He grinned massively, eyes wide, and Lucas wondered how he'd ever looked on that smile and seen it as anything other than deranged. "No more rats, no more cavemen. Just this world—and England. A new start, where we get to set the rules. We have just shy of a thousand people back at the base, all hand-picked for their health and loyalty. We have a warehouse full of rat technology to give us a leg up. Besides, by the time we march south to recruit and re-establish order, there'll be no real resistance."

"Sixty million people will roll over, will they?"

"There won't be that many, by then." Rove's voice was all solemn regret about the necessity of someone else's sacrifice. "I don't think much of the underground infrastructure came through, if I recall Charen's models. Running water, power, all of that will fail sooner rather than later. Fuel will run out, there's nowhere to import food from, no medicine. And, of course, no real government, nobody keeping the peace, no emergency services. Give them half a year, they'll fall over themselves to pledge fealty to anyone who promises them discipline and peace." He suddenly looked hungry, dangerous, the veneer of civilization wearing thin. "When I first met Charen and realized what she'd discovered—more than she ever did, idiot savant that she was—do you know what I felt? When I stood, like Alexander, and looked out over that vast expanse of many worlds? It was ghastly. Because it wasn't an emptiness. Everywhere you looked, there were *things*. You've seen some of them, the vermin and the monsters. The universe was *infested*. And we weren't the great power we thought, either. They were stronger than us. Any one of them could have marched into our world and taken it from us, exterminated us. We'd lost our place at the centre of the universe. It's not the way the world should be, Lucas. I could tell immediately that it was a mistake. Creation is for humanity, not for crawling things."

"But you worked with the rats."

"Do you think I wanted to? Subhuman creatures that would

lord it over us because they arose *earlier*? But they had so much we needed, and they ate up my promises about giving them access to the Earth. I already knew the Earth, our Earth, had no future. Weakness, Lucas. It was overcome with weakness, all those petty minds . . . But now we have a new chance, a new Jerusalem. We can put it to rights, make a new world that we can be proud of, a world for the strong."

Surely he was practising his rhetoric so he could brainwash his troops? But no, Lucas suspected he was finally seeing the real Daniel Rove. *Is this all?* he thought numbly. *Is this petty provincial dictatorship what you moved Heaven and Earth for?* It all seemed inexpressibly sad. Looking ahead, he wasn't sure what would be the worse outcome: Rove living three hundred years as the unchallenged god-king of his own Aryan personality cult, lording it as emperor of a broken, feudal England, or a young usurper cutting the man's throat after ten years because they wanted a chance to wear the big hat and sit on the fancy chair. Both options seemed equally unappetizing.

"Well, congratulations, sir," he heard himself say. *And perhaps it's the best that could have happened. If Khan and the others couldn't save the whole house, at least we have our fucking shed in the back garden.*

They returned to the base, and the corps spent the rest of the day unboxing and setting things up. There was a generator and petrol, though Lucas knew that wasn't going to last long. There was accommodation to sort out, and he watched without much amusement as the pretty boys and girls played one-upmanship to get whichever were perceived as marginally better digs. There was more squabbling over the rota to muck out the privies and wash the dishes; Lucas reckoned Rove had brought him along as sergeant major as much as anything.

Leaning on the tenuous authority he carried as someone who walked in Rove's shadow, he waded in and started giving orders. There were plenty of mutinous looks, and he knew that whatever line these jackbooted children had been sold, it hadn't included scrubbing the dunnies. They weren't forces types, that was for sure. They hadn't had that kind of obedience drilled into them. By the time night fell, Lucas was uncomfortably sure that he'd have to watch his back. When you told people they were the inheritors of the world, none of them imagined *sharing*.

Still, day one down and nobody had needed punching in the face, which felt like a victory of sorts. He retired to the mess hall, where some of the women were serving mac'n'cheese from cans. *Hunting rota tomorrow*, Lucas decided, because presumably most of the animals were edible and had no real fear of man. They could make it a good bonding exercise, maybe a reward for the best and boldest. Also tomorrow they could see about clearing ground for planting. There were books, Rove had said, on how to do it, and they could raid south for tinned goods—to keep them going until they'd figured it out. Lucas felt like going to investigate which crates contained the beer, but he reckoned that would be a dangerous precedent right now.

When the chorus of voices rose from outside, at first Lucas thought it was high spirits. Then more joined in and he recast it as panic and hurried outside. Because it was entirely possible that Rove was wrong about this world and an army of angry rhino-men or some damn thing had just broken out of the trees. No enemy was at the fences, though. Nobody was rushing about looking for where they'd put the guns. Instead, people were staring upwards, pointing. Voices that had been shouting had sunk to whispers by the time Lucas joined them.

"What? What's going on?" He could distantly hear Rove's querulous demands, but his boss was no longer a priority. Even when a thin hand shook him by the shoulder and Rove was shouting in his ear, all he could do was stare up at the clear night sky.

"Lucas, damn you!" Rove snapped, and slapped him across the face. Lucas barely felt it.

Above them, the stars were going out, darkness spreading across the cosmos.

The pace of extinction sped up, until he realized that it wasn't just—just!—the stars that were being snuffed out. A whirling tide of chaos and nothingness was racing towards them, unravelling everything in its path. It hadn't worked, and all that sacrifice had been pissed down the drain for nothing. This insane Little England was as doomed as everything else in the universe. As Rove rained threats and exhortations upon him, it all came down and there was nothing more.

17/2.

I

"So what good *is* she?"

"Every manner of good, Lucas." Rove's look had an iota too much condescension in it, and Lucas felt his blood pressure notch up another few points. "Did you never wonder how I ran rings around the rats, for all their lauded technological superiority? Charen was walking in and out of their data systems on the back of the ice-world machine. If you can access a system from elsewhere on the dimensional axis, you can circumvent any kind of security and just run rampant." There was more, because Rove was tired, so the inner man could claw its way out more readily. And what the inner Rove really wanted was for the universe to appreciate how clever he was. So there was a Russian-sounding woman who was doing all the work, and Rove was stringing her along, same old same old. The thought made Lucas feel that he and this Volkovska bint probably had a fair amount in common. He stood there, surly, as Rove waxed smug about the plans he'd made, the resources he'd stockpiled, the people he had in readiness. All very convincing, on first blush, but Lucas reckoned that if he prodded any part of it too hard the whole thing would fall apart. Like the universe, apparently.

"All in place, Lucas, all waiting," Rove assured him blithely. "If only Khan and her menagerie can do their damn job." The man let out a long breath, eyes closed. For a moment he looked twenty years older, the real Daniel Rove, shorn of the youthful twinkle he saved for the cameras. "Bugs and monkeys and vermin and queers," he said softly. "What sort of a way is that to run a universe? I'll be glad when we're rid of them."

Lucas stared down at him, knowing that *this*, *now* was the moment he could turn back. He wasn't as smart as Rove, and he lacked the man's vast influence and ambition. But he had two strong hands, one of which was superhuman in its capabilities, and Rove's neck was thin. He felt the will to do it rise in him, a sudden surge of violence born as much from personal frustration as from a desire to do the right thing.

Something long suppressed spiked in him and he wrapped his fingers around that lily-white throat. Rove's eyes flashed open and he grasped Lucas's wrists, grimly pulling them apart, kicking at his attacker's shins. He was remarkably strong, far more so than his frame should have allowed, and Lucas belatedly remembered the rats had given Rove's body quite the upgrade. But Lucas had leverage. More than that, he had killed people before and done all manner of wrongs, many of them on Rove's orders. He felt he should triumph for the sake of sheer poetic justice.

Yet Rove managed to jab his shoe into Lucas' groin, then dragged his hands apart, silent save for hissing grunts of effort. His face was purple now, not from the strangling but from sheer outrage at the betrayal. Lucas had a moment of genuine worry. Then he remembered what he was capable of and twisted his artificial hand, breaking the man's grip.

He bore down with all his weight, pinning his victim to the wall, before punching Rove full in the face.

He broke Rove's teeth and jaw with his black hand, Rove's vicarious gift to him, and barely felt it. Adrenaline cheering him on like a gladiator's bloodthirsty audience, he punched again and again, marvelling at how he could shatter bone and barely feel the impact. Shorn of reciprocal pain, the feeling was intoxicating.

After the fifth blow, he realized he'd probably done enough. Rove was a smart man, but those brains wouldn't cause any trouble now, not after they'd been spread half across Cam's chitinous wall and up Lucas's arm to the elbow. He stood up, feeling his savagery subside.

Rove's phone buzzed from where it had skittered across the floor. A spike of fear, self-loathing and resurgent rage rushed Lucas. He stamped on it, smashing the screen to shards and flattening the case. If he spared a thought for Charen Volkovska it was *Be free*, as though she'd been a genie trapped in that latest-model lamp.

And then: *Oh fuck, what now?* He was of absolutely no use to anyone on his own. He wasn't a boffin and he had no friends on board. Without Rove he was, not to put too fine a point on it, screwed.

He had the wit to clean up, washing the residuum of Rove from his hands. He also changed clothes, then went to find Sabreur and Matchell, the government bods. They were talking to the thuggish caveman who'd given him so much trouble before. Not ideal, but beggars couldn't be choosers.

"Right, listen," he said. "You're going home, right? 'Real Earth' home?"

They were frowning at him, as he'd interrupted their

conversation. But he reckoned what he had to say was way more important. The woman, Matchell, was narrow-eyed though, and he had the sudden premonition that she somehow *knew* what he'd done.

"I want to make a deal," Lucas said hurriedly. "With MI5. I know a crap-ton of what Rove's been up to and I can help you dismantle his entire operation. In return, I want a pardon, a new identity. A deal."

"Where's Rove?" Matchell asked slowly, and Lucas knew he couldn't dissemble. Not with the bloody evidence in the next room.

I

"Spiker," Alison said, and then nothing else.

Julian found his arm had slipped down until it was around her waist, and her hip and thigh were pressed against his. Her head was turned slightly, lips an inch from his cheek so that he could feel the flutter of her breath. All terribly genteel. Yet under the skin, he found that he wanted her in a way that was more powerfully physical and erotic than anything he had allowed himself to feel in a decade. *We are at the end of the world. Civilized considerations need not apply.* Right now, there was nothing preventing the two of them just finding a chamber within Cam and tearing each other's clothes off. Nothing beyond the checks they carried within themselves.

Julian felt the moment stretch, excruciatingly aware of Alison's own stillness. Knowing that she was waiting to see what path they would take, and that if he said *yes* then she would say *yes* too. Then they'd have committed themselves to the one thing that had been the elephant in whatever room they'd shared for years. Julian fancied he could hear the universe holding its breath.

It took the slightest shift of his head to bring his lips round to hers. He left her room to back off at any point, and she didn't, and they kissed. He'd imagined the moment far too many times. And afterwards, every time, all the spectres of his regulated existence had risen from their unquiet graves to castigate him. This time, Alison Matchell's lips still carried a faint sheen of cold from her communion with elder, ancient things. Even as they came together she had to shift awkwardly, because she'd been in one position for slightly too long. She ended up accidentally butting him in the temple and then almost biting him. It was, hands down, the most romantic moment Julian could remember. And in the next second he was pulling her to him, her reciprocal grip almost painfully tight. Years of suppressed longing sprang free of their shackles, running rampant through all the primal parts of his brain.

They broke apart, and he was suddenly aware that Cam's grotesque avatar was right there—regarding them placidly and thinking who knew what. With a start he made to pull away, but Alison wouldn't let him. She had already worked out that if Julian Sabreur had a moment to think, he would clam up again and that would be that. And he didn't want to clam either. He wanted Alison. He wanted to throw propriety out the window this once and have what he wanted, what they both wanted.

They backed out of the avatar's presence and found a suite of deserted windowless chambers. Here they claimed one of the leathery, yielding surfaces Cam had manifested for them to sleep on. Not exactly a honeymoon in a four-star hotel, and they were both short of a good wash. They also felt tired, old and unutterably insignificant beneath the shadow of vast events. But it just meant that what they did didn't matter: they were free. He laid her down and she practically dragged him on top of her, wrestling with his belt as his hands slipped under her blouse.

When Kay came to find them, later, she was utterly delighted.

I

"The timing will be the trickiest thing," Kay explained, looking over her impromptu audience. Mal and Lee, Stig and Auruthmer, all sitting there like schoolkids; Alison and Julian still pretending they weren't an item. And at the back were Rove and his brute, because every Eden needed a serpent, apparently. Kay had never been terribly good at explanations to the uninitiated, but she'd prepped carefully, because this wasn't going to be news any of them wanted to hear.

"It's like this: we planned to do all the hard work over here, before slipping back to our home branches to finish up. Everyone getting to go home happy. We've spent more time and sweat than you can imagine, trying to make that plan work in theory. Cam's lot don't really care, because they fully intend to fuck off back to the stars when we're done. It doesn't affect them much which universe they're in, but it's a big deal for the rest of us." She suppressed a yawn. At this point she'd been up for almost forty-eight hours, and was due another dose of the amphetamine-type drugs Cam had fabricated for her. "So reality check time. We've gone over the maths and there is too great a chance that going home will compromise the plan. Meaning it's bye-bye universe." She felt like crying, suddenly, because damn it...she had tried so *hard* to square that circle. It had come down to her casting vote—and she'd really wanted to go home. She wanted to *live*. After all, she'd only worked out how to set her life straight two-thirds of the way through it. She had a lot of living to catch up on, that miserable Khurram Amir Khan had never dared to try.

But the whole universe was a precious bauble to balance against a few more parties at Camden Lock, a few more liaisons in understanding bars and another couple of pride marches. Never let it be said that when it came to the crunch, Kay Amal Khan was selfish.

"So it's like this," she told them all. "We're going to do it all from this side. We're going to nail the doors shut, with us still inside the house. Even then it might not work. I'm not going to lie to you, this is stuff that nobody—not Cam, not Ertil, not Murther and certainly not me—can claim to have mastered. But we think we've got the maths down and we're playing the odds. This is a suicide mission. I'm sorry. We didn't know when we set out."

She was looking specifically at Julian and Alison, at Mal and Lee, who needn't have come. They could have stayed in the Cousins' world. They could have been repatriated to the shattered streets of London. They could have...any number of things, really. But now they were sentenced to exile and probably death, just like her.

"So...what, then?" Julian asked after a contemplative pause.

"Well, we stick with Cam, I guess. Live on in a trilobite's gut. I think it's used to the idea of having company, now. So maybe that can be a thing. We'd suffocate pretty damn quick outside, so I don't really see any other option. I really am sorry. We all are."

Nobody took it well, and they kept on not taking it well for the next week, as Cam's peers constructed what they needed and liaised with the Ice Mind. On the Outerward branches, Kay knew, the Cousins were preparing their own engines to support the healing process. There were plenty of Cousin science teams who would end up stranded on this world or that. They accepted it as part of their duty, more sanguine than Kay's own people at the prospect of giving their all for the greater good.

Nobody was speaking to Kay except Auruthmer and Murther either, and she felt vastly aggrieved that she was the lightning rod for all that disgruntlement. *It's not my fault*, she wanted to shout. *This is our best chance to save everything!* But they couldn't really understand, and so in the end she found herself on the cusp of preserving the universe, feeling as alone as she ever had.

She watched via Cam's intricately constructed displays as great engines were thrown into motion, taking hold of the complex fields the Ediacaran was generating. Their constructions had to try and align these fields into a stable configuration, one that would survive the death of the entity generating them. And not a moment too soon, because a huge, morbid cascade was now sweeping this world, this true original Earth. There was a critical threshold of living material to monitor. Below this, by Kay's calculations, the Ediacaran would be unable to sustain itself and its pet realities. Perhaps it would then continue as a collection of basic life forms. Reduced to an assortment of quilted bags on the sea floor and crusty lichens on land—no longer a singular entity at all.

She watched in real time, through Cam's mediation, as the fields aligned and shuddered under their ministrations. Murther was at her side as they parsed the data, shoulder to shoulder. Kay felt a swoop of triumph as everything fell into place as their models had predicted, all the straws leaning against one another just *so*, so that each one balanced the next in a great round. Every timeline was abruptly separate and whole, their metaphorical walls sound and solid, every branch an island.

And then they experienced the bleak depths of despair as their great experiment failed. As it all came apart, cracks proliferating, the complex waveforms of the different timelines collapsing rapidly into oblivion. All those different Earths, all those lives, those minds, those histories…unwritten and unwound until nothing was left and as if none of it had ever been.

She'd given it her very best shot, sacrificed everything, and still the grand plan had disintegrated into shards and splinters.

Kay Amal Khan took a deep breath and stepped back from the damning display. Elsewhere aboard the living ship were other people waiting to hear that their own sacrifices had been worth it. That the plan that had doomed them—denying them any last chances to say goodbye to friends or family or their lives—had worked. She couldn't face them. She couldn't tell them the truth.

"Cam," she said hoarsely, "would you open me a hatch to outside, please? I feel the need to go for a walk up top. I may be some time."

I

Several new trilobites had made the jump across, as far as Alison understood it. And there was practically a shuttle service between here and the Cousins' timeline to bring materiel and experts over. Daniel Rove had even been back to the rat world, and now the rats seemed to be contributing to the universal repair effort.

When Kay finally approached her and Julian, Alison knew what she would say. Julian wouldn't like it, true. But it would only be one more thing for him to explain, amongst so much else.

"I've made a bit of a decision," Kay said.

"You're staying with the Cousins when this is done," Alison concluded for her.

Kay blinked, put out. "Talk about stealing a girl's thunder, Matchell," she said peevishly. "But yes. I mean, they offered. It's tempting because they're way ahead of us, scientifically. And what's more, there's no guarantee that this fix of ours will be permanent. They're going to set up a whole institution dedicated to interdimensional theory, watching for cracks. That's something I can contribute to. And…"

"And…?" Julian prompted testily.

"You knew Murther was a man, right? Biologically a man?"

Alison hadn't known that, although with the Cousins' heavy physiology it was harder to read these things.

"She knew about me—it was her call to recruit me in the first place, to send Mal out to make contact. From what she says, the Cousins have had a broad view on things like that since the year dot. Comes down to priests, she says. They had priests for death rites and vision quests and all that jazz, and they were always women. Except some of them were men, only they had to *become* women to do the priesting—wear the clothes, walk the walk, all that, and that made them women. So as far as they're concerned, it's all part of the way the world works—your gender is like your calling." She was aware she was talking too quickly, but pressed on. "And when she said *that*, I couldn't stop thinking about people like Billy fucking White. All the shit I got every bloody day, just because of who I am. I thought I'd fit in better with the Cousins, even though they're a different subspecies. So I'm sorry, Julian, but I'm not going back when this is done."

Alison watched Julian warily, not sure how he would take this, but in the end he shrugged.

"Communist transsexual cavemen," he said. "Hind really would have a fit." He took a deep breath, as though steeling himself against the extra paperwork. "I hope it works out for you, Kay. It's been a privilege to work with you." He stuck out a hand, but Kay hugged him fiercely instead.

"You're one of the good guys, Julian, you really are."

I

"Mr. Sabreur," Rove said, "you're a good servant of the Crown, are you not? A loyal man? You've seen the sort of circus they're running here, a zoo where all the cages are open. I can't believe any of this sits well with you. We are facing the destruction of everything we know. But even if this ludicrous plan of Khan's succeeds, do you really think that the things we truly value will survive? Do you think life can go on as before, with our country riddled with rat-creatures and cavemen and who knows what else? Do you honestly think that once our 'host' has dropped us off in England this monster will just go away? Why should it, when it has us to lord it over? The Earth was a prehistoric wasteland when it left, and now there's a whole planet of slaves which it can get to treat it as a god. There'll be religions and cults dedicated to it within a week, once we're back. And you know how these cavemen have been infiltrating our society for decades...That woman has a seat at a U.S. university, for God's sake. Do you really think they haven't been pulling strings elsewhere, in the Oval Office, at Downing Street? Believe me, I've been opposing their machinations for a long time."

"So what's your alternative?"

"Reset the clock, Mr. Sabreur. Burn away the rot that's been degrading our society, this monstrous fifth column. Rebuild something truly human, English, from the ruins. After all, you saw how things were collapsing back home, when we left. What state do you think things are in by now?"

Julian said nothing, and Alison waited for his rebuttal. For him to follow the line that Hind had been taking towards any and all of Rove's machinations.

"We can't save everything," Rove said softly. "It's too late for that now, whatever Khan says. But we can save England, Mr. Sabreur. We can save what we love."

Something shifted in Julian, just slightly, and yet it opened up a great gulf of space between him and Alison. She wanted to shout at him; she wanted to tell him about the great sliding blocks that were slotting into place in the ice, co-opting Khan's work to serve Rove's plan. But she remained frozen, wordless, and at heart she knew that Julian's weakness was also her own. Rove had a plan; she and Julian had none. They were surplus to the requirements of this scenario, utterly without significance or power. The only way they could take control of their destiny was to choose a side.

"Explain," Julian said, but the aggressive tension was leaching out of him. Alison knew that in her silence she was just as complicit as he was and that they were bad people after all.

I

"Charen seems to think everything is in order," said Rove, pocketing his phone. "We may need to move quickly when the moment arrives. And I have no doubt that some of our fellows here will get in the way."

"I'm ready, sir," Lucas confirmed. "You're happy this Charen can deliver, though?"

"Charen is in deep with the ice-computer that these cavemen use to get from place to place," Rove replied, closing his eyes. "She's in so deep that she's in suspended animation, at round about zero degrees centigrade in a secure facility back home. Has been for a couple of years now—but that just means she can communicate constantly with the ice-machine. It's what she would have wanted, probably. But it gives her unparalleled access, and she's tractable enough in that state. She doesn't have any desires, really, little enough conscious volition. She just does what she's told—because as far as she's concerned she's already achieved her nirvana, the thing she was always chasing. She thinks she's found God, poor deluded soul."

Lucas felt an unwanted kinship with Charen Volkovska, as witless stooge of Rove's plans. "So she does what, exactly?"

Probably, had Rove not been so worn out, the man would have fobbed him off with some platitude. But instead, he said, "She's saving a little piece of England for us, in a place I've picked out where we can start again. The rest can go to hell."

Again, Lucas could have pretended to accept that. But play the thug as he might, that didn't mean he was actually stupid. "Doesn't that mean she screws herself out of her religion, though? I thought that the ice-computer thing was on one of the other Earths. The ones that will end up being destroyed?"

Rove snorted, half opening his eyes. "Your point, Lucas?"

He had nothing to gain by pursuing this line of enquiry. He owed this Volkovska woman nothing, after all. "None, sir."

Rove's phone buzzed, and he took it out again, a satisfied look already spreading over his face. But it was quickly replaced with a frown.

"Sir...?" Lucas prompted, and his breath ghosted from his lips, visible for an instant in the chilly air.

Rove was tapping at his phone screen, languidly and then with increasing urgency. And Lucas saw on the curved chamber wall behind him lines of frost flowering into existence. They formed one word in letters a metre high.

NO

Rove had his phone to his ear now and was speaking into it hurriedly. Then he hissed and dropped it. By the time it struck the ground it was so cold that it shattered into pieces. Lucas saw ice crystals actually forming in the air, and distantly he heard the cries of the others.

The word *NO* was appearing all over the walls and ceiling, repeated in a multitude of sizes and drawn at various angles, formed from lines of gleaming ice. *NO NO NO NO NO.*

He blundered out of the chamber, cannoning into Sabreur and Matchell. Their host lurched, throwing them into a wall that was abruptly bristling with sharp lances of frost. Cam shuddered around them, faltering in the air, and Lucas imagined ice building on its carapace, freezing the colossal creature in the iron-hard grip of winter.

They were falling, and he knew the sea they dropped towards would become a frozen tomb the moment they struck the waves. He, Rove, Khan, the cavemen, none of them would ever get the chance to put anyone's plan into action. The best intentions of the greatest minds were all moot.

I

When the time came to say their goodbyes, Lee actually felt a little tearful. Given that she and Mal had contributed precisely nothing to the high-level science, and had instead spent the time renewing their relationship, she suspected that they'd been the only ones having even a halfway good time. As a result, they might be the only ones who'd miss this weird interlude.

"There won't be any magic, you know? Afterwards. It'll just be us," she said. But her fellow humans, apart from Mal, of course, didn't seem to care.

"We could go with the Nissa," Mal suggested. "Last chance."

"Is that what you want?"

"I want what *you* want."

"No, but seriously. You've...seen some crazy things, we both have. Are you going to be happy with just one Earth?" It was a serious question. Lee knew Mal, after all. She wasn't someone who took limitations well.

Mal looked thoughtful at that. "I'm going to have to be, aren't I? Whichever Earth we pick. I don't want to live with the Birdmen forever, that's for sure. And the Nissa...I like them, I like Stig. I reckon we'd be okay there, but...it would be a bit dull, maybe, all that community service and no small talk?"

Lee nodded, and felt a huge wash of banal and domestic relief, to which she would never admit.

"If there's anything you wanted closure on, though, now's your chance," Mal said, half joking. "Any secrets of the universe you were wondering about. Because in a short while there won't be anything but us, as you said. And we humans are pig-ignorant, apparently."

Lee frowned. "Actually, there was something..."

She went to Cam's avatar, because the Nissa had already jumped ship. The weird, humanoid shape hung there like a manikin, jumping into crawling animation when she ducked into its chamber.

"Lee," it said, its face emerging from the writhing surface of its head.

"I want to ask something..." She wished she'd dragged Dr. Khan over, because she wasn't sure Cam could do layperson's explanations. "About time travel. Into the past."

"This is, of course, impossible," Cam explained smoothly.

"Well, that's what Auruthmer said, but Murther seemed to think there was some way. And Murther's their top scientist.

And I was thinking…we're about to cut ourselves off from everything, from all those other worlds. I understand it's necessary, if that's the only way to save everything. But what if we could go back, somehow? If we could change things before they got so bad, maybe there would be another way…?" She let her voice peter out under a withering stare that was almost certainly in her head. *Stupid girl asking stupid questions again, being interested in time-wasting things, you'll never make anything of your life.* She suddenly felt just like she had at school, or back at home. Like she did with anyone except Mal.

"Nothing can travel backwards in time," Cam pronounced. "However, the formation of parallel timelines does in itself involve the collapsing of a waveform of potential here and now. This mandates the existence of a deviation point, prior to the moment that the waveform collapses. Nothing can travel backwards, but the new timeline's divergence is anchored in the past, sometimes considerably further back in the past. Murther knows this, because she oversaw the project by which her people generated your Earth's parallel. By this means, they discovered that their own genetic line had become functionally extinct in their newly created time-line fifty thousand years before their experiment was initiated in their own."

"So could we make a branch where the collapsing-timelines problem was *fixed* fifty thousand years earlier?" Lee demanded. "I mean, maybe if someone had thought about it then, we wouldn't have to…?"

Cam hung there for a long moment. "I do not know what would happen, should that be attempted. I suspect it may be impossible to bring into being a timeline with a past that interacts with all the other timelines—or else it would have been accomplished already. And we would have observed the effects. However, the question is a worthy one, and if we had more time...My calculations suggest that at this late stage in the morbidity of the originating life form, we are out of time. The only new branches that could be generated would be rooted in the very recent past. This would afford us dwindling possibilities, meaning that the opportunity to reset events is now profoundly limited."

Lee blinked, digested that, blinked again. "Would we know?" she asked.

A pair of toothed arms clicked down over Cam's compound eyes, then up again, copying her. "I do not understand your question, Lee."

"Would we *know* if this was happening to us? If new timelines were being created, resets put into motion?"

"I..." And then Cam fell silent, and Lee had a weirdly triumphant moment: *I've thought of something that nobody else has considered.*

I

Once, there was a species of fish-like creatures that had been the masters of their world. But that Earth had died, in part because of their overreaching technology. And yet the fish-creatures themselves persisted, even though they no longer *lived*, because their last act had been to make their world their greatest work, their archive, their mausoleum.

Sometimes Alison felt she had cast her lot in with a genie or demon, all that power reduced down to something she could petition. It was impossible to shake the impression she was dealing with a personality rather than a system, too, no matter how hard she tried to be distant and professional about things. Right now she was monitoring local traffic: the trilobites, Murther, Ertil, Khan and Rove. She had missed Rove's input for too long though, not because his signal was hidden in the noise but because another user was deliberately obscuring his activity. When she'd tried to investigate, she'd met access issues for the first time: *someone* had more privileges than her. Only one person that could be, if they were pushing Rove's agenda.

Hello, Charen, Alison thought. She'd intended the words to remain prisoners inside her head, but a spike of pain stabbed deep into her mind, even cutting through the usual dreamy numbness that accompanied communion with the Ice Mind.

"Hello, Alison Matchell. I remember you."

Alison cut the connection immediately, rubbing at her face, where ice crystals were gritty as sand. *Gone too far, gone too far, really—*

"I need to talk to you, Alison." She realized now that the voice was in her ears, not her head... There was something there, flickering, just where she could catch it in the corner of her eye.

Do I really want to see what this is? Because if her life had become a horror movie, this would be when the monster struck.

But she wasn't eight, and she was insatiably curious, so she turned.

She remembered Charen Volkovska from all those years ago, a reserved Slavic woman with a flat voice. This current representation of her wasn't very accurate, but maybe this was how Charen saw herself now, rather than how the world had seen her. She was an image composed entirely of glittering ice crystals, which formed and reformed as Alison watched. The figure broke up like static only to coalesce a moment later: a tall, pale woman in a spike-edged gown, diamonds glinting on her brow. The Snow Queen—of course she was the Snow Queen.

"Has Rove sent you to . . ." It occurred to Alison, somewhat belatedly, that if Charen could do *this*, she could probably kill someone easily by freezing select parts of their brain or cardiovascular system, blood clots that would melt before the autopsy discovered them.

"You have so few words left." The voice did not come from the image's mouth but from its whole, ringing like bells as the ice crystals vibrated and rubbed against one another. "Do not waste them. Return to the machine. You must bear witness."

Alison didn't want to do anything on Charen's say-so—but if the woman's goal was a dead Alison Matchell, there was nothing Alison could do to stop her. "Return to what, though?" she asked.

"Everything." Charen's otherworldly voice sounded like frozen grief, and the woman radiated a dignity and grace she'd never possessed in person. "The end of everything, again. Come, see, while there are sands still in the glass. See, and then carry word of it to the others."

"I thought you were on Rove's side?"

For a moment the spectral image of Volkovska shattered apart into a million sparkling motes of chaos, a very human temper tantrum. The temperature dropped another five degrees and she reformed—visibly fighting to remain coherent.

"I am on the side of everything," she said, garbled and distant. "Come to the edge of the ice, Alison. You must see."

With profound misgivings, Alison reached out for her interface and let the cold in.

Instantly a complex architecture ópened to her, a trove of buried information she hadn't even suspected... *Or was this even here before? Is this new?* She couldn't make anything of it, other than seeing that a colossal amount of information had somehow been compressed to fit here. Then Charen, impatient, did something that changed the way it was manifesting. Alison's mind conjured up a filing system, a library, showed her books she could draw out and open, videos to be watched, experiences to be relived.

She was abruptly on the couch with Julian, without any sense of transition. They had ice cream, probably the source of her splitting headache, and they were flicking between trailers for TV shows. Charen Volkovska was standing behind the couch, staring at the screen as particles of ice drifted down from her hair. This seemed normal as Alison just watched the shows, which were all variations on the same theme. A bunch of people were stuck in a weird living ship trying to save the universe. They were failing over and over. One of the people was her.

In one episode, Rove's thuggish minion murdered him. That was a good one, she thought. Then there was "The One Where Alison and Julian Get It Together." That was acutely embarrassing but also thrilling, because she'd always wanted to know how that would pan out. Then there was... and then there was... and then... and...

"Do you understand what this is?" Charen hissed, blasting Alison's ear with a gust of icy breath. "This is how it could go; this is how it has gone. The Initiator has placed these thoughts within us." And that "us" meant the Ice, which apparently wasn't

THE DOORS OF EDEN

separate to Charen, as far as the woman was concerned, and the "Initiator" was...

"You mean the...thing, the Ediacaran?" *The thing that made us all.* The god of all the universes.

"It is telling us how we failed. But we have to learn! Nothing we have done has helped."

Alison had just watched "The One Where Charen Kills Everyone," and very much didn't want to get on the wrong side of her.

She could see how to make this information accessible to Cam too, if only because Charen was giving her a roadmap. Cam would then be able to make it accessible to everyone else, even if he had to act it out, shadow puppets style, with his little legs.

And she wouldn't be able to edit this "footage" either. It would come warts and all, so people would see her being shallow and selfish, being intimate, and all those other things that people hid from one another. She would be absolutely naked. They all would.

"Yes," she told Charen. "Yes, let's do it."

"Be swift." The hallucination, the couch, Julian, everything, was receding. "There isn't much time."

Then Julian, the real Julian, was shaking her, shouting her name. She'd collapsed on the floor, shivering violently, on the verge of hypothermia.

"Get everyone together," she told him, croaking out the words. "In Cam's room. There's something you have to see."

17/3.

I

In the end, Cam hadn't needed to act out all their branching infidelities, treacheries and failures. Charen Volkovska had taken the initiative, gripping the forward compartment with a fist of winter to manifest a shimmering silvery screen of ice crystals forever drifting downwards while the images displayed upon it glimmered, luminous as old film.

There was a lot of noise at the start: complaints, demands, Khan insisting that she had work to do—you know, just saving the actual *universe*, nothing that couldn't be interrupted, love. Rove was snarkily dismissive, wanting to return to whatever he was doing, a private plot that Alison already knew inside out. Except that plot needed Charen, and Charen wasn't playing any more.

The screen began showing them themselves, and everybody quietened down. Charen had taken information deposited by the Ediacaran, all their failed timelines, and reconstituted it into familiar images. Now they were all able to see themselves on TV—or whatever the equivalent was for the various sentients watching. This time, now Alison wasn't receiving the information via the Ice Mind, she felt... echoes, perhaps. It seemed that when the "her" on screen said a thing or did a thing, a kindred string was plucked within her. A shadow of that alternate Alison's emotional state bled through. Glancing at her fellow voyeurs, she guessed something similar was happening for them.

It all played out, branch by branch, the recursions of the world tree's final shoots. Kay Amal Khan saw her schemes go south. Rove saw his own backstabbing come back at him. And there were other alternatives, too. In one, Cam and his people gave up and flew away into the vastness of space, abandoning everything, returning to solitary and unthinkable lives amongst the stars. In another, the rat kings came thundering through the interdimensional boundaries with their machines and their numbers, dead set on reclaiming Ertil for retributive justice, and the rent they tore in reality expanded until there was nothing left of anything. The branching universe came to this point of final collapse again and again, leaving only a singular cosmos containing a dead Earth somewhere within its uncaring vastness.

"We..." Julian said, sitting beside Alison. "We actually..." He couldn't look at her, or at anyone else—given that the entire crew was now voyeur to his foibles. "Matchbox, I'm sorry. I don't know how I could..."

"You could," she said firmly. "That's the point. We went there. It was a thing we might have done, that we didn't in this timeline. Like all the other scenarios."

"I don't know how to process this," he complained. "I'm feeling guilty over something I decided not to do. That's... Actually, that's damned unfair."

Alison hugged him, one-armed, her eyes still on the glittering screen. "It's okay, Spiker. *We're* okay. Well, the whole of creation is falling apart...but you and me, we're golden."

He didn't answer, and she knew he would be thinking through the maze of it. At least part of him would be trying to work out whether—if the damage was already done—it gave him a moral get-out clause, should he fall again... That was the sly suggestion her own id had been making ever since.

From behind her, she heard Rove curse. "Lucas, you... *killed* me?"

"If you're going to fire me, I fucking resign," Lucas said flatly. "Jesus, *that* was your plan?"

At last it was all done, every iteration played out, and in not one of them had the universe been saved: not in the branches where Khan, Rove or someone else had actually put a plan into action; certainly not where they had been interrupted. After all the personal embarrassments and outrages had burned themselves out, that message remained. They were going to fail.

Kay, Ertil and Murther had a bit of a confab after that, with Auruthmer standing between them to translate. Everyone else drifted away for half an hour or so. And Alison sat with Julian and tried to be there for him, whilst also tapping back into the Ice Mind. Now she'd met Charen there, it felt as though she was stepping into the lair of a dragon— one that might or might not be hungry. Off Rove's leash, she didn't know quite *what* Charen wanted, save to preserve her communion with the Posticthyan entity. If there'd been a scenario where she could've let the rest of the timelines unravel but held on to that one, Alison had no doubt she'd have done it.

"That is correct."

She jumped. That voice was in the room again; Julian was on his feet, glancing wildly around.

"I have modelled the logistics of preserving a single secondary timeline," Charen continued. "It was part of the job Rove set me. I had thought it would be possible when I was subservient to him." Charen's voice lacked the contempt Alison would have expected, remaining graciously regal. Her Snow Queen avatar shimmered and danced briefly before fading. "Given what we have seen, I do not think it is possible now. The waveforms always collapse to zero. You cannot isolate and preserve a single timeline. You cannot maintain the separation of one, or some, or indeed all of the timelines. Without the constant intervention of the Ediacaran, they all decay to entropy."

"Oh, that's jolly," Julian muttered. "So why show us all those failures? Was it just to rub them in?"

Charen's icy face waxed visible again. "I don't know." And then, more human than Alison had yet seen her since their long-ago face-to-face meeting: "I was never very good at knowing why people did things. People never interested me like things did. I knew where I was, with things."

Right then, Kay burst in, scattering the icy particles of Charen's image to the four winds, asking for everyone to come back in.

"We've examined the information stored in the ice," Khan began. "And, in light of that, we've looked into how the Ediacaran is exerting force on the fields that maintain the timelines. We'd already noted a lot of fluctuations, but we'd kind of written it off as the thing, you know, dying off. We thought it was simply on its last legs—not that it has any. Except *now* we think it was creating new temporary branches. One after the other, over and over, dozens of them. Or one of them, dozens of times, might be a better description. It springs a new timeline, then another one on the heels of the first, and then...like you've got a length of rope and you're shaking loops in it over and over. Each one gets to the point of failure and collapses, but there's another one a moment behind where things were done differently, little changes, new outcomes. Basically it's doing what it did before, whatever the fuck it did, to bring all our timelines into being. But now it's gone into complete overdrive." She was making wild gestures, trying to encompass the ocean in a nutshell. "Everyone with me?"

Ertil and Murther seemed to be following, and presumably Cam; everyone else was decidedly glassy-eyed.

"Where does this get us, though?" Lucas asked. It was the first time he'd actually addressed the floor, and he was standing on his own now, no longer in Rove's shadow.

"We look through what we did, in other waveforms, for stuff that didn't work. We find out what went wrong. We refine our equations. We keep an eye on the ice archives for more data. Because we've been given another chance, maybe not even for the first time. We adapt. That's what life does," Kay explained.

But Alison was recalling Charen's words. *The waveforms always collapse to zero.* They were all living in what was simply a possibility. All of reality, which had seemed so robust and enduring, was merely the fevered dream of a dying god. In much the same way, a single-celled creature might see its drop of water as a vast and eternal ocean even as the sun came out of the clouds to dry it up.

II

Evening found Mal and Lee sitting atop Cam's carapace, looking at the strangely underwhelming sunset. The sun was descending into the western sea without fuss or fanfare. And although it would rise again here, who knew if any other Earth would see the dawn. All the rituals and invocations Dr. Khan and the rest could devise were insufficient to guarantee another day.

They had their masks on, ones Cam had made, which also added an unusual dimension to the experience. Lee did her best to stop this detracting from the moment as she held hands with Mal, trying to ignore the faint prickling of alien air on her skin. Below them she could see that both land and sea, where shallow enough, were carpeted with corrugated and quilted patterns. But within these patterns were enormous denuded circles, where life was already mouldering or dead.

"You know what, though?" If Mal leant in to her, mask to mask, they could carry on something of a conversation. "If you look at all those splinters of timeline, all those versions of *us* . . ."

"Mm?"

"We never fucked it up, between us." Mal hugged her tight. "In not one did we have *that* argument, the one we couldn't come back from. We never broke up. You and me against the world, all of the worlds, every single time."

"We argued, though, in some of them."

"And we made up. *Seriously* made up, in some cases."

"Which everyone saw." Lee hadn't known where to put herself.

Mal, predictably, hadn't cared much. "Screw them," she said casually, giving Lee a squeeze. "You reckon that means we're destined?"

Lee had something scathing to say on that topic, but she bit down on it. Destined, why not? Now all they needed was a universe to be destined *in*.

"Poor old dying sponge-god," she said, staring into the sea, those depths that only hid more decay. "Does it think we can save it?"

Mal paused, then said, "Does it *think*, even? Does it want anything? Or maybe it just *is*...Maybe this whole business of producing timelines is like breathing? Just a thing it does— rather than being entertainment, or something else. Maybe the process even generates some by-product it feeds off, and creating *us* is just a side effect."

"No." Lee's reply was immediate, automatic. She had to go back and examine precisely why she thought this. "Because it's trying to help us. Why give us all this other timeline data, showing us how we got it wrong? That's active, that's it *doing* something. It's aware of us..." She stared down past the slope and spines of Cam's shell, feeling suddenly very small. *It knows us.* "It's as if we were a part of its immune system, or something—except we're part of its 'many-worlds' system. Although that doesn't help us know why it built this system in the first place."

"Change," Mal said.

"What?"

"It encompassed a whole world and it was alone, so it wanted to make something new."

"That's a very human view."

Mal laughed. "I only *have* a human view. But who says a

human-level view is as irrelevant as all that? We're all part of the great programme. Let's say the Ediacaran had been alone for millions of years, this singular thing, and it was self-aware. Maybe it did think, 'What if there was something else?' And because it *could*, it created. As to why it did this, why does Yahweh make the world? Why does Odin carve up the bits of some giant? Why do any gods light the blue touch paper, in the end?"

"You're saying it was bored?"

"I'm saying...maybe it was static. It saw the possibility of something dynamic and different, and it preferred that. It sure seems to want to preserve that difference, now it's on the way out. And it needs us to do it. We are the things it dreamt, and now it needs us to keep the dream alive, after it dies." And then she ruined the profundity by adding, "*Vive la différence,*" with a snicker.

"I can get behind that," Lee agreed tentatively. She realized that she'd been looking for just that difference herself. Hunting big cats on the moors, searching for lake monsters, for bigfeet: prying into the corners of the world because she'd wanted more world than there was. She'd always wanted that mystery, the sense that there was *something* hidden out of sight. If she'd been able to, perhaps she'd have been budding off timelines like there was no tomorrow too. Except now there was no tomorrow.

"Let's go in," she said. "I want to talk to Cam."

They found the trilobite's avatar hung up like an off-season wicker man, looking weirdly untenanted and fraying. Lee spoke its surrogate name a couple of times before animation returned and its fabric of interlocking limbs twitched and tightened.

"Time travel, then," Lee said. "In one of those other time-lines, we talked about that."

"That was another waveform that failed, I am afraid, Lee." Its facial expressions seemed more authentic now, making Lee feel it was taking her more seriously. "I have no memory of that."

"Well, I mean, I don't either," Lee said, slightly thrown. "That's the point of other timelines, isn't it? They're what we might have done but didn't."

Cam regarded her for a moment. "I appreciate this now. I had thought that your consciousnesses had integrated the parallel experiences. I, or at least my larger consciousness, has been trying to accomplish the same feat."

Lee goggled at it. "No, no, we're all in the same boat. Which is...less than helpful, given you're the boat we're all in, but hopefully you—"

"I have absorbed the figure of speech, along with other data pertaining to your language," Cam confirmed. "Consider it understood. Time travel, then? It also remains impossible, I'm afraid, for entities."

"But—"

"But we have witnessed a very specific circumstance under which information *can* be moved backwards in time. This is entirely outside my own experience, and I had not believed it possible. However, having now examined the evidence, it would appear that the Ediacaran is repeatedly seeding time-lines within the same possibility-space. This is creating multiple temporary waveforms—each of them with the potential to be a functioning, permanent timeline. Owing to the nature of such coalescing potential timelines, as we discussed in that alternate past we neither of us have memories of, the inception point forms prior to the conception point, so that when the conceiver—the Ediacaran—beholds the new time-line, that timeline is found to have diverged from the parent universe sometime *before* the date of access. Just as Murther's people found when they accessed the timeline they created, in which your people had supplanted hers. We, you and I now, are part of one of these temporary waveforms. And the Ediacaran has been able to seed this timeline with information gleaned from the collapse of prior waveforms. Thus it has used the principles of timeline generation to provide us with cautionary information about how our future might transpire if we take certain actions."

"So where—or no, *when* is the Ediacaran, in its own timeline, when it's creating these new lines?" Mal pressed tentatively.

"At the end," Cam said solemnly. "At the very end of its existence, in its last seconds. Otherwise it would not be able to assess the success of our various efforts. Or rather, to learn from our failures."

"So this is happening when it's given up and is letting go," Lee said. "And so everything is starting to fall over where it is..."

"But it's still generating waveforms before it hits the ground," Mal finished for her.

"That reflects our best assessment," Cam confirmed. "With the caveat that, frankly, we are all very much out of our depth." And it gave them what was just recognizable as a human smile. Cam had come a long way too.

"Good figure of speech, there," Lee said.

"I try. It is what I am for."

"We need to talk to Kay, maybe?" Mal pressed. "Bring her

in on this, because half a degree in English did not prep me for this. Let me go hunt her out."

Lee was left with the trilobite's avatar, which had started to lose tension and return to its corn doll state, all bristling angles and spines. Struck by a sudden thought, she said, "Cam?"

It cocked its head, a small motion, but she knew it would have shifted its entire body to compensate.

"How much of you is *here*, paying attention to this? I know I'm talking to some really fancy antennae, right? It's just... you've become like a person, to talk to. Take that however you want, good or bad."

For a moment Cam just dangled there, and she saw the flurry of parts moving within. "This is very little of me," he said at last. "This *I* is merely an organ, apparent to the whole only when I fail to perform my function. In the same way that you only attend to your stomach when your digestion is inadequate." It paused. "Yet, my wider mind is much the same. My consciousness lacks the illusion of unity that governs yours, Lee. Every individual aspect of my existence is governed by a separate centre of cognition. These meet as a council does, to report and make decisions. But their everyday business remains separate. I do not believe this is a native state, but it has come upon my species through our long lives. I am over one hundred million years old myself. Some of my kind are twice that. Gone so far into the cosmos that we will never hear from them again." Cam stopped, and Lee wondered for the first time if it had wanted to make that journey too.

"It was hard to make this part of me, this *I*, so I could speak to you," Cam continued. "But the greatest difficulty was not in absorbing your culture and language, alien as these were. It was in remembering how and why I should communicate with *anything*...outside the congress that makes up my own mind. I have spent millions of years travelling the stars, experiencing *everything* that there is. I've heard a thousand voices...and all of them are mine. But now there are others. It is hard to listen, yet after we part company—if we are successful in our task—there will be a part of my mind that speaks with your voice. For as long as I live, an impression of you will exist within me."

Mal came back with the news that Dr. Khan had, apparently, gone *out*. She found Lee quiet and wide-eyed, without words.

Kay Amal Khan was up top, on Cam's shell. By the time they finally located her, though, the moon was up, close to full. They could see her masked figure sitting, watching the stars. As they approached, she lifted her mask up. She hastily put something to her lips, then let out a cloud of what looked like smoke. The mask snapped shut.

"Dr. Khan," Lee said, weirdly scandalized. "Are you... smoking?"

Khan was distinctly unamused. "No, I am *vaping*, love," she said. "Because our beloved 'transport' digested a century of health warnings along with our language. So it won't let me light up inside. Only, after it sent me out here to this majestic bloody smoker's oubliette, I remembered there isn't enough *oxygen* out here to light up. So I am making do, love. I am making bloody do."

"We need to talk to you, Dr. Khan."

"Kay, sweetheart, just Kay." Khan went through the laborious task of taking another drag. "I'm handing my doctorate back," she said, sounding dog-tired and miserable. "Can't even do a simple thing like save the world, can I? I've gone back over *every* parallel where I put my plans into action. Nothing worked."

"Are you...drunk?" Lee asked.

"Little bit. Lucky Cam didn't take prohibition as seriously, right?" Khan sighed. "Not as drunk as I fucking want to be. What's up, kids?"

"We wanted to talk about the cracks between the worlds," Mal said.

"What's the matter? My maths not magical enough for you?" Khan demanded. "Wish I could conjure up a wardrobe and we could all escape through it? It ain't happening." Her head hung loosely, and then she shrugged. "Sorry. None of this is your fault. You shouldn't even *be* here. So talk, kids. What can Auntie Kay help you with?"

"These cracks, everyone's treating them like a symptom, right?"

Kay Amal Khan nodded. "It's how we know this whole universe is falling apart, sure."

"Is that the only way we know it's broken, though?" Lee pressed. "You had that proof...the one the Nissa sent you, that convinced you to go over to them. Was it about the cracks between worlds?"

"Not just that. There are other measurements that allow you to measure the deterioration. But having a fucking dinosaur or a giant bug monster turn up on your doorstep is more of a red flag, frankly." Khan examined her makeshift vaping device critically, then hurled it away. They watched it clack across the creature's shell before it bounded into the void. "What?" she demanded. "If you're going to lecture me about littering then you can f—"

"No," Lee said hurriedly. "But Mal and I were thinking..."

the Ediacaran is trying to communicate, using these timeline alternatives. Right?"

Khan shrugged. "Is that for certain? No. Is it likely? Maybe. But so what? It hasn't had anything useful to say, has it, other than 'You're not good enough. Try harder.'"

"And if it wasn't for the cracks between the worlds, the Nissa would never have found you, or the ice world... or anything. Everyone would have had a piece of the puzzle, but nobody would be able to solve it." Seeing Kay about to say nobody *had* solved it, Lee added hurriedly, "We couldn't even try."

Kay regarded them, her masked face unreadable. At last she said, "You think the Ediacaran was driving in those wedges itself, to make us all pool our resources?"

Lee spread her hands. "Just a thought. Because there have been cracks for millennia. So what if they're not a symptom, but part of the plan?"

"To wake us up?" Khan sounded halfway closer to sober than she had a moment ago. "The whole thing, from the Stone Age or whenever, just in case we ended up with some kind of science that could help? You've heard Auruthmer on what the Neanderthals found out there, right? All those worlds, and on most of 'em they're not exactly working up the general theory of relativity any time soon. There's only a handful of us that are even close to that, and we humans are the junior partners."

She looked down at her hands, and the moonlight shone across her visor. Tentatively, Lee and Mal sat down next to her.

"Only, we had a thought," Lee tried.

"Oh, did you." There was nothing in Kay's voice that

suggested she wanted to hear any thoughts. "I must have missed the bit—when Murther, Ertil, Cam and I were talking higher maths—where you had a contribution."

Lee was already halfway to her feet with a "Sorry to bother you" on her lips. But Mal wasn't having it.

"You said yourself, we're the junior partners," she snapped. "So what do *you* have to offer, Kay? Does human maths have somewhere to go that the Nissa haven't been stomping all over since the Bronze Age, or whatever? No, it's because you think differently to them. Same numbers, different ideas... and *we* had a different idea, and it's nothing like what anyone's been talking about. Probably it's bollocks. But what the hell, right? I mean, we have just been very firmly told that nothing we've tried has worked, right?"

Kay stared at her, all manner of hostility to be read in the cant of her mask. But then she said, "You're right. I am a fucking mean drunk, and I apologize. Sit, kids. Tell me what you've got. Literally cannot do any harm right now, you know?"

After ten minutes of mostly coherent explanation, Kay hauled them inside their host. They encountered Ertil first and started the ramble again, for his benefit. After that, it was time to call Murther. It was the middle of the night, but they made enough noise to ensure that nobody was sleeping. Kay had quite the audience by the time Murther clambered down into the avatar's chamber.

"So we have a new plan," Kay addressed them all grandly. "Maybe, possibly, a new plan. Everyone awake and ready?"

She visibly braced herself, looking at her audience. A mixture of sceptical, optimistic and hopeless faces looked back, their usual complement plus Murther.

"It's been put to me by our two brave kiddos here," Kay

said, still sounding slightly drunk, "that the Ediacaran might be opening rifts between timelines *deliberately*. To get the gang together. No cracks means no meeting of minds. So either the Ediacaran is taking advantage of this symptom of collapse, or... it's not a symptom, after all?"

Murther raised an objection, which Auruthmer translated. Their measurements proved that breaches affected timeline integrity. So breaches *must* cause timeline malfunction, rather than being messages.

"Which is right," Kay allowed. "But we've also all made a grand stinker of an assumption. One that is absolutely unconscionable in any serious scientist—correlation versus causation, right? What if we screwed the pooch right off the bat, guys? What if the medium *is* the message?"

Lee seriously doubted Khan's metaphors were making it through translation intact, but at least they baffled any potential critics into silence. Kay grinned wildly and met Lee's eyes. "What if maintaining timeline integrity *isn't* actually the answer? What if the Ediacaran is trying to lead us somewhere different... What if—wait for it—we're supposed to make the breaches worse rather than heal them?" She hastily waved down the swell of disagreement. "No, listen. They're connections between different timelines, after all. Like, you've got a load of poles that don't stand up straight, but you tie them together, cross-brace them, and they're just fine. And the breaches are the only things we've got that link the timelines together. So we don't get rid of them, we multiply them, make them our scaffolding.

"Huh?" she added, because the silence after her words was oppressively total. And then, after another few dragging seconds, "Well, how about it?"

"Do you have any models to support this?" Murther said mildly.

"Almost, yes. No. I have half of one." Kay's replies came in quick succession. "Look, this is all new thinking. I'm hoping you'll come in with me to work on the numbers, or else I'll still be plodding through them when the world ends. I have some preliminary equations that suggest it's not impossible . . . that we could reach a stable state when the timelines are interconnected. We thought the same would happen when the worlds were separated. But we've tried that. It's fallen over every single time. We can't save just one world. We can't save them all while maintaining an ivory tower isolation. So what are we left with?"

By that time, everyone else had caught up. Everyone had an opinion, too: they didn't like it. The two government types were against it; Stig was shaking his head and slapping the floor. Even Cam seemed to be raising an objection. Kay was trying to argue with everyone at once from sheer force of personality, with visibly diminishing returns.

"But then we've got *nothing*!" she insisted. "We can't keep repeating ourselves. We don't know how many more goes around we've got left!"

"That's right. We don't!" Murther confirmed. "We cannot waste our time on this. We need to refine our existing plan." She was jabbing at Auruthmer's shoulder as though that would get the translation out faster.

"We *have* refined it," Kay said flatly. "We have spent more time on this plan than the universe actually contains. We have done it forwards and sideways and ass-backwards. We cannot make it work."

"There is a great distance between 'cannot' and 'have not

yet,'" the Nissa scientist insisted. Then it seemed as if Auruthmer was arguing with *her*. Next everyone was talking over everyone else, the hard-walled chamber ringing with a babel of discordant voices and languages.

The cold came first, and the walls glittered as frost flowered across them in intricate, interlocking patterns. Then Charen Volkovska exploded into being halfway across the room. Everyone except for Cam's avatar quickly dropped back. She came in full regalia, a translucent, gleaming figure, crowned and robed and pale as death. Her eyes flashed and her face was set in an expression of regal displeasure. It stilled every voice.

"We have been here before," Charen said. As if to emphasize the force of her words, her image fuzzed briefly in and out of focus. "I have seen this moment a dozen times. I have seen this woman shouted down, over and over." A spectral hand singled out Kay. "We *fail*, each time. We *die*, each time. We are burning up our chances. Each new timeline starts closer to the inevitable end. Just try—try what she says. Try *something* new, because nothing else is working."

She was fading again. The tides of connection were carrying her further away, along that axis on which the parallels were strung. Lee saw her lips moving, but her voice was gone, and then so was she.

"Fuck me." Kay cleared frost from her eyebrows. "I guess that's more proof that the Ediacaran is watching us now... seeing if it gets to add this idea to the mix tape. Murther?"

The Nissa scientist stared at the ground, then let out a huge breath. When she replied, even Lee could translate it as "Yes."

And then Rove said, "No."

He had his phone in his hand. And Lee wondered if Charen's sudden vanishing had been something more than the vagaries of dimensional connections. Rove had seen Charen betray him before, after all, and who knew what safeguards he'd built into their relationship. Lee hadn't pegged him as a trusting man.

"We can't do this," Rove said flatly. "Whatever would be left, even if this plan worked, wouldn't resemble our world in any way. We can't just hold open the doors and let the monsters walk in and out as they wish." That his audience included several "monsters" didn't seem to register. "The only *point* of this circus is to save what is valuable to us. What you're proposing would destroy everything we are."

"And...save everything that there is," Kay responded uncertainly. "I mean, you understood that bit, didn't you?"

"The *sacrifice*," Rove pronounced deliberately, "is not worth it. Not to share it all with beasts. Find another way."

"We have tried," Kay said, as one would to a child. "That is the *point*. What I'm saying is—"

"I know what you're saying," Rove snapped. "Small wonder *you'd* prefer the sort of mongrel chaos you're proposing. Lucas, your gun."

"I am done working with you," Lucas said flatly.

Rove seemed to take that in his stride. In the next instant he had a gun of his own, a gold-plated thing that was obviously a surprise even to Lucas. "Then perhaps you'd put your own weapon on the floor," he suggested, "and kick it over to me."

"What's the plan here, Rove?" Julian asked. Lee could see various people around the room preparing to act. She tried to pluck at Mal's sleeve to dissuade her, but her friend was out of arm's reach, inching closer to Rove.

Rove's gun was aimed directly at Lucas, who slowly drew his own pistol out and placed it on the floor.

"The plan," Rove said, "is to preserve our world, Mr. Sabreur. *Our* world—as it should be preserved. To save our institutions, customs and way of life. Not to live in a world where the unspeakable is around every corner. And I'd have thought you'd agree. Do *you* really want to live in the world they're proposing?"

"Not really," Julian admitted. "Sounds like the lesser of two evils, though, compared to annihilation."

"But they *can* make it work!" Rove spat. "I've seen the maths. Until this latest nonsense from Khan, they were perfectly happy to keep trying, too. Mr. Sabreur, look at who you're standing with here. Not your sort of people, not at all. You can't just let them waltz in." He indicated the Cousins, Ertil, Cam...but his gesture might have taken in Khan, Lee and Mal too. And to Lee's amazement, Rove's voice trembled a little, a genuine mote of sentiment making itself known. "They're stronger than us, Sabreur. They'd make us their slaves, destroy us, colonize us."

"But you said they're not like us," Mal said, still inching nearer. "You seem to think they're *just* like us."

"Lucas, *kick over your gun*," Rove snapped, his pistol whipping to aim at Lucas's face.

Mal went to grab it just as Lucas flicked the weapon with his boot, and it span off across the room. Rove grabbed Mal's collar and pressed the gun to her temple.

"Now," he said, "we are going to go back to the original plan. Or I will start with this filthy sapphist here, and keep going."

"What are you going to do, force me to do maths with a

gun to my head?" Kay said, stomping forwards. Julian tried to get in her way, but she wasn't having any of it, and then the pistol jabbed in her direction.

"What?" she demanded. "You'll shoot me, now? Who'll do your precious thinking then?"

Rove snarled, a man who'd backed himself into an ideological corner. Suddenly, Mal bucked underneath him. Rove was slightly bigger and heavier; Mal was strong from four years spent hunting and gathering in a harsh world. She slung him off, sending him sliding across the floor. As Lee reached to grab Mal, Rove swung the pistol and pulled the trigger three times, his face purple with outrage.

The thunder of the gun was deafening in the enclosed chamber. Lee gathered Mal to her, looking for the blood that must surely be there, searching for the telltale holes in her clothes. There was nothing. Mal was shaking with shock, not from a hit.

Stig was kneeling before Rove, head down and arms wrapped around himself. She wasn't sure if the big man had been going for Rove already, or if he'd deliberately put himself in the way. He wasn't dead, but he hadn't been wearing body armour either.

Rove aimed the pistol at Lee and Mal over Stig's lowered head.

"I. Will. Shoot," Rove spat out. His eyes were bulging, lips drawn back from his neat white teeth. "I will shoot every last one of you. You will *not* do this to me."

"Put the gun down, Mr. Rove." Julian levelled Lucas's gun at Rove, who switched aim to return the favour.

"Mr. Sabreur," he said, forcing courtesy through his teeth. "You, of all people, should be on my side. We can force them to keep England sacred. We've all seen you come over to me, in one of those alternates. You're like me, inside." When Julian remained composed, he added with a nasty smile, "I know you're not going to pull the trigger. You're a desk-and-papers man, Sabreur."

"I would bring you back to face justice," Julian said, "but there aren't laws to cover what you've done...and your friends in high places would make sure you were just fine." His hands were shaking. Lee had assumed he was a steely-eyed James Bond type, but he'd almost certainly never held a gun in his life. He'd certainly never used one on another human being.

Rove's smile ratcheted up a notch. "Put it down, Mr. Sabreur. Or I will shoot you. That would be a waste, wouldn't it? Or perhaps I'll shoot Dr. Khan, who seems to be the architect of this intolerable situation."

He shifted to point his gun at Kay, and Lee saw his finger tighten on the trigger. Then Stig straightened up with a bestial roar. One meaty forearm knocked Rove's gun arm aside as he squeezed his throat. Rove squeaked, sounding more animal than human. Then Stig's broad fingers clenched. The resulting crack was almost as loud as the gunshot that followed.

Lee looked around frantically, in case Rove had posthumously killed Dr. Khan after all. Instead, the bullet had gone into Cam's avatar, blasting away a chunk of its head. Fragments of disarticulated limbs trickled from the hole. Even as she watched, more legs were winding through the mass, weaving its cranium back into shape.

Stig dropped Rove's limp body and sat down heavily. There was a lot of blood across his midriff, and Lee hoped that the small calibre of the gun and the dense Neanderthal musculature would preserve him. Auruthmer, Julian and Mal rushed over, peeling back his gory poncho to look at the damage. Lee sagged against the wall, awash with sheer panicky adrenaline—and Kay slumped down beside her, her face bleak.

Before she could say anything, Lee said, "Not your fault."

"My idea," Kay said hoarsely. "Fuck me, you don't get this kind of heckling from the Royal Society."

"Not your fault," Lee repeated, and then they were both in Murther's shadow, the Cousin prodding Kay with one foot.

"Time to do the hard sums, I guess," she said, letting Murther help her up.

Postscript

I

"We are facing a period of unparalleled disruption," Dr. Khan said gravely, staring at the camera. She had dressed up for the occasion, immaculate suit, hair neatly styled, every inch the serious scientist. There wasn't a half-finished cigarette in sight. They'd even found a desk for her to sit at, positioned before shelves of leather-bound books. The memes of the academic at work, reinforcing this message to the world. "The word 'catastrophe' may not be out of place," she went on. "Thankfully, all calculations show that we have a little time to prepare, perhaps a decade, perhaps less. Certainly no more. The timeline integration that I've described is inevitable. It *is* going to happen. The governments of the world can either prepare or ignore it and suffer the consequences. I'd hope that there is an obvious choice out of those two."

She glanced to her left, where Ertil was sitting. The rat-creature's double-thumbed hands were resting on the desk, and he glanced towards Khan and nodded periodically. Watching as Cam recorded her speech, Julian had felt the monster possessed the solemn poise of a newsreader. But watching it now, played back, the effect was far more of a glove puppet. It added a horribly inappropriate air of farce to Khan's statement.

"We are going to see colossal environmental changes as time goes on," Khan continued. "Invasive species from other timelines will be turning up all over the world. And we won't be able to eliminate these new arrivals or prevent them from coming. We'll have to work with what we've got.

"And there will be some intrusions that will require the action of diplomats, not conservationists. There will be intelligent entities who stray into our world by accident, and those who come here because they are fleeing privation or persecution. There will be people from our world who fall through the gaps to elsewhere, and those who choose to leave. There are worlds out there that will need protecting from us, and worlds we will need protection from. We are entering a new age of our planet's history. And while we have staved off Armageddon—for now—that doesn't rule out this being an extinction-level event for humanity.

"If the governments of Earth, our Earth, can get their act together and put away their rivalries, we can rise to face these challenges together. And the time to start working on these future problems is today. I can't stress this strongly enough. Speaking as an academic, a scientist, I have no power to force such cooperation or such foresight. I can only state my case as forcefully as possible and hope that sane minds prevail. But that's on you, all of you."

She took a deep breath and leant back in her chair. She was drumming the fingers of one hand on the desk, which Julian knew meant she was desperate for a smoke. The recording had taken nineteen attempts, after all. Everyone involved had been getting short with one another.

Ertil tapped politely at Kay's elbow. "This is Ertil," she explained. "His people live next door to our world, or just about. Some of his people are already in our world, and there will be more. They're also ahead of us, technology-wise. They've cured cancer! How about that? They could potentially do a load of good for everyone." She glanced to her other side, and Murther shuffled into view.

"Murther's people have been skipping from Earth to Earth for ages." Khan eyed the Cousin scientist. "They have a lot of great tech too, and they've solved all sorts of problems that we haven't. And they'll help, if we behave ourselves! This is our big opportunity to be part of something bigger and get all the good stuff." Someone obviously made a signal to her off camera—Julian remembered it had been him, in fact— because Kay rolled her eyes and shrugged. "Loves, I am all out of this diplomacy stuff. What more can I say? This is a thing that's happening." She looked directly to the camera once more. "Along with my 'Christmas Message,' you're getting my proofs, my equations, all nicely set out. Any physicist who wants to double-check these signs of impending doom can do so. They can then confirm to their local representatives that yes, this phase of Earth's history is on its way out. And no, you can't do anything to stop it. Believe me— and feel free to check the workings in the appendices—we looked at every other damn possibility. We checked if we could carry on in splendid isolation, and it was a bust." She grinned abruptly. "That's it, I'm done, loves. Show it to your presidents, show it to the Queen. Show it to the chairmen, your premiers and the Pope." She got up abruptly, forcing Ertil to scrabble at the tabletop to remain seated on his high stool. "Peace out," were the last words of Dr. Kay Amal Khan's message to the human race.

Leslie Hind had watched this in her office, stony-faced, as

Julian and Alison shifted awkwardly in their seats. After the recording ended, she regarded the static on the screen for a long time.

"I dearly want," she said at last, "to ask if this is a joke, in incredibly poor taste. But we have the RAF all over the sky above London right now. That alone is ample evidence that it is not." She stared at them both in turn. "What am I supposed to do with this, Julian? Alison?"

Julian squared his shoulders. "You'll have to take it to the Home Secretary. Who has to take it to the Prime Minister. Who will have to take it to the UN. And this recording isn't just with us, either. Every government will have a copy by now. I'd guess you have maybe two weeks before it starts appearing on YouTube, if that. What we have to do is act on this information. Start talking, making plans. Decide whether we're going to accept help from our new neighbours—working with whatever price they set—or go it alone, hoping we'll be able to manage."

Hind stared at them. "And you saw all this, did you? These...other Earths?" For a moment there was a hint of wistfulness in her voice, that she had been sat behind a desk while her subordinates had been off having...adventures.

"Yes," Julian confirmed, and it struck him that his reliable if unimaginative reputation was finally coming into its own. "It's all true. Rat-creatures, dinosaurs, cavemen and, well, you've seen..."

"We've all seen," Hind confirmed bleakly. "Perhaps you can explain just what we're seeing." Her eyes didn't even stray to the window, where the hardest possible evidence of all was putting the Thames in its shadow.

"That's Cam," Alison explained. "It's a person from another Earth where sentient life evolved a lot earlier. And it's here

590

because it has...humans on the brain? Maybe that's the best way of putting it. It had to learn how to interact with us, and now it's interested in us. It has kin scattered across a half-dozen Earths right now too. Maybe tomorrow they'll all get bored and return to deep space—yes, they can do that—or maybe they'll stick around and become the backbone of a new interdimensional United Nations. Or teach *us* how to reach deep space. Or some other thing. It's not as though we can force them to do anything."

"What's to stop this 'Cam' from destroying London with its laser vision or whatever the hell it's hiding under the bonnet?" Hind asked.

"Absolutely nothing," said Alison, which wasn't the reassuring answer Julian had lined up. "But it has no reason to kill us all. It's a self-sufficient entity with the universe at its disposal, and now there are a slew of extra universes for it to investigate. We have nothing it needs—it's just interested in our uniqueness as life forms. That's something we can trade on without any cost to ourselves...and we might get all manner of invaluable information in return. If we're bold enough. If we're open-minded enough." She was looking at Hind, her expression willing her to understand. "Leslie, do you remember your poets? Andrew Marvell? 'Had we but world enough, and time...' As a species, we're facing the greatest challenge to our existence we've ever known, to our societies, our beliefs, to everything we hold dear. But as Dr. Khan said, it's the greatest opportunity too. There *is* world enough, *and* time now. All we have to do is work together." She lapsed into silence, hoping her boss was with them.

Hind paused. "And you retain your...privileged status, with the alien computer you described in your report?"

"Oh, yes." Alison nodded.

"And Dr. Khan. Where is she now?"

Her subordinates let a few seconds pass, waiting to see who would field the thorny question.

"On her own recognisance, right now," Julian confirmed at last. "She'll be back, I'm sure. Although I suspect she'll want to set some conditions. She has just made herself the lightning rod for every dissatisfied nut job and angry government on the planet."

"Yes, I see that." Hind's profoundly troubled look lasted whole seconds before being banished behind her customary unflappable reserve. "I'll arrange to speak with the Home Secretary as a matter of urgency. Given the situation out there"—she eyed the sky above the Thames—"I think he'll be delighted to hear even the most tenuous explanation. Currently we have three terrorist organizations and a cult trying to claim responsibility. Interdimensional aliens is almost a more palatable alternative. As for you two, not a word of this to another living soul." And, seeing something rebellious in them, she added, "For now. I'm well aware this cannot remain a secret, but at least give me a running start. But you'll have people to call who need to know that you're home and safe. I trust you both to do that without a handler listening in." She permitted herself one-third of a smile. "You've done as well as anyone might, given what can only be considered extremely adverse circumstances."

*

Nineteen days had passed since Kay and her confederates had put their new plan into action.

Nineteen days without any obvious deviation in the relationship between the timelines. As Kay had explained, the connections between them would grow from intermittent cracks to permanent doors, binding them all together. And according to their predictions, they would do so in a way that left each Earth intact but permanently linked at a multitude of points with its interdimensional siblings. Julian found himself thinking of Mal and Lee's half stone circle, where both ancient dinosaur descendants and ape descendants had worked to mark out a crossing. That place would be a permanent full circle soon enough, a door from here to there. Perhaps many ancient ritual sites would gain fresh significance. The New Age pagans would go bonkers, he knew. So would the conspiracy nuts and the UFO guys and every different flavour of fundamentalist. In fact, going bonkers was probably a rational response to what was happening.

"You put the report in about Lucas May?" Alison pushed.

Julian nodded. "All filed. Leaves something of a bad taste in the mouth, all told. Especially as he shot me that once. But it's not about how I feel." Lucas was currently being held in custody, in reasonable comfort. Given what he knew about Rove, Julian had recommended cautious overtures of recruitment. He didn't like the man, but Lucas did seem to be competent, and turning against Rove counted for something.

Standing in the office lobby, with the daily bustle of the department going on oblivious around them, they both let out a long sigh of relief.

"What now?" Alison said. She looked as flat as he felt, he thought. Turned out coming back down to Earth was a bit of an anticlimax, even if it was a hugely welcome one.

"I have to call Josie," he said automatically.

They stood there, Alison nodding reasonably.

"I should probably call Derek. Later. After a drink, maybe. Or a week. Where the hell are *we*, Spiker?"

He wanted to pick her up and carry her off, was what he *wanted* to do. He was absolutely bursting with the need to tell her...just how much he loved her. The one time they'd got together, for real—that was the true him. That was the man who'd finally shaken off the shackles and followed his heart. Instead of words, which would just have stuck in his throat, he reached for her, and they held each other.

"I'll call Josie," he said finally. "I'll go home and be a responsible human being. But then we need to talk about us. You, me and Josie need to have that talk." All beautifully worded to avoid committing to any particular proposals.

Alison nodded, squeezed his arm and then let go. "You do that," she agreed, as respectable as ever. But they were both smiling, somewhat shyly. And as she was turning to go, she said, "You know how much polyamory there is in Josie's books, right? Just saying."

II

Stig looked utterly sour when he came out to greet them, but Lee reckoned she knew him by now. There was a glint in his eye and a certain tilt to his head when he scowled off into the distance which said he was pleased to see them.

He was still moving gingerly, and his abdomen was bulked out with what was probably more complicated than a bandage. They hadn't had the full Nissa medical kit with them on board Cam, so he was healing slower than he might, but he was already back on his feet. He wouldn't be on any active expeditions for a while, but would instead be tutoring new recruits for the interdimensional-explorer business.

"Still want to do this, do you?" he muttered, as though they were either mad or had been stringing him along.

"Absolutely." Lee clasped Mal's hand. They were robed like natives, hoods up against the drizzling rain. It hadn't let up since they'd arrived.

"Not going to be easy," Stig went on mournfully, rivulets finding paths down the lines of his face. "Worlds out there, they won't ever have seen a hominid before. Worlds been at war for a thousand years, worlds that're nothing but ruins. All kinds of bad stuff."

"Don't oversell it, there," Mal said. "Anyone'd think you didn't want to see the back of us."

"Besides, we'll have one of Cam's lot watching over us, like a mothership," Lee pointed out. "It'll be like Star Trek. And you'll be able to talk to us wherever we are, right? You've got the tech for that."

There was already a network of Nissa expeditions, spanning many different Earths. It was part of a programme they'd been pushing for generations. Of all the different civilizations that had arisen, on all the different Earths, only the Nissa had grown up from barbarism to civilization knowing that they weren't alone. There were colossal machines across the Nissa's home world that could open portals with the expenditure of vast quantities of energy. Other machines drew energy from the world tree, from the interaction between its branches that could power everything they needed.

This begged one question that Lee had been mulling over.

"If the first plan had gone through, and all the worlds had been separated, what would that have done to your people, Stig?"

His eyes swivelled about, the usual embarrassed-looking act the Nissa put on. "Nothing good," he said at last, spreading his big hands. "Lose a lot of what we have, probably. Lights going out, transport stops, still a little power coming in but mostly we have to make do without."

"Nobody said that. Ever," Lee pointed out. "Murther, Auruthmer and you—you never said, 'We can't do this, it'll destroy us.'"

"We thought, if we don't do it, everything gets destroyed. Where's the choice, then? But this is better. Thanks to Dr. Khan. And you."

It was Lee's turn to feel awkward, but she was saved by a sudden drop in temperature. Rain turned to sleet in a column of air three metres across. The shimmering figure of Charen Volkovska appeared, hazy as a ghost. She seemed simultaneously bounded within that circle and far, far away along some ethereal axis. Mal and Lee were getting their outward fare paid this way, without drawing on the Nissa's reserves of power.

"Are you ready?" Her voice was faint, but the dashes of sleet seemed to shiver with the rhythm of her words.

"Good to go," Mal confirmed.

"Then your carriage awaits."

Lee still wasn't sure about Volkovska. Whether she was still human or not at all. Perhaps her final translation into the ice meant they were communicating with something completely other, her image as shallow a mask as Cam's dangling avatar.

Mal gripped her hand tightly. "Shall we?"

As Lee nodded, Charen raised a wisp of a hand. "I should warn you. In recent days, my hosts have begun to take notice. They've realized their work has been involved in affairs beyond its original purpose."

Lee took a moment to disentangle her words. "You mean the fish-people are waking up?"

Charen tilted her head. "They are paying an interest. What that means is beyond my ability to guess at present. I hope to act as an intermediary though, if circumstances permit. Does this change your minds at all?"

Lee and Mal exchanged one quick glance, and they both shook their heads.

"Good." Charen's indistinct face was smiling. "We who have been to the ends of the Earths and returned...we have many leagues further to travel."

An eye blink later, there was just Stig, standing outside the domed house in the rain.

SPECIAL ACKNOWLEDGEMENTS

Andrew McGrouther for assistance with police procedure.

Simon Roy and Memo Koseman for their "dinosauroids," which were (with permission) a significant inspiration for this book.

Brian Third for advice on computer intrusions and hacking.

Maxwell Barclay, Dr. Megan Williams, Dr. Emily Mitchell, Michael Czajkowski and @JUNIUS_64 for their advice on matters palaeontological and biological.

Olivia Michaud and Eliska Bejrova for a tour of the Mount Pleasant Mail Rail system.

Also:

Stephen Jay Gould for his always inspirational *Wonderful Life*.

Curtis Congreve, Amanda Falk and James Lamsdell of the podcast *Palaeo After Dark*. Autun Purser for his superb artwork. John VandenBrooks of Arizona State University.

And the usual suspects, who have held my hand and allowed me to get away with this sort of thing for years: Annie, my wife, Simon Kavanagh, my agent, and Bella Pagan and everyone at Pan Macmillan.

And finally:

The staff of my local Cielo and Waterstones cafes for providing such pleasant writing environments. And coffee.

extras

meet the author

Photo credit: Ante Vukorepa

ADRIAN TCHAIKOVSKY is the author of the acclaimed ten-book Shadows of the Apt series, the Echoes of the Fall series, and other novels, novellas, and short stories including *Children of Time* (which won the Arthur C. Clarke award in 2016) and its sequel, *Children of Ruin* (which won the British Science Fiction Award in 2020). He lives in Leeds in the UK and his hobbies include entomology and board and role-playing games.

Find out more about Adrian Tchaikovsky and other Orbit authors by registering for the free monthly newsletter at www .orbitbooks.net.

if you enjoyed
THE DOORS OF EDEN

look out for

CHILDREN OF TIME

by

Adrian Tchaikovsky

Who will inherit this new Earth?

The last remnants of the human race left a dying Earth, desperate to find a new home among the stars. Following in the footsteps of their ancestors, they discover the greatest treasure of the past age—a world terraformed and prepared for human life.

But all is not right in this new Eden. In the long years since the planet was abandoned, the work of its architects has borne disastrous fruit. The planet is not waiting for them, pristine and unoccupied. New masters have turned it from a refuge into mankind's worst nightmare.

Now two civilizations are on a collision course, both testing the boundaries of what they will do to survive. As the fate of humanity hangs in the balance, who are the true heirs of this new Earth?

1.1   JUST A BARREL OF MONKEYS

There were no windows in the Brin 2 facility—rotation meant that "outside" was always "down," underfoot, out of mind. The wall screens told a pleasant fiction, a composite view of the world below that ignored their constant spin, showing the planet as hanging stationary-still off in space: the green marble to match the blue marble of home, twenty light years away. Earth had been green, in her day, though her colours had faded since. Perhaps never as green as this beautifully crafted world though, where even the oceans glittered emerald with the phytoplankton maintaining the oxygen balance within its atmosphere. How delicate and many-sided was the task of building a living monument that would remain stable for geological ages to come.

It had no officially confirmed name beyond its astronomical designation, although there was a strong vote for "Simiana" amongst some of the less imaginative crewmembers. Doctor Avrana Kern now looked out upon it and thought only of *Kern's World*. Her project, her dream, *her* planet. The first of many, she decided.

This is the future. This is where mankind takes its next great step. This is where we become gods.

"This is the future," she said aloud. Her voice would sound in every crewmember's auditory centre, all nineteen of them, though fifteen were right here in the control hub with her. Not the true hub, of course—the gravity-denuded axle about which they revolved: that was for power and processing, and their payload.

"This is where mankind takes its next great step." Her speech had taken more of her time than any technical details over the last two days. She almost went on with the line about them becoming gods, but that was for her only. *Far too controversial, given the* Non Ultra Natura *clowns back home.* Enough of a stink had been raised over projects like hers already. Oh, the differences between the current Earth factions went far deeper: social, economic, or simply *us* and *them*, but Kern had got the Brin launched—all those years ago—against mounting opposition. By now the whole idea had become a kind of scapegoat for the divisions of the human race. *Bickering primates, the lot of them. Progress is what matters. Fulfilling the potential of humanity, and of all other life.* She had always been one of the fiercest opponents of the growing conservative backlash most keenly exemplified by the *Non Ultra Natura* terrorists. *If they had their way, we'd all end up back in the caves. Back in the trees. The whole* point *of civilization is that we exceed the limits of nature, you tedious little primitives.*

"We stand on others' shoulders, of course." The proper line, that of accepted scientific humility, was, "on the shoulders of giants," but she had not got where she was by bowing the knee to past generations. *Midgets, lots and lots of midgets,* she thought, and then—she could barely keep back the appalling giggle—*on the shoulders of monkeys.*

At a thought from her, one wallscreen and their Mind's Eye HUDs displayed the schematics of Brin 2 for them all. She wanted to direct their attention and lead them along with her towards the proper appreciation of her—sorry, *their*—triumph. There: the needle of the central core encircled by the ring of life and science that was their torus-shaped world. At one end of the core was the unlovely bulge of the Sentry Pod, soon to be cast adrift to become the universe's loneliest and longest research post. The opposite end of the needle sported the Barrel and the Flask. Contents: monkeys and the future, respectively.

"Particularly I have to thank the engineering teams under Doctors Fallarn and Medi for their tireless work in reformatting—" and she almost now said "Kern's World" without meaning to— "our subject planet to provide a safe and nurturing environment for our great project." Fallarn and Medi were well on their way back to Earth, of course, their fifteen-year work completed, their thirty-year return journey begun. It was all stage-setting, though, to make way for Kern and her dream. *We are—I am—what all this work is for.*

A journey of twenty light years home. Whilst thirty years drag by on Earth, only twenty will pass for Fallarn and Medi in their cold coffins. For them, their voyage is nearly as fast as light. What wonders we can accomplish!

From her viewpoint, engines to accelerate her to most of the speed of light were no more than pedestrian tools to move her about a universe that Earth's biosphere was about to inherit. *Because humanity may be fragile in ways we cannot dream, so we cast our net wide and then wider...*

Human history was balanced on a knife edge. Millennia of ignorance, prejudice, superstition and desperate striving had brought them at last to this: that humankind would beget new sentient life in its own image. Humanity would no longer be alone. Even in the unthinkably far future, when Earth itself had fallen in fire and dust, there would be a legacy spreading across the stars—an infinite and expanding variety of Earth-born life diverse enough to survive any reversal of fortune until the death of the whole universe, and perhaps even beyond that. *Even if we die, we will live on in our children.*

Let the NUNs preach their dismal all-eggs-in-one-basket creed of human purity and supremacy, she thought. *We will out-evolve them. We will leave them behind. This will be the first of a thousand worlds that we will give life to.*

For we are gods, and we are lonely, so we shall create...

Back home, things were tough, or so the twenty-year-old images indicated. Avrana had skimmed dispassionately over the riots, the furious debates, the demonstrations and violence, thinking only, *How did we ever get so far with so many fools in the gene pool?* The *Non Ultra Natura* lobby were only the most extreme of a whole coalition of human political factions—the conservative, the philosophical, even the die-hard religious—who looked at progress and said that enough was enough. Who fought tooth and nail against further engineering of the human genome, against the removal of limits on AI, and against programs like Avrana's own.

And yet they're losing.

The terraforming would still be going on elsewhere. Kern's World was just one of many planets receiving the attentions of people like Fallarn and Medi, transformed from inhospitable chemical rocks—Earth-like only in approximate size and distance from the sun—into balanced ecosystems that Kern could have walked on without a suit in only minor discomfort. After the monkeys had been delivered and the Sentry Pod detached to monitor them, those other gems were where her attention would next be drawn. *We will seed the universe with all the wonders of Earth.*

In her speech, which she was barely paying attention to, she meandered down a list of other names, from here or at home. The person she really wanted to thank was herself. She had fought for this, her engineered longevity allowing her to carry the debate across several natural human lifetimes. She had clashed in the financiers' rooms and in the laboratories, at academic symposiums and on mass entertainment feeds just to make this happen.

I, I have done this. With your hands have I built, with your eyes have I measured, but the mind is mine alone.

Her mouth continued along its prepared course, the words boring her even more than they presumably bored her listeners. The real audience for this speech would receive it in twenty years' time: the final confirmation back home of the way things were due to be. Her mind touched base with the Brin 2's hub. *Confirm Barrel systems*, she pinged into her relay link with the facility's control computer; it was a check that had become a nervous habit of late.

Within tolerance, it replied. And if she probed behind that bland summary, she would see precise readouts of the lander craft, its state of readiness, even down to the vital signs of its ten-thousand-strong primate cargo, the chosen few who would inherit, if not the Earth, then at least this planet, whatever it would be called.

Whatever *they* would eventually call it, once the uplift nanovirus had taken them that far along the developmental road. The biotechs estimated that a mere thirty or forty monkey generations would bring them to the stage where they might make contact with the Sentry Pod and its lone human occupant.

Alongside the Barrel was the Flask: the delivery system for the virus that would accelerate the monkeys along their way— they would stride, in a mere century or two, across physical and mental distances that had taken humanity millions of long and hostile years.

extras

Another group of people to thank, for she herself was no bio-tech specialist. She had seen the specs and the simulations, though, and expert systems had examined the theory and summarized it in terms that she, a mere polymath genius, could understand. The virus was clearly an impressive piece of work, as far as she could grasp it. Infected individuals would produce offspring mutated in a number of useful ways: greater brain size and complexity, greater body size to accommodate it, more flexible behavioural paths, swifter learning... The virus would even recognize the presence of infection in other individuals of the same species, so as to promote selective breeding, the best of the best giving birth to even better. It was a whole future in a microscopic shell, almost as smart, in its single-minded little way, as the creatures that it would be improving. It would interact with the host genome at a deep level, replicate within its cells like a new organelle, passing itself on to the host's offspring until the entire species was subject to its benevolent contagion. No matter how much change the monkeys underwent, that virus would adapt and adjust to whatever genome it was partnered with, analysing and modelling and improvising with whatever it inherited—until something had been engineered that could look its creators in the eye and understand.

She had sold it to the people back home by describing how colonists would reach the planet then, descending from the skies like deities to meet their new people. Instead of a harsh, untamed world, a race of uplifted sentient aides and servants would welcome their makers. That was what she had told the boardrooms and the committees back on Earth, but it had never been the point of the exercise for her. The monkeys were the point, and what they would become.

This was one of the things the NUNs were most incensed about. They shouted about making superbeings out of mere beasts. In truth, like spoiled children, it was *sharing* that they objected to. Only-child humanity craved the sole attention of the universe. Like so many other projects hoisted as political issues, the virus's development had been fraught with protests, sabotage, terrorism and murder.

And yet we triumph over our own base nature at last, Kern reflected with satisfaction. And of course, there was a tiny grain of truth to the insults the NUNs threw her way, because she *didn't* care about colonists or the neo-imperialistic dreams of her fellows. She wanted to make new life, in her image as much as in humanity's. She wanted to know what might evolve, what society, what understandings, when her monkeys were left to their own simian devices . . . To Avrana Kern, *this* was her price, her reward for exercising her genius for the good of the human race: this experiment; this planetary what-if. Her efforts had opened up a string of terraformed worlds, but her price was that the firstborn would be *hers*, and home to her new-made people.

She was aware of an expectant silence and realized that she had got to the end of her speech, and now everyone thought she was just adding gratuitous suspense to a moment that needed no gilding.

"Mr. Sering, are you in position?" she asked on open channel, for everyone's benefit. Sering was the volunteer, the man they were going to leave behind. He would orbit their planet-sized laboratory as the long years turned, locked in cold sleep until the time came for him to become mentor to a new race of sentient primates. She almost envied him, for he would see and hear and experience things that no other human ever had. He would be the new Hanuman: the monkey god.

Almost envied, but in the end Kern rather preferred to be departing to undertake other projects. Let others become gods of mere single worlds. She herself would stride the stars and head up the pantheon.

"I am not in position, no." And apparently he felt that was also deserving of a wider audience, because he had broadcast it on the general channel.

Kern felt a stab of annoyance. *I cannot physically do everything myself. Why is it that other people so often fail to meet my standards, when I rely on them?* To Sering alone she sent, "Perhaps you would explain why?"

"I was hoping to be able to say a few words, Doctor Kern."

It would be his last contact with his species for a long time, she knew, and it seemed appropriate. If he could make a good showing then it would only add to her legend. She held ready on the master comms, though, setting him on a few seconds' delay, just in case he became maudlin or started saying something inappropriate.

"This is a turning point in human history," Sering's voice—always slightly mournful—came to her, and then through her to everyone else. His image was in their Mind's Eye HUDs, with the collar of his bright orange environment suit done up high to the chin. "I had to think long and hard before committing myself to this course, as you can imagine. But some things are too important. Sometimes you have to just do the right thing, whatever the cost."

Kern nodded, pleased with that. *Be a good monkey and finish up soon, Sering. Some of us have legacies to build.*

"We have come so far, and still we fall into the oldest errors," Sering continued doggedly. "We're standing here with the universe in our grasp and, instead of furthering our own destinies, we connive at our own obsolescence."

Her attention had drifted a little and, by the time she realized what he had said, the words had passed on to the crew. She registered suddenly a murmur of concerned messages between them, and even simple spoken words whispered between those closest to her. Doctor Mercian meanwhile sent her an alert on another channel: "Why is Sering in the engine core?"

Sering should not be in the engine core of the needle. Sering should be in the Sentry Pod, ready to take his place in orbit—and in history.

She cut Sering off from the crew and sent him an angry demand to know what he thought he was doing. For a moment his avatar stared at her in her visual field, then it lip-synced to his voice.

"You have to be stopped, Doctor Kern. You and all your kind—your new humans, new machines, new species. If you succeed here, then there will be other worlds—you've said so yourself, and I know they're terraforming them even now. It ends here. *Non Ultra Natura!* No greater than nature."

She wasted vital moments of potential dissuasion by resorting to personal abuse, until he spoke again.

"I've cut you off, Doctor. Do the same to me if you wish, but for now I'm going to speak and you don't get to interrupt me."

She was trying to override him, hunting through the control computer's systems to find what he had done, but he had locked her out elegantly and selectively. There were whole areas of the facility's systems that just did not appear on her mental schematic, and when she quizzed the computer about them, it refused to acknowledge their existence. None of them was mission critical—not the Barrel, not the Flask, not even the Sentry Pod—therefore none were the systems she had been obsessively checking every day.

Not mission critical, perhaps, but *facility* critical.

"He's disabled the reactor safeties," Mercian reported. "What's going on? Why's he in the engine core at all?" Alarm but not outright panic, which was a good finger in the air for the mood of the crew all around.

He is in the engine core because his death will be instant and total and therefore probably painless, Kern surmised. She was already moving, to the surprise of the others. She was heading up, climbing into the access shaft that led to the slender central pylon of the station, heading away from the outer floor that remained "down" only so long as she was close to it; climbing up out of that spurious gravity well towards the long needle they all revolved around. There was a flurry of increasingly concerned messages. Voices called out at her heels. Some of them would follow her, she knew.

Sering was continuing blithely: "This is not even the beginning, Doctor Kern." His tone was relentlessly deferential even in rebellion. "Back home it will have already started. Back home it is probably already over. In another few years, maybe, you'll hear that Earth and our future have been taken back for the humans. No uplifted monkeys, Doctor Kern. No godlike computers. No freakshows of the human form. We'll have the universe to ourselves, as we were intended to—as was always our destiny. On all the colonies, in the solar system and out, our agents will have made their move. We will have taken power—with the consent of the majority, you understand, Doctor Kern."

And she was lighter and lighter, hauling herself towards an "up" that was becoming an "in." She knew she should be cursing Sering, but what was the point if he would never hear her?

It was not such a long way to the weightlessness of the needle's hollow interior. She had her choice then: either towards the engine core, where Sering had no doubt taken steps to ensure that he would not be disturbed; or away. Away, in a very final sense.

She could override anything Sering had done. She had full confidence in the superiority of her abilities. It would take time, though. If she cast herself that way down the needle, towards Sering and his traps and locked barriers, then time would be something she would not have the benefit of.

"And if the powers-that-be refuse us, Doctor Kern," that hateful voice continued in her ear, "then we will fight. If we must wrest mankind's destiny back by force, then we shall."

She barely took in what he was saying, but a cold sense of fear was creeping into her mind—not from the danger to her and the Brin 2, but what he was saying about Earth and the colonies. *A war? Impossible. Not even the NUNs...* But it was true there had been some incidents—assassinations, riots, bombs. The whole of Europa Base had been compromised. The NUNs were spitting into the inevitable storm of manifest destiny, though. She had always believed that. Such outbursts represented the last throes of humanity's under-evolvers.

She was now heading the other way, distancing herself from the engine core as though the Brin had enough space within it for her to escape the coming blast. She was utterly rational, however. She knew exactly where she was going.

Ahead of her was the circular portal to the Sentry Pod. Only on seeing it did she realize that some part of her mind—the part she always relied on to finesse the more complex calculations—had already fully understood the current situation and discerned the one slim-but-possible way out.

This was where Sering was supposed to be. This was the slow boat to the future that he—in a sane timeline—would have been piloting. Now she ordered the door to open, relieved to discover that this—the one piece of equipment that was actually his particular business—seemed to have remained free of Sering's meddling.

The first explosion came, and she thought it was the last one. The Brin creaked and lurched around her, but the engine core remained stable—as evidenced by the fact that she herself had not been disintegrated. She tuned back into the wild whirl of frantic messaging between the crew. Sering had rigged the escape pods. He didn't want anyone avoiding the fate he had decreed for himself. Had he somehow forgotten the Sentry Pod?

The detonating pods would push the Brin 2 out of position, drifting either towards the planet or off into space. She had to get clear.

The door opened at her command, and she had the Sentry hub run a diagnostic on the release mechanism. There was so little space inside, just the cold-sleep coffin—*don't think of it as a coffin!*—and the termini of its associated systems.

The hub was querying her—she was not the right person, nor was she wearing the proper gear for prolonged cold sleep. *But I don't intend to be here for centuries, just long enough to ride it out.* She swiftly overrode its quibbles, and by that time the diagnostics had pinpointed Sering's tampering, or rather identified, by process of elimination, those parts of the release process that he had erased from its direct notice.

Sounds from outside suggested that the best course of action was to order the door closed, and then lock the systems so that nobody from outside could intrude on her.

She climbed into the cold-sleep tank, and around that time the banging started; those others of the crew who had come to the same realization as her, but slightly later. She blocked out their messaging. She blocked out Sering too, who was obviously not going to tell her anything useful now. It was better if she didn't have to share her head with anyone except the hub control systems.

She had no idea how much time she had, but she worked with the trademark balance of speed and care that had got her where she was now. *Got me leading the Brin 2 facility and got me here in the Sentry Pod. What a clever, doomed monkey I am.* The muffled banging was more insistent, but the pod only had room for one. Her heart had always been hard, but she found that she had to harden it still further, and not think of all those names and faces, her loyal colleagues, that she and Sering between them were condemning to an explosive end.

Which I myself have not yet escaped, she reminded herself. And then she had it: a work-around jury-rigged release path that avoided Sering's ghost systems. Would it work? She had no opportunity for a dry run, nor had she any other options. Nor, she suspected, any time.

Release, she ordered the hub, and then shouted down all of the different ways it was programmed to ask "Are you sure?," until she felt the movement of mechanisms around her.

if you enjoyed
THE DOORS OF EDEN

look out for

NOPHEK GLOSS

by

Essa Hansen

When a young man's planet is destroyed, he sets out on a single-minded quest for revenge across the galaxy in Nophek Gloss, *the first book in this epic space opera trilogy by debut author Essa Hansen, for fans of Star Wars and* Children of Time.

Caiden's planet is destroyed. His family gone. And his only hope for survival is a crew of misfit aliens and a mysterious ship that seems to have a soul and a universe of its own. Together, they will show him that the universe is much bigger, much more advanced, and much more mysterious than Caiden had ever imagined. But the universe hides dangers as well, and soon, Caiden has his own plans.

He vows to do anything it takes to get revenge on the slavers who murdered his people and took away his home. To destroy their regime, he must infiltrate and dismantle them from the inside, or die trying.

CHAPTER 1

TENDED AND DRIVEN

The overseers had taken all the carcasses, at least. The lingering stench of thousands of dead bovines wafted on breezes, prowling the air. Caiden crawled from an aerator's cramped top access port and comforting scents of iron and chemical. Outside, he inhaled, and the death aroma hit him. He gagged and shielded his nose in an oily sleeve.

"Back in there, kid," his father shouted from the ground.

Caiden crept to the machine's rust-eaten rim, twelve meters above where his father's wiry figure stood bristling with tools.

"I need a break!" Caiden wiped his eyes, smearing them with black grease he noticed too late. Vertebrae crackled into place when he stretched, cramped for hours in ducts and chemical housing as he assessed why the aerators had stopped working so suddenly. From the aerator's top, pipes soared a hundred meters to the vast pasture compound's ceiling, piercing through to spew clouds of vapor. Now merely a wheeze freckling the air.

"Well, I'm ready to test the backup power unit. There are six more aerators to fix today."

"We haven't even fixed the one!"

His father swiveled to the compound's entrance, a kilometer and a half wide, where distant aerators spewed weakened plumes into the vapor-filled sky. Openings in the compound's ceiling steeped the empty fields in twilight while the grass rippled rich, vibrating green. The air was viciously silent—no more grunts, no thud of hooves, no rip and crunch of grazing. A lonely breeze combed over the emptiness and tickled Caiden's nose with another whiff of death.

Humans were immune to the disease that had killed every bovine across the world, but the contaminated soil would take years to purge before new animals were viable. Pasture lots stood vacant for as far as anyone could see, leaving an entire population doing nothing but waiting for the overseers' orders.

The carcasses had been disposed of the same way as the fat bovines at harvest: corralled at the Flat Docks, two-kilometer-square metal plates, which descended, and the livestock were moved—somewhere, down below—then the plate rose empty.

"What'll happen if it dissolves completely?" The vapor paled and shredded dangerously by the hour—now the same grayish blond as Caiden's hair—and still he couldn't see through it. His curiosity bobbed on the sea of fear poured into him during his years in the Stricture: the gray was all that protected them from harm.

"Trouble will happen. Don't you mind it." His father always deflected or gave Caiden an answer for a child. Fourteen now, Caiden had been chosen for a mechanic determination because his intelligence outclassed him for everything else. He was smart enough to handle real answers.

"But what's up there?" he argued. "Why else spend so much effort keeping up the barrier?"

There could be a ceiling, with massive lights that filtered through to grow the fields, or the ceiling might be the floor of another level, with more people raising strange animals. Perhaps those people grew light itself, and poured it to the pastures, sieved by the clouds.

Caiden scrubbed sweat off his forehead, forgetting his grimy hand again. "The overseers must live up there. Why else do we rarely see them?"

He'd encountered two during his Appraisal at ten years old, when they'd confirmed his worth and assignment, and given him his brand—the mark of merit. He'd had a lot fewer questions, then. They'd worn sharp, hard metal clothes over their figures and faces, molded weirdly or layered in plates, and Caiden couldn't tell if there were bodies beneath those shapes or just parts, like a machine. One overseer had a humanlike shape but was well over two meters tall, the other reshaped itself like jelly. And there had been a third they'd talked to, whom Caiden couldn't see at all.

His father's sigh came out a growl. "They don't come from the sky, and the answers aren't gonna change if you keep asking the same questions."

Caiden recalled the overseers' parting words at Appraisal: *As a mechanic determination, it will become your job to maintain this world, so finely tuned it functions perfectly without us.*

"But why—"

"A mechanic doesn't need curiosity to fix broken things." His father disappeared back into the machine.

Caiden exhaled forcibly, bottled up his frustrations, and crawled back into the maintenance port. The tube was more cramped at fourteen than it had been at ten, but his growth spurt was pending and he still fit in spaces his father could not. The port was lined with cables, chemical wires, and faceplates stenciled in at least eight different languages Caiden hadn't been taught in the Stricture. His father told him to ignore them. And to ignore the blue vials filled with a liquid that vanished when directly observed. And the porous metal of the deepest ducts that seemed to breathe inward and out. *A mechanic doesn't need curiosity.*

Caiden searched for the bolts he thought he'd left in a neat pile.

"The more I understand and answer, the more I can fix." Frustration amplified his words, bouncing them through the metal of the machine.

"Caiden," his father's voice boomed from a chamber below. Reverberations settled in a long pause. "Sometimes knowing doesn't fix things."

Another nonanswer, fit for a child. Caiden gripped a wrench and stared at old wall dents where his frustration had escaped him before. Over time, fatigue dulled that anger. Maybe that was what had robbed his father of questions and answers.

But his friend Leta often said the same thing: "You can't fix everything, Caiden."

I can try.

He found his missing bolts at the back of the port, scattered and rolled into corners. He gathered them up and slapped faceplates into position, wrenching them down tighter than needed.

The adults always said, "This is the way things have always been—nothing's broken."

But it stayed that way because no one tried anything different.

Leta had confided in a nervous whisper, "*Different* is why I'll fail Appraisal." If she could fail and be rejected simply because her mind worked differently, the whole system was broken.

The aerator's oscillating unit was defaced with Caiden's labels and drawings where he'd transformed the bulbous foreign script into imagery or figures. Recent, neatly printed labels stood out beside his younger marks. He hesitated at a pasted-up photo he'd nicked from the Stricture: a foreign landscape with straight trees and intertwined branches. White rocks punctured bluish sand, with pools of water clearer than the ocean he'd once seen. It was beautiful—the place his parents would be retired to when he replaced them. Part of the way things had always been.

"Yes, stop everything." His mother was speaking to his father, and her voice echoed from below, muffled and rounded by the tube. She never visited during work. "Stop, they said. No more repairs."

His father responded, unintelligible through layers of metal.

"I don't know," she replied. "The overseers ordered everyone to gather at the Flat Docks. Caiden!"

He wriggled out of the port. His mother stood below with her arms crossed, swaying nervous as a willow. She was never nervous.

"Down here, hon." She squinted up at him. "And don't—*Caiden!*"

He slid halfway down the aerator's side and grabbed a seam to catch his fall. The edge under his fingers was shiny from years of the same maneuver. Dangling, smiling, he swung to perch on the front ledge, then frowned at his mother's flinty expression. Her eyes weren't on him anymore. Her lips moved in a whisper of quick, whipping words that meant trouble.

Caiden jumped the last couple meters to the ground.

"We have to go." She gripped a handful of his jacket and laid her other hand gently on his shoulder, marshaling him forward with these two conflicting holds. His father followed, wiping soot and worry from his brow.

"Are they sending help?" Caiden squirmed free. His mother tangled her fingers in his as they crossed a causeway between green pastures to a small door in the compound's side. "New animals?"

"Have to neutralize the disease first," his father said.

"A vaccine?" His mother squeezed his hand.

Outside the compound, field vehicles lay abandoned, others jammed around one of the Flat Docks a kilometer away. Crowds streamed to it from other compounds along the road grid, looking like fuel lines in an engine diagram. Movement at farther Docks suggested the order had reached everywhere.

"Stay close." His mother tugged him against her side as they amalgamated into a throng of thousands. Caiden had never seen so many people all together. They dressed in color and style according to their determinations, but otherwise the mob was a mix of shapes, sizes, and colors of people with only the brands on the back of their necks alike. It was clear from the murmurs that no one knew what was going on. This was not "the way things have always been." Worst fears and greatest hopes floated by in whispers like windy grass as Caiden squeezed to the edge of the Flat Docks' huge metal plate.

It lay empty, the guardrails up, the crowds bordered around. Only seven aerators in their sector still trickled. Others much farther away had stopped entirely. There should have been hundreds feeding the gray overhead, which now looked the palest ever.

Caiden said, "We'll be out of time to get the aerators running before the vapor's gone."

"I know…" His father's expression furrowed. The grime on his face couldn't hide suspicion, and his mother's smile couldn't hide her fear. She always had a solution, a stalwart mood, and an answer for Caiden even if it was "Carry on." Now: only wariness.

If everyone's here, then—"Leta."

"She'll be with her own parental unit," his father said.

"Yeah, but—" They weren't kind.

"Caiden!"

He dashed off, ducking the elbows and shoulders of the mob. The children were smothered among the taller bodies, impossible to distinguish. His quick mind sorted through the work rotations, the direction they came from—everyone would have walked straight from their dropped tasks, at predictable speed. He veered and slowed, gaze saccading across familiar faces in the community.

A flicker of bright bluish-purple.

Chicory flowers.

Caiden barked apologies as he shouldered toward the color, lost among tan clothes and oak-dark jerkins. Then he spotted Leta's fawn waves, and swung his arms out to make room in the crowd, as if parting tall grass around a flower. "Hey, there you are."

Leta peered up with dewy hazel eyes. "Cai." She breathed relief. Her knuckles were white around a cluster of chicory, her right arm spasming, a sign of her losing the battle against overstimulation.

Leta's parental unit wasn't in sight, neglectful as ever, and she was winded, rushed from some job or forgotten altogether. Oversized non-determination garments hung off one shoulder, covered her palms, tripped her heels. She crushed herself against Caiden's arm and hugged it fiercely. "It's what the older kids say. The ones who don't pass Appraisal're sent away, like the bovine yearlings."

"Don't be silly, they would have called just the children then, not everyone. And you haven't been appraised yet, anyway."

But she was ten, it was soon. The empathy, sensitivity, and logic that could qualify her as a sublime clinician also crippled

626

her everyday life as the callous people around her set her up to fail. Caiden hugged her, careful of the bruises peeking over her shoulder and forearm, the sight of them igniting a well-worn urge to protect.

"I've got you," he said, and pulled out twigs and leaves stuck in her hair. Her whole right side convulsed softly. The crowds, noise, and light washed a blankness into her face, meaning something in her was shutting down. "You're safe."

Caiden took her hand—firmly, grounding—and back-tracked through the crowd to the Flat Dock edge.

The anxious look on his mother's face was layered with disapproval, but his father smiled in relief. Leta clutched Caiden's right hand in both of hers. His mother took his left.

"The overseers just said gather and wait?" he asked his father.

"Someday you'll learn patience."

Shuffles and gasps rippled through the assembly.

Caiden followed their gazes up. Clouds thinned in a gigantic circle. The air everywhere brightened across the crowds more intensely than the compounds' lights had ever lit the bovines.

A hole burned open overhead and shot a column of blinding white onto the Flat Docks. Shouts and sobs erupted. Caiden stared through the blur of his eyelashes as the light column widened until the entire plate burned white. In distant sectors, the same beams emerged through the gray.

He smashed his mother's hand in a vise grip. She squeezed back.

A massive square descended, black as a ceiling, flickering out the light. The angular mass stretched fifty meters wide on all sides, made of the same irregular panels as the aerators. With a roar, it moved slowly, impossibly, nothing connecting it to the ground.

"I've never..." His mother's whisper died and her mouth hung open.

orbit

Follow us:

f **/orbitbooksUS**

/orbitbooks

/orbitbooks

Join our mailing list
to receive alerts on our
latest releases and deals.

orbitbooks.net

Enter our monthly
giveaway for the chance
to win some epic prizes.

orbitloot.com